UNFAMILIAR TERRITORY

R. LINDSAY CARTER

A new adventure awaits!

R Lindsay C

ROCK AND FLOWER PRESS

First Edition Hardcover

Cover design by Angelee van Allman

ISBN
Hardcover: 979-8-9859072-0-9

Paperback: 979-8-9859072-2-3

Ebook: 979-8-9859072-1-6

www.rlindsaycarter.com

CONTENTS

To Mercedes
Thanks for being my companion for twenty-one years.

CHAPTER I

Midnight. The witching hour. A time when most people are tucked into their beds, or at the very least safely ensconced behind locked doors.

I'm not most people. Not by a long shot.

Instead of secure walls and windows enclosing me, I was surrounded by tall trees and overgrown brush, driving my wooden wagon on a nearly forgotten road at the base of the Hooded Mountain. The ancient forest, prolific and dense, turned the dusty road into a tunnel, with only a small break far above to allow a fraction of the light from the full moon to enter. The gloominess didn't bother me for a couple of reasons. For starters, I had my lantern hanging on a hook to the left of me, and as it swung slightly with the motion of the wagon, it emitted a warm glow.

The other reason was a bit harder to explain.

The woods on either side of me were silent, unnaturally so. Having spent a good amount of my life in forests such as this one, I knew I should hear the nocturnal activities of various woodland denizens. Instead of crickets chirping, frogs cheeping, and owls hooting, the only sounds reaching my ears were the muffled clip-clop of Humbert, the aging dapple gray Percheron horse in front of me, and the creaking of the wagon he pulled.

I remained alert in the eerie quiet, keeping all of my senses open and active.

And suddenly, I heard it. Off to my right, a good half mile away. A long, low-to-high primitive melody that could only be one thing: the howl of a wolf. It was music to my ears.

My companion within the wagon must have heard it too, for the old wooden vessel gave a great lurch to the side, nearly taking two of the wheels off the ground. The lantern swayed dangerously by my head, forcing me to lunge to the side. I pulled on the reins quickly.

"Whoa, Humbert," I called. The large horse complied immediately, the rhythmic staccato of his hooves ending abruptly. His ears flicked but he remained placid as usual. Any other horse would have spooked at the sound of howls, but Humbert wasn't easily spooked, which made him an excellent employee. He was, however, most likely annoyed at working late into the night, so I made a mental note to reward his overtime with extra honeyed oats later.

The recently stopped wagon should have been motionless, but now it shuddered violently from side to side. I set the reins down and steadied the lantern by my head as best I could while trying to keep myself balanced upon my seat. I opened the hatch to the interior behind me and surveyed the pitch-black inside.

"Calm down, won't you!" I admonished the darkness within. A low deep growl answered me. I rolled my eyes in exasperation as I relatched the hatch and got down from the seat. At least my rebuke had worked, because the wagon had stopped rocking.

I smoothed out my trousers and vest and quickly stretched my back to work out some kinks that had taken occupancy during the wagon ride. Because I am short, I had to use the step of the wagon to reach my lantern, but once I had it off the hook, I made my way to the rear of the wagon.

My wagon was of simple design, basically a box with no windows. I obtained it used, so I'm not sure what its original intent was, but I'm fairly certain it had been a hearse at one time, because it was just long enough to store something approximately coffin-sized. I never painted anything on the side because I preferred not to advertise my services. I liked having the element of mystery on my side.

The back was comprised of double doors, again with no windows. They were latched, but the lock was not engaged at the moment. In the alcove above the doors was another lamp hook. It took me standing on the ladder and reaching as far up as I could to hook the lantern upon it, but I had gotten surprisingly good at that maneuver. With my hands once again free, I placed one on the latch. Intense energy on the other side radiated, just waiting to burst out.

"Please don't go charging off," I called out. "Give me a moment to gather my things, at least."

A faint whuff sounded through the doors. I mulled over how to interpret the sound. Resignation, with a heavy dose of frustration? I nodded to myself, convinced of my understanding and satisfied by said sound, and slid the latch over.

I flung the doors wide and leapt out of the way as a very large, dark mass bounded out of the wagon and started sniffing the air. With my companion out of the wagon, I quickly jumped into the open back and, opening the shallow cabinet on the wall, found the silver shackles in their rightful place. I grabbed them, clipped them to my belt, slid back out, and relatched the wagon. While I doubted any thieves were out here, I also locked it. My companion regarded me with impatient yellow eyes while I did this task. He growled again, very low in his throat. This I knew was not a threat, despite its intensity, but rather a frustration over having to wait. I ignored him while I slipped the key back into my vest pocket. I was used to his impatience.

The eerie howl once again reverberated through the forest, electrifying the both of us. Meeting his eyes, I gave a nod of my head, and my companion instantly tore off into the woods. I followed.

He, of course, was much faster than me and I almost instantly lost sight and sound of him. But I wasn't worried. We had long since worked out a system in which he would purposefully dig his claws into the ground as he ran, leaving a noticeable trail of churned detritus for me to follow in his wake. Tonight was no different. Although I had left the lantern back at the wagon and the light of the full moon wasn't strong enough to penetrate to the forest floor, I had little problem seeing the trail of freshly disturbed dirt and leaves. After all, my night vision is better than any human's I know.

In situations such as this, time is always of the essence. I ran along the trail at a steady pace, keeping my senses alert to avoid low-hanging branches and fallen limbs in my path. While my soft and comfortable leather boots pounded a quiet rhythm on the forest floor, the silver shackles jangled and bounced against my trousers as an accompaniment. The faint trail led upward through the forest at a mild incline, which made me thankful I was in good shape.

Perhaps seven minutes into the forest, my ears picked up the first sounds of an altercation. I quickened my pace, adrenaline sharpening my reflexes that much more. I burst through some shrubs and into a small clearing at the top of the hill, the sudden light of the full moon momentarily dazzling me. I paused to adjust to the light, panting mildly. As soon as my vision cleared, I saw I had reached my target.

Two large canine bodies took up the middle of the clearing, rolling together in fierce battle. I couldn't distinguish who was who as they tumbled about, snarling, biting, and clawing their way to hopeful victory. As I watched, the mass of limbs separated enough for me to make out the opposing forces: one, a massive black shaggy ball of canine anger, and the other a slightly larger, grey wolflike creature whose limbs rippled with muscles. They were my cohort and our quarry—the werewolf.

I'd seen a few such skirmishes over the past year, but, like every other time, I couldn't help but admire the form of the two components involved, especially the werewolf. While werewolves were terrifying monsters, the savage elegance of such beasts was something I could appreciate from afar. This particular individual was no different. About the size of a small horse, the lycanthrope moved with a deadly, predatory grace. Its lupine snout snarled at my companion, showing off pointed, pearly teeth in the moonlight. The limbs of the beast were a mix between canine and human: slightly longer in the back, and the front ending in what could pass as hands.

To the casual observer, it would appear to be a fair fight. I knew better than that, though. While the lycanthrope had size and ferocious strength to its advantage, the other had cunning and stamina. Already, I could discern the supernatural creature was tiring. Finally, with one last slobbery and exhausted howl, the werewolf backed away from the fight, a clear sign of surrender. My companion, however, refused to acquiesce. When the werewolf turned its back to flee, the black canine leapt onto said back and clamped his large jaws around the neck of the wolf creature.

With a mighty groan, the lycanthrope collapsed under the weight of its unrelenting tormentor. With its neck still held in the vice of the black beast above it, it gave a whimper. Shuddering once, the wolflike body began to change. It shrank into itself as hair became sparse, and muzzle, tail, and clawed appendages morphed into something much more innocuous.

After fifteen seconds, the mighty and terrifying werewolf was gone. In its stead lay a relatively hairy, yet balding middle-aged man, naked and shivering with fear as his face was pressed into the soil by the weight of the beast that still held his neck in its jaws.

I had stayed at the edge of the clearing the entire time the fight had ensued, my presence unneeded. But now it was my turn to act. I approached the scene boldly, opening the silver shackles as I went. My companion met my eyes as I advanced, and he silently shifted his body to one side to expose both arms of the man, keeping his grip on his neck all the while. Swiftly I grabbed the man's left arm and clasped the cuff over his wrist before reaching across to do the same to his other arm, shackling them together behind his back. Only when I gave a nod did my companion release the neck, but he stayed hovering over the shaking form. The man stayed frozen for a heartbeat more before slowly raising himself to his knees, still facing away from me.

I unclasped the neck shackle and slowly fit it to the back of his slobbery neck. As I latched it with a concluding click, I spoke a memorized speech in my best authoritative voice, "Edward James Collier, you are under arrest for the murders of Johnathan Meyer, Agatha Meyer, Colin Meyer, Lance Dubosse, Carlotta Henessey, and Patricia Vance, and for the wanton destruction of property in the form of three separate flocks of sheep and the houses of the Meyer family and the Henessey Family."

Upon hearing my statement, the naked man fell forward onto his face and sobbed loudly from his prostrate position. "I didn't know," he cried into the dirt. "God, please forgive me!"

"I am not God, nor am I one of his agents, Mr. Collier," I responded with harsh glibness. "It is not my job to weigh your soul against your actions, but merely to bring you in for others to do so."

At this, the hapless man stilled a beat, and then craned his neck to the side to look up at me for the first time. He had obviously failed to notice the delicate timbre of my voice during my arrest speech, but it seemed to register with him after my second comment. He stared at me with frank confusion, then, to my amusement, terror.

"But you ... you are a ... who *are* you?" He shifted his body to one side to get a better look at me. A warning growl came from behind him, and the man froze. More shakily, he asked with a slight whimper, "And what is that *thing*?"

I get this reaction a lot. We are an unusual pair, after all. I kept my face stern and authoritative without a hint of the smile that threatened to surface and drew myself upright.

"I am Cressida Curtain, professional bounty hunter, Mr. Collier. And this," I gestured behind him with a wave of my hand, "is my business partner, Grimm. He is a Lycanhund."

Mr. Collier blanched noticeably in the moonlight at the breed's name. I nodded at his reaction.

"No doubt you thought them a myth, yes? As you can attest, he is very real. And he is still very angry, Mr. Collier, so I would not try any funny business if I were you."

As if to authenticate my words, Grimm growled low at the man, showing off his impressive teeth in the moonlight. The captured man flinched again, and I could immediately tell he carried no notions of funny business. This was a beaten man. He cringed and sobbed some more, resting his face on the clearing floor. I knew he wouldn't dream of reverting back to werewolf form even if the silver shackles hadn't been physically preventing this.

"Very good, Mr. Collier," I continued. "It is my business to deliver you to the sheriff of Veradale, in which the aforementioned crimes were committed. Once I deliver you our business is concluded. Now then, we have a bit of a walk ahead of us. Are your legs still sound? Yes? Good. I understand that your tussle with Grimm has left you winded, but I suspect you won't delay us too much."

He shook his head earnestly. Grimm took two steps back to give the man some maneuvering room. Bound as he was, Mr. Collier had lost all of the grace he had possessed with his lycanthropic body, so in the end I had to grab him under an arm to help hoist him to his bare feet. Once he was steady, I motioned for him to follow my lead. With Grimm bringing up the rear, we began our trek back to the wagon.

Just another successful job.

Walking downhill with a naked man whose hands were secured behind his back and who did not possess night vision or even callused feet made the hike back to the wagon a long one indeed. My bounty was a small-statured man, but his recent diet of numerous flocks of sheep and a few people had caused him to bulk out substantially. Twice Edward Collier stumbled on the path, and twice he was saved by my quick reflexes as I turned to catch him as he fell into me. Both times I had to push him by his hairy chest back into an upright position. I found it rather distasteful, what with all the dirt and slobber mashed into his plentiful, wiry chest hairs.

To his credit, Mr. Collier did not complain during the journey, and even thanked me when I prevented his falling each time. I went slow, mindful of his condition. The night was beginning to take its toll on me, however, and I was very happy when at last I could discern the end to our trek.

Funny enough, Mr. Collier did not notice his lack of clothing until we got to the road's edge, which was bathed in the soft glow of the wagon's lamp. By this time, I was already on the road, making a beeline for the wagon and eager to be done with this part of the business. I stopped, however, sensing no movement behind me, and turned to see the nude man still standing at the edge of the road, trying to hide his genitalia behind a bush and blushing furiously. Even with Grimm giving him a subtle nudge with his cold wet nose on his bare behind, Mr. Collier didn't budge.

Apparently, the presence of the light had reminded Mr. Collier of his nudity and the fact that he was in the company of a lady, even if she was a bounty hunter.

I rolled my eyes and sighed with exasperation. "Mr. Collier, I am flattered by your modesty, but I can assure you that in this line of work I have seen such fare as yours, and it does not offend, nor does it tantalize me in any way. Now, there is a blanket waiting for you in the wagon, so if you please!"

But he did not please. Even with the threat of the Lycan dog at his backside, he refused to move. "I'm a lifelong bachelor, miss," he stated with more gumption than I had given him credit for, "and I won't add indecent exposure in front of a member of the fair sex, especially one so young and pretty as yourself, to my list of sins."

In the end, I retrieved the blanket from the wagon and walked it over to the man, making sure not to offend his sense of propriety by keeping my eyes on his face. I made sure to give him my best glare as I wrapped the blanket carefully around his midsection, taking care to make as little contact with his skin as possible.

Now that he was properly covered, Mr. Collier offered no more resistance and meekly followed me to the wagon and clumsily climbed into the back.

I took the lamp off its pole and placed it on a hook inside the wagon, illuminating the interior. The unfortunate man had already hunched himself into a corner where a plush mat was placed.

"I must inform you that Grimm will be riding in back with you," I told him with a touch of gentleness. "As long as you behave yourself, I guarantee no harm will befall you while you are in our care."

He said nothing but nodded without looking at me. A barely discernible whimper escaped his lips. The paunchy man had started to shiver, now that his lycanthropy had been temporarily nullified by the silver shackles and his blood had cooled to a human temperature. Mr. Collier, naked and trembling, with filth covering his body and his head hanging low, looked quite pathetic. I fought a pang of sympathy for him before recalling the many people he had killed and eaten in various murderous rampages during the three nights when the moon was fullest.

I turned and met Grimm's eyes. Soundlessly, the black dog jumped into the wagon. I studied my partner for a second, checking for noticeable injuries from the fight. Nothing stood out as obviously wrong and I breathed a sigh of relief.

Satisfied with my quick inspection, I latched and locked the double doors, and then hoisted myself into the driver's seat. Humbert, who had been snoozing patiently during our absence, shook his head once and started to move the instant my hands got a hold of the reins. He knew where to go; the reins were nothing more than a symbolic gesture.

I sighed heavily and leaned back against the wagon, letting my mind wander and my senses relax a bit. The pockmarked road led us on a slow decline, the density of the trees starting to thin as we descended altitude. It was very early morning; sunrise would occur in a handful of hours. It had been a productive night, but we weren't finished yet. I could only hope that the sheriff of Veradale would handle things efficiently so that I could collect our reward, drive to a secluded spot, revert to my true form and purr myself into a deep and deserving sleep.

Oh yes, I forgot to mention—I'm a cat.

CHAPTER 2

The world I live in is not the same as yours, but rather a sister dimension. Being such, there are many similarities, true, but vast differences as well. One of the biggest differences is the fact that in my world, magic exists, and things that are regarded as myths and legends in your realm are very real here. Werewolves and vampires? They are ordinary nuisances here, and the only reason other dimensions even know of their existence is that on occasion our worlds can connect. For instance, about a hundred years ago a man from your world opened a temporary gateway to mine and for some reason gifted us with free energy. That man, Tesla, sure changed our world in a big way.

As it is, we still don't have much use for highly advanced technological capabilities because some of the population is gifted with a variety of magical talents, some small, some big. These talents can often replace the need for technology; why invent a fancy icebox when you can use an enchanted entropy-free box to keep your groceries fresh? Or what use is there for heavy farming machinery when some people are gifted with plant manipulation? The types of magics are as varied as the people who wield them: spell casting, enchanting, elemental magic, mind magic, and innate magic, just to name the common ones. Magic is simply a way of life here, and magic users of all types live side by side with the mundane. It's usually no big deal.

But on occasion, magic can be a very big deal. Let me tell you a story.

Once upon a time, approximately five hundred years ago on the eastern coast of Vinland, there lived a witch of frightening power. She was known as Annie Coddle, and her reputation induced fear in even the bravest of souls. Annie did not use any of her magical ability to benefit anyone else, but rather for her own interests.

Now, it is common knowledge in my world that witches with a certain threshold of magical talent have the ability to summon to themselves a being of energy. These beings, once arriving in our plane of existence, create a body for themselves, which always takes the form of a small animal, house cats being the most popular model for some reason. These beings are known as familiars. Annie had power in spades, and so it took her no time at all to summon her own familiar, a cat spirit by the name of Glivver. Now, familiars are usually emotionally attached to their witches, protecting them from unwanted attention and aiding in their spells. Annie, though, was into cheap labor. Instead of treating Glivver as an equal or protector, the witch swiftly downgraded the familiar's status into nothing more than a slave.

There is only so much that an ethereal cat can do around the house, even with magical talent, and Annie wanted Glivver to do all the dirty work, quite literally. So, the old witch devised a spell that turned Glivver into a human woman at Annie's will. That way Glivver was forced to do all the cleaning, cooking, ingredient gathering, and basic spell preparations while Annie focused on her one and only aspiration: world domination.

The witch proved to be quite adept at the one thing she set her mind to. Annie Coddle quickly turned her small corner of the country into a hell hole. Magic users began to die of mysterious circumstances and mundane people lived in fear of enslavement and harsh punishment. Crops withered. Even the mighty forests began to die as Annie's influence over the natural realm stripped the trees of their organic magic. And her evil influence spread ever wider and at an alarming pace.

But there was one little detail that she overlooked.

To say that Annie's relationship with her familiar was an unhealthy one would be an understatement. Glivver despised Annie from the moment the witch first forced her into a woman's body. While in this state, the familiar was stripped of her powers and vulnerable. To make matters worse, Glivver was hardly ever allowed to revert to her cat form as Annie kept her constantly busy. This angered Glivver to no end. But Annie, bent on enslaving the planet, was too busy to notice her slave's feelings.

One day, as the witch perfected her immortality potion (for what fun was ruling the world if you had to die some day?), Glivver made a simple potion of her own. Annie swiftly finished her recipe, unaware of her familiar's goings on, and, feeling generous, allowed Glivver to change back into a cat. This was the moment Glivver was waiting for. While Annie Coddle ladled her precious potion into a mug and began to sip it ritualistically, Glivver murmured a few words over her own concoction and activated its magical qualities. Then, as Annie tipped the dregs of her potion into her greedy, wide-open mouth, Glivver propelled her potion into the witch's face. The majority coursed down her throat.

The results, they say, were fantastic, but I don't know the specifics.

What I do know is even though Annie Coddle managed to drink enough of her potion to achieve everlasting life, Glivver's actions banished her to another dimension where she could no longer do harm in this world. Before she left, Annie vowed she would find a way back from her banishment and finish the job she started. Glivver was no dummy—she knew Annie meant what she said. So, she used a little-known tool that familiars possess to create a prophecy:

"By Glivver's blood the witch is bound,
By Glivver's word the witch must obey,
So long as the daughters of Glivver remain,
So long as the cat that walks as a woman lives,
The witch Annie Coddle can never return."

Glivver, sacrificing the last of her power, stole the shapeshifting spell from Annie and internalized it, successfully allowing Glivver to change from cat to human and back again at will. Aside from this new magical ability, Glivver lost all her power. She ceased to be a familiar and became a mortal cat. It was the price to pay for freeing the world of evil tyranny.

Despite the amount of abuse Annie Coddle had heaped upon Glivver, the witch had kept her familiar a fiercely guarded secret. Nobody knew of her existence, either as a cat or a human. Glivver could not have waltzed into society as a mortal cat, for no one would have been able to understand that Annie was truly gone. No, Glivver needed to access her human side, which was why the shapeshifting spell was worth her immortality.

She wasted little time in setting out in her human form to spread the word of her successful banishment of Annie Coddle. Changing her name to Gilva, she claimed to be the powerless slave of the witch who happened to be lucky enough to learn of a way to dispose of Annie during her imprisonment. Her story spread far and wide, and it wasn't long before the heads of state lauded her as a hero.

It also wasn't long before men came out of the woodwork to ask for her hand in marriage, for Gilva's human form was quite lovely to look upon, and her status had skyrocketed. Popularity and beauty made her quite the catch, but love wasn't exactly a factor in any of these proposals.

Gilva, of course, knew that the prophecy required her to bear offspring in order to keep Annie at bay. What she didn't know was that sometimes prophecies take on a life of their own and form some of their own rules. In this particular case, the requirement was that Gilva could only procreate with a man that was her one true love.

It didn't happen overnight, but eventually Gilva did indeed find a suitor worthy of the title. She married him and had a very happy three months with him before learning the next rule.

Since she was a cat first and foremost, it was of the utmost importance that she revert back to her true form every now and then. This was of course done in secrecy as her husband did not know of her true state. One day, Gilva told her beloved that she was going to take a stroll through the woods, a pastime she often used as an excuse to get some alone time. Once safely away from any prying eyes she shifted back into her cat self and spent a wonderful hour hunting and frolicking. When she tried to change back, though, she was unable to. Instinctively, she knew the reason why: she was pregnant.

A developing embryo must stay the same species as its mother, and changing forms during growth could cause severe damage to the budding life in the womb once it was past the single-cell stage. With this logic, it only made sense that the mother's body would have a built-in mechanism to deny shapeshifting during the entire pregnancy. Glivver (for she still identified with that name as a cat) was a bit saddened by this revelation, for she had not properly said goodbye to her husband. She had to settle for approaching him while he worked outside and rubbing up affectionately against his leg. He in turn gently nudged her away and shooed her from his sight, unaware that this would be his last glimpse of his wife.

Approximately nine weeks later Glivver delivered a healthy female kitten. She was once again able to transform into Gilva, but she no longer felt there was a reason to. Her daughter, upon reaching maturity at eight months, obtained the ability to shapeshift as well. And thus, the lineage of Glivver came to be.

Which brings me to, well, me. I, Cressida Curtain, am the last in a very long line of feline shapeshifters. I am the latest descendant of the familiar Glivver. And if the prophecy from five hundred years ago is to be believed, I am the only thing standing in the way of Annie Coddle's return. No pressure, right?

I was born two years and almost six months ago in a long-abandoned barn in the woods, a tiny kitten of pure white, save for two small black markings resting between my ears on my forehead. My mother raised me there, catching a variety of rodents and birds for her own sustenance while I was still nursing, and then teaching me the feline art of hunting as I got older.

She also taught me about humans and their rules, laws, etiquette, and all other important tidbits, even though I had never even met a human before. Mom also told me stories of how she could shape-shift into one, and how I would too when I became old enough. I begged her to change into a human for me to see, but she never did. At times I felt like the whole humanity thing was all a big lie my mother told me.

But when I was around eight months old, I woke up one day feeling different. I had been maturing from a fuzzy blue-eyed kitten into a sleeker medium-haired cat with a wonderfully fluffy tail. At that moment I had crossed an invisible threshold, one that forever barred me from kittenhood and ushered in the primitive maturity of teenage-dom.

That day, Mom led me to a small clearing in the woods, far away from any prying eyes. She took a deep breath and her form *shimmered* before me. I could no longer see her in the indistinguishable glow that lasted just a mere second before the shimmer enlarged and went away. Standing before me was an unusual creature. A human.

Despite her vast change in appearance, I knew she was still my mother. Excited to try for myself, I concentrated on changing shape. From my open eyes I could see the shimmer happening, and then suddenly I was much taller than I had ever been in my young life. Concentrating again, I managed to transform back into a cat.

I practiced all day that day until I had perfected my transformation. Once I had mastered that, it was time for my mom to up my studies, which included learning to speak in the human language common to this region, reading, and writing as a human.

And throughout my first year of life, there was one lesson upon which my mother placed the most emphasis: I must keep my true nature a secret. No one can know what I truly am. She broke it down into three simple and easy to remember rules:

1. Always pretend to be a plain mundane human.

2. Never shift if any human can see you.

3. If you screw up 1 and 2, never give them the whole story.

Now, I'll be the first to admit that I have already broken the first two rules with two humans, but the third is still intact. And of course, Grimm knows the whole truth, but he's a dog. I asked my mom why I must live in secrecy, and her only comment was that while Annie has never returned since her banishment, there may still be some unsavory characters out there who are hell-bent on trying to destroy the prophecy and allow Annie Coddle to return.

And there's one other time where I'm allowed to break the rules, if I wish. When I find the one man that is my true love, I *could* tell him. But I am nowhere near ready for that level of commitment. I'm still young, I have time, and it's best not to dwell on those types of things.

After all, I have a business to run.

CHAPTER 3

I
t was still dark, of course, as Humbert and the wagon made
their way down the mountain road. But with the full moon
and my magically sensitive eyes, I could see well enough to be at
ease. The dense trees that had enclosed the road for so long finally
began to taper off, giving way to scrub and farmland on either
side.

While Annie Coddle and Glivver had resided in the eastern
portion of the country of Vinland, at some point in the last five
hundred years my ancestors had traveled west. I was born in the
Oracune Region, about a hundred miles inland from the vast
Serenic Ocean. I might have been a bit biased being a native
and all, but I surmised this area of the country to be one of the
prettiest, especially with the Hooded Mountain looming close
by.

I let my tired mind wander as I took in the scenery. We reached
Veradale an hour from where we had apprehended our quarry.
To call Veradale a town was to give it more status than it deserved.
There was a simple wooden sign on the outskirts, engraved with
the words, "Welcome to Veradale, pop. 300." The engraving had
once sported bright colors but most of the paint had peeled off
and faded away.

Humbert followed the road as it became the main—and only—drag through the little burg. A tiny oval village green split the lane in two at the very heart of the town. At the widest point sat a handful of businesses: a post office, a police station, and a grocery store on one side, with a restaurant, a general store, a bar, and a church on the other side. I noted with a small amount of amusement that the bar and church were next door neighbors. I wondered if that had been planned. A small number of houses surrounded these buildings before giving way to farms and sheep fields on either side.

The town green housed a quaint tall clock upon an iron post, the most interesting focal point of the entire place. The clock told me the time was 3:29 in the morning. I fervently hoped that someone was working at the police station at this hour. It wouldn't be the first time that I would have to knock on doors to wake people up in these micro-towns. That didn't mean I enjoyed doing it.

Thankfully, as I rounded the green and slowed Humbert to a stop in front of the police station, I spied a light within. With the strict laws enforcing the use of free energy, I surmised nobody would be stupid enough to waste their allotment by leaving the light on without anybody working there.

Humbert fully came to a stop, blowing a great horsey sigh from his lips. It had been a long night for him, I thought with a pang of guilt. I got down from my perch and stretched some of the kinks out of my spine once again. Leaving Grimm and Mr. Collier in the wagon, I pushed open the peeling, beige wooden door and entered the station.

There *was* someone working there, but he was fast asleep at the front desk. Given his youth, he must have been a deputy working the graveyard shift. Occasional werewolf aside, I bet there wasn't much need for round-the-clock law enforcement in a town so small. I surmised he was only here tonight due to special circumstances. I could hardly fault the man for sleeping on the job. But I was weary myself and wanted to end this business as quickly as possible.

A tarnished bell rested on the counter. I struck it smartly, and it let out an alarmingly clear and loud ding. The young man startled at the sound and nearly tumbled off his chair. He blearily glanced around before resting eyes on me. Upon seeing me, he leapt to his feet in a rather uncoordinated way. He ran a hand around his belt to check that his shirt was properly tucked in before fixing his full attention on me. His eyes leapt straight to my hair and stayed glued there for far too long.

Ah yes, the stare. I was well used to it by now. My unusual magical genetics translated my medium-length white feline fur into straight, fine hair of a practically white platinum blonde shade that fell just below the tops of my shoulders. But because my true form had those two black spots marking my forehead, my human counterpart's locks included two small jet-black streaks that grew from just above my temples at the hairline. For someone with such pale hair, the streaks were incredibly noticeable and rather jarring. Most strangers assumed I dyed my hair that way on purpose.

And if it wasn't my hair that caught looks, it was my eyes. They retained the vivid sky-blue shade of my cat form, a color that was highly unusual in a human. Coupled with the fact that my lashes and eyebrows were of a darker shade than my platinum hair, my eyes really stood out. I suppose this, along with my petite five-foot-three-inch stature and wiry, athletic build, had generally led to me being labeled by humans as "cute." It was mostly a distinct downside for my chosen profession, unfortunately.

I quietly allowed the deputy's visual perusal as his brain slowly warmed back up. Still mentally dusting off the cobwebs and obviously at a loss, he finally mumbled, "Uh, can I help you, ma'am?"

I hated the word "ma'am;" it never failed to make me feel old. I was anything but old. But I ignored it and smiled as sweetly as I could, albeit with too much teeth showing. "I spoke with Sheriff Jones earlier today and I have a delivery for him. Could you get him for me?"

The deputy only stared with obvious befuddlement, allowing his mouth to gape and close like a carp without emitting a word. I rolled my eyes in weary exasperation. Leaning toward the deputy with the toothiest smile I could muster, I enunciated with a slight growl, "Get. The. Sheriff." I paused, then added, "Please."

He must have seen the metaphorical blood in my eyes, for the young man jumped up and with a curt "Yes'm," and ran out the door. I sighed and stretched my arms above my head, and then waited as patiently as I could. I didn't dare sit on the only other chair provided, exhausted as I was.

To give the deputy credit, I did not have to wait long. Sheriff Jones, bleary-eyed and scruffy, came in with the younger man at his heels. He was a large man, not fat but large in body and presence. I made eye contact with the Sheriff, who gave me a little nod.

"Miss Curtain," he boomed. "To what do I owe the pleasure this time? I figured after our little talk yesterday I wouldn't be graced with your presence again."

He was referring to the previous afternoon, when I showed up to discuss the bounty on Mr. Collier. His "little talk" consisted of assuring me that the problem would be handled by a professional very soon and not to get involved because (and I quote), "I would hate to see that pretty face of yours get mangled."

My response to the clear misogyny was to ask the man if the bounty was still open, and if so, to make sure it would be rewarded with all fairness once it was claimed. He did verify this to be true. I left without punching him in the face to take a nap before I drove out to the last known whereabouts of the werewolf. A very professional approach if I do say so myself.

Now, from my vest pocket I pulled out the crinkled sheet of paper with Mr. Collier's mugshot on it. I unfolded it before showing it to Jones. "I have your man, Sheriff. I've come to collect."

The sheriff blinked at the dossier before looking at me. "You have him?"

I suppressed my urge to strangle the man. "Sheriff, I was trying to tell you this afternoon that despite my gender, age, and my looks, and despite still being a bit fresh to my chosen occupation, I *am* a professional. Meaning, your job has been handled just as you had hoped."

The big man rubbed the back of his neck. "Now, Miss, no need to take offense. If what you say is true, then I'll admit I was wrong."

"That's awfully big of you, sir."

"But," he held up a finger to ban me from interrupting, "Seeing is believing. Let's have a peek at the man, shall we?"

I nodded, annoyed that my word wasn't enough, but pleased that I was about to make him metaphorically eat his hat. Sometimes I had to celebrate the little wins. I folded up the wanted poster and placed it in my pocket.

Sheriff Jones motioned for his deputy, who had been standing uselessly to the side. "Bloom! You come too; we might need an extra set of hands." Deputy Bloom jumped at his name, but dutifully followed us outside to my wagon.

A canine huff emitted from within, followed by a low growl. The noise was just loud enough and with enough of a threat behind it that both men stopped well away from the wagon. I rolled my eyes again.

"It's just my partner," I explained, marching up to the wagon with no fear. As I unlocked the back doors I said, "Cool it," to Grimm. The interior of the wagon quieted immediately. I opened the doors and allowed some space for Grimm to jump out. He soundlessly and obediently trotted to me and sat by my side.

"Your partner?" Deputy Bloom mimicked my words with disbelief in his voice. He hadn't been around in the afternoon like the sheriff had, and therefore hadn't met Grimm yet.

This was a reaction that we encountered on a regular basis, Grimm and I. For starters, Lycanhunds are not easy to ignore. Despite belonging to the hound group, Lycanhunds more resemble border collies, with a slightly squarish long muzzle, three-quarter-pricked ears, shaggy fur, and intelligent yellow eyes. Except they are all black, slightly leggier, and much, much bigger than a collie. Grimm was over three feet tall just at his shoulder. He had also perfected his "don't mess with me" demeanor, and smart people tended to keep their distance.

And to be partnered up with me, a petite young woman—well, the visual juxtaposition seemed to blow people's minds.

So, I just nodded at the deputy's incredulous question, shrugged my shoulders nonchalantly, and then ignored him. It was my go-to response. I gestured to the sheriff to check out my catch. Sheriff Jones gave Grimm a nervous look but strode over to peer into the wagon's interior.

Mr. Collier had barely moved from his hunched position in the far corner of the wagon. He turned his head to meet the sheriff's gaze. "He-hello, Gordon," he stammered.

Sheriff Jones sighed at the greeting. He seemed to deflate a little at the sight within the wagon. "Ed," he responded, although more to himself. Straightening, the sheriff turned to me, nodded his head, and then called out, "Bloom! Grab the man out of there and bring him into the station."

Deputy Bloom didn't move. He only blinked once, glanced at me, then settled his full attention on Grimm before peering at the wagon with a look of dread on his face.

Grimm seemed to sense his trepidation and let out a soft growl, adding fuel to the proverbial fear fire. Bloom turned white. "Uh, sir..." he stammered.

"It's safe, Bloom. Get a move on!" Jones ordered. The younger man finally listened to his boss and moved, albeit reluctantly. He cast another look in my direction. I couldn't discern what made him more nervous, Grimm or the has-been werewolf.

"My partner won't hurt you and the werewolf is harmless at the moment. He can't morph with the shackles on," I informed him.

With that information Bloom moved with a bit more confidence. While he crawled into the back of the wagon, I noticed the town had started to come awake at the commotion. Sleepy, disheveled citizens formed a ring around us. Sheriff Jones beckoned to a boy of around twelve years of age over to his side.

"Andy, go fetch Amelia," he told the boy in a low tone. "Tell her we need the potion."

The boy nodded, wide-eyed, and cast a glance at the wagon before sprinting off. Jones turned back to the wagon. "My boy," he informed me without a glance in my direction. I made a small noise in my throat as a means of acknowledgement.

Bloom finally managed to guide the shackled Collier out of the back of the wagon, having reapplied the blanket around the naked man's waist. The gathering crowd murmured amongst themselves. Grimm, by my side, growled deeply, drawing attention back to himself. The crowd of looky-loos took a fearful step back in unison, as if choreographed. I bit the insides of my cheeks to prevent myself from smiling and placed my hand on top of Grimm's head to soundlessly tell him to shut up. He stopped instantly.

The deputy led Mr. Collier into the station, with the sheriff directly behind. Grimm and I brought up the rear. I was pleased to see that no one followed us inside. Grimm sometimes came in handy for keeping unwanted crowds at bay.

In the light of the station, Mr. Collier was white and ashen, his face gaunt and his body streaked with dirt. His eyes became shiny with unshed tears as he turned toward Jones. "Gordon, I—" he began to whimper.

Sheriff Jones raised his hands, his face hard. Mr. Collier ceased talking, but still let out faint snivels. "Ed, you have the right to remain silent. Your judgment will come soon enough but save your pleas. Amelia will be here soon to ..." Jones's speech was interrupted by a loud knock on the door. Jones nodded curtly at the deputy, who sprang into action and almost ran to open the door. An older woman with steel-gray hair in a loose braid over one shoulder entered. She was still wearing her nightgown, with a dingy, cream-colored robe wrapped around her. She held a small vial in her hand.

"Good morning, Sheriff," she greeted, her tone somber.

"Amelia," Jones responded with a trace of warmth. "I see you have it?"

She held up the vial and carefully swirled the murky contents within. "Wolfsbane," she announced. "I made it just last evening in hopes of such an occasion."

"Wonderful. Amelia, might I introduce you to Miss Curtain? She is the one that tracked and captured Ed." He turned to me. "Amelia is our resident herb woman."

"Herb woman," or sometimes just "herbalist," is another name for a lesser witch, someone who has the knowledge and skill to make minor potions out of plants but no talent for any other magic. For some odd reason I never understood, many of these small or tight-knit communities saw witches of any caliber in a negative light, despite any benign intentions that most witches might have. Therefore, this more polite term was conceived to use for a respected member of one of these communities, which did away with the so-called negative connotation of being dubbed a witch.

I thought it was stuff and nonsense, personally. The names were interchangeable in my mind. As long as one wasn't a power-grubbing, familiar-enslaving harridan, I did not see how being called a witch was insulting.

This woman had a look about her that suggested she would be the type to take offense to being called a witch, however, so I kept my opinions to myself. It was just as well, because Amelia clearly didn't warm up to me on sight alone. She looked me over upon Jones' introduction, pursing her lips and narrowing her eyes slightly. Her body language screamed that she did not trust my presence.

"My pleasure," she said, although there was no pleasure in her tone.

I refused to give her the satisfaction of cowing me. I gave a curt head nod and replied, "Ma'am."

She then turned her attention to Grimm by my side. Her stiff and unwelcoming demeanor lifted slightly. "A Lycanhund," she murmured appreciatively. She took another glance at me, appraising me anew. "It takes a strong will and determined hand to own such a dog."

"Oh, I don't own him," I replied with an offhanded shrug. "We just work together."

The herb woman made a small grunt in return, scowling at my flippancy. She turned away from me to focus on the task at hand, clearly dismissing my presence.

False niceties met, Amelia asked the sheriff if she should administer the potion now, to which Jones gave his permission. I took this opportunity to wrap up my business and, politely grabbing Jones's arm, steered him a small distance from the proceedings.

"My end is done, Sheriff," I stated, keeping my tone professional. "It's been a long night and I'd like to be on my way."

"Oh yes, of course. What is it that I owe you? Five hundred?"

I sighed and did my best to prevent rolling my eyes. Low-balling bounty hunters was the oldest trick in the book. I once again removed the folded-up piece of paper. Opening it and smoothing the creases, I displayed it to the sheriff, pointing out the sum at the bottom. "Nine hundred. Not a penny less."

He knew better than to argue. "Of course. Wait here." He retreated to a back room.

While I waited, I watched the herb woman as she tipped her wolfsbane potion down Mr. Collier's throat. I was no stranger to witnessing the effects of the wolfsbane, since my partner was bred to hunt werewolves and it happened to be our specialty. This was the fourth time I had viewed its administration. Unfortunately, it was not the most pleasant thing to observe, and Mr. Collier's case was no different. Within seconds of swallowing the liquid, he doubled over, groaning. The veins at the surface of his skin turned a deep violet as the herb destroyed the werewolf taint within his blood. He fell to the floor, gasping and writhing in sudden agony.

Sheriff Jones returned with a cloth bag just as Mr. Collier's blood vessels faded back to a normal color, indicating that the lycanthropy was fully destroyed. While Collier lay on the floor, panting with exhaustion, I counted my money and doublechecked that the receipt was also tucked into the bag. Satisfied, I turned to Jones, who was looking rather green. I doubted he had ever seen the wolfsbane at work.

I cleared my throat to get his attention. Sticking out my hand to shake, I said, "A pleasure doing business with you, Sheriff. Good luck with him." I tilted my head at Collier. Jones, still riveted on the goings-on, didn't seem to notice my comment but robotically shook my proffered hand, still clearly shellshocked.

I turned to go, frustrated by my treatment during this whole affair. Between the blatant discrimination based on my appearance, the attempt to short-change me, and now a limp-handed dismissal, I was leaving the situation in a sour mood.

Honestly, it wasn't the first time I had been treated this way. It shouldn't have surprised me.

"Oh, Miss Curtain?"

I turned around at the sheriff's call, putting my dark thoughts on temporary hold. My feelings must have been etched upon my face, however, because the man took a slight step back upon meeting my eyes. He rubbed his sweaty forehead with the back of his hand, finally giving me his full attention. "My apologies, Miss," he said sheepishly. He gave a half-chuckle of discomfiture. "I'll be the first to say I didn't think you had it in you. This is a bad affair for this town. There aren't that many of us here and I didn't need any more embarrassment to reflect badly on this community. Ed here is my cousin, and I didn't want to draw more attention to his ... mistakes than was needed. I worried a lady like yourself might only aggravate the problem at hand by getting herself injured."

I stood stock still, doing my best to rein in my emotions and keep my face neutral. "Okay."

"What I'm trying to say, and failing because it's late and I'm wrung out, is that you did a better job than I imagine even a seasoned hunter would do. Thank you for that. Veradale owes you a debt beyond what I just paid you. I want you to know that you are always welcome here, you and your dog, that is. I'd be happy to recommend you to anyone with a similar problem too. And, God forbid, if something like this ever happens again you will be the first person I contact to take the job."

A large chunk of apprehension I had been holding evaporated at the second half of his speech. I allowed myself a small smile. "Thank you, Sheriff. I appreciate it. If you ever do need help, I would be honored to work with you again. Have a good night."

He tipped his head at me as I turned away. Before leaving the station, I approached the hapless Collier, who was still recumbent and groaning softly. I carefully unlocked my silver shackles from his neck and wrists, once again attaching them to my belt. Giving him a quick head nod when he locked eyes with me briefly, I stood.

"Keep the blanket," I told the room in general. Partner at my heels, I left without a second glance at the proceedings behind me.

CHAPTER 4

A part of my magical heritage that I haven't yet discussed is my unusual way of aging. First of all, while mundane cats have an average lifespan of fifteen years, give or take a few, my family lives much longer. How much longer? Well, it's hard to say exactly what our lifespan is because of one amazing fact: we only age when we are in cat form. That means the more I stay human, the slower I age. I could easily extend my life by an extra forty or fifty years if I spent the majority of that time in my non-natural form.

The only rub in this plan is the fact that the longer I continuously wear my human form without taking breaks to be a cat, the more unpleasant I feel. I liken it to wearing an already uncomfortable suit. It's not so bad when you first put it on, and any discomfort is easy to ignore. But then, after a couple of hours, imagine somebody comes along and pours sand down the back, massaging it around the inside of the clothing. Later on, they add more sand, and then still later they switch to placing biting ants in the clothing. Lastly, they blow smoke in your face every five minutes. By the end, all you desire is to strip off the offending article, thoroughly bathe yourself, and be comfortable at last.

My record was about twelve hours in one go as a human without any cat breaks. It was fairly horrible by the end. This time, between all the driving to and from Hooded Mountain, stalking the werewolf, and dealing with the town of Veradale, I was approaching my sixth hour. Nowhere near as long as my record, but I was definitely feeling the strain.

It was, by now, about five in the morning. The darkness that had persisted through our nighttime encounters was just giving way to a grayness that hinted at a beautiful late-summer dawn. I could tell it was going to be a glorious day, but in the moment, contemplating the weather was the furthest thing from my mind. I needed rest. I needed to dehumanize myself. I needed my real body back.

We had traveled in our wagon for a good hour to get enough distance between ourselves and Veradale. This was a habit of mine. It's not that I thought the townspeople would do something bad to us, but human nature was not something I put a lot of trust into. Especially in small, tight-knit communities, sometimes the drive to protect their own causes people to react violently. It was always better to be safe and exhausted than sorry.

Luckily for us, I found a perfect little pull-off from the main road that was nicely hidden by young trees lining the roadside. Once the wagon was safely settled, I had to see to my employee's comfort before even thinking about my own. I unharnessed Humbert and hastily curried him. As a bonus means of thanks for all his hard work, I fetched a bucket of apples and carrots from the back of the wagon and politely dumped them at his feet.

Only after he began to munch on his well-earned bonus, did I jump up back onto the driver's seat of the wagon. There, after one quick glance at my surroundings to verify utmost privacy, I transformed.

Ah, pure bliss. After wearing my human form for so many hours, I had been getting quite achy and uncomfortable. To be my true self again felt like stripping out of that sand and ant-infested suit and slipping into a plush robe made of clouds. Not only that, but my olfactory and hearing senses instantly sharpened, barraging me with myriad scents and sounds that had previously gone undetected by my inferior human organs. I gave my furry head a brisk shake before taking a deep relaxing breath, soaking up the returning bodily comfort.

My belly made a squelching sound of hunger, intruding on my Zen moment. Humbert swung his massive head in my direction, his jaw working on an apple or carrot. I breathed in deeply to sniff his horsey breath. Based on the sweet smell wafting my way I could discern with accuracy that it was an apple being crunched between his massive teeth. I closed my eyes for a brief second, affirming my trust in my equine employee.

I opened them again. Humbert tossed his head at me, still chewing with pleasure. "Thank you, Mistress," he said to me. Despite our differences in size and species, I thankfully had no problem understanding him when I was a cat. This wasn't true of all species. For instance, I had a very hard time understanding prey animals such as rodents. I assumed it was a built-in mechanism to make cats not feel guilty about killing sentient beings for sustenance.

"Thank *you*, Humbert," I replied. "And sorry for the late night. Good work out there. Get some sleep. There's a stream nearby, and I trust you'll feel comfortable to forage on your own?"

"Delighted, Mistress," he returned. "Goodnight."

Humbert was a simple soul, and a devoted employee. From the start he refused to call me anything but "Mistress," an obvious indication of his devout loyalty to me. His speech and mannerisms were slow and deliberate, and he was never quick to anger, even when I pushed him hard, which I tried to avoid. Despite his advanced age, he still enjoyed being useful, and I was glad of the fact that I had saved him from a certain "retirement" involving dog food and glue.

Wishing him a pleasant rest, I jumped through the opened wagon hatch into the cozy interior. The wagon, our home away from home, was small, just big enough for a tall man to lie down comfortably. We kept the wagon sparse: just a couple of thin mattresses on the floor for the comfort of ourselves and for the hapless humans we occasionally transported. On the side wall I had hung various tools of the trade, such as the silver shackles. A shallow cupboard held food and toiletries at the front of the wagon, below the window hatch.

I surveyed the contents of the cavelike interior from my cupboard perch. Grimm was already in there, taking up much of the space, and the lamp was still on, buzzing softly with the free energy. Jumping down onto the mattress, I transformed back into a human to tend to a few chores.

First thing, I bolted the inner lock on the doors with my key, and then safely tucked the key into my vest pocket. This was a safety precaution that I performed every time we slept within the confines of the wagon. I figured it was foolproof for one reason: I did not need to strip my clothes off before becoming a cat. This was yet another unique trait of my heritage; whenever I shifted back into my cat form whatever I happened to be wearing disappeared, but when I became a human again it automatically reappeared. I didn't fully understand how it worked but I imagined that the shimmery bit of my transformation acted as an interdimensional pocket that stored whatever I happened to be clothed in while I was my true self. Whatever the machination was, it was awesome. I saved a fortune on clothing because I didn't change daily. The best part was that as long as I groomed myself thoroughly as a cat, my human body and my clothes stayed sparkly clean, so I never had to do laundry.

And this bit of magic applied to anything that happened to be in my pockets at the time of transformation too. In other words, the key that locked us in would stay in my interdimensional pocket until I chose to shift back to human. There wasn't a being I knew of who could thieve from *that*.

Having deposited the key in my pocket, I opened the cupboard and took out a good supply of jerky and a jug of water for both Grimm and me. Two bowls were next to be taken out of the cupboard; a dainty porcelain one that I had procured at a flea market, and a deep mixing bowl for the large canine. These I filled with water, and then set everything on the bare floor of the wagon, slightly away from our sleeping area in case one of us got a little sloppy with our drinking habits. (Hint: I wasn't talking about myself. Cats never slosh water out of their mouths, unlike messy canines.)

I reverted to cat form to eat and drink. Naturally, I ate less as a cat than I would as a human, so our food supply lasted us longer on the road. I had also found that my taste buds vastly differed between my human body and my true form. While I always packed backup food for our work excursions, there were times that we ran out before our job was finished. It had become habit to rely on my hunting skills and live off rodents, birds, or even reptiles in a pinch, while we traveled. As a true cat, these small animal bodies tasted just fine to me, minus certain organs. As a human, however, the thought of consuming a raw mouse absolutely repulsed me.

Luckily, jerky tasted delicious in either of my forms. It wasn't the most amazing breakfast, perhaps, but the dried meat soothed our bellies after the physical activity of the night. It would do until we made it back to home base, our ultimate destination after we got some sleep.

Once our meal was finished, I shimmered up again in order to return the water bowls to the cupboard. I also extracted the earnings from this venture from my vest pocket and made a mental note to divvy it up accordingly: forty percent for me, forty percent for Grimm, five percent for Humbert's wages (with which I paid for his food and care), and the last fifteen percent for our manager, Fleurette. For now, though, I was too exhausted to calculate any sums, and I was content to simply stash the money in the small lockbox in a hidden spot within the cupboard.

Lastly, I turned off the lamp, plunging the two of us into complete darkness and eliminating the faint yet annoying buzzing sound. Then I shed my humanity for the final time before sleep.

Grimm was sprawled on his side, a large furry mound of warm dog flesh for me to cuddle into. I stretched luxuriously and nestled into his belly, giving myself a hasty grooming. I was too tired to tend to my whole body, so I settled for a quick face wash, mentally noting to do a more thorough job once I was more rested. I tucked myself deeper into Grimm's side, letting out a subtle purr.

"Good job out there," I mentioned with a yawn.

He grunted softly. "Same to you. That werewolf was softer than most. It was easy. He didn't get a single bite in. How about you? Did the man try to bilk you?" He was referring to Deputy Jones.

Good old Grimm. He always had my back. I stretched out a front leg, claws extended for maximum reach.

"Always. He lowballed me by four hundred, the fleaball. They have to try, don't they?" I laid the arm over Grimm's elbow, keeping my claws politely tucked.

Grimm's side rumbled with a very low growl. He repositioned himself, sitting his body more upright and curling around me, lowering his head to be closer to my body with his chin touching the mattress. He jostled me with his movement, which was rather irritating, but I quickly found my groove in his side and resettled myself. In the near darkness of the wagon, I caught a twinkle of light as his left eye moved over me.

"Just say the word and I'll bite the next one that tries to stiff you," he gravely informed me.

"Aww." I licked his ear that was closest to my face. "I appreciate it, but sometimes I need to fight my own battles. How else are they going to learn that I'm not just a dumb and pathetic female?"

Grimm snorted. "Smartest cat I know. Human too, for that matter."

I purred lazily, pleased by his comment.

"'Night, partner," I murmured as my purrs dwindled.

"'Night, Cress," he sleepily replied.

I realize that Grimm and I made an unusual pair. We were a study of opposites; I was small, a mere eight pounds, and Grimm was huge. I was white, he was black. Female versus male. Cat versus dog. Cheerfully sarcastic versus grumpy and brooding.

But we made it work. We were a dream team together, and most importantly, we enjoyed our partnership.

Even for those who only knew me as a human, our differences seemed very jarring to people. When I was occasionally asked how I found myself partnering up with a Lycanhund, one of the rarest and most magical breeds of dog, I usually gave the questioner a quick and vague answer of, "I saved his life and he saved mine." It's the truth, but the whole story is more complicated than that simple explanation. Allow me a walk down memory lane.

It was just over a year ago. I had left my mom, with her reluctant blessing, at the abandoned barn because I was restless. Even knowing that my life had a grand (although abstract) purpose, I wanted to do something more, something tangible, with myself and my magical gift. And so, I had recently decided to be a bounty hunter, as I figured it would allow me an adventurous life while simultaneously doing some good in the world by capturing wanted criminals.

I had been warned by Fleurette, my new manager, to start out small, but I didn't want to listen to reason. After all, secretly being able to morph from cat to human and vice versa gave me a huge advantage over my competition, in my mind. I was still very young and very inexperienced with life in general. And a tad impetuous, perhaps, looking back.

So, I ignored the advice and chose for my very first hunt not a thief or a domestic abuser, but a man wanted for murder.

His name was Amos Frost. He was wanted, dead or alive, for the grand total of three thousand dollars for the killings of five different individuals spanning four different small towns in the Sunrise Mountain region of Vinland. His last known whereabouts had been outside a town called Jet. The artwork on his wanted poster showed a gaunt man with a large pockmark on his right cheek and horsey, crooked teeth. The artist had done his best to make Frost appear angry and scary, as if to frighten people away from the thought of apprehending him. But I wasn't scared; I was captivated.

I didn't have my wagon yet, nor Humbert. The easiest way to travel was to hitch a ride on an unsuspecting wagon in my true form. It took two days of this hitchhiking to reach Jet, where I resumed my human form to ask for news.

Declaring myself a bounty hunter, I went about seeking answers. But I was only met with derision. Nobody took me seriously. The sheriff of Jet threatened to send for my parents if I didn't stop sticking my nose in serious men's business. His words, not mine. Frustrated by the misogyny being thrown my way, I transformed back into a cat to try a different approach. Nobody took any notice of a new stray in town, although I did attract the attention of some of the local cats. One of them told me she had smelled "the bad man" in town not long ago, although the scent had dissipated quickly. She said the scent had been found at the back of the town, where a path led into the surrounding forest. I was worried about how long ago the cat had actually discovered the scent. Time is a hard thing for many mundane animals to grasp. I assumed she meant days ago, but it could have been mere hours or as long as a month when she had first noticed the scent. However, a lead was a lead, so I thanked her and went to look for this path.

It was easy to find as it had a sign marked, "Jet Valley Nature Trail, Sunrise River two miles." It was obvious that the residents of Jet had no desire to do any nature walking, as they had barricaded the start of the trail off. I paid no attention to the barricade but slipped past it with ease.

It was late afternoon by the time I reached the trail's end by the river. There were no signs anybody had been there for some time. I almost gave this lead up as a dead end when my cat ears picked up a very faint sound coming from upriver to the left. It sounded to me like a pained whine.

I picked my way through the brush near the river, thinking it safer to keep hidden. I slinked along in this fashion for fifteen minutes before the brush thinned to a clearing, where a shack sat hidden from the river's view. A rusty fence with cruel barbs lined the perimeter. A disturbing scent of decay and filth permeated the property and I wondered if this was the smell of the 'bad man' the cat had told me about. If so, it was very fresh. I sat and observed, a statue of catliness, for many minutes before hearing once again the sound that originally drew me to this place.

It came from within the shack. It was an animal in pain—that much I could surmise. My senses picked up no other signs of activity. Steeling myself, I crept under the wire and sneaked over to the shack.

I didn't want to risk transforming here in the open, and I assumed the door was locked anyway, so I scouted around for an alternative way into the interior. There was a broken window on the left-hand side, hidden from my previous vantage point. The jump was doable, even if the window ledge was narrow. I crouched and sprang. I grabbed the ledge with my front claws, using my back claws to hoist myself up the rest of the way. Once I was properly stationed, I looked through the broken pane.

It was my first glimpse of Grimm. He was crammed into a steel kennel that was almost too small for him, with a muzzle on his snout that was definitely too small for him. The muzzle was so tight that he could only open his mouth enough to stick his tongue out and lick frantically at his nose. I imagined the insides of his lips were painfully abraded from digging up against his pointed canines. A bowl of water was placed in front of him, but he could barely wet his tongue, snout-bound as he was. From the window I could see his coat was matted, soiled, and he was malnourished and dehydrated.

I did some fast thinking. It angered me to no end to see a beast imprisoned like this. Clearly, he was dying. But, given his grand size, was he trustworthy? After all, he could easily kill me in my natural state, and even in my human form if he was so inclined. I weighed the pros and cons for about a minute before deciding what to do.

As sick as he was, he hadn't heard me at the window despite my noisy jump. I leapt down into the shack, which caused him to startle. He tried to sit up in the crate. A lackluster growl came from his throat.

"Hush!" I reprimanded. "Do you want my help or not?"

His eyes became huge. "You aren't ordinary, are you?" he asked, staring at me and twitching his nose.

No, I was not, and neither was he, that much I could tell the moment he spoke to me. Despite his disheveled appearance, he had a way about him, like he was a prince among dogs. I shook my head in answer, a very un-cat-like gesture, and he understood me in a very un-mundane doglike way.

"Yes, please help me," he responded after a moment's hesitation.

I took a breath. "Okay, stay calm," I replied. Closing my eyes, I shimmered into a human before him. I opened my eyes to see his yellow ones boring into me, slightly fearful but resolute and hopeful. He gave a curt head nod. I returned it and unlatched the crate. He painfully extracted himself from it and then sat on his haunches before me, waiting.

I looked him directly in the eye. "I trust you," I said, although my heart fluttered, and my hands shook. He stood stock still as I fumbled with the clasps of the muzzle. At last, the straps came free, and I slowly moved it off his face. He stayed still even then, keeping our eyes locked. I dropped the muzzle on the floor of the shack. Then I transformed.

"I am in your debt," he said immediately. "I have been locked up for nearly two weeks, and the muzzle hasn't come off once. I've barely been able to drink with it on and I haven't eaten anything but the thinnest gruel. The evil man had wanted to take the muzzle off, but every time he tried, I attempted to kill him. I don't think I would have lasted much longer had you not come along."

"We aren't out yet," I responded quietly. With a large dog in tow, I didn't think the broken window was an option for escape. I glanced at the door. A deadbolt caught my eye. I turned back to him. "I'll get you out of here and find your owner."

He started to say something, but I was already turning into my human counterpart, and I could no longer understand his canine language. Once I had hands, I undid the dead bolt and cautiously placed my hand on the knob to open the door.

The door, seemingly under its own volition, flew wide away from me. Taken by surprise, my hand never left the knob and I was yanked forward out of the shack. I lost my grip and fell to my knees. I heard the door latch shut behind me as a boot on my back pushed me to the ground. From inside the shack, I could hear furious barking, muffled by the closed door.

"So, I've caught a little fly," a voice sneered over me. Rough hands grasped my shoulders and flipped me to my back. Standing over me was a very dirty man with a puckered pockmark marring his face. Amos Frost. His wanted poster hadn't done him justice. He was much scarier in real life.

Upon seeing my face, Frost smiled and licked his lips. "Such a pretty fly, too," he added lecherously. "It's almost a shame to have to add you to my list. Oh well."

The barking within continued, taking on a frantic note. Frost ignored it and took a step toward me, the ugly smile never leaving his face. Gathering what wits I still had, I raised my knee back and kicked out with all my might, connecting my foot with his shin. Frost bellowed with pain and rage, the creepy smile finally dissipating. I tried to get up, but he fell on top of me as soon as I had rolled back to my hands and knees, making me fall back to my stomach as he trapped my body between his legs. Frost grabbed a massive fistful of my blonde hair, tugging my head back at a painful angle.

"You're going to regret that," he threatened into my ear, his breath contaminating the air with such putrescence that I gagged a little. From the corner of my eye, I witnessed him reaching behind himself with his free hand and removing a long, curved knife from his belt. I admit I whimpered at this point, too petrified to act rationally. He tilted my head back even more with a vicious yank on my hair.

I screamed, a high hoarse sound with no power behind it, given the angle of my throat. As the scream left my mouth, the unmistakable sound of glass breaking erupted behind us. I closed my eyes, expecting to feel the sharp kiss of the blade on my throat, but instead the weight of Frost's body was abruptly gone. The hand holding my hair yanked one more time, taking a few strands with it. I opened my eyes at the sound of another scream. Frost's. The dog stood over him, growling and holding the man's neck in his teeth. In one swift movement, the black beast ripped out Frost's throat. The scream turned to gurgles as blood spurted haphazardly out of the gaping wound. Death was quick if not quite clean.

Blood dripping from his muzzle, the dog looked at me. I let out a single body-heaving sob before becoming a cat. I tried to make myself as small as possible, cowering into a ball with my puffed-up tail wrapped about me, a flimsy security blanket against the terror I had just been subjected to. I blinked my wide blue eyes at the black dog before me.

"You saved my life. Thank you."

He shook his head ineptly and padded over to me, each step ungraceful. The jump through the window and ensuing activity had taken its toll on him in his emaciated state. "Just returning the favor," he said before falling over in exhaustion.

If I didn't do something fast, he wouldn't survive, of that I was sure. I couldn't tolerate that. I sprang back up into human form and grabbed the dish that had been in his kennel. I ran to the river and filled it with fresh water. On my way back to the dog, I spied two freshly killed rabbits near the fence gate. Frost must have been coming back from checking his snares when he realized he had unwanted company. I made a quick detour to grab the rabbits too, then fell to my knees in front of the dog.

"Here," I said as a human, offering the water first. He understood me and began lapping up the water in big, long slurps. The fresh blood that coated his muzzle quickly turned the water pink. I had to look away to quell the sudden queasiness the sight gave me.

"Not too much at once," I cautioned, not sure how much the dog could understand of my human tongue. Even if the words didn't make sense, the canine paused in his lapping. I had been right about his superior intelligence.

The dog was becoming hydrated, but he needed fuel to heal his body. I glanced around and spied Frost's knife, my would-be murder weapon, lying on the grass a foot from the corpse. I hustled over and grabbed the knife by the handle. Feeling suddenly squeamish, I used the curved blade to cut open the belly of the first dead rabbit. I let the entrails spill out a bit before placing the carcass in front of the dog. "Here. Eat."

Not waiting for a response, I got up and went into the shack to look for something with which to carry the corpse back to town. My pickings were slim, and I finally settled for an old, stained quilt that had adorned an equally old and stained mattress in one corner of the room. Quilt in hand, I went back outside and laid it on the ground next to the body. I did not want to touch Frost again, but I worked up the nerve to drag his stinking corpse onto the blanket, and then folded it over him to hide him from view.

By that time the dog had made quick work of the rabbit. I fetched him a bit more water and then changed to a cat. "Better?" I asked him.

"Better." He still sounded exhausted. He laid his head down on the grass and licked his muzzle. I kept my distance still, unsure of what I should do. It was twilight by then, and the adrenaline that had coursed so freely through me now left me weary.

"My name is Grimm." This statement came out of the blue as I watched him.

"Cressida. Curtain," I added.

"Come here, Cressida," Grimm beckoned, giving his tail a small, gentle wag, "I'll need your body warmth tonight."

I hesitated for a second, trying to determine if he was as friendly as he sounded. I finally concluded he meant well, and I awkwardly nestled into his side. With the corpse of a bad man just a few feet away and the stars above us, we both slept the exhausted sleep of survivors.

I awoke at dawn, and with the mountains in the background I saw firsthand why they were called the Sunrise Mountains. Even with my slightly color-compromised cat eyes, the sky was brilliant. I briefly transformed into a human to fully appreciate the complete majesty of the sight. The pinks and oranges mixed with the blues and purples over the mountain tops in a symphony of natural splendor.

I was transported back to reality when from behind me, Grimm groaned and stretched his legs out. I went back to cat form so that we could talk.

"Good morning," I greeted warily, unsure how much the dog would remember of me.

"Cressida. Good morning." Well, he remembered my name. That was a good sign.

"I'd like to go back to town today. With the body. Are you well enough to walk the distance?"

"With more water and maybe the other rabbit to eat, I could walk it, yes."

We spent the morning resting, gathering up Grimm's strength. I tested him by having him walk to the river to drink and relieve himself. I also dunked his soiled coat carefully, washing away two weeks of dirt and oil, along with the remaining blood from his recent gruesome kill. Back at the shack's yard, he told me his story as he ate.

His mother was owned by a monk who lived alone in the mountains. Not the Sunrise Mountains, Grimm clarified, but some range much, much farther away. The monk bred the Lycanhunds, a breed of dog with a small amount of natural magic in their blood. This magic allows them to live much longer lives than mundane dogs, but negatively affects their fecundity. Grimm's litter was only his mother's second, and she was approaching the age of twenty years at his birth. Grimm was one of three puppies in his litter, the other two being females. When he was two years old, still very much a puppy for a Lycanhund, Grimm was sold to a man who had made the journey to find the monk. Grimm told me his new master was a kind man who, although he didn't treat Grimm as a pet, gave him a good life with plenty of food and exercise and a warm home.

"I was happy with my master," he said. "The monk had started my werewolf hunting training and Master continued it. Master was very adroit with his teaching."

This idyllic life lasted for three years. Grimm had by then reached maturity and was proficient in his skill. But then, while out in the woods for a walk near the base of one of the Sunrise Mountains, Grimm felt something sting his flank. He turned to go back to his master but suddenly felt sleepy and heavy. Just before he passed out, he witnessed his master's murder by the knife of Frost. When he came to, he was muzzled and in the kennel.

"Frost tried to break me. He wanted to use me to hunt, but all I wanted to do was kill him. He would have killed me either by starvation or something else unpleasant in the long run." Grimm shuddered. "And now, I have no master. I have no home to go back to."

At this last statement, Grimm oozed despair. A working Lycanhund was a happy Lycanhund. A Lycanhund with no purpose was a dog at loose ends. In that moment I felt a small amount of kinship with him.

With this unsatisfactory conclusion to his story, I decided it was time to leave this place of unhappy memories. A human again, I grabbed the corners of the quilt and dragged the corpse behind me. Grimm brought up the rear. It was a hard two miles, and we were both exhausted by the time we reached Jet. I dragged Frost over to the sheriff's station. He saw me coming and made to shoo me away again, but something in my face made him stop. Without a word, I flung the quilt off the body.

"I've come to collect," I said.

The following days were a bit of a blur. I remember seeing respect in the sheriff's eyes and that was the best reward of all. Of course, the three thousand dollars was lovely as well. I rented a room in the inn and insisted that Grimm stay by my side the entire time. At first the sheriff contended that the dog was the property of the deceased owner's family, but Grimm had told me his master had no living family, and this was seconded by the townsfolk who knew his master. In light of this, I told the sheriff the dog could be with whomever he wanted. Grimm backed this up by growling menacingly at anyone who wasn't me. In the end, they agreed with my reasoning and let us alone. We stayed perhaps a week at the inn, sleeping, eating copious amounts of food, and recovering Grimm's strength. We talked a fair bit as well when locked in our room together. Despite being a tad overeager with this bounty and having it nearly mortally backfire, I was convinced I wanted to continue as a bounty hunter. I had told Grimm he was a free dog, but we had bonded over the course of our journey, and Grimm was reluctant to leave me. It gave me an idea.

"What if we worked together?" I asked him the day before we left Jet.

"You mean I would work for you?" Grimm mulled this idea over.

"No," I replied emphatically. "I mean *together*. As equals. I am not your master, and I will never own you. You deserve the bounty for Frost as much as I do because you were the one to bring him down. And many of the bounties I've seen are for werewolves and other supernaturals. You'd be indispensable to me."

"So, partners?"

"Fifty-fifty."

"I accept."

And that was the beginning of our professional career. And, as it turned out, a pretty incredible friendship.

CHAPTER 5

S leep was awesome. After a grueling job like the one we had just finished, I could have slept all day. But fate had other plans.

I was dreaming that Mr. Collier had escaped and was a werewolf again, but instead of Grimm hunting him down, I was jumping on the werewolf in human form, pummeling him with my bare hands until he shrank into a tiny mouse, shivering and squeaking. I morphed into my cat form and pounced, claws extended, feeling their sharp tips sink into the soft flesh of the quivering rodent...

WHUMP!

Something landed on the roof of the wagon with enough force to jar me from my dream. My eyes opened wide, taking in the small amount of light coming from the cracked-open hatch. I perked my ears to catch any stray noise, keeping the rest of my body as unmoving as a statue.

Sure enough, the staccato ticking of walking claws caught my attention. This was followed by my name being cawed in a very familiar voice.

"Rupert," I muttered.

The noise woke Grimm too, who stretched his recumbent legs on either side of me and groaned largely. "Go catch that bird for our lunch," he grumbled.

I stretched my body, first rump up, and then spine curved up. With bleary eyes, I made my way up through the hatch, pausing on the seat to allow my sensitive eyes to adjust to the brightness of the morning. Based on the look of things, I guessed the time to be around seven, which meant I only had two hours of sleep under my belt. Not nearly enough, damn that bird. Eyes suitably adjusted, I jumped up onto the roof.

Rupert the crow had his back to me. He was peering over the ledge at the back, ruffling his wing feathers. I watched him for a moment, remembering the thrill of hunting that my dream had left me in, and thought for a moment about pouncing on the unsuspecting bird from behind. Fleurette would not be happy with me if I gave into my base urges, however, so I ignored the desire.

Rupert's role in our operations was a bit of an enigma. He had been a package deal, albeit a bit of a reluctant one, when Fleurette became my manager. He basically acted as a messenger whenever we were otherwise unreachable, such as this morning. No matter where we were, he had an uncanny knack for finding us. He and I didn't exactly get along, so I never bothered to ask how he managed it. I simply chalked it up to how the crow flies.

"This better be important, Rupert," I grumbled after watching him for a moment.

The crow jumped and swiveled, eyeing my appearance with sudden nervousness. "Ah, g'morning, Cressida! Did-did I wake you?" He blinked his dark eyes and did a little anxious hop to the side.

I merely stared at the ebony bird and lashed my tail from side to side, my ears tucked slightly back in annoyance. My body language was not lost on the corvid.

"Right! Sorry about that!" he fidgeted a bit. When I still didn't reply, he continued, "Fleurette found another job for you. She tried to reach you on your message mirror, but it wasn't working."

That would be because my mirror was in my vest pocket. On my human body. Which was tucked away in an interdimensional pocket. The magical artifact didn't work at all while it was in there. I didn't mention this to Rupert, however. He continued, "She'd like you to make your way home as soon as you can. Of-of course," he added with a sidelong glance, "you can keep sleeping longer if you like."

I sighed. "How thoughtful of you." I yawned theatrically, showing the crow all of my teeth. Rupert fluttered a bit. "Tell Fleurette we'll be on our way just as soon as we are sufficiently rested. Say, closer to noon."

"Will do!" His message delivered, Rupert leapt into the air with his wings unfurled. Flapping to gain altitude, he made a swift exit over the treetops.

I watched him fly for a few seconds before returning to my cozy den.

"New job?" Grimm asked sleepily as I crawled on top of his rib cage. I began kneading his side, careful not to dig my claws in too deep. He sighed, his great chest raising me a few inches before lowering again.

"Mm-hm. Sleep now, job later," I replied as I positioned myself securely onto my warm canine mattress.

Grimm and I slept for another three hours. I would have gone for more, but the thought of Fleurette wanting me back so soon had started to nag at me and impact the quality of my sleep. Besides, by that time Humbert had gotten a good bellyful of grass and other clippings and was ready to depart. Grimm and I ate another hasty meal of dried meat, and I harnessed up Humbert. Less than twelve hours after capturing our last quarry, we were on our way to learn about the next.

It took Humbert about three more hours to travel into the town of Knobby Hill. Once we entered town limits, my horse employee picked up a little speed, knowing that home base was just another twenty minutes away.

This home base was in truth a stone-and-wood cottage about two miles outside of the town of Knobby Hill. It was situated on the north side of a road that led directly from the town westward. The road had the odd name of Rabbit Hole Road. I had never seen a rabbit hole anywhere near the road, and believe me, I checked, so I have no clue why it was dubbed thusly. The locals tended to shorten this to R.H. Road, as the full name was a bit of a mouthful. The road, no matter its name, stopped being paved about half a mile in, as most locals had no reason to travel on it further. And, while Rabbit Hole Road did continue past the cottage's property, it didn't amount to much more than an old pothole-ridden wagon wheel track surrounded by woodland on either side after a half mile or so. On my days off it was a favorite pastime of mine and Grimm's to walk that direction and explore those woods.

Home base didn't have any close neighbors; in fact, the closest neighbor lived one and a half miles closer to town, right where the road stopped being paved. There were plenty of open fields and a few sparse patches of trees, however, between the cottage and town.

The cottage was built about one hundred years ago as a simple stone structure, with the main sitting room in front and a kitchen in back. Over the years its residents had added a room here and there, sometimes matching the original stonework, and sometimes lowering the cost by building with wood instead of stone. It evolved over time as well; when indoor plumbing became the new best thing, the dining room located to the left of the kitchen was converted into the bathroom, and a new dining room was eventually built to the right side of the kitchen. The cottage's most recent floor plan consisted of the original sitting room and kitchen, the dining room and a tiny workroom off the kitchen to the left, and a T-shaped hallway on the right that gave access to the bathroom and two bedrooms.

The cottage sat one hundred feet back from the road. Its stone and wood façade were aged to perfection, the front door freshly painted in a cheerful shade of plum. A small wooden stoop with three steps led to this cheerful entrance, with plant life flanking either side. The cottage was surrounded by an untidy front yard dotted with shady trees and messy flower borders. A vast herb and vegetable garden, lush with greenery, took up much of the space to the right side and wrapped around to the back of the house. Farther out, more outbuildings dotted the property.

The whole look of the property was an odd contradiction of tidy disorder, or disordered tidiness, depending on how one wanted to view it.

This was Fleurette's home, and I loved it, no matter how neatly untidy it was.

On the dirt road, rounding the last bend of our journey, Humbert's ears perked up and his tired feet sped up slightly more, his anticipation at being home palpable. I too relished coming back to Fleurette's after an especially grueling job, even if just for a day or two. I always felt like it was welcoming me home, a salutation for a job well done. As the property came into view, I found myself smiling. Grimm, who had decided to walk the last two miles from town, emitted a small bark before putting on the speed to beat us to the cottage. He felt its welcome too.

The place looked as green and lush as ever. While the property exuded a wildness with the dense garden, it also was very obviously a contained and maintained chaos. There wasn't an overly long blade of grass or a scraggly shrub in sight.

I led Humbert to the left side of the cottage opposite the mighty garden, where the fence line ended. Hopping down from my seat, I patted the horse affectionately before beginning the process of unharnessing him. As I worked, I heard the front door open and shut, followed by a raucous caw. I glanced over my shoulder as Rupert landed on the wagon's roof and gave me a sidelong glance. I turned back to see Fleurette approaching me with a large smile on her tan face.

Have you ever heard the adage that a person doesn't choose their cat, but the cat chooses their person? It's completely true, take it from me. Sure, a human can go and pick up a cat and claim it as their property, but if that human doesn't have the cat's blessing, the relationship will never be meaningful. We cats are picky that way. We only adopt humans that we find to be worthy in some significant way, whether it's trust, kindness, or some other special quality.

A year ago, I adopted Fleurette as my human.

Sure, Fleurette may have been my business manager, but she was also my closest human friend. She was kind, she was trustworthy, and she exuded a calm warmness that made me feel at home every time I was there. I would have been crazy not to choose her. Of course, I never told her any of this. It was in my best interest to stay a proud, aloof feline.

Oh yes. She also knew I was more than human. That's right; she was the first human with whom I broke Rules Number 1 and 2. Fleurette was an honorable woman, however, and promised to keep my secret safe. As much as I trusted her, though, she still believed I was a simple shapeshifter, instead of the only being who was somehow preventing an evil megalomaniac from returning to this dimension. In this regard, I had kept Rule Number 3 intact. It was better that way.

Fleurette rounded Humbert to stand in front of me. She was dressed in her usual fashion: a long, flowy patterned skirt paired with a white peasant blouse that enhanced her curvy figure.

"Welcome back!" she greeted, embracing me. She was a good five inches taller than me, and so it seemed that her whole essence engulfed me whenever we hugged. She smelled like fresh herbs, flowers, and churned earth, as always. Her thick chestnut brown hair, wild and curly, was braided down her back, but some of the unruly wisps had escaped and framed her face. There was never a chance of fully containing those locks of hers. Her skin was a healthy tan; I once thought it was from the sun until I learned about her mixed heritage.

I typically wasn't the hugging type in my human form, but when it came to Fleurette I could never say no to one of her embraces. They were incredibly comforting.

She released me and I stepped back. "How was the job?" she asked with sudden seriousness, studying my countenance with the focus of a mother cat cleaning her kitten.

I shrugged. "Super easy. Right, Grimm?" I glanced around when I didn't hear a customary chuff of agreement from my partner. I spotted him at the edge of the property, following his nose about for any new smells that might have accumulated since we were gone. I turned my attention back to Fleurette, angling my head at the wagon. "I've got the bounty in the safe. I didn't have time to divvy it up yet."

Fleurette waved the idea of money away. "Don't worry about that just now; we can handle that later today."

Time to figure out what was going on that was so important as to hurry us back home.

I gazed up at her face. "Fleurette, what was the rush?"

I didn't mean to sound quite as snippy as I did, and I immediately regretted my tone when I saw her face fall a bit. She looked upward and sighed.

"I know I usually give you a bit more time between jobs," she began, "but this one ... well, I feel like you should get there first." She straightened a little and smiled. "I have a feeling you two are hungry. Come on, let's get some food in you first. I'll explain over lunch."

She walked ahead of me into the cottage but stopped short at the doorway. I craned over to the side to see what had caught her attention. A creeping fig had been planted on the left-hand side of the doorway years ago. It now took up a large portion of the front wall surrounding the purple door, clinging tightly to the outer façade. A creeper had started to trail outward toward the door. Fleurette had taken notice, which had triggered her impromptu stop. I watched as she extended her hand carefully and touched the tip of her finger to the vine's edge. The vine trembled faintly at the slight pressure, and then began curling inward like a retracting worm, before hiding itself in the surrounding branches of the fig.

That was another important thing about Fleurette. She was not just my manager and my friend, but also, she was a minor witch, her specialty being plant magic. She had, in my opinion, the world's greenest thumb. Her garden, in all its wildness, was the happiest garden on the face of the planet. Each plant in her domain had been meticulously cared for. I didn't have the foggiest clue how her magic worked; as far as I knew she was born with this talent. The best way I could describe it was that she somehow communicated with the plants, and they responded by doing what she asked.

When she wasn't acting as my manager, Fleurette made a living two other ways: she sold seeds and seedlings to the local folk at the Knobby Hill Saturday Market in the springtime, and she produced herbal tinctures and salves to heal various minor ailments, which she sold year-round. She lived rather simply, however, and a little money went a long way. Therefore, the traffic to her cottage was kept at a minimum, which suited her—and me when I was there—just fine.

Having asked the fig to tuck back its errant vine, Fleurette entered her abode. I followed her through the small and cozy sitting room filled with mismatched stuffed chairs, a loveseat, and small house plants hanging from the ceiling or in pots on every available surface. Just past the sitting room was the kitchen, which faced the back of the cottage. The kitchen had an airier feel to it than the previous room, probably because it wasn't stuffed to the gills with furniture, although the windowsills were also chock full of greenery.

I breathed in the scent of chicken soup, one of my favorite meals. Sure enough, a large pot sat on the apple-green stovetop ahead of me, the contents simmering and releasing the aroma of chicken, onions, garlic, and veggies into the air. The smell was drool-inducing. Fleurette made her way to the oven, picked up a wooden ladle and stirred the soup. She smirked as she turned to look at me.

"You are just in time," she said. "Nothing like a good home-made soup to lend some comfort!"

At this moment Grimm, who had caught up with his 'news' around the property, made an appearance. He walked to my side and sat at my heels, acting the obedient dog. Fleurette laughed. "Grimm, welcome back!"

Fleurette understood that my partner was more than an ordinary dog, and always treated him as an equal, which made her that much more special in my mind. I knew that Grimm also appreciated her. He never growled at her or gave her gimlet eyes but treated her as a respectful member of his pack.

"Did the smell of soup get to you too?" she asked him playfully. Grimm chuffed in response and Fleurette laughed again before getting bowls down from the cupboard to dish up lunch.

Bowls filled, we sat at the dining room table, off to the right of the kitchen. The room was a heavily windowed addition, which made it light, bright, and warm on sunny days such as this. Fleurette had already opened most of the windows to allow a cooling breeze through the room. It infused the scent of chicken soup with that of grass and flowers.

After our last few meals of jerky, the soup was ambrosia. Even Grimm got his own bowl, magically cooled off by Fleurette before he scarfed it down. I was so hungry I focused solely on my spoon, knowing that talk would have to wait, no matter how curious I was.

But eventually my belly was satisfied, and just at the right time too, considering I was scraping the last of the broth into my mouth. It was time for information.

I gave Fleurette a serious look. "What's the job?"

Fleurette was still eating, by virtue of not having been starving. She glanced up at me as she added another spoonful to her mouth. She chewed thoughtfully, gauging my rising impatience.

Finally, she carefully placed her spoon in her bowl and let out a small sigh. She then leaned to one side to fish into her flowing skirt's pocket, pulling out a piece of folded up paper. It was something I was familiar with.

"You know I normally don't pull you for a job this quickly," she began, still keeping the paper in her hand, "but I saw this on the board yesterday, and this one seemed important."

"Important how?" I queried, reaching for the paper.

She paused another heartbeat before leaning over the table to pass me the sheet. "As in, I think you should be the first to get to him because I know you'll treat him better."

This was unusual. Fleurette may have donned the mantle of manager when I first decided to pursue this career, but mostly it was in title only. Typically, she left Grimm and me to our own devices when it came to choosing our jobs. In fact, the only time she intervened was when we were asked for by name for a specific bounty. Otherwise, she typically didn't even peruse the available bounties on her own.

Did that mean she was lying to me when she said she just happened to stumble upon it on the message board? That didn't seem like Fleurette's style. Curiosity thoroughly piqued, I gave Fleurette one more look before unfolding the paper and scanning it quickly.

A very crude drawing of a face looked back at me: a nondescript squarish jaw, angry eyes and lips, and just a line to hint at a nose. All this was framed by ear-length hair that was filled in with black. This was nowhere near realistic enough to be a speculograph, a magically taken picture of someone. Nor was it an eyewitness approved artist's rendering. That by itself spoke of mystery in this case. No one really knew what the perp truly looked like.

"'Boy burglar, wanted for theft..." I read in confusion. "Boy burglar?"

"My thoughts exactly. I don't know how old he is, but the dossier seems quite strict for petty crime. Cressida, you have a bit more of a gentle hand. Something isn't adding up and I worry that another bounty hunter will take everything at face value."

I reread the paper in my hands. "It says here that all the crimes were committed in Chargrove, but Knobby Hill Corrections is the one processing the criminal. That's a bit odd." I may not have had a solid grasp on this region's geography, but I did know that Chargrove was not exactly close to Knobby Hill.

"I agree."

I nodded absently, still thinking things through. This typically wasn't the kind of bounty I usually went for; the reward was relatively small, and I liked to focus on the more supernatural criminals that others had a hard time acquiring. This just didn't seem challenging, but at the same time Fleurette was right. Something wasn't adding up on multiple accounts. It was time to make a decision: let this small fry go or reel in in?

"I accept," I said.

"Excellent!" Fleurette exclaimed. She stood up briskly, collecting our messy dishes with enthusiasm. "We should head to town and visit the courthouse as soon as possible. The dossier was only posted yesterday evening, so I bet not many other hunters have reacted to it yet, but time is of the essence on this one."

I internally groaned. I hadn't really gotten a fulfilling amount of sleep since the last job. The thought of starting this new one immediately wasn't exactly making me jump for joy.

"Should I leave for Chargrove this evening, then?" I asked reluctantly, raising my voice so that she could hear me in the kitchen.

Fleurette bustled back into the dining room and took her seat again. She shook her head. "I don't think that's necessary. Everyone else will be taking the main road from Knobby Hill to travel to Chargrove. It's a nice flat road that can be traveled at a faster pace, but it also takes you farther out in order to connect with other towns along the way. I happen to know of a shortcut."

"A shortcut?" I cocked my head.

Fleurette smiled knowingly. "This road here just so happens to be a direct route to Chargrove."

I frowned. "Your road? As in the one right outside that goes into the woods?"

She gestured toward the front of her cottage. "Yes, silly. Did you not know that? If you take a left out of my place, Rabbit Hole Road takes you to Knobby Hill, as you well know. But turning right takes you to Chargrove. It used to be the main way to get there before they built the newer, wider, but much longer road. This way, it's about a twenty-five-mile drive. I did it once when I was younger. I do recall it's a rough road in the middle, but it should still be drivable."

I pondered this. "So, if I take this back road, I should beat any competition there, right? What are the chances that anybody else will know about this alternative route?"

Fleurette shrugged. "It was more widely used about fifty years ago, before the main road was constructed. Seeing as how I hardly ever get traffic past my house, I think it's a safe bet that most people don't know about it anymore. And I guarantee they don't put it on maps anymore."

"Great." I nodded my head as if to cement the plan. "How soon can we go and arrange things at the courthouse? I should try to leave first thing in the morning if I want any sort of advantage."

"I plan to drop off some more tonics at the Apothecary. I just need to gather some things together, once I clean the kitchen. Give me half an hour?" Fleurette hedged.

I glanced at Grimm, who was lying on his large haunches and licking his paws. "Perfect. that will give me time to tell Grimm all the details." At the mention of his name, my intelligent partner lifted his head and gazed into my eyes with a serious demeanor, although I did see his tail wiggle in an almost-wag.

"Speaking of..." Fleurette added, almost hesitant. I swiveled my head to look at her. "Dad's told me it's time for Grimm's checkup. Can you stop by there after our town errands today?"

Fleurette's dad was a veterinarian, our own personal doctor as well as a trusted friend.

Grimm, while not fully understanding human language, knew more words than the average dog to piece together 'Dad' and 'checkup.' His ears drooped in a pathetic way as he glanced at the woman. I chuckled.

"No problem," I answered.

CHAPTER 6

"Look, I know I'm a good boy but please tell me I don't need a shot!" Grimm complained.

We were in the sitting room, lounging on the love seat. It was a good thing I was so small because he took up practically the whole thing. Fleurette was tidying up the kitchen after our big meal and told us to vamoose out of her way, so I wasted no time stripping off my human form and getting comfortable for a bit before we ventured into town.

I purred a little to placate the dog's uneasiness. "You wrestle werewolves into submission, but a little needle poke scares you?"

Grimm blew out a breath through his black wet nose. "I was born to wrestle werewolves. Needles? Not so much."

"Sorry, partner, I can't tell you one way or another. It's up to Lyle, not me, whether you are due or not. A tiny poke is better than a life-threatening disease, right?"

Grimm groaned in response, dropping his head and trying to hide his face with a paw. Then he shot back up, perking his ears a bit, adding, "But I can't get fleas. What makes you all so sure I can contract regular dog diseases?"

It was true, fleas hated Grimm. I chalked it up to the small amount of magic running in his veins. Magic must be a natural flea deterrent. I wasn't complaining either, because fleas hated me just as much.

Still. "Fleas are easy to see. Microbes are not. Just suck it up and it will be over. Better to be safe than sorry, right? Before we go, can I tell you about the new job?"

"Sure. What is it this time?"

"It's a little out of our wheelhouse," I began, and thought back to the dossier, which I had already memorized. I rattled it off to Grimm, "Wanted alive or incapacitated: boy burglar, name: unknown; age: under eighteen; magic: unknown; distinguishing features: dark hair of either black or brown color, thin build. Last seen in Chargrove. Crimes: theft of large amounts of food from locals, both stores and private; theft of clothing from Chargrove; assault of Henry Whitman of Chargrove. Reward: $800. Payable by Constable Fletcher of Knobby Hill Corrections."

"Not much, and yet, they usually don't bother with bounties for small stuff," Grimm observed.

"That's why I'm interested. We're going to town today, and then we'll leave first thing in the morning. That will give you enough time to recover from your checkup."

Grimm groaned.

It was the tail end of summer in Vinland, and in our little patch of the Oracune Region, that meant delightfully warm days enhanced with intermittent cloud cover. We were reaching the end of the dry time, and the almost incessant rain would be starting within a month, two if we were lucky. Because we locals never took glorious days for granted, the three of us decided to walk to town instead of hitching Humbert back up.

I had spent so much of my time as a human with this last job, that I decided to do the bulk of the trek as a cat. The warm sun felt wonderful on my white fur, with my two dark spots on my head soaking up the rays even more. I felt a little sorry for Grimm, as he must have been quite hot in his shaggy black fur. He was accustomed to his permanent coat, however, and the only sign of discomfiture he displayed was a bit of light panting as we walked.

Fleurette didn't mind that I chose my cat form. She simply enjoyed the animal company on the walk. Occasionally she would speak to us about something that crossed her mind. I could understand human speech in my true form, but I did have to concentrate more on the words than I otherwise would as a human. Grimm only caught the gist, so he often asked me to translate for him if something didn't make sense.

Soon enough, we came close enough to town that it became prudent for me to be in my human guise. I ran off into the ditch, just in case, and came back out on two legs. We continued our casual stroll until we reached the edge of town, at which point Fleurette parted ways, promising to meet us back at the cottage after our visit to her father.

Knobby Hill wasn't a large town by anyone's measure, but it was substantial for what it was. It also boasted a state-of-the-art courthouse, which made it the unofficial head for criminal investigations in Tinuka County. Many of the neighboring towns came here to post their bounties, and to judge and prosecute many of the bigger trials, even if the crimes committed were far away.

The stately white courthouse featured an expansive lawn out front: lush, green, and meticulously maintained. On nice days like this, it was a beacon for those of the town that were searching for a little sun and relaxation.

The lawn also contained the town notice board. It was tucked to one side instead of in the middle, so as not to mar the view of the regal building behind it. The board was rather long, and double sided. One side was for general postings: lost pets, items for sale, and upcoming events in Knobby Hill. This was the side that faced the street and got the most attention.

I wanted to scope out the other side.

That section was strictly for postings pertaining to the courthouse and the law in general. In other words, it held all of the bounties that were available: my bread and honey.

Bounty hunters like myself thrived off the dark side of notice boards. Although sometimes the bounties were slim pickings, most of the time there was a glut of options to choose from. Today, it was somewhere in between.

I scanned the various papers, giving each bounty a brief once-over. Most were small-time things; some were just for questioning a mark. Those didn't provide much of a bounty but would at least pay for a meal or two if one were in dire financial straits. Many times, the supernatural bounties were the best to take because they tended to have a more dangerous quality to them, and therefore needed an extra bonus for most bounty hunters to risk it. Those were naturally the cases I gravitated to, seeing as how both myself and my partner were also considered supernatural. But alas, none graced the board today.

As a matter of fact, the bounty I already held in my hand was the highest paying one. That concerned me a bit, because it would automatically make it more appealing to my fellow hunters, and competition wasn't my goal.

Clashes with other hunters was something I had to put up with a lot, however, seeing as how Knobby Hill not only contained the region's courthouse, but it was also the home of the Northwest Bounty Hunters' Guild. I was a member of said guild, but only because I had to be in order to be a bounty hunter. The laws in our region made it clear that "rogue" hunters were not eligible for the bounties. I surmised this was the guild's way of making more money, since dues were owed annually. As it was, I felt enormously uncomfortable stopping by the lodge, as some members rented out rooms and chose to lounge there between jobs. It was a boy's club, for sure, as I was the sole female member. My guildmates made sure to make me feel welcome on my first day by leaving a dead mouse in my mail cubby. It was meant to freak me out with the hopes I would quit. The joke was on them, though; I picked it up, took it with me back to Fleurette's, and had a nice little meal in the privacy of her backyard as a cat.

It was delicious.

The Guild Lodge just happened to be located across the street from the message board, which was convenient for any hunter passing by. Yes, competition could be fierce.

As if to drive the point home, I sensed someone approaching me from behind. I spun and tried to hide the paper in my hand, but I wasn't quick enough.

The man towered over me, all brawn. He was in his mid-thirties and had a slightly raised scar on his left cheek. He smiled as he met my eyes, but it was the look of a bully who was about to get some pleasure belittling someone smaller. Like me.

"Well, well, well, it's Baby Bounty Hunter! Still in one piece, I see," he said cheerfully as he gave me a quick once-over.

Here's the thing about my chosen profession: there were a lot of jerks in it. Big, muscled, testosterone-ridden jerks. Most of them were older than me, had been doing this for longer, and, last but not least, could pee standing up. That made me, younger, smaller, and female, the brunt of many of their jokes, despite the fact that I had more than proved my capabilities over the last year.

And so, the responsibility fell to me to make sure my fellow hunters didn't get complacent with their misogynistic views, and above all, that their views weren't justified by any ineptitude on my part.

It was often exhausting, but then again, I clearly relished a good challenge.

I plastered on a smile, the one that showed off way too much teeth. "Why, Allan, hello! Still avoiding showers, I smell. What brings you here?"

Allan guffawed. I had to give it to him—he wasn't the worst man out there in terms of bullying. He may have liked to flick verbal crap at me, but I could tell that deep down he held a nugget of respect for me. I couldn't say the same for many of the others.

It also helped that we rarely crossed paths while out in the field. Allan liked to stick to the more mundane ever since he tangled with a rather nasty specimen of a rogue shifter. Hence the scar he sported. I rarely viewed him as strict competition.

Allan answered my question with an exaggerated wink. "Why, this is where I pick up all the pretty lady hunters, naturally."

Well, that was different. My desire to banter suddenly fled as I grappled with a surge of discomfort. I waved my bounty paper like a tiny white flag in front of me. "Well, good luck with that. I need to get inside to ask about this one."

Allan scrunched his eyes to try to read the moving paper. He puzzled out a hint and found it on the board, tearing a copy off for himself. He narrowed his eyes as he read the description.

Finally, he met my gaze over the top of his page. "This one, huh?" He mused aloud. "Too far out for me. But just a head's up, I saw St. Cloud grab this one too, just an hour ago."

I groaned. Out of all the bounty hunters out there, Gavin St. Cloud was the one I liked least of all. He and I almost always clashed over bounties, and he was good. He was also a jerk.

"If you want to go after this one too, you might want to get a move on. Gavin plans to head out tomorrow, I think," Allan added with a slight raise of his eyebrows.

"Um, thanks for the warning," I replied, frowning a bit at him. Why was he being so nice to me?

Allan smiled again, a real smile without the cruelty. "Any time, Baby B. Listen, if you have a few to spare, maybe you and I could go get a drink at Lucky's Pub."

Huh? Was he asking me out for a drink? This was entirely too weird. As nice as he was being, I had no interest in doing anything remotely social with him. I was taken off guard, and my uneasiness increased.

"Thanks, but no. I don't drink." I finally replied. It wasn't a lie, either. I'd never touched the stuff in my life. Alcohol smelled repugnant to me in my cat form, and not much better while human. I'd stick to water or, if I was feeling lively, a little bit of dairy.

Allan stepped forward, encroaching on my personal bubble a bit. "Aw, c'mon. I thought that was a nice tip I just gave you. Surely you can see it in your heart to have one little drink with me."

Okay, now I was getting annoyed. I was about to tell him that I didn't owe him anything, and to leave me alone, but a loud growl answered for me. Grimm, who had been lounging on the sunny side of the board during this time, had clearly sensed my discomfort and stalked to my side like a silent yet vengeful shadow.

Allan instantly backed up a step. "Or maybe not," he replied with a nervous undertone. "Next time, perhaps? Stay safe out there, Baby B." He speed-walked away.

I waited until Allan was gone from my line of sight, and then let out a breath. "Freya's furballs," I muttered. I swiveled around to pet Grimm's head. "Good timing, partner," I told him. He tried to lick my hand. "Let's go get this over with."

Satisfied that there were no other bounties we wanted, the two of us approached the courthouse.

Inside the grand front doors, a guard approached. Since I was a regular to the Bounty Office, we recognized one another.

"Miss Curtain, welcome." He greeted me with a professionally honest smile.

"Hey, Frankie," I greeted back. I bent over to remove the only weapon I ever carried. It was a knife, about six inches in length, that I kept in a special pocket in my right boot. After the incident with Amos Frost, Fleurette got a little concerned for my safety, even with my new giant dog partner. In order to let me continue this line of work, she insisted on me carrying some sort of protection. Guns gave me the heebie-jeebies, so the knife was a compromise. It wasn't just an ordinary knife, though. Fleurette had it enchanted. All I had to do was make the tiniest cut on my foe. The knife would react to the blood on it, and the next wield would be a fatal blow to the owner of said blood. The enchantment would only last for one enemy before it would wear off. It was always my last resort. I called it Hail Mary.

Straightening back up, I slipped Hail Mary out of my boot and placed it on the table next to me without being asked. Then I held my arms out to my sides and widened my feet a bit. I stared straight ahead and asked Frankie, "Who's working the office today?"

Frankie waved a small crystal orb over the front of me, and then over Grimm's back. It stayed a clear color, which was the favorable outcome. In the presence of a dangerous weapon, magical or physical, the orb would have darkened to a soot black. Hail Mary would have set it off in a heartbeat if I hadn't removed it from my person.

Frankie straightened, satisfied with the results of his weapons check, and shot me another smile. "It's Angie today," he said with a tiny shrug. He picked up Hail Mary and tucked into a cubby behind him for safe keeping.

"Hmm, well, could be worse." I waved my hand in farewell as I took the left hallway, and went through a door that said, "BOUNTY OFFICE" in bold letters.

The office reminded me of a small bank lobby, with wood paneling coming up halfway and the rest of the worker's area ensconced by delicate metal bars, much like a large bird cage. And, behind the cage, sat the noisiest canary of them all.

"Why, Miss Curtain!" Angie Barton gleefully called out. "What a pleasant surprise! I wasn't expecting to see you so soon. Whatever can I do for you today, hon?"

Angie, bless her, was a talker. That woman could pack in more words per square inch than anybody else I have come across. I usually left the office with a mild twitch after being in her presence for five minutes. But she had a heart of gold, and a soft spot for me as well, given that I was the only female hunter in the area and, as Angie liked to say, "We womenfolk have to look out for each other."

I approached her cage with a forced smile. "Hi, Angie," I greeted with less enthusiasm than she had shown me. I slid the wanted sheet into the paper-width narrow slot at the bottom of the cage. "What can you tell me about this one?"

Angie took the paper from me and studied it. Her blonde ringlets fell forward into her round face as she bent her head. She blew one of them to the side rather ineffectually, as it bounced right back. Her forehead creased.

Angie turned to her left to grab a key from a hook by the door that gave her access to the hallway. She bent down to insert the key into a filing cabinet that lay directly underneath the hook.

I had seen her do this before to access files on the bounties that were posted here in Knobby Hill. Sure enough, she rummaged through the open cabinet until she came across a folder and pulled it out. She took a moment to peruse the file.

"It's an odd one," she began, somewhat slowly paced for her. "All I have on it is it came in two days ago from a private source, not directly from Chargrove. An independent is footing the bill on this one, but through us instead of hiring privately like they normally do. Once the criminal is apprehended, a trial will be held here. But we also have to send a telegraph to the independent source once the criminal is detained here. I imagine the wronged Chargrovers will have to come here to testify. I'm not sure why they aren't keeping to their own jurisdiction, though. It's all a little fishy to me."

"Hmm," I got in.

"Not my place to say anything, of course, but it's a strange way to go about it, if you ask me. All this for a little petty theft!"

"Don't forget the bludgeoning," I pointed out.

"Well, yes, I suppose that's a bit more serious. But it's not like anyone was murdered or anything. If knocking someone over the head was a serious offense, I would think most of the pubs in this country would have serious troubles!" She laughed quietly and took a breath. "But anyway, if you want this one, be quick about it. We haven't had too much interest in it, but enough. Particularly from a certain somebody." Angie rolled her eyes theatrically, and then winked at me. She knew about my personal nemesis.

"Yes, so I've been told already." I rolled my eyes as well. "Any other bits you can tell me?"

Angie opened her mouth but was interrupted by her office door opening. She instead clamped her lips shut as she looked at the interloper.

It was the head bounty clerk, a stern, upright woman by the name of Miss Clark. While Angie adored me, Miss Clark clearly felt the opposite. She was so unfriendly that after more than a year of first meeting her, I still didn't even know what her first name was. I had done nothing to peeve this woman, but the older clerk simply did not like me, and used her words and body language to prove it.

"Miss Curtain," she practically barked, "how many times must I tell you to keep that dog outside?"

Oh yes. Her dislike of me also extended to Grimm. I was also fairly certain Miss Clark was the only human alive that intimidated my partner. His ears drooped at her tone.

"Uh, at least once more?" I hazarded with a shaky smile to prove I was trying to lighten the dismal mood Miss Clark had brought with her. Miss Clark was not amused, however. I looked at Grimm and walked back to the hallway, motioning for him to wait outside when I opened the door. He instantly complied.

As I took care of "the problem," Miss Clark had begun to berate Angie over some minor infraction. I tried not to eavesdrop.

"Yes, Miss Clark," Angie replied, her tone meek and shoulders hunched. Satisfied that her indomitable will was still being enforced, Miss Clark nodded her graying head, glanced at me with poorly hidden disdain, and marched back out of the door, clicking it neatly shut.

Angie let out a small breath and looked chagrined. She sheepishly glanced my way. "Sorry about that," she resumed, forcing her usually cheerful demeanor back into her words. "Where were we?"

"The Chargrove case. Anything else you can tell me?"

Angie snapped the folder shut, as if Miss Clark could see through walls. "Sorry, hon, no, the rest is confidential." Sympathy laced her voice.

Angie had probably already given me more tidbits than she was supposed to. Her mouth sometimes worked against her work protocol like that. If I had gotten Miss Clark from the get-go, I would have gotten much, much less. Still, there were things about this case that simply were not adding up, and more clues would have been most welcome. I tipped my head at Angie all the same with a smile on my lips.

"Thanks for your time, Angie," I cheerfully called out as I turned to leave.

"Any time, dear!" was her exuberant reply.

CHAPTER 7

D r. Lyle Williams, just Lyle to his friends, was Fleurette's father and closest neighbor on Rabbit Hole Road. He owned a small farm that was situated to the right side of the woodland only half a mile outside of Knobby Hill, the last major stop on the way out of town.

Lyle was the local veterinarian. He saw to the health of Knobby Hill's pets and livestock, from cats and dogs to cows and horses. And instead of renting a space within the town limits, Lyle had the room to hold his practice on his own property. He also did house calls on a regular basis.

On his farm, there was a small herd of three sheep, one milking goat, a couple of horses, and a large flock of chickens, but only two people called it home: Lyle and his housekeeper. Lyle, or Dr. Williams to his clients, was well known and well-liked by the community. His housekeeper, however, was a bit of a mystery. No one from town had ever met her and she wasn't from the surrounding areas. Nobody even knew what her name was. I imagine that tongues wagged a bit when she first appeared, especially since she never spoke to anybody, and she was only ever seen through the windows of the house, and never in town.

But she was no mystery to me. She was my mother.

Belinda Curtain was an aging calico tabby cat who was now living the good life. After she left my father—who I've never met—and produced me, she decided human life was too complex to keep up with. We were basically feral while I was a kitten. After meeting Fleurette and Lyle, I convinced her to retire in a little more comfort. She was a stubborn one, but I eventually won out.

Lyle and Belinda's agreement was that she could live in the barn rent free on two conditions. One, Mom had to keep the barn free of rodents. And two, once a week she had to become a human and give the house a good once-over. The rest of the time, she could be a lazy barn cat and nap in the sun to her heart's content. It was a good deal, considering that Lyle didn't need a constant companion, and my mom was more than happy to while away her time in isolation, although on occasion she would go up to Lyle if he was in the barn to demand a little petting. Lyle always complied with a smile on his face.

This afternoon I found my mother lounging outside of the house on the porch swing. At fourteen years of age, she was starting to show some feline maturity, and napping and lounging were her two favorite hobbies. As I stepped onto the porch in my human form, she opened one eye into a slit before noting my presence and closing it again. I rolled my eyes at the lackluster greeting before knocking on the door.

At this, she let out a little chirrup in my direction. Grimm, by my side as usual, chuffed back. I waited another second to see if anyone would answer my knock before I transformed and jumped up onto the swing's other cushion.

"Lyle's out back in the clinic. He told me to tell you to find him."

"And I missed you too, Mom. Yes, it was another successful job, thanks for asking!"

Grimm snickered. Mom ignored him, which is what she did about ninety percent of the time. She was of the mind that cats are superior to dogs. She instead stretched theatrically before settling into a sitting position, regarding me with half-closed green eyes.

"Hello, Cressida, child of mine. Tell me, please, are you of sound body? Has the world stayed safe from the Coddles of the world?"

Oh, sarcasm. Two could play that game. "Yes, Mother dear. Grimm and I triumph over evil yet another day!"

She leaned in and started grooming my ear, a rusty purr coming to life in her throat. "I *am* glad you are well, Cress," she murmured in a more motherly fashion. "Although you know how I feel about your line of work. That's all."

Yes, I did know. Mom made it abundantly clear what she thought of my job. I believe I once heard her describe it as "Cressida playing the hero and saving the world, one villain at a time. With a dog." Personally, my entire existence hinged on keeping a great evil out of this world. And her existence, too. Because nothing bad had ever happened on her watch (or the watch of any of our lineage, come to think of it) Mom had developed a complacent attitude toward the whole prophecy thing.

But, not one to get into an argument with my mother, at least not half the time, I dropped the subject. "Anything new here?" I asked her.

"Let's see ... not much, although I did see that Lyle got a shipment of brand new super sharp hypodermic needles." She glanced in Grimm's direction.

He gave a theatrical shake of his body and stalked off, muttering something about evil cats. It's just as well I couldn't hear exactly what he was saying, given that he was making derogatory remarks not only about my mother, but my species. Still, I chuckled.

"You are terrible, Mom," I chided.

She gave the feline equivalent of a shrug. I licked her forehead affectionately. "I'd better help my partner get through his exam. Behave yourself, Mom!" I jumped down from the swing and resumed my second form. Waving at my mother, who was already getting comfortable for another nap, I turned and started for the back of the house, in the direction Grimm went.

"Sit, Grimm," Lyle commanded.

Grimm sat dutifully.

"Shake."

Grimm extended his paw for Lyle to hold.

"Other paw, Grimm."

Grimm extended his other paw for inspection.

"Say, 'ahhhhh.'"

Grimm opened his mouth wide.

This routine always tickled Lyle pink. He grinned as he inspected Grimm's teeth.

"I wish all my patients were this compliant," he said to me. I had stayed in my human form to more easily communicate with Lyle. The veterinarian continued his exam with the very accommodating canine, running his hands down flanks, lifting his tail, and palpating his abdomen. Finally, Lyle stood up.

"For a large intact male approaching the age of seven, he is in excellent shape," Lyle praised. Grimm wagged his tail hesitantly, liking the positive tone of his doctor but unsure what might come next.

"But seven is still considered young for Lycanhunds," I argued.

Lyle nodded in agreement as his eyes continued assessing Grimm. "That it is, which goes against every other dog breed I know. Usually the bigger the dog, the shorter the lifespan."

I fake-coughed into my fist and let out a quick, "Magic!"

The veterinarian grinned at me. "I know, I know. I'm a mundy. And so are most animals. Magic isn't something I encounter a whole lot in this line of work." He surveyed the two of us, adding, "Present company excluded."

I grinned. Grimm's tail gave another half-hearted wag. Clearly, he was still a tad uneasy.

"I hardly think of you as a mundy, Lyle," I told the older man. The term referred to people with no magical skills. It was slang for mundane. "After all, look at your daughter."

He smiled and shook his head. "I can't take any credit for her skills. That was all her mother."

At that, he went silent, perhaps thinking of his wife who, as I had been told, left Lyle and Fleurette years ago and never returned. I couldn't help but feel that I had inadvertently stumbled upon a sore subject. The silence became a tad awkward.

Lyle shook off his short air of melancholy, however, and changed the subject with slight inelegance. "No shot today," he told the big dog directly, shooting both of us a grin.

Grimm immediately lost all apprehension and jumped up and turned a quick circle, looking more like a puppy than a regal Lycanhund. 'No' and 'shot' were definitely a part of his vocabulary.

"Thanks, Doc," I said. He waved a hand dismissively and started picking up his instruments. Lyle's clinic was an outbuilding that had been retrofitted to care for his smaller patients if his clients chose to travel to him. Grimm, weighing in at nearly one hundred and fifty pounds, barely qualified as a smaller patient.

"And how is my other favorite patient doing today?" Lyle asked me with a friendly wink.

Fleurette's father was the only other human to know that I was more than what I seemed, although like his daughter, I let him assume I was just a shapeshifter and nothing else out of the ordinary. When Fleurette had first brought me to his home, I wanted to keep everything from him, but Lyle was no dummy and knew immediately there was something more to me than meets the eye. He patched me up and he'd been my trusted doctor ever since.

Lyle was a solidly built Black man in his late fifties, with a bit of a paunch and a receding hairline. What hair he had left was un-ruly curls, just like his daughter's, although his was salt-and-pep-per instead of brown, and kept trimmed short. He was only slightly taller than Fleurette. His daughter must have taken after her mother more in looks, for the only thing that she seemed to have gotten from her father, besides the hair, was his kind eyes, although his were a shade darker than hers.

I waved one hand in a dismissing gesture, a smile gracing my lips. "Just fine, doc," I bantered. "How's life for you?"

He rubbed his goateed chin. "Well, I'm fine," he mused, "but, just between you and me, your mother has been awfully per-snickety. More so than usual, I mean." He let out a chuckle before sobering again. "I don't suppose you could see what was wrong with her, would you? She won't even shift most of the time to chat with me."

I rolled my eyes. Mothers. "Sure, Lyle, I'll do it right now. Are you sure Grimm doesn't need a shot?"

I shimmered down as Lyle let out a large laugh. As I ran back toward the house, Grimm yelled out at me, "That was a low blow, furball!"

Chuckling to myself, I reached the porch in no time and came to a sudden halt in front of my still-recumbent mother. I jumped up and stared at her. "Okay, Mom, what's the deal? Lyle said you weren't talking to him."

"Hello again, Cressida. Back for more?"

I wouldn't let her sway me. "Spill."

She stretched out a front leg, claws splayed, and then tucked it back under and glared at me through heavily lidded eyes. "Cressida, how old am I?"

"Um..." The question had caught me off guard. "Fourteen, right?"

"And how old are you?"

"I'm two, Mom."

"And how much longer must I wait to see my only daughter finally settle down and pass the torch?"

Oh, sweet Freya, help me. My ears flattened. "Not this again, Mom."

She hadn't blinked this entire time. Now she did, slowly. "You asked what was bothering me."

"Mom—"

"I was *looking*, Cressida—actually looking—for my mate for years. I was seven when I met your father."

I had heard all this a thousand times. Yes, my mother didn't find her true love until she was seven years old. His name was Roger Curtain, and he was an accountant. Not exactly thrilling, I know. Anyway, they got married and tried to start a family but after a few years of trying with no results, Mom began to wonder if perhaps she had married the wrong man (keep in mind that there must be true love between the couple for the magic to grant a child). Before I was even conceived, she had written a letter to my dad explaining that she could no longer be with him, etcetera, and placed it somewhere within easy access of a cat. Finally, after five years of marriage, Mom found out she could no longer shift back to human, which could mean only one thing. She retrieved the letter and placed it on Dad's desk and left her home forever, never to look back. I was born shortly after that, out in the woods in that abandoned barn.

"Mom," I stated, my voice firm. "I am young. Younger than you at this age because I spend a lot of time as a human. I have loads of time to find The One. I want to do something in this world before I settle down. He's out there, I'm sure, but I have plenty of time to find him."

I jumped down, ignoring the angry stare and flattened ears my mother was throwing at me, and ending this rancid discussion. "Now, be nice to Lyle; he just wants to help you. I'm heading back to Fleurette's. I'm off to save the world again first thing in the morning!"

I stormed off like a petulant kitten, rushing down the driveway to the road before my mom could get another word in edgewise. I was out of sight of Lyle's homestead before I heard familiar toenails clicking down the road at a fast pace behind me.

"Cress, hold up!" Grimm called out, his mouth open in a mild pant.

I slowed to a walk while Grimm caught up. "She is without a doubt the most irritating animal on the face of the planet!" I fumed out loud.

Mirth rolled off Grimm. "So, in other words, the apple doesn't fall far from the tree?"

I glared at him, my ears flattening. Cats are good at glaring. He just stared right back. "You want a claw in the eye? Maybe then Lyle will *have* to give you a shot."

My threat did not much faze the big dog. Instead, he went into play position, rump up, front legs splayed down low, mouth open but no teeth on display. "You have to catch me first!" he declared before tearing off down the road, kicking up little pebbles with his speed like a giant puppy.

I sighed and started running after him. I didn't push myself, knowing there was no way I'd catch up to the beast. Before long I had reached Fleurette's house. Grimm lounged at the foot of the front door, tongue lolling to the side as he panted heavily. "I won."

I just stared with fake contempt. "You cheat, dogbrains."

"Furball."

"Stinkmuffin."

"*Stinkmuffin*? Are you just making up insults now?" Grimm's tongue went back in his mouth as he sat up and shook his coat.

"Looks that way," I snarked. I transformed into a human before Grimm could say anymore. "Ha. Looks like I got the last word." Grimm growled at me, but it was his playful growl. I patted his head affectionately as I passed by to open the front door. He swiveled his head up to lick my wrist and followed me inside, jumping up on the sofa to lounge.

I found Fleurette in her workroom, a tiny room off the kitchen. I imagine it served as a pantry before Fleurette came to live here. The walls were lined with every herb imaginable, dried or in the process of drying. At approximately six feet long and four feet wide, there was only enough space for Fleurette's worktable and a chair, which sat at the back of the room. There were no windows in here, so Fleurette had an electric lamp on the table, with the brightest bulb possible powered by limited free energy.

The worktable was always a bit of a mess, with papers piled haphazardly in one corner, various glass vials and stacked books toward the back, and used tea and coffee mugs strewn about. There was also a perch near the back for Rupert, and although he always went outside to defecate, a few loose ebony feathers always found their way to the table's surface and added to the mess. Fleurette referred to her space as "organized chaos."

She was in the middle of grinding up something in her heavy marble mortar, her back turned to me and her hair pulled back in a loose ponytail. I leaned in the doorway and rapped a knuckle softly on the frame.

"Knock, knock."

"Hey, Cressida. Be a dear and hand me the funnel, will you? It's hanging on the wall to your right." Fleurette didn't even look up.

I located the funnel and placed it on her table next to her. "Fleurette, was your mother annoying?" I asked her without preamble.

She let out a low laugh. "She left us when I was young, so I don't remember if she was annoying or not," she replied. Whoops, I had forgotten that detail of Fleurette's past. I hoped it wasn't a sore subject. Based on her reaction, it didn't seem to be.

"Oh."

"Since she didn't have any compunction about leaving her family, though, my guess is that yes, she would have been annoying. Why do you ask? What did Belinda say to you?" She turned in her seat to look at me, a small smile gracing her kind face.

How anyone could have left this woman as a child was beyond me. I marveled at the amazing job Lyle had done as a single father to raise such a caring soul.

"The usual," I responded with a sigh. "Mom wants to know why, as an adult barely out of childhood, I might be more interested in being single and living my life on my own terms rather than immediately setting out to find my perfect mate."

"I see."

"I mean, look at you! Here you are older than me, at thirty-one, and still single. It's not like you are rushing all over Gaia's green world trying to find a man!"

I swear I saw her face fall just a bit before she swiveled back around to focus on her table. Her hair, while held back in a loose ponytail, still fluffed up enough to hide her face from view. "Well, that's a little different."

Uh-oh. I felt like I had inserted a paw into my mouth. "What makes it different?" I asked softly.

In a very quiet voice, she answered, "Because this is a small town and nobody is right for me here, and I don't have the chance to get out and see the world like you do. So, it looks like the single life is for me."

"That doesn't mean you'll be single forever. If it's fated to be, Mr. Right will find you."

Still hiding behind her hair, she chuckled sadly. "I wish I had your optimism." She turned again to look at me, determination etched in her face. "But listen, enough about me. Be kind to your mother. She just wants what she feels is best for you. Just because what you feel is right for your life and what she feels is right don't match up, doesn't mean one of you is wrong. You both are vastly different people with vastly different views on the world. The bottom line is that she loves you, no matter what. Don't go out on another job being mad at your mother because you never know what the future will bring."

Fleurette had a way of putting things into perspective. I wanted to stay mad at my mom, like a moody kitten. But my friend had a point. Feeling properly chastised, I nodded at her wisdom.

"Wow, Fleurette. You're absolutely right. While I'm gone, can you tell her that I love her? I really do."

Fleurette stood and gave me a quick squeeze. "Of course, Cress."

CHAPTER 8

It's amazing what a full night's rest can do for a body. Grimm and I both slept on the spare bed, as we always did, starting an early bedtime of eight o'clock in the evening. By the time four in the morning rolled around, we were both refreshed and ready to tackle another job.

I spent a good half hour grooming myself thoroughly, since I didn't always have the opportunity on the road. With ablutions finished, all that was left to do was eat a quick breakfast and hitch up Humbert. We had already packed supplies—mostly extra food in case we were successful, and if our quarry needed to eat—the night before.

We were ready to roll by five, just as the sky was turning from deep purple to rosy pink. Fleurette held a cup of coffee in her hands as she sleepily shuffled out into the yard in her robe. She gave me another smile as I rechecked Humbert's gear one last time.

"Stay safe out there," Fleurette said by way of goodbye.

I headed to the back of the wagon to open it, since Grimm had informed me earlier that he wished to ride for a while, the lazy dog. Fleurette followed behind me, waiting for my response. As Grimm jumped up, I turned to her. "Of course! You know how I am."

"Impetuous with no sense of personal safety?" Fleurette laughed while I shut the wagon door and glared at her, before cracking up and smiling along with her mirth.

I climbed up into the seat, grabbing the reins. "This will be a walk in the park. I'll see you in a couple of days," I told her. Waving, I flicked the reins at Humbert, who clopped into motion, leaving Fleurette behind in her yard waving back at me.

I was so used to turning Humbert left out of the yard that I had to stop and purposefully think about what I was doing. But turn right we did, and soon enough Humbert was plodding along at a steady pace, as the sun peeked over the horizon and started the day in earnest.

I had only ever come this way with Grimm on foot, and even then ventured on this road for about a half mile or so. I knew that the right-hand side held grassland, and the left was young deciduous woodland, because often we did a little hunting in this area when we had a day off. The monotony of the scenery, along with the rhythmic clop of horse hooves, lulled me into a state of mild torpor for the first few miles.

But soon enough, as the cooler morning air gave way to a cloudless sunny sky, the grassland to the right changed into the same forest as the left. After another hour, the grass was swallowed up completely by the thickening forest. Rabbit Hole Road also ceased to be, turning into a dirt path just barely wide enough for the wagon. It was obviously disused much of the time, although there were some signs of activity near the more rutted areas. My senses sharpened back up as Humbert carefully navigated the pockmarked path.

At noontime, the road grew even worse. Up until this moment we had been able to skirt around the larger potholes, but the road was especially narrow in this area. Despite urging Humbert carefully, the wagon lurched to a sudden halt. I swore under my breath. Requesting the horse to hang tight, I hopped down from the seat to investigate.

There was a prickly feeling on the back of my neck as I walked to the rear of the wagon, but my human side told me to ignore it. After all, I was in the middle of nowhere, so what could it be? I assumed it was just me getting squirrely, considering I had been human for about seven hours at this point. Already I could feel my eyes getting itchy and my skin starting to ache. I would just go see what the problem was and perhaps take a little break as a cat to unwind before continuing on.

Just as I thought. When I rounded the back of the wagon, I could see the wheel was trapped in a very deep rut. A good push to the back while Humbert carefully pulled would do the trick. I put my right hand on the door latch to see if Grimm could help.

"Don't move!" shouted a voice behind me. I obliged, my hand stilling on the door handle, my left making sure it could be seen by my unknown assailant. So much for being alone out here. I mentally kicked myself for allowing my human side to be so complacent.

"Turn around." Again, I obliged. "Slowly," the voice hissed. I turned halfway, enough to see the owner of the voice, a tall and skinny middle-aged man with shaggy blonde hair, a scraggly beard, and a very obvious hygiene deficiency. His clothes looked like they hadn't seen a washer, nor any body of water, ever. Although he stood about six feet away from me, the breeze wafted a smell of putrid body odor in my direction. He held a long dagger in his hands. It had undeniably seen cleaner days.

Some days, I cursed my petite frame and non-threatening features. After all, it led to a lot of my fellow hunters not taking me seriously. But other times, it was a bonus. For instance, at this moment. I observed the man from my frozen position through slightly downturned eyelashes. I wanted very much for him to not view me as a threat. He must have liked what he saw, for his craggy face broke out in a smile, showcasing discernable gaps in his heavily stained teeth. He moved forward, a seemingly dominant predator, until he was right in front of me. The knife, now inches from my body, was covered in rust and dried blood.

"I'm unarmed," I said meekly, shying away from the man. I tried to look as helpless and non-threatening as I could. I took a quick glance at my surroundings to see if he was alone. Chances were high he did not operate solo.

The highwayman grinned lewdly, and I was up close and personal with his lack of a full set of chompers.

"Well, well, well, what do we have here?" he breathed on me. I tried to hold my breath as his halitosis hit me in the face. "It's dangerous for a pretty girl to be out here alone. I've heard there's bandits about."

A guffaw from the left side of the path gave away the location of a second man. I risked a quick glance in that direction, keeping the mask of fear on my face. As I did, a burly individual, just as dirty as Skinny, came out from behind a tree. He too held a dagger in his meaty ham hock. He gave my body a once-over and smiled vacuously. I held my gorge.

So, two guys. No pistols or arrows. Dirty blades.

Ever the actress, I asked timidly, "What are you going to do to me?"

Skinny grinned again and scratched his head with his free hand. "We'll have some fun, but first we're going to relieve you of all your worldly possessions. Knutson!" he yelled at Burly, "keep an eye on her while I check the wagon!"

"Can do," Knutson replied in a lazy manner as he lumbered closer to me.

That's when the fun started, but probably not in the way these bozos had envisioned.

As Skinny started to turn the handle, I stepped away from the wagon, toward Burly, who was not expecting his victim to approach him at such a rapid rate. The minute the handle turned, the wagon doors exploded outward as a large, black, flying projectile launched itself directly at Skinny. As Grimm landed on Skinny's chest, I whipped downward, jabbed Burly in the groin with my pointy elbow, and plucked the dagger out of his hand. I pirouetted up and behind him. As his face turned red and his knees began to buckle, I jabbed the point between his shoulder blades, just enough to let him know it was there.

I glanced over at my partner, who was snarling into Skinny's face, flecks of spittle flying into the man's mouth every time he opened it to scream, which was at least every two seconds. I noted that the second dagger had flown out of the bandit's hands the moment the massive dog had hit him in the chest.

In the meantime, Knutson was moaning, but otherwise doing an excellent job of staying still.

"Wow, guys, that *was* fun!" I called out. "Now, how about we get you into the back of my wagon? I know that's where you wanted to be anyway."

Rounding them up was easy.

Nobody expects the pretty girl to be their doom.

Chargrove, once upon a time, was a bustling community built around a small gold claim that paid big for about one hundred years. Once the gold mine dried up about fifty years ago, so did much of the town. Now, it either took a special breed of courage or stupidity to live a full life there. It wasn't quite a ghost town, but the existing Chargrovers were few and far between. They made for a tight-knit community that looked out for each other no matter what.

The town was shaped like a U, with the main road coming in at the top and a small back road bifurcating the shape at the very bottom. A genuine well sat in the very middle, surrounded by the saddest patch of grass I had ever seen. All the buildings looked the same: ancient, wooden structures with no signs to detail what might lay inside. There were plenty of townsfolk around, although as my wagon rattled into the heart of the dying town, I saw more than a few people scurry inside the nearest doorway, like cockroaches escaping light. The braver individuals simply stopped whatever they were doing and stared, their disbelief at my otherness boring into me. I stopped in front of an elderly woman, who glared up at me.

"Pardon me, ma'am," I said as politely as I could, "would you direct me to the sheriff's station?"

The old woman did not take her eyes off mine, as if I'd transform into a monster and devour her if she did, but she pointed one gnarled finger to the opposite side of the U. I thanked her graciously and led Humbert to the sheriff's station, which apparently doubled as his house judging by the multiple children running in and out of the door. Two of the smaller ones stopped to watch, their little noses running freely. I hid my disgust as best as I could. Poor personal hygiene was a sore spot for me.

As Humbert rolled to a stop, I reached into my vest pocket for my watch. Three o'clock, almost on the dot. It had taken me ten hours to get here, and I mentally patted myself on the back for the speedy travel. I surmised that taking the known road to Chargrove would add at least five hours, more likely eight, to that travel time. Still, I felt the clock ticking. If I was going to beat the other hunters to the reward, I needed to be quick.

Grimm was in the back of the wagon, making sure my new friends were behaving themselves. Leaving them to stew for a little while longer, I walked boldly through the door by myself and stopped to survey my surroundings. An aging man, his bald pate gleaming in the sunlight streaming through the window, sat at a desk positioned directly in front of me. He did not look up from his work but kept scribbling away on a sheet of paper. He had a fringe of dusty hair that bobbed in the air as he wrote. Watching this partial halo of hair dance on the air was almost mesmerizing.

The station was dead silent, except for the pencil scratching. "Helen, what's—" he started to say, but cut himself off at the sight of me. His eyes grew large and I thought his mouth might open to make a little O of surprise, but he quickly straightened and neutralized his face, minus the mien of outsider distrust that everyone I had encountered here so far had perfected. "Can I help you?"

There was an old wooden chair placed by his desk. I crossed over to it and sat down without being asked.

"Sir, I am Cressida Curtain, and I am a professional bounty hunter." As I began my spiel his eyes immediately glazed over. I'm sure every Tom, Dick, and Harry who arrived out of the blue was a so-called professional bounty hunter. I could barely blame his obvious dismissal.

"What is this about, Miss Curtain?" he drawled at me, his cadence barely making the words into a question. He had gone back to perusing his paperwork, not even giving me his full attention.

"I recently obtained information about a wanted individual last seen in these parts. I was hoping to work with you to find said person."

He practically rolled his eyes as he glanced my way. "I am sorry to disappoint you, but there's a reason my office didn't post the bounty in the first place. We really don't want to be bothered by such trivial matters. You should take it up with the station that put up the bounty. Good day."

Just like that I was dismissed.

I didn't move, however. "I was under the impression that your job was to serve and protect your community. I assumed that helping a hunter to track down a potentially dangerous criminal would fall under that category, no matter how trivial his crimes may seem. As it stands, I have already apprehended two such criminals on my journey here. Given the location of their arrest, I'm most certain they fall under your jurisdiction. But, seeing as how you don't really care about the safety of these townsfolk, I'll set them loose. Sorry to have bothered you." I stalked out before he could reply.

He did not directly follow me out, as I had predicted he wouldn't. By this time, my presence had attracted a small crowd, which I assumed to be the majority of the townsfolk. They had closed in tightly around my wagon, so I had to shove my way through. Once I got to the back of the wagon, I unlocked it and opened the doors.

Grimm stood at the opening, blocking the goons from view with his large body. The townspeople murmured amongst themselves at the sight of my partner. But then, from within, came the wild voice of Skinny. "Help us, she's trying to kill us!"

If the collective gasp of the town hadn't done it, the sudden ravings of Skinny would hopefully be enough for the sheriff to leave his nest and see what was happening.

Predictably, the sheriff did burst out from his station and pushed through the crowd toward me, metaphorical blood in his eyes.

"What is the meaning of this?" he bellowed at me, getting close enough for me to smell his breath, which had the sour odor of an empty stomach. I flinched away imperceptibly to breathe some fresh air.

Once my lungs had been fortified, I turned toward his wrath and smiled politely. "These two men waylaid me on the back road, on a section that is,"—I lifted my voice to a higher pitch—"technically part of Chargrove property. Their intention was to rob me, at the very least"—I eyed Skinny, squinting my eyes at him in scrutiny—"and I believe rape and even possibly murder might have also been on their minds."

I faced the sheriff again. Wide eyed, he squinted into the darkness of the wagon. "But, sir, now that you've so blatantly told me your position on these matters, I was just about to let them go. Grimm!"

"Now, now, now, let's not be hasty!" sputtered the lawman. During my little speech, his eyes had adjusted to the inner gloom enough to see the two criminals. Turning back to me with an improved disposition, he said, "These two have been a thorn in this community for some time. Young lady, let's get them safely behind bars so that we can discuss the matter of the bounty you needed information on."

"Sir, you are too kind," I replied. The crowd had started to back away but still stayed close, watching the entertainment unfold. A little name dropping wouldn't hurt. "As I said, Cressida Curtain at your service."

The man tipped his bald head in my direction. His fringe danced merrily in the breeze. "Jeremiah Boggs, Sheriff of Chargrove, at *your* service."

Service with a smile, at last.

Sheriff Boggs sat me down once the two bandits were tucked away. Grimm came along because I never left him out of a discussion, even if he didn't fully understand every word. The sheriff initially balked at having the dog with me, but I made it clear it was happening with or without his approval, and Grimm's yellow-eyed stare said he was not to be trifled with. So here I was, back in the wooden desk chair, across from the sheriff while Grimm sat at my side.

There was a sandwich on the desk, which I was reasonably sure had appeared since my last visit to the inside of the station. Egg salad, by the smell. I noticed Grimm's nose twitch appreciatively and I tried not to do the same. Sheriff Boggs glanced at it, almost embarrassedly. "The missus. She always brings me my dinner about this time," he explained.

I nodded. "This won't take long. What information do you have? Can you point me in a direction to investigate?"

Boggs took another peek at his sandwich. I could have told him just to eat the damn thing, but I was still a little rankled by my earlier treatment. He sighed before answering.

"It was all petty little stuff up until a week ago. Annoying, but not worth our time, really. Sometimes vagabonds come through here and steal a little food from our community. They never stay long, and the amount of stuff they take isn't worth an investigation." He took his focus from his sandwich to look me in the eye. "That changed last week when Henry got the stuffing knocked out of him."

"That would be Henry ...Whittaker?" I hazarded, trying to remember the details of the rap sheet.

"Whitman. He owns a farm on the outskirts of Chargrove. He's an old timer." Boggs chuckled to himself, adding, "I guess we're all old timers, to be living here. But Henry's family has been here before Chargrove was even founded." The sheriff opened a folder on his desk, one that he had pulled from a file before we had sat down for this chat. "Said he went to milk his cow first thing, sat down at the stool, and got pummeled from behind. A real kerfuffle. Poor Henry didn't even get a good chance to see his attacker except at the end when he saw the kid running out the barn door."

"And this kid had black hair?" I asked.

Boggs nodded. "Yes ma'am. According to Henry, anyway. Shaggy black hair, and with the height and build, Henry assumed a teenager."

I pursed my lips. "Tell me, Sheriff, if you didn't put this bounty out, who did?"

Boggs glanced at his sandwich as if it held all the answers. He shrugged his shoulders. "Honestly? Beats me. It wasn't anybody in this area. Some high-falutin' guy in a suit drove into town the day after it had happened, took a similar statement from me as I just gave you, and left. He said his client had been wronged by the same mystery person and they were collecting evidence to build a case for a bounty. I gave him my two cents about not bothering, as Henry turned out to be fine and all, but this man basically told me to mind my own business." He scratched his fringe. "I've been Sheriff of Chargrove going on thirty years. Weirdest encounter I've had to date."

"Hmm. Indeed. Well, Mr. Whitman's farm seems as good a place to start my search as any." I tapped my chin thoughtfully. Grimm huffed softly, causing both myself and Boggs to stare at him, although our expressions were vastly different. I nodded decisively at my partner before leveling my head at the man opposite me. "Might you give me the address to Mr. Whitman's farm?" I asked, my tone sweet.

The sheriff was still watching Grimm with a huge air of trepidation. He finally managed to move his head away from the beast to meet my eye. "Of course," he replied unsteadily. He got out a scrap piece of paper and scribbled on it with the pencil from earlier. Then he handed it to me. "Just take the south road from the square. Follow that until the road forks. Take the left fork. Can't miss it."

I glanced at the paper and stuffed it in my breast pocket. "One last question," I added. "Have you talked to any other bounty hunters about this particular case?"

Boggs shook his head. "You are the first and only. And hopefully the last, God willing."

I internally breathed a sigh of relief. I had officially beaten out my competition. So far, anyway. Standing, I thrust out my hand. Boggs hesitated but took it before the pause became insulting.

"Sheriff, I appreciate your help. My wish is to not come back to bother you any time soon," I said with polite sincerity.

He smiled. "Young lady, that is my wish too. I know I said the meeting with the well-dressed man was my weirdest encounter, but being interviewed by a girl and her giant dog might just top that. It must be my lucky week." He smiled. "Good luck to you."

CHAPTER 9

The farmhouse in front of me may have once been white but was now more of a dirty beige, and the front door's paint had flaked off nearly everywhere. The sagging porch was littered with various liquor bottles, all empty. There was no welcome mat to speak of, literally or figuratively.

I had followed Sheriff Boggs' instructions to the letter, so I sure hoped this was the right place, seeing as there weren't any other farms in this direction. I knocked on the door and waited.

"Yeah, what do you want?" This rather rude greeting was issued at me through a peephole of the closed door. I assumed the bloodshot blue eye staring at me belonged to the man I needed to talk to—Henry Whitman.

I suppose I should have been grateful that there wasn't a shotgun pointed at me, all things considered.

"Mr. Whitman?" I ventured. "I am on the trail of the criminal who assaulted you. Can I take a few moments of your time?"

The eyeball stared at me for just a moment longer before disappearing as the peephole closed. I worried for a moment that the man attached to the eye had ignored my request until I heard the scraping sound of a lock disengaging. The door opened with a protesting squeak as another scrap of paint flaked off and drifted to the ground.

"What do you need?" Henry Whitman grunted.

He wore an undershirt that must have been white at some point but had succumbed to the same dinginess that the house suffered from. His stained dungarees were unbuttoned, I noticed. Whitman had quite the impressive gut, carried by legs that looked too skinny for his body. What remained of his hair was light and flowy, and fell down into his eyes. He did not seem to notice.

At his spoken words, the heady aroma of booze and onions rolled off him in attacking waves. I did my best not to react to the stench. Not breathing too deeply, I said, "My name is Cressida Curtain. I'm a bounty hunter. This is Grimm," I added with a head jerk to my partner on my right side. Whitman glanced at him and then back at me, unfazed. Not a typical reaction, but I continued. "I understand that you were attacked in your barn, is that correct?"

Another grunt, which I interpreted as a yes. I forged on. "May we see the barn?"

Whitman eyed me for a second, as if debating whether I was worth his time. He picked at something in his teeth before answering, "C'mon." He stepped off his porch and sauntered toward the largest outbuilding on the property. We followed.

The path to the barn took us by what was once a generously sized vegetable garden enclosed by a rustic fence made of sticks. As with everything else on this property, the garden was poorly maintained. In fact, as I walked single file behind Whitman, I could see that nearly everything within was practically dead from lack of water. Everything, that is, but the plants that were immediately next to the fence bordering our path. I noted peas, beans, and some sort of squash alive with vibrant lushness, a stark contrast to the rest of the dying plants. Whitman must have only been able to water what was easiest to reach. An odd choice, but, judging from the two minutes of knowing him, certainly not out of character.

We came to a halt outside the dilapidated barn. Pushing the odd garden design out of my mind, I turned my attention back to our host.

Taking a key out of his pocket, he unlocked the massive barn door and held it open for us. Grimm sauntered in first, looking relaxed but I could tell he was alert. Mr. Whitman gestured for me to enter. I scanned the area, knowing full well that he could easily lock us in the barn if he wanted to. But that was just how my mind worked. Cats tend to be suspicious in nature. Shaking off the trepidation, I walked inside the musty barn. It smelled of cow dung, mold, and old hay. I suppressed the urge to sneeze.

To my relief, the farmer did not lock us in but followed up the rear leaving the door wide open for a bit of fresh air. He walked over to the milking stall against one wall.

"This is where it happened," he muttered. "One minute I was getting ready to milk Veronica, and then wham!" He mimed being hit on the back of the head. "I was out for a solid minute. When I come to, the weasel was running out the door. Almost missed him."

"And he matched the descriptions of the other robberies?" I asked.

Whitman shrugged, and then nodded. "Black hair, like raven's wings, was really all I could see. But the way he run, gangly-like, he was a youngster."

"And Veronica is your cow?"

"No, she's my wife." Whitman deadpanned to me. He gave me a second of utter confusion, before adding, "Of course she's my cow! What kind of dumb question is that?"

I ignored that jab. "Is your cow in the barn right now?" She might have been a witness to the scene, and I thought it would be helpful to talk to her.

Whitman stared at me with a quizzical frown forming on his otherwise inscrutable face. "No," he said slowly, "she ain't. She's free roaming this time of day."

I shrugged, trying not to look like I had a screw loose. "Just trying to get a picture formed, no worries." Whitman just kept staring, making me a tad nervous.

Grimm also stared at me, but not in the crazy-person way. He really needed to talk, I could tell. I did some quick thinking. "Uh, thank you, Mr. Whitman, for your help. Might I have a moment to look around?"

He said nothing for a beat before shrugging again. "Not sure what else you'll find. It's been almost a week. But go for it. I'll be on the porch. Don't steal anything." He turned and lumbered out.

The moment he was out of sight I ran over to a hay bale, hid behind it, and shimmered down. I ran back out to Grimm. "What did you find?" I asked him.

Grimm grimaced. "That human has problems."

"What? The boy? How can you tell?"

"No, not the boy. The farmer. He smells like he's two days away from dying." Grimm half-sneezed to purge the scent from his nostrils.

Cats don't naturally roll their eyes, but I've picked up a few human traits. "Focus!" I yelled. I sniffed the air, my curiosity piqued. While my feline nose was no slouch, I didn't have Grimm's gift for smells.

Grimm sniffed the air again. "I caught a scent the moment we got on the path to the barn. It's stronger in here. Male, young, dirty, green."

"Green?" I asked.

Grimm did the canine equivalent of a shrug. "Like earth, like living things. Fleurette smells green all the time too. Except when she's just taken a shower. Then she smells of soap."

"Okay, not important." Time was getting short. "Can you track it?"

"Let me see." Grimm lowered his head and made a beeline for the barn exit. As soon as he was outside, he yelled back, "I've got it! I think I can figure out which way he went!"

"Excellent!" I hastily transformed to human and followed Grimm out. He continued down the path but instead of going straight toward the farmhouse, he turned the corner of the mostly dead garden and made a beeline across an overgrown grassy field toward the road. Grasshoppers flew in a mass exodus from his path as he barreled through the yellow grass. He stopped at the road and yipped at me, the unusually high timbre of his bark a sign that the trail was still present. I nodded and made my way to the house again. Stopping short of the porch but within eyesight of Whitman, I did a courtesy head bob.

"Sir, thank you for your time. We are going to try the road for clues. Are there any other roads or stops in this region that we should investigate?"

Henry Whitman scowled and rubbed his scraggly chin in thought.

"If you noticed coming here, there's a road that connects to this one. There's an old abandoned school from Chargrove's heyday out that way. It's haunted to bits, though, so nobody in their right mind would go there."

"Haunted?" I asked dubiously.

The old man nodded. "Oh, 'bout fifty years ago when the prosperity dried up. Those rich folks still kept sending their kids there even as the town started to die. I was a youngster myself then, but my folks weren't rich, so I stayed on the farm. But then the haunting started and let loose some nasty diseases. Kids and teachers alike started dying, as I recall." He paused to scratch his grizzled chin again as he squinted at the horizon in thought. "The folks pulled the rest of the kids and everybody else left in a hurry. They didn't even bother to remove the stuff from the school or lock the doors."

"How sad," I commented. Whitman glanced at me as if he had forgotten I was there.

"Sad, nothing," he responded rather harshly. He gave a loud snort to dislodge something from his throat, then spat to the side away from me. "Somebody messed with things they shouldn't have. This town's had a death mark on it long before that. Those hoity-toity school people should have seen the signs sooner."

He paused again, pursing his lips. "No matter now. Could very well be that the school is exactly where a young criminal might go. It'd seem like a safe place if you didn't know the history. 'Course, he could also be long gone by now too. Go on back the way you came, missy, and take the left fork instead of the right. Ain't nothing else but that school out there, but if you stay on the road, it eventually loops back to town."

I gave more thanks for this information and trotted to my wagon. Time was of the essence in cases like these. Plus, if I was being honest with myself, I wanted to put some distance between myself and this creepy farm with its presumably dying man.

Grimm stayed on foot, his nose to the ground as I followed with the wagon. Sure enough, his remarkable sense of smell led us to the left fork in the road, just as Whitman had predicted. Once off the wider road we had been following, this branch became a bit more swallowed up by the surrounding woods. The oldest trees here were perhaps seventy years old, with plenty of space in between for saplings to try to grow. Being late summer, the shade of the bigger trees felt nice. The sun peeked out pleasantly between the leaves.

It was clear that no one ventured this way very often. Once we had traveled into the seclusion of the forest, I pulled Humbert over to the shoulder and hopped down. I got a bucket of water and some carrots from the back of the wagon for the old horse. It had been a long day, and he needed a break. Once he had consumed his refreshments, I turned into my true self.

"Humbert, Grimm and I are going to scout ahead. Are you okay to stay here for a while?"

"Delighted as always, Mistress," he replied, ever stoic.

Grimm snuffled the ground. "It's getting stronger," he said.

Heart pounding with anticipation, I urged Grimm to continue his search, keeping hot on his heels as he made his way down the lane.

Presently we found the old school. It was a relic of a bygone era: three stories tall, square, complete with a cupola at the front and a wide stone stairway to the grand—if shabby—double doors that marked the entrance. Many tall windows faced the front of the building, and the whole thing was covered in a red brick façade. Where once a large yard surrounded the outside of the building, now there was a mess of tall blooming grass, brambles, and saplings that encroached upon the crumbling building. It would have been a stunning piece of architecture back in its day, but now it was just a sad ghost of itself. Many of the tall windows had been broken, and some of the bricks were tumbled down.

We paused at the start of the stone stairs, surveying the school.

"Do you think it's really haunted?" I asked Grimm, trying to sound nonchalant. I had filled him in on what Whitman had told me while we walked toward the school together.

His nose twitched in the air. "I don't know. Could be, but then again, sometimes humans are prone to mass hysteria. What if it was just a bad illness and not something supernatural?"

"True. Can you smell ghosts?"

Grimm glanced at me with humor in his yellow eyes. "No." He pointed his nose back toward the building. "But I *can* smell our bounty."

"So, he is here?"

Grimm began sniffing the ground, turning in circles. "At least up until recently. I do smell activity closer to the door but it's stronger over ... this way." He turned and padded off to the right and continued behind the school. I followed.

Grimm stopped once he got to the edge of the woods, where the saplings gave way to older trees. I could discern a small path leading deeper into the wilderness. Grimm began to follow the path.

I stayed put, turning my attention back to the dilapidated school. "Why don't you go on ahead? I'd like to stay and check out the building for clues."

He grunted. "Fine by me. This trail is fresh, by the way. I'll follow it and let you know where it takes me. I'll meet you back at the school." He ambled away, still following his nose.

I once again approached the double front doors, which, as Whitman had said, were not locked. I couldn't budge the heavy doors in cat form, however. Sighing, I shimmered up. I had to admit that my human form had some perks, opposable thumbs being one of the biggest. I grasped the tarnished handle and pushed, easing myself into the dark hallway.

I'm not going to lie; it was spooky in there. I could almost hear the echoes of children long gone, either now old or, most likely, dead by this time. Whitman's story did not help, either, as I imagined the ghosts of the deceased children trailing the halls for eternity. Perhaps they were waiting for unsuspecting people to enter their school, upon which they would grasp the victims in a cold embrace, chanting, "Come be our new play mate, for ever and ever..." I shivered theatrically.

I collected my wits with a stern internal talking to and surveyed my surroundings. I stood in what must have been the foyer. Directly in front of me sat a grand staircase to the second floor, complete with a dusty and dingy carpet runner. To the left of the staircase was what I assumed to be the office. A small sitting area and a fireplace stood to the right of the stairs. Flanking me on both sides were dark hallways.

Decisions, decisions. Which way to go first? At random, I chose the right-hand corridor and cautiously began walking. It was a spacious hallway at least, with faded green paint above wainscoting on either side. Glancing at the first few doors I came across, I established that I had found a classroom wing.

The hallway turned a corner, and I continued to follow it. After a couple more classrooms I came across side-by-side bathrooms, one for boys and another for girls. There was one last doorway at the very end of the hall. Another classroom, from the looks of it.

The door to this classroom was open, unlike all the other doors I had passed. My innate kitty curiosity began to pester me. I quietly crept up and peeked in.

The room was positioned so that upon entrance, the teacher would have stood off to the left of the door in front of the chalkboard and the students would have sat to the right. A wall of windows faced me from my position in the doorway. The teacher's stately and solid desk took up the far left-hand corner. At the very back of the room there was a long table filled with beakers and test tubes. There was a human skeleton, hanging out, quite literally, in the corner by the chalkboard. I hoped it was a replica and not the real thing.

Even with my limited knowledge of human schools, the whole setup screamed "science class" to me.

The desks were shoved into the room haphazardly. I crept forward slowly to investigate; while the majority were completely covered in dust, there were clean spots on certain surfaces in the shapes of finger smudges and handprints. Someone had definitely touched these recently.

I glanced toward the windows, noting the line of cabinets underneath them. Plant pots perched on top—some empty, some filled with dirt, and some containing the remains of dead plants. And, at the far end of the cabinets, a whole cluster of plants—bright green, happy, and healthy—flourished in their pots.

Intrigued, I approached this collection of plants. My time with Fleurette had helped me get to know my botanical species a little better. I could see that some of these pots held lettuce and spinach, and others contained tomatoes and berry bushes, which bore delicious and robust fruits upon them. I touched a lettuce, marveling at the healthy coloration of the leaf. Thriving plants were not what I had expected to find in an abandoned school. How did they get here?

A noise from behind the teacher's desk had me stiffen and turn. If I were my normal self my fur would be standing on edge. Trying to be brave and not think about ghost children, I inched toward the sound. My arms broke out in goosebumps. I could hear breathing from the corner of the room.

"Hello?" I ventured meekly.

Something shot out from behind the desk and ran cheetah-fast past the chalkboard and out the door. That something was child-sized, and definitely corporeal, because it had rattled the skeleton as it ran past.

I froze for just a moment, stunned.

"Furballs!" I muttered to myself as my body unlocked and gave chase. I stopped at the doorway, peering into the darkness of the hallway. I made it just in time to see a door closing with the telltale squeak of unused hinges. Bingo.

I took my time walking the hallway, treading softly. My instincts told me the figure had most likely gone into the girl's bathroom, and sure enough I could hear labored breathing from within the lavatory once I reached it. I waited a heartbeat.

"Hello?" I tried again from outside the bathroom, hoping that this was the only way in and out of the room. "I'm not going to hurt you; I just want to talk. My name's Cressida." Silence. The labored breathing had ceased. "I'm going to come in now," I continued in the friendliest, most non-threatening voice I could muster. I placed my hand on the door and gave it a small push.

The door squeaked but gave way easily enough. I peeked in, my senses on alert. Natural light filtered in through large, frosted windows on the far wall from me, a few cracked and one with a sizable hole in the corner. They showed off a grimy yet elegant lavatory done up in shades of white and mint green. This bathroom must have been at the height of modernity at the time of its creation. A row of wash sinks lined the wall immediately to my left. Stalls lined the opposite, with a very small alcove directly to my right. I almost didn't see the girl because the door initially blocked my view.

She was hunkered down in the corner, knees drawn up to her chest with her arms hugging her whole body. I let myself in so she could get a good look at me. I wanted to appear harmless.

This girl obviously was. I was bad at guessing the ages of humans because I age so differently, but I would have put her at around twelve years of age. She wore simple clothes, layers of shirts, a smock, and leggings, all of it filthy. Her hair was chestnut colored and long, and were it not for the naturally sleek nature of it I'm sure rats could have moved in in a fortnight. Her face was rounded with a petite nose, and she was covered in grimy smudges. The dirtiness of her countenance made her hazel eyes stand out, shining with fear.

She stiffened as I entered. I held up my hands. "No, no," I soothed, "it's okay. I want to make sure you are all right. Can I help you?"

She didn't move at first, but as I inched toward her, she seemed to lose a little of her fear. I held out my hand to her. She stared at it in apprehension, and then reached out to grasp it. Standing, she was just a few inches shorter than me. She said nothing, but still stared with wide eyes.

"Hello," I tried in a friendlier tone. "I'm Cressida."

"What are you doing here?" the girl asked. Her voice seemed fearless, a direct contrast to her body language. Honestly, the question threw me off guard.

"I..." Verbally stumbling, I thought frantically. Honesty seemed to be the best policy. But maybe I should focus on getting her out of here instead of having an odd conversation in the bathroom. What was the best route? I realized I didn't have any experience with kids.

I began to slowly turn her toward the door.

"As I said, I'm Cressida. I'm investigating a criminal in these parts and his last known whereabouts were near this school. So, I was checking out the building. I didn't expect to run across a girl like you."

The girl had been amiable about moving as I spoke, but now she put the brakes on and spun on me. "Criminal?" she asked, cautious again.

I tried again to usher her toward the door. She was not budging, and she was in front of me. Perhaps I shouldn't have mentioned the criminal. Clearly, she was afraid of any potentially dangerous activity. Perhaps she had even already had a run-in with him.

"Yes," I explained. "Have you seen someone around here? Black hair, young? Are you in trouble?"

She stared at me with a stony expression. Ever so slowly the blank face turned to one of pure rage. My skin prickled. Obviously, I had said the wrong thing. I frantically thought over possible damage control options.

"*Criminal*?" she repeated with high-pitched venom. "No, I'm not in trouble. But you are."

At those words, this sweet young girl began to grow. Her limbs became longer, her muscles expanded, and hair sprouted all over her body. Within just two seconds I was staring at the biggest, ugliest werewolf I had ever seen. And it was blocking the only exit.

CHAPTER 10

The werewolf roared at me in challenge. I tried not to pee myself.

Mastering my bladder, I backed up as quickly as I could while the great beast continued bellowing in the most terrifying way possible, the sound reverberating through my bones. And then it started swiping its arms at me; razor-sharp claws stretched from each fingertip. The reach of those long arms was incredible, and unluckily for me I bumped into the radiator that lived in front of the windows. I was out of backing-up space.

The werewolf took its fury out on the first stall it came to. With a mighty swing it bashed the side in. The broken divider crumbled to pieces, a huge chunk falling and blocking the underneath of the existing stalls. With one stall demolished, the werewolf locked eyes on me again and started advancing.

As a hairy arm swung in my direction, I ducked and dove toward the last stall, flinging the door open and wrenching it shut as quickly as I could. I closed the lock just as the massive fist beat on the door. With a pounding like that, though, I wasn't going to stay safe in here for long.

"Think, think!" I chided myself, but thinking was difficult with all the stall bashing and roaring that the werewolf was doing.

Luckily, the werewolf had decided to take its anger out on the middle stall before going after mine again.

I had my knife in my boot. I nearly reached for it, but two thoughts made me pause. First, I had to nick the beast with it in order for Hail Mary to be effective. The chances of getting clobbered first were quite staggering.

Second, I could still remember the image of the little girl this beast had been just moments ago. The idea of attacking a child was too harrowing, no matter what she had become.

So, the knife stayed in my boot. I thought harder.

Finally, a break-through.

The broken window. The tiny hole in the corner. It was my only hope.

I jumped up on the closed toilet and shimmered down. The door was stronger than its fallen brethren, but it was buckling significantly. The fur along my back was standing up. It was now or never.

I sprinted forward, squeezed under the stall door, jumped up onto the radiator, leaped for the windowsill, scrabbled with my grip momentarily, and then put all of my effort into escaping through the hole without getting shredded to bits, either by the monster or the broken glass.

Time seemed to slow down.

I squeezed the first half of my body through the hole, but my middle got stuck.

The massive hand swung down toward me.

The air current caused by the downward momentum of the falling hand brushed the soft hairs of my tail. With a final sucking in of the gut, my body became unstuck.

The massive hand made a grab at my tail as I leaped forward, but it closed on nothing but air and about three hairs from

113

the very tip of my tail, ripping said hairs free as I plummeted downward.

And then I was on the ground outside and time resumed as normal. The monster roared with frustration from within the demolished bathroom. I wanted to taunt the beast with my lucky escape, but time was wasting, and I wasn't completely stupid. I dashed off in the direction Grimm had taken.

Cats are built for short bursts of speed. As I zipped away from the school and into the woods, my spine worked like a spring to make my strides as long as possible. There was no real way to track Grimm's scent at my madcap pace, however, and besides, sprinting is extremely taxing. I coasted to a quick stop to smell the air, resisting the urge to pant. Grimm's unique odor was not hard to track. Of course, it helped that he had not strayed from the path behind the school. I increased my speed again, keeping my eyes and ears open.

Eventually, though, I lost my will to keep running. I was still on the path, but when I searched for eau de dog, it just was not there anymore. My cute little kitty nostrils flared in between necessary air gasps. I may not have the amazing nose that Grimm has, but I was able to find the scent again, off to the left of the path. I bolted again in that direction.

"Grimm! ... Grimm! ... Grimm!" I called hoarsely as I ran.

At last I saw him, a dark shadow in a sunny forest. He turned to face me, confusion rolling off his body. I stopped in front of him, winded.

"Cress? Your tail is giant." He had the nerve to chuckle.

"There's a ... werewolf..."

"A what?" he asked.

"Werewolf ... in the school."

He stared at me. He straightened his nose to smell the air, as if he could scent it from this great distance. "Are you sure?"

I wanted to swat him. "Yes!"

The one thing about Grimm was that he trusted me, no matter what. It only took one second guess to believe me. "Let's go."

My legs felt like jelly after so much exertion. "I can't run again..." I started.

He stopped and turned his head in my direction. "Get on my back."

Not one to waste any more time, I did as he asked. He flinched. "Ouch! Grab onto my fur, not my skin!"

"Sorry," I readjusted my claws. Satisfied, he bounded off.

Unlike cats who are born to sprint, dogs are built for endurance. He got back to the school in record time. My canine companion barely had to pant at the end, for which I was just a teeny bit jealous. He took us straight to the front doors instead of the broken bathroom window. The front door was still slightly ajar from when I had entered as a human. Grimm, being much stronger than a cat, nosed it wider to let himself in. I hopped down from his back, still puffy from my experience but at least in control of my legs again.

"It was in the girl's bathroom," I stated in hushed tones, looking nervously down the right-hand hallway. Grimm turned his head in the direction I was staring and cautiously padded down the corridor. Sure enough, sounds of carnage emanated from the end of the hall. With baited breath we ventured on, but once we reached the dreaded bathroom, we found it empty. Trashed, but no monster within. Another muffled crash reached our ears from farther down the hall, however. Treading lightly, we walked on, stopping just outside of the science room. The door had been mostly closed.

From inside it sounded as if multiple beakers were meeting their end. Grimm stared into my eyes, his yellow ones aglow with determination. I nodded my feline head, giving him the go ahead.

He did a quick nod back, a gesture that seemed very undoglike, before peeking his head into the cracked door. For a second, he stood stock still, his head invisible to me, but his tail gave a shallow wag before he bravely pushed his way into the room.

His mannerisms did not fit his normal, crazed animal persona when he was about to battle monsters. It greatly confused me, which of course piqued my curiosity. As terrified as I was to be back in the same room as the werewolf, my interest in the situation won out over fear of death. It's no wonder curiosity killed the cat, as the saying goes.

I stationed myself behind Grimm and peeked between his legs. There the monster stood, its back turned to us as it took its aggression out on inanimate objects within the classroom. It did not realize we were there, much to my relief. I took a moment to tear my eyes away from it to look at my partner.

Grimm watched its movements as if spellbound.

"Well?" I asked him, "Aren't you going to do your thing?"

"Fascinating," he replied, still not taking his eyes off the sight, "but not a werewolf."

"What!?" Didn't he have eyeballs?

He pointed toward it with his nose. "It doesn't smell right. And it's broad daylight. How many werewolves do you know that can transform without the moon?"

"Oh." I had not thought of that. "Then what is it?" I countered.

"It smells human. Female. Young."

"Yes, it *was* a little girl before she changed into … that."

"Not was. Is. Still is."

I stared at the monster before us, its back still turned and unaware of our presence. "You're telling me that's a human girl? How?"

He stared harder, cocking his head to the side. "It's an illusion."

I turned to stare at Grimm, who continued to watch whatever it was as it tore up the classroom. "An illusion?"

He nodded his black nose in its direction. "I could be wrong, because I've never seen one before, but my mother told me she once saw one. She said there's an extremely rare magical talent that only a handful of humans possess. They are called projectionists. I never thought I'd see one though."

"But it tore up the bathroom!" I countered fiercely. "You can see it picking up objects. And it swiped at me when I escaped. Pulled out a couple of hairs. I could feel it! How could an illusion do that?"

"Illusion isn't exactly the right word," Grimm explained. "They are called projectionists because they can project an image, or even themselves in a very real way. So yes, even though she isn't actually a monster, she is projecting the monster arm to reach out and tangibly touch objects."

I just stared at him. He turned his head down and to the right to make eye contact. "It's hard to properly explain."

"I bet," I murmured. "So now what? We can't just leave her like this."

"Try talking to her? Calm her down?"

"Talking to her is what made her this way."

Grimm chuffed. "I've got your back this time. Try it."

Approaching the girl/beast was the last thing I wanted to do, but I was at a loss. I fully entered the classroom and transformed.

"Hey!" I yelled with more gusto than I thought I had in me.

The monster turned at my voice and saw me. It growled low in its throat and started advancing.

"Uhh, Grimm?" I half-moaned.

Grimm, true to his word, did have my back. He sprang in front of me, hackles raised, growling menacingly. I knew that stance. The next step would be to engage and tackle it to the ground if need be.

The beast stopped for a moment, assessing. Then it roared in response to the new threat. Okay, definitely not good.

Grimm responded by increasing the volume of his growl and bunching his muscles. He barked a deep, low woof, a "back off" bark if I ever heard one. With the monster still ignoring his threats, he prepared to spring.

Somebody shouldered past me, knocking me slightly off balance, and thrust himself in between my determined partner and the crazed monster. Everything happened so quickly I could not decide whether he was the bravest person ever or merely the stupidest.

Holding one hand out to me and Grimm and the other behind him, he cried out, "Stop!"

The monster behind him became silent and straightened, cocking its head in confusion. A heartbeat later it started shrinking. Grimm straightened as well but kept his guard up. I stayed where I was, too dumbfounded by the goings-on to even think about moving.

Within seconds the girl was back, looking disheveled and exhausted. "Fal?" she asked timidly. And then she fainted. The new person, a teenaged boy with raven black hair, caught her as she sank to the ground.

CHAPTER 11

As Grimm guarded the classroom door, I paced the hallway. The girl had been out of it for about ten minutes. She was still unconscious, and the boy was not going to voluntarily leave her side while she was in that condition. I had taken one look at the youth to know he was my bounty, but I couldn't just swoop in and arrest him. There was clearly more to this story. So, I paced.

I was at a loss, to be honest. So far my bounties had been morally easy for me. Bad guy? Nabbed. Werewolf? No problem. Vampire? Obviously guilty. Teenage boy devoted to a younger girl who I could only guess was his sister? Whose only crime was petty theft and knocking a curmudgeon over the head? This was unfamiliar territory.

My duty was to uphold the law as a bounty hunter. It was not in my responsibility to act as judge and determine whether someone was guilty. But something was fishy about this whole scenario.

I needed answers to assuage my newfound crisis. But answers would have to wait, so I paced.

It wasn't terribly long before Grimm rumbled at me, his stiff posture making it clear that my presence was needed in the room. I hurried over to the doorway and looked inside. The girl was awake and sitting upright with the help of the boy. Both stared first at Grimm, but their eyes moved to me. I flashed a smile.

I broke the silence. "Hiya. Can we chat?"

I nervously watched the girl, who glared at me. However, it was apparent she was exhausted, and I was fairly certain she wouldn't morph again. The boy hesitated a moment, and then nodded.

I entered the room slowly, then crouched down to their level a good four feet away from them. I quickly examined them before speaking, noting the same shabbiness of the teen's clothes, the very shaggy quality of his dark hair, and the general dirtiness of his skin. His eyes were the same shade and shape as the girl's.

Meeting those eyes, I asked my first question: "Is she alright?"

He looked at the girl resting in his arms, and she at him. He nodded. I continued, addressing the girl, "I'm sorry to have upset you earlier. I didn't realize I was describing your ... brother?"

She sighed heavily, wearily. "My brother," she confirmed in a tiny voice.

I looked back at him. "My name is Cressida Curtain. I am unfortunately in a sticky situation. Before I say anything more, I want you to be aware that the black dog behind me is my partner, and he will not allow either of you harm me, or leave, until we get this sorted out. This is not a threat, merely a statement. I do *not* want a repeat of what happened earlier."

There was a small flare of fear in the teen's eyes. Normally, I thrilled to see that in a criminal's face, knowing I was the cause. I hated it this time.

He schooled his features and nodded. "I understand."

"Are you aware, young man, that there is a bounty out on your head?"

He shook his head, thought for a moment, and gave a small nod. "I guess it shouldn't surprise me."

I nodded at his answer. "I don't like mincing words. I am a bounty hunter."

"Don't take him!" The girl cried out, her voice wavering.

"Hush, Wren," her brother soothed. She quieted again and he looked back at me, his expression troubled.

"I need you to understand something," I continued. "It is my job to apprehend those with bounties on their heads and bring them back to the law. If I don't, someone else will." I stopped for a moment, grasping at the right words. "I don't know anything about you, but I feel there is more to this story, and I find myself in a peculiar position."

The teen gazed at me, his look uneasy. "So, you aren't going to apprehend me?"

I sighed. "It's not that easy. The bounty is for only you. There's no mention of the girl. But I can't just let you go. You do have a bounty out. I think you should be grateful that I was the first hunter to find you. Because I want to do what's right. Trust me, I know other bounty hunters." I shook my head. "Most would scoop you up without any questions asked. They'd collect the money and not give two figs about your situation. They might even just leave your sister behind, since there's no bounty on her. No, I want to do the right thing. But I just don't know what that is yet."

He nodded but the confusion was still clear on his face. "So, you *are* going to apprehend me?"

The girl looked into her brother's face, shaking her head adamantly and trying not to cry. He shushed her softly again.

"I think...if we could come to an agreement, say, I do apprehend you but in the nicest way possible and in the meantime, you shed some more light on your ... circumstances? That way I basically save you from another less charming bounty hunter and

I possibly get myself out of a moral pickle. Win-win?" There. My cards were on the table.

"And if I say, no thanks?" he countered.

I slumped a tad. "Then I still arrest you and damn my morals. And my curiosity. Because I really, really am curious about ... this." I gestured in their general direction.

I saw a ghost of a smile. "Morals are important in this world," he said. "If you treat us fairly, we promise to go with you, even if it means incarceration."

"Fal, no!" his sister objected.

"Wren, is it?" I asked her. She glared just a smidge as she focused her attention on me. "I promise I will do what I can to see that your brother is not wrongly accused. And believe me, this is not what I usually do. But for some reason I want to help you two. Will you trust me?"

She stared hard, nearly enough to make me squirm. After all, I did already piss her off enough for her to sort of turn into a raging monster. But she sighed and slumped back into her brother before uttering one small word. "Fine."

"Great!" I stood up, wiggling my ankles to get the blood flowing. "Let's get out of here as soon as possible. Knobby Hill is a long way off and as I mentioned, there are most likely other hunters on their way."

Grimm, noticing the change in my tone, came trotting over. I glanced at him. "Right, first thing's first: introductions. You know my name already. This is Grimm. He is my partner, and he will protect you both so long as we all follow the rules."

I held out my hands in a 'your turn' way. The youth sighed. "I'm Falcon. Falcon Rambert. I go by Fal. This is Wren, as you know."

"Falcon and Wren..." I trailed off.

He shrugged. "Our parents had a thing for birds."

"Okay then," I replied, waving the conversation away. "Seriously, can we get moving? It's getting late in the day," I said, looking pointedly at the dimming light level out of the window.

Wren yawned. Fal looked at her, still in his arms. "I think, if it's okay with you, Wren needs to stay put until the morning. She's completely taxed her system today."

I furrowed my brow at his request. Staying until the next morning seemed like a huge mistake. I mulled it over and was about to object until I caught sight of the girl's exhausted face.

"I'll bet," I said. "Very well, but we leave at first light. Some of those other hunters are too good at their job and I didn't have much of a head start. Show me your sleeping arrangements."

Fal stood up awkwardly, helping Wren to stand in the process. I still did not trust the child and I was hesitant to even touch her. But Fal didn't need the help. He managed to get a good grip on her and lift her into his arms, even though she was not that much smaller than him.

"Follow me," he said.

Fal's path led us up the main set of stairs, which creaked ominously but held. The stairs opened into an upstairs hallway, which seemed to be staff lodging. In the very last room down the hallway, Fal nudged the door open with his foot. We followed him into a small dark room with a single bed, upon which he laid Wren down. She snuggled in willingly as he drew the blankets over her form. She began breathing heavily almost immediately.

For the first time, I noticed the knapsack on Fal's back. He took it off now and opened it, removing a single yellow apple, which he placed on the nightstand by the bed. I was touched by the thoughtfulness of the gesture and surmised that Wren was likely to be very hungry when she woke.

Fal motioned quietly for me to step out with him. Grimm stayed by my side pace for pace as we made our way across the hallway to a large sitting room, presumably the teachers' lounge. There, he sank down into a very ragged and dusty sofa. I took the one opposite him.

Digging through his knapsack again, Fal withdrew a second apple. He froze, looked at me pensively, and then offered the apple to me with an eyebrow raised. I shook my head with a small grin. He shrugged, almost with relief, and then took a giant bite of the apple.

We sat in silence as the teen devoured the fruit. When he was finished, he gazed at the two of us.

"You have questions, I know," he began.

"Yes."

Fal sighed. "About Wren?"

I nodded. "That's at the forefront, certainly."

"It's a little difficult for me to simply open up to a total stranger. No offense, but you are here to arrest me, after all."

I raised my hands in a placating gesture. "No offense taken. We all have our secrets. Let's start with the list of crimes. Are you guilty of them, or am I apprehending the wrong black-haired boy?"

Fal squirmed a bit. "It was food," he finally confessed. "We needed to eat. Just a loaf of bread here, a cooked chicken there. We were trying to get milk from the cow at that farm. Nothing more."

"But you hit that man over the head!" I exclaimed. Fal met my eyes with a small hint of anger. It was the first time I saw any strong emotion from him. "Did you do it because you thought you had been caught red-handed?"

He stayed silent, sheepishly looking down. Finally, he shook his head, refusing to meet my eyes.

Interesting.

"We haven't stolen anything to eat since then," he continued in a low voice. "I ... found some potted plants to eat for food, and I also found an apple orchard. That's where I was coming back from this afternoon."

I nodded, mulling over what he said. Clearly, living off of apples and lettuce would not do in the long run. These kids needed protein and fats. I glanced out of the window, noticing the diminishing light.

"Listen, it's getting dark out and I need to bring my wagon and horse someplace unnoticeable. Would you be able to help me with that? We could chat on the walk."

Fal rubbed his chin, as if unsure of what to say. "Wren..."

"I can leave Grimm to guard over her. It won't take long." Besides, if Fal took the opportunity, however ill-advised, to try to escape, I'd still have leverage with the girl in my possession.

He nodded. I turned to Grimm. "I'm bringing Humbert in. Don't leave Wren's side."

Fal furrowed his brow as Grimm gave his head a small nod and padded out of the room toward Wren's door. "That's some dog you have."

I shrugged. "He's not mine. We just work together."

Clearly the teen thought I had screw loose, based on the raised eyebrow he sported. But he shrugged it off and followed me outside.

The air was chillier than previously, with wooded shadows darkening the old road. Crickets were just starting their evening serenade in the background. I stopped at the front of the school and held my breath, listening for any sounds that were out of place and watching for any shadows that moved. Fal, to his credit, stayed perfectly still and silent while I surveyed the road in either direction. Only after I had started moving again did he make any noise.

"So, spill," I said in hushed tones as we walked down the silent lane. "Is Wren a projectionist?"

Fal didn't answer for a heartbeat. "I'm surprised you know about them," he replied.

"I hear things." *Like, earlier in the day.* "I admittedly don't know much though."

"They are incredibly rare, as I'm sure you know. It can run in families, skipping generations before reappearing. Our great-grandmother was one."

"I've never seen one in action until today," I pondered. "She was pretty terrifying."

Fal was silent. I looked at him in the failing light and could see the struggle he was internally suffering from. I stopped walking, turning toward him. "What is it?"

Fal stayed mute, shaking his head. I sighed. "Fal, I can't help if I don't know what's going on. What's eating you?"

He still didn't answer, but I could see his resolve cracking. "Look," I said a little more intently than I meant to, "I get that I'm a perfect stranger you only just met, and I'm taking you into custody to boot. You don't trust me." I started walking again, and he dutifully followed.

"Miss Curtain," he began, his voice cracking.

I interrupted, rolling my eyes. "It's Cressida to you. If you insist on calling me Miss Curtain, I'll be forced to call you Mr. Rambert and that just won't do."

"Sorry," he apologized needlessly. Back to silence.

I felt the need to break it, and I blurted out the first thing that popped in my head. "How old are you, fourteen?"

"Sixteen. Wren will be twelve in a month." His tone was short.

Oops, I guess I hit a sore spot there. I often forgot how important age could be to humans. "Sorry, I'm bad with guessing ages." I waited for him to answer my original question, for him to burst open with honesty about the situation, but he didn't, and I didn't want to push him. Yet.

The wagon was now just around a bend. The light by this time was nearly nonexistent. I could still see fine, but I could tell that the teen was having to focus more on his foot position to prevent tripping. As we rounded the bend, Humbert gave a small whinny, happy to smell a familiar being. I pushed down a spot of chagrin. Grimm and I had left while the sun still shone. I assumed we would come straight back to the wagon, but instead Humbert had patiently waited hours for our return, and now he waited in the dark.

"Here we are," I said cheerfully as I made a beeline for the lamp that still hung from its front pole. Turning it on, I bathed Humbert in its soft glow. I patted the horse's side. "Sorry for the delay, Humbert. We're going to move you to a more secure spot."

Humbert whickered and tossed his head in Fal's direction. "Oh, I nearly forgot. Humbert, meet Fal. Fal, Humbert."

The teen stared at me, the lamp's glow dancing across his face. "You are strange," he said. "I mean, no offense. Do you always talk to your animals like they're people?"

I stifled a giggle. In actuality, Humbert couldn't really understand me in human form, just as I couldn't understand him. But he could pick up on vocal cues and body language. I couldn't exactly explain this to Fal, though. "It's impolite to leave anybody out of a conversation," I said as way of explanation.

Fal gave a little shake of his head. He turned his attention back to Humbert, who nickered softly again.

"Wow," Fal breathed, his eyes large. "He sure is big."

"Humbert is a Percheron, a draft horse. Have you never seen one before?"

The youth shook his head. "No, actually. The only horses I have been familiar with were riding horses."

"Oh, well," I responded, at a loss for words. Much of this area, Tinuka County, and even the larger Oracune Region, had use for draft horses, and they tended to be a familiar sight. Where were these kids from? I shook the question off and diverted the subject. "Now, let's get this show on the road. I'm sure Humbert would appreciate getting unharnessed for the rest of the night."

I looked up at the lamp above me, and then over at Fal, who was taller than me. "Do me a favor? Can you lift the lamp down from the hook?"

Fal grinned as he easily maneuvered the lamp down for me. He handed it to me without a word.

"Thanks," I said. "I have to jump up onto the seat to reach. Short girl problems."

Lamp in hand, I led Fal to the back of the wagon. I took my key out of my vest pocket and unlocked the back. With the interior alight thanks to the lamp in my hand, Fal sucked in a breath.

"Huh," he softly murmured.

"It's not much, but it's home away from home," I replied. "You can climb in and sit back here or ride up front with me."

He was about to answer, but my ears picked up a noise that seemed very out of place. It was an extremely faint hum, similar to that which the lamp was emitting, but this wasn't coming from the lamp. It came from the outside, behind the bend in the road. A motor.

Fal must have seen my change in body language because he became rigid and silent. I reacted an instant later as the hum's volume increased slowly.

"Quick!" I hissed. "Get in the wagon! Don't make a sound!"

Thankfully, instead of acting surly to my sudden demands, Fal obeyed instantly, his gangly limbs working double time to get himself inside the interior. I shut the doors and locked them but kept the lamp with me. Heart pounding, I walked over to

Humbert and ahead of him as casually as I dared. Once I was a good ten feet in front of the wagon, I stopped and waited.

Mere seconds ticked by before the reason for the hum came into view from the opposite direction. Sure enough, it was a motorized carriage. A relatively new invention, these were gaining popularity in the more urban settings but were rare to come by in the vast rural and wildland locales. I personally hated them. They ran on free energy, but because there was a limit to the amount of energy any given machine could use, the MCs (as they were often called) could not go very fast at all. A galloping horse was just as fast, if not faster, and a horse did not produce that annoying hum. I'm certain the noise these machines emitted didn't bother human ears, but there was an unmistakable and vastly irritating quality to the mechanized drone when heard by superior feline ears. In other words, I considered motorized carriages to be completely pointless.

This particular MC I hated more than the rest. It was only a two-seater but had been modified with a decent cargo space in the back, just big enough to hold one person comfortably or two people uncomfortably. The exterior had been painted a shiny black with cherry red highlights on the wheel casings and bumpers. It was one-of-a-kind. And the owner was a one-of-a-kind tool.

The MC, lights glaring, slowed to a stop neck and neck with my wagon. I pretended to be walking towards it, holding the lantern out in front of me. The engine of the carriage cut out, but the lights stayed on. The door opened.

"Gavin St. Cloud," I called out, trying hard not to spit the name out like it had a dirty taste.

Gavin St. Cloud was a fellow bounty hunter. In appearance he was only a few years older than my human form. We had met a handful of times before, and battled over the same bounty twice now, both times figuratively colliding into each other. He beat me to the first one with a sneer and a swagger that instantly made him my enemy. On the second one, I edged him out just barely, which probably put me on his enemy list. He oozed condescension over that second one, commenting about how I'd gotten lucky. I hated his guts.

"Why, Cressida Curtain!" he called back with mock friendliness as he exited his vehicle. "Whatever brings you out here?"

I approached him with a small swing in my hips, which I swear I didn't tell my body to do. He was a good-looking man, I'll admit, with dense dark hair like rich umber, a bronzed complexion, and wide eyes of a deep amber hue that hinted at a partial Eastern Continent descent. The problem with those eyes was that every time they looked at me, they seemed to be ogling me and mocking me simultaneously.

I stopped directly in front of him. He was only five inches taller than me, on the short side for a man, but he was broader of chest and his body belied strength. He was wearing trousers and a tight button-up shirt that outlines his muscles. He also had a holster strapped to one leg, showing it off in plain sight. I hated firearms and refused to carry one, despite the inherent risks of my job.

I scowled at him as his eyes continued their sweep over my body and face. "I could ask you the same thing, St. *Clod*."

He smiled widely at the jab, showing off perfect teeth. I wanted to punch that pretty mouth and the thought made me grin a bit. At that, Gavin took a step toward me, destroying my personal bubble. I desperately fought the need to take a step back, since I knew that was what Gavin wanted me to do. In a battle of wills, I was determined to beat the bastard, so I stood my ground.

"Ah, ah, ah, Miss Curtain!" he exclaimed. "That would be telling! Although, it's no coincidence that we are meeting in the middle of nowhere, is it?"

"I suppose not," I said, pretending to ponder something. "I *will* tell you that if you are thinking about checking out that school, don't bother. Where do you think I'm walking back from? Dead end."

"What school?" He laughed. "It's so sweet of you to share information with me, and so out of character. And where is your little dog?"

"Off hunting in the nearby woods," I lied. "Did you talk to the old farmer? He told me that there's been a sighting closer to town. I won't say where; that'd be cheating. I'm off to investigate just as soon as Grimm joins me."

"Uh-huh." I could tell St. Cloud was not exactly buying it. Darn. This could get messy. "As much as I'd love to take your word for it, Miss Curtain, I think I'd better investigate this school anyway. I'll let you follow your lead, I'll follow mine, and we'll see who comes out..." he paused to suck air through his teeth as he beamed an unsettling smile at me, "... on top, shall we?" The slight sexual innuendo was not lost on me, but Gavin luckily did not extrapolate further on it. He took a step back and tipped an invisible hat my way. I scowled a little at him. "A pleasure as usual to run into your lovely self, Miss Curtain."

The smug handsome bastard turned to get back into his MC. I yelled at his backside, "I wish I could say the same thing!"

Gavin laughed as he swung into the driver's seat and slammed the door. He began the process of starting the engine. I sauntered over to the side of his vehicle, and, because I was feeling rather childish, I called out, "The school is haunted, by the way. Just thought you should know."

Gavin didn't answer but instead gave me a saucy wink as his MC rumbled to life and headed down the road. I simply stared at his slow departure, remaining calm on the outside but roiling on the inside.

Once the carriage finally swung around the curve, I darted over to the doors and unlocked them as fast as I could.

"Fal!" I exclaimed, trying not to let the panic creep into my voice as I opened one of the doors. "I need to get back to the school and fast! Stay near the wagon and whatever you do, don't go near the school! I'll be back as soon as I can!"

I barely had time to see the panicked look on his whiter-than-usual face before I placed the lamp on the floor of the wagon and sprinted into the darkness, where I transformed into my true self. I made my second mad dash of the day.

CHAPTER 12

I kept to the side of the road, hoping my speed could beat that of the mechanical engine. I practically flew over the ground, my toes barely making contact on the dirt as my spine worked like a well-tuned spring. As focused as I was on speed, I almost didn't hear the electrical motor until the noise of it suddenly cut off just a hundred feet in front of me.

Damn, I was slightly too late to beat St. Cloud to the school. In fact, as I came to the once-grand front lawn, I could see him slowly walking up the steps to the front door with a small light in his hand. I did not let that deter me, however. As nimbly as I could, I raced up behind him, just keeping my distance. He stopped at the doors, inspecting them carefully, before swinging one open.

Here was my chance. As he entered the dark school, I let out an ear-piercing screech from behind. St. Cloud jumped visibly, and as he began a clumsy swing around to investigate the terrifying noise, I bolted forward, leaping over his foot and barely brushing against his leg with the fluffy tip of my tail. I was three-quarters of the way up the stairs before I even heard him mutter, "What in the...?" And I was at the top before he resumed entering the building.

I hoped I had given him a real case of the heebie-jeebies. Served him right.

Stamina visibly flagging now, I rushed to the end of the hallway. No Grimm stationed outside. Cursing his kind for just the briefest of seconds, I regained my sense and saw that the door to Wren's room was ajar. Familiar canine scents emitted from within. I went in.

"Grimm! We have company! St. Cloud is downstairs, and we have to get out of here now!"

He stared at me, almost terrified, which was not an expression I typically saw on him. It was then that I realized the room was not entirely dark. A very small lantern, most likely supposed to be used as a nightlight, sat on a table near the bed and created a faint glow around the room, illuminating everything just enough for human eyes to see. With this in mind, I looked up to the bed where Wren should have been asleep. Instead, she was sitting up awake and staring at me, the cat that had just waltzed into her room in an obvious panic and was now standing fearlessly in front of a giant dog. She did not say a word, but simply scrutinized us, her expression unreadable.

In any other situation I would have been panicked by such an error on my behalf. But unfortunately, we had bigger fish to fry this time.

Grimm finally communicated back. "Seriously? How are we going to do that?"

Perplexed, I shook my head, a bad habit I picked up from my human side. "I'll change to human to warn Wren. We just need to be sneaky, I suppose."

"You'll be sneakier as a cat, but we can't communicate to Wren this way."

"We don't have time to argue! Whatever happens, you and I need to stay out of Gavin's sight! I told him we already checked this place." Before Grimm could discuss more, I dashed out of the room and into the hallway, transformed, and barged back in.

"Wren! We need to go now!" I whisper-yelled at the girl.

She stared at me, eyes narrowing. "Where's the cat?"

"What cat?" I hoped I sounded convincing as I continued my tirade. "Seriously, there's a bounty hunter in the school right now looking for your brother. We need to get you out!"

Her eyes widened and she jumped from bed, obviously re-freshed. "What do we do?" She whispered back with an edge of panic in her voice.

"Stay with Grimm. He'll sneak you out. I'll stay back to look out for the hunter." I paused to think for the briefest of seconds. "Is there only one staircase?"

Wren shook her head. "There's a faculty staircase in the up-stairs lounge that leads to the kitchen."

"Good. Take it."

Grimm chuffed encouragingly at the girl to get her attention. She glanced at him and then back at me. She nodded.

I breathed a sigh of relief. "Keep a hold of his tail. He'll keep you safe."

As she did as I said, Grimm started for the door, cautiously nudging it open the rest of the way and peering out before lead-ing his ward into the hallway.

As they disappeared from view, I whisper-called out, "Good luck!"

With my newfound privacy, I turned off the light, stuffed it in my trouser pocket, and morphed into a cat again. I waited until I was sure the duo had gone into the lounge before peeking my head out into the hallway. With no sign of anybody out there, I nimbly pranced down the darkened hallway and down the stairs. I needed to find Gavin so that I could run interference if need be.

After checking the landing and not finding him, I cursed hindsight, since it would have been faster to get Wren out this way. Nothing could be done about it now, though. I stopped and listened to figure out which way to go.

Silly human, thinking he was being so quiet. I could easily hear him off to my left and down the hall. I ran to find him.

As soon as I turned the hallway corner, there he was. I skidded to a halt and watched him, keeping far away from the glow of his light. Gavin was checking each and every door as silently as possible, opening them a crack, peering inside, and then moving on. I threw out a silent prayer that he would continue to do so and keep far away from Grimm and his ward.

I guess when you aren't really religious, prayer doesn't work.

As Gavin started to check another door, a faint clatter could be heard elsewhere in the school. He straightened immediately, his hand reaching for the pistol at his side. He strode across the hall to the door closest to the sound, reading the inscription on the door. He nodded as if affirming something before pushing it open and bounding in.

Crap, crap, double hairballs. I chased after him, vaguely noting that the sign said, "Kitchen, Faculty Only." Luckily, the door was mostly open, so I breezed through without a problem. I had a bad feeling this would be the only easy thing about this whole development.

The kitchen was immense, as I surmised it would be. After all, this place had to feed a lot of kids back in the day. Just as with the rest of the school, it had not been emptied out. There were no windows, so the only light in the room came from Gavin's handheld. It did a good job of illuminating much of the center of the kitchen, leaving massive black shadows in the periphery.

"Okay, wherever you are, come out with your hands up!" Gavin barked. He had his pistol at the ready now, the light trained to follow its sweep as he moved cautiously forward. I had to hand it to him; he was a pro at his job.

I kept creeping up behind him, racking my feline brain as how to best get us out of here in one piece. So far Grimm and Wren had stayed in the shadows, somewhere. But this was bad. My brain refused to cooperate.

I had decided the old screech and scare tactic might be our best bet. I realized it was a bit weak and the outcome would be unpredictable, but I was doing my best to talk myself into it.

I was a bit too late.

A roar split the air before I could act, reverberating through the large room. Gavin and I both froze. As a large shadow off to the left emerged, the bounty hunter swung the light in that direction, revealing a large monster standing on two legs. It was bear-like in looks, with a gaping maw filled with too many sharp teeth and red eyes, but it looked diseased or undead as patches of fur and skin sloughed away all over its body. Sharp spines emerged from various spots on its head, shoulders and back.

I had to give the girl credit for originality.

Wren's monster roared again as the light illuminated it. I glanced at it for a second before returning my attention to Gavin.

I did not like what I saw. He was terrified, naturally, but he still had the pistol trained on the beast. Wren's new form may have been out of a nightmare, but Gavin was keeping enough wits about him, and he was not about to turn tail and run. Unfortunately, if he fired his weapon, I had no way of knowing if it would actually harm the girl, and I couldn't let myself find out.

I bounded forward and barreled my small body into the back of Gavin's knees. His legs collapsed forward and he lost his balance. As he fell backward his finger pulled the trigger, and the sound of the gunshot filled the space. Luck was on my side, however. I heard the bullet ping off to the right, too far away to hurt anybody.

The wind was clearly knocked out of Gavin. He had dropped the light, which spun in a small arc out of reach of his out-stretched left hand. But the pistol was still clutched in his right. I needed to remedy that, and fast. Steeling myself, I rushed to that hand and swiped my claws across his wrist, cutting deep enough to instantly draw blood.

Gavin let out a string of profanities but dropped the weapon as he raised his arm up. I took this opportunity to jump onto his diaphragm solidly, eliciting a "Woomph!" from him that stopped his cursing. I think he made to grab me, but I jumped off as quickly as I had jumped on and ran to the left side of the room.

Grimm came out of hiding then, as I screeched to a halt in front of the bear-thing. "Time to go!" I yelled.

Grimm looked up at the monster, who looked back at the two of us. Grimm chuffed once and pranced forward slightly. Nodding its head, the bear-thing began to follow our mad dash for the door. As it ran, it shrank back down, so that by the time we reached the door it was Wren again. I noted with approval that the entire time she had held onto Grimm's tail, even as a monster.

Back in the hallway, I paused for the briefest of seconds. "Just go this way to the main doors. I'll meet you out there!" I dashed off ahead of them.

Outside again, with the dark fully settled into night and the nocturnal creatures in full chorus, I switched my form again. Not three seconds later Grimm and the girl burst out of the school. Even in the dark I could see the fatigue on the girl's face. I frowned.

"Wren, get on Grimm's back," I commanded. She hesitated only a bit before realizing her own limits and then she straddled the dog and wrapped her arms around his neck. I nodded my approval, met Grimm's eyes, and tilted my head to tell him we should get out of here *now*. That was all it took for the two of us to break into another run, back to our wagon.

We ran all the way back to the wagon without encountering any problems, a real blessing. Fal, to his credit, had stayed out of sight in the wagon and he only came out once he knew it was us.

"Wren! Wren!" he called out with brotherly concern. He rushed over to the large dog and his rider, grasping her arm.

I was beat. All that running and adrenaline was finally catching up to me. I bent over with my hands braced on my thighs to catch my breath. Grimm was panting profusely. As I recovered from our sprint, I watched Fal pull Wren off Grimm and into a loving hug, which she returned, albeit with less gusto.

"You're all right," he murmured into her long hair.

"I'm fine," she replied breathlessly, "just tired. The cat saved me."

Those words hit me like a figurative punch to the gut.

Fal didn't say anything, but a look of confusion swept his face momentarily. He glanced in my direction without breaking the hug. I shrugged nonchalantly, at least that was what I was going for. There were tears shining in the light of Fal's eyes. Once the quizzical look passed, I could see a grateful smile through his sister's hair.

My breathing back to some semblance of order, I picked up the lantern and started in with my boss voice. "St. Cloud is still at the school. We need to get out of here now."

"Fal?" came Wren's small voice. "So sleepy."

I strode to the back of the wagon and got in, setting the lamp in its usual spot. I pulled out the mattress and blankets and arranged them semi-neatly.

"Fal! Bring her in here!" I said. He was already making his way over with the girl in her arms. It was difficult for him to climb up into the interior with his bundle, so I held out my arms to him.

He hesitated.

I sighed. "Please?"

He acquiesced, and between the two of us we hoisted Wren inside. She was already nearly out of it again, but she managed to walk two steps to sink into the mattress. Fal tucked the blanket around her prone form.

"Fal, I don't know if we can trust her. She's a cat." Wren whispered.

Fal glanced up at me, but I pretended I didn't hear the girl's words, even though my heart was pounding in my chest. He looked back down to Wren.

"Don't talk nonsense, Wrenny. You just need sleep." Fal laid a small kiss on her dirty forehead and by the time he had straightened up she was asleep.

I looked at the teen. "We need to put distance between us and this place. Stay back here for a while?"

Fal nodded, and I let out a heavy sigh of relief. I pulled the night light out of my pocket and handed it to Fal, who turned it on and placed it between himself and his sister. I grabbed my own lamp before scooting out of the wagon and closing the doors behind me. Grimm, nearly lost in the dark save for his shining yellow eyes, snuffed once, a sound I took to mean that he would run alongside for a spell.

I did not dally in turning the wagon in the opposite direction of the school.

CHAPTER 13

Once we had been traveling for about a half an hour and had gotten back onto what would eventually be Rabbit Hole Road, I called for Humbert to stop. Jumping down with the lantern, I spotted my partner's glowing eyes off to my left. Grimm was panting from the night's exertion but otherwise seemed fine. I walked swiftly to the back and opened the doors softly. Shining the soft glow of the lamp inside, I met Fal's hazel eyes, shining nearly black in the low light. Beside him, Wren was still fast asleep.

"I think I'd like to ride up front for a while," he hesitantly stated.

I shrugged. "Sure, there shouldn't be anyone out tonight where we are going, and I'll have Grimm ride back here to keep Wren safe. I just feel that it's best to travel a little further before we stop for the night."

Fal looked almost relieved, as if he had not thought I'd say yes. He nodded and, after one more quick look at his sister's prone form, he made his way out of the wagon.

Grimm sat patiently by my side as Fal exited the back. Once the teen was out of the wagon, the black dog looked at me, the sunflower yellow of his eyes shining in the light. I flicked my head at the wagon. "Wren duty."

Without a sound, Grimm jumped up into the interior. I closed the doors firmly, latched them, and spun around to make my way to the front, only to find Fal blocking my path with a dumbfounded look on his face.

"What?" I asked.

"How...?" Fal started but shook his head. "I just don't get it."

"C'mon," I said with a combination of force and compassion. I grabbed his forearm to steer him to the wagon seat. He meekly obeyed. Once he was up onto the seat, I handed him the lantern and made my own way up. Fal had already figured out where to hang the lamp. I picked up the reins and barely flicked them. "Let's go, Humbert!"

As the large horse moved forward, I saw another slight shake of Fal's head. I sighed. "What?"

"Is there ... is there such a thing as an animal witch?"

"You mean like an herbalist, but with animals?" I asked to clarify.

"Yes, like that."

I shook my head. "I'm sure there is, but I'm not one if that's what you're thinking."

He glanced at me. "Then, how are you able to boss these animals around?"

I winced. "First of all, it's not bossiness. It's called taking the lead. Grimm and I are partners. He can be just as bossy as me, trust me." Fal frowned. I continued, "Grimm is special. He understands more than the average dog."

"He's bigger than the average dog, that's for sure," Fal mused out loud. "Okay, but what about the horse?"

I thought about it. "Humbert has been working for us for a while now. He knows my cues. Trust me, it wasn't this easy in the beginning."

Fal fell silent beside me. I could almost see his thought process about whether or not to believe me. Finally, he shrugged, and I was surprised by the amount of relief I felt from the gesture.

We rode in silence for another five minutes.

"Uh, Miss Cur...Cressida?"

I smiled toothily at the dark road in front of me. "Yes?"

Another pause, then: "Thank you. For, for keeping Wren safe. For *this*." He gestured to the seating arrangement.

My smile became more pleasant. "You are welcome. I gave you my word. And you gave yours."

Fal fidgeted beside me. When at last he spoke, he kept his voice low. "She projected again, didn't she?"

I nodded heavily. "We were almost caught in the kitchen. She scared him off with another beast form."

He sighed. "You know, I didn't quite believe you about the whole bounty thing until I heard you talking to that other hunter. It made it all very real to me."

I fished into my vest pocket, finding the rap sheet. I pulled it out and offered it to Fal. "Here. I should have shown you this earlier."

He took it and unfolded it. There was silence for a moment before he let out a strained chuckle. "It's real all right. You were right, I'm glad you got to us first. I was so scared. I thought I heard a gunshot come from the school."

"You did." Fal turned quickly at that, and I hastily added, "It went off in the air! Nobody was hurt! St. Cloud was too close for comfort, so I, uh, pushed him from behind and knocked him over. After that we got out safely."

Fal let out a shaky breath, almost ending in a laugh. "Again, thank you."

"Are you kidding? I got one-up on St. Clod. I should be thanking you."

This time he did let out a chuckle. The humorous undertone didn't last long, however, before the mood settled into an awkward silence that lasted a hair too long.

Just as I was about to break the horrible uncommunicative pause, Fal beat me to it with a huge sigh.

"She's changed," he exhaled.

"Wren? How? In what way?"

"Earlier this evening you had described Wren as terrifying. That isn't how she used to be. She ... she used to be so happy. She only projected innocent things. Fairies and unicorns, or she'd turn her room into an enchanted forest. She used to tell me stories. She was so positive, until just before our parents died." He sighed.

"So, what happened? What changed her?" I asked softly.

"I'm not sure." He looked at his hands, which were clasped in his lap. "She only makes monsters now. She's unpredictable with her anger. And now she makes things up. She lies to me. She thinks you are a cat; I'm worried about her mental health."

Skirting around the cat issue, I asked, "Has she made up things before?"

He nodded slightly. "She started telling me stories about new places she would go. She called them her new worlds. She started to get angry at me when I referred to them as stories."

I stayed silent, thinking.

Fal broke the silence first. "It was Wren that knocked out the farmer."

I didn't expect that statement, and I swung my head over to look at him. He looked ashamed. But now that he had said it, it made perfect sense.

"We went there to steal some milk, that much is true. When the farmer interrupted us to milk his cow, I was planning on staying hidden until he was gone. He was so drunk that we could have easily snuck around him. But Wren got a look in her eye and ran up to him before I could stop her. I watched her pick up an empty pail and bash it over his head. As soon as she did, I shooed her out of the barn first and chased after her."

"So that's why Whitman saw you and not Wren?"

He hid his eyes in a sigh of despair. "She had never done anything like that before! I had no clue she was even capable of such violence! I started leaving her behind after that whenever I needed to gather supplies. I couldn't risk her hurting another person."

"That ended well for me," I muttered to myself. Fal let out a little guffaw tinged with chagrin.

"I saw the bathroom. I don't know how you got out of there in one piece."

I clammed up on that subject.

But he had one more thing to say. "But I'm glad you did."

CHAPTER 14

We rode mostly in silence for another two hours, taking it slow for Humbert's sake. There was much more to the Ramberts' story, but we still had a good day's journey left, so I didn't press. Before we reached the part of the road that was heavily pitted with ruts, I stopped the wagon. Even in my human form I could feel Humbert's appreciation for calling it a night. Traversing that stretch would have been too dangerous for the old horse in the dark. I winced, realizing he had been harnessed since five in the morning. I'd have to make it up to him soon.

"Sorry, good sir," I murmured to him as I slid off the seat, plucking the lantern off its pole. Fal must have been getting used to my odd ways, because he didn't react to my words. Instead, he yawned widely and stretched his arms in the air. He followed me off the seat.

I handed him the lantern, which he readily took. I began to unbuckle the horse while Fal stood by, unsure what to do.

I said to him, "Go on in the back. Grimm and I will sleep under the wagon tonight. We'll be leaving again first thing in the morning."

Fal paused. "Are you sure?"

I nodded curtly. "We'll be fine."

"Don't you need the lantern?"

I shook my head. "I can do this with my eyes closed." Technically a fib, but the real reason would not have sat well with the youth. Normal people cannot see in the dark.

Before the teen turned away, I held up a finger to pause him. "Hang on, you should have this too." I dug into my vest pocket and snagged the key. Handing it to him, I said, "This locks the wagon doors from the inside. And the outside, but that doesn't really matter right now. Be sure to lock the doors tonight. Just to be on the safe side."

"Thanks," he said as he accepted the key. He gave me a small smile, then stood there staring at me awkwardly for a few seconds. Finally, clearly at a loss for what etiquette would dictate, he added, "Well, then, goodnight." He turned away, the glow of the light receding as he went around the back. As Humbert was slowly freed from restraints by my hands, I could hear the doors being unlatched and Grimm jumping down from the wagon. "Goodnight, Grimm," I heard Fal say softly as the doors closed and the lock snicked shut. I smiled to myself. The boy was starting to talk to animals too.

I finally got the last of the gear off Humbert and spent extra time currying his coat to show my gratitude for the long day. Grimm sat nearby, watching. I paused when I was finished, listening for errant sounds, and searching for wayward light. All was quiet and dark, so I shimmered down with a breath of relief.

"Humbert, thank you for your service. I apologize for the long day, and I regret to say that we'll need to leave first thing in the morning. Please get some good grazing in and then rest as much as you can."

"My pleasure, Mistress. Good night." Good old Humbert. He never complained.

Grimm had crawled under the wagon to settle down for the night. It wasn't a very cozy spot to sleep but it was more protected than out on the open road. I stretched my front legs, my rump in the air, and then my back legs with my chest puffed out. I crawled into his doggy warmth and proceeded to groom myself.

"Bleh, road dust," I muttered while my tongue caressed my fur.

Grimm chuckled, his side rumbling softly. "You got some filling in to do, CC. I tried to listen to your conversation, but I couldn't understand most of the words. What's the scoop?"

In the solitude of our animal kinship, I told him everything that Fal and I had discussed since leaving the school.

"There's still so many things I don't understand," I admitted. "Why is Wren like this? I have the feeling she doesn't like me very much. Could it be because of the way we started off?"

Grimm was silent before cracking his jaw in a big yawn. "Dunno," he replied sleepily.

I purred at him. "Get some sleep. Long day."

"Tomorrow might be longer."

Sometimes I hate it when he's right.

The problem with sleeping outside of the wagon is the lack of security. Any critter and its mother could disturb us, and for that reason alone I had a very hard time turning my little animal brain off. My ears kept pricking at every single sound and it took complete exhaustion to finally pull me under enough to fully sleep.

That was why I did not fully awaken to a small disturbance above. The wagon creaked ever so slightly, but my sleepy brain told me it was just one of the occupants inside shifting position. My ears flicked at a distinctive sound: a lock slowly turning. I woke fully when footsteps stepping down from the wagon finally alerted me that something was amiss.

I threw my eyes wide, taking in what little light the moon was casting. A figure watched me.

My hackles rose. My nostrils flared and my eyes grew huge.

It was Wren, my senses determined a second later. She was crouched down, peering under the wagon.

She was watching me, specifically. My hackles got even higher, and I involuntarily arched my back a little as her face contorted into a knowing grin. I flattened my ears instinctively. She stayed to watch me for a couple of seconds before straightening and walking away into the darkness.

Grimm, usually much more alert to disturbances than me, was still sound asleep. I did not want to wake him just yet, as I had no clue what exactly was happening. I was a bit surprised by my gut reaction, and I wasn't so sure if I should trust it or not. One thing was certain: Wren was up to something.

I waited for a moment, then slowly crept out from under the wagon. My tail was still puffy, and my heart beat too rapidly. I followed after the girl.

It took me a bit to catch up with her. She had made a beeline into the surrounding woods, walking much too fast for this to be an innocent midnight stroll. I stalked her from behind until I was close enough to see her, and then I transformed, leaping forward to grasp her arm, heedless of the noise I made in the process.

Wren spun with a slight yelp, the fear on her face quickly morphing into an angry scowl. I scowled back at her.

"What do you think you are doing?" I accosted her, keeping my voice low.

"Let go!" she retorted, angrily flinging her arm out of my grasp. I let her, knowing I could catch her again if necessary and hoping my cooperation would enable hers. She huffed like a spoiled princess. "I just needed to go to the bathroom."

I scoffed. "A little far out for that, don't you think?"

"Ever hear of a little thing called privacy?" she shot back, vehemence lacing her words.

"Ever hear that the woods are dangerous at night?" I countered, just as angry. "There are things out here that go bump in the night and might find a little girl a tasty midnight snack. I don't care how much privacy you want—this is too far. You and your brother are under my protection, and right now you are making my job difficult!"

I also couldn't help but think she was lying, but to what end? What other possible reason would she have to be skulking about in the woods in the middle of night? I shook my head.

"C'mon, we're going back. Will you come peacefully, or do I need to hog tie you and drag you back to the wagon?"

She glared heavily at me, her eyes flashing murder. I knew she didn't know I could see her that well, which made her facial expression all the more chilling. I was looking at her true face, with no sweet girl mask in place. This kid definitely creeped me out.

She did not answer me for a moment. "You couldn't."

"Try me." I grabbed her arm to turn us back. "Don't try any funny business. I'll call for Grimm, and next time he won't go easy on you." It was a bit of an empty threat, but she did not need to know that. Luckily for me, she allowed herself to be led.

As she approached the wagon, I heard a soft voice call out: "Wren?"

We emerged from the bushes by the road. I called out, "She's here. She just needed to use the bathroom." I turned to Wren. "Where's the key?"

She seemed puzzled enough about my covering for her that she took a moment before responding, her voice coming out less menacing and more little-girl-like. "I left it with Fal."

"Good." At least it wasn't lost in the woods. "Let's keep it that way."

I helped her into the wagon. Wren shot me one last glance as she crawled into the interior. I couldn't quite place the look, as it seemed a mixture of hatred warring with confusion and gratitude. It bothered me, but I chalked it up to late-night oddness and left it at that.

Fal was sitting up while Wren snuggled back into the covers. "Thank you for looking out for her," he whispered to me. I merely nodded, although I was sure his human eyes could not spot the gesture in the light of the waning gibbous moon.

After a pause, I whispered back, "Fal, would you please lock the door and keep the key safe?"

I closed the doors without waiting for his answer but heard him shuffle out of the blankets and crawl to the wagon doors, upon which I heard the satisfying click of the lock engaging. Appeased, I yawned widely before shimmering back down and crawling up against Grimm, who had woken up when Fal had stirred.

"What was that about?" he asked me, his tone gruffer than usual.

"Tell you later," I murmured before settling in.

One last thought came to me, though. Should I have covered for her? Or was I simply feeding a monster with my compliance?

Once again, I played the try-to-get-to-sleep-while-out-in-the-open game. And, once again, it took a little while, especially given my unsettling encounter with Wren. When I did fall asleep, I dreamed of blissfully chasing big rats around a room. The room suddenly vibrated, and I panicked, thinking there was an earthquake. But the vibrating woke me out of the dream, and I realized it was Grimm growling so low and deep that I could feel it more than hear it. I opened my eyes to see that it was still mostly dark out, but the sky would be turning from purple to gray very soon.

"What's up?" I asked, my senses coming fully awake.

"Those clowns that we arrested yesterday. The thin one and the large one. They're back."

"Ugh, what?" All that hard work down the tubes. But he was right. I could smell their foul odor of dirt, blood, sweat, and tooth rot. "Does the Chargrove jail have a revolving door? How could they have been released already?"

Grimm sniffed the air. "Don't know. They walked right by the wagon, whispering. They didn't see us, and I didn't let them know we were here. They stopped briefly and tried the door latch, but it's still locked. Then they kept walking. I think an ambush down the road is in our future."

"I think you're right."

Grimm gave another sniff. "Do you think they were aware it's the same wagon?"

I pondered a moment. It was for reasons exactly like this that I chose not to decorate the outside of my boring transportation.

Unlike St. Cloud and his unique MC, I enjoyed having the slight edge of anonymity.

"Chances are good that they don't recognize it. Let's have some fun with them."

Grimm groaned softly. "I think your idea of fun might be a little different from mine. But I'll bite. Maybe literally."

We discussed our plan until it truly became apparent that morning had arrived. We would continue as normal, except instead of Grimm being in the back of the wagon like last time, he would be hiding in the side brush to give the goons another good scare. What we did with them after we caught them for a second time, however, was up in the air, considering that the wagon interior was now occupied. I figured inspiration would strike when the time came.

Once the sun was up, Humbert came strolling out of the trees like a giant gray unicorn, ready to start another day. Grimm told me he was going hunting for his breakfast and took off into the surrounding woods. I was a tad jealous, but it was more important for me to play nursemaid.

With Humbert back and Grimm gone, it was time to officially start the day. I made doubly sure that I was not being watched before I morphed to human, especially with a strange girl in the wagon somehow putting two and two together. I made sure that the back of the wagon was still closed, just in case.

At least I felt refreshed as I became my human form; even with the disturbance in the night, the amount of sleep I did manage was enough to invigorate me. I had a feeling I was going to need all the help I could get today.

I knocked on the back of the wagon and called out in my best singsong voice, "Rise and shine! Let's get some food in us before we head out!"

From inside, I heard the shuffling sound of blankets being thrown off sleepy bodies. If I concentrated, I could probably hear their bellies growling with the thought of breakfast, something these two had clearly gone without too many times as of late. The inner lock clicked open, and I backed up a few paces to allow the doors to swing ajar. I saw a raven-haired head for just a moment before it was withdrawn back into the darker recesses.

"Too bright," Fal groaned as he lay back down again. I paid the withdrawal no mind, instead turning my attention inward with thoughts of the day ahead. Forcing an attitude of cheerfulness upon the youngsters, I hummed a little ditty while I rummaged through a sack near the door, looking for the dried goods that I could turn into a quick breakfast.

Hands grabbed both of my arms from behind me and I was flung back from the wagon. I let out a little yelp of surprise. It only took a split second to realize that the planned ambush hadn't been for down the road after all. The highwaymen must have recognized my wagon.

I really should have been paying more attention to my surroundings, but perhaps I was a little more sleep deprived than I had initially thought. So much for plans.

After being goosestepped back a couple of paces from the wagon, a familiar stench and person wafted into view. He was showing off his lack of teeth again in a wicked grin while brandishing a newer looking and less bloody knife in my direction. I briefly tested my bonds with a quick and obvious struggle. Burly, from behind, was expecting it and held on tight. Time to play along.

"Skinny, Burly, back so soon?" I asked as casually as I could.

"Shut it! We've got a bone to pick with you!" Skinny spat at me, quite literally. I grimaced as the flecks hit my face. He held the knife closer to my chest. "Now, where's your dog?'

"Gone. I sold him in Chargrove," I lied with a straight face, raising my voice as much as I dared. I hoped Grimm wasn't quite out of earshot and would circle back. "How'd you get back here so soon?" I stayed perfectly still while I chatted.

A low chuckle brushed my ear. Skinny met his partner's eyes over my shoulder and grinned.

"That place is a joke," he replied. "They couldn't keep us in if they wanted to."

"I'm pretty sure they wanted to. Couldn't you come up with a wittier reply?"

Skinny frowned at me. "You've got quite the mouth on you, dontcha?"

The banter called for a shoulder shrug, but I refrained, still keeping my body ragdoll loose. Burly's grip seemed to be getting a little relaxed, but I couldn't quite be sure.

"It pays the bills."

Skinny laughed, giving me another spit shower. "I'll just bet." The lecherous quality was back in his voice. He licked his lips in a way that made me want to vomit into my mouth. "Maybe we should be putting that mouth of yours to work, huh?"

I mentally sighed as I kept my face neutral. Some men are simple pigs.

Skinny took my neutrality as a sign of me finally giving in. "You and I are going to try this again, now that we've got a good hold on you. Be a good girl this time, hmm?"

The knife was still brandished near my face. Just over Skinny's shoulder I could see the opening of the wagon, with two scared faces at the back. I did not think Burly would have been able to see them with the amount of darkness within, but that was not a problem for me. I made eye contact with Fal, who nearly looked like he was going to spring up. I pleaded with my eyes and the barest of head shakes not to get involved.

Still looking at Fal, I said, "Sorry boys. I don't play well with others!" And then I kicked out and high, connecting my boot with Skinny's jaw while twisting to the side to wrench myself free of Burly. The twisting motion half worked, enough for me to smash an elbow into the big lug's gut while simultaneously jamming the back of my head into his Adam's apple. Burly dropped my other arm to wrap around his midsection, wheezing heavily as he did. But Skinny had kept a hold of the knife, miraculously, and he made a half-hearted stab at me, aiming for my neck.

I instinctively raised my arm to deflect it. The knife connected, and I let out a hiss of pain as it sliced into my forearm. I forced the sting into the back of my mind. I cocked back my other fist and punched Skinny on the nose as he lifted the knife again. Where a little jaw kick had failed, a broken nose succeeded. He stumbled back with a grunt of pain, dropping the knife and holding his face with both hands. Burly, to my right, was fleetingly incapacitated, trying to get air back in his lungs.

Grimm charged through the brush a distance off, still too far away to be helpful. I paced away from Burly's backside; he glared at me with a healthy dollop of fear in his eyes before skittering over to Skinny's side. It would seem that the big guy had a brain in there after all.

"My dose!" Skinny shrieked. He clung to his ruined countenance but joined Burly in the glaring, murder easily readable in his eyes. Apparently, any amorous ideas had been completely wiped away. "You are going to pay for that, you bitch!"

I stared at the two bandits. Grimm was seconds away from barging to my rescue, I could tell. But, considering the two bandits had already gotten the drop on me, I figured it was time for Hail Mary to make an appearance. Extracting the knife from my boot, I took a step forward. Comically, both men took a step back toward the opening of the wagon, hitting their rears on the door lip.

I snarled at them. "I am *not* a bitch. I'm a damn queen."

Three things happened all at once. Both men frowned in confusion at my words (seriously, people? Look it up). From behind me, the bushes parted as Grimm bounded out in ferocious glory. Lastly, I watched in horror as Wren popped into view within my wagon, an expression of pure malice on her girlish features. Before I could react, she clamped a hand down on each man's shoulder. The bandits only had a half-second to turn toward their new assailant before the unthinkable happened.

Wren and the two men disappeared.

It was almost as if time itself slowed down. One moment they were there, confused looks on the outlaws' faces, and then Wren seemed to pull their shoulders toward her body, and the two men somehow *folded* into Wren, and Wren *folded* into herself before completely vanishing.

What was left at the scene was one bleeding woman (me), one befuddled dog who had ground to a sudden halt at the disappearance of his quarry, and one teenaged boy who froze for a second before screaming out his vanished sister's name.

CHAPTER 15

Fal's heartwrenching cry shook me from my stupor. I rushed over to where Wren and the bandits had been just seconds before. Fal met me at the entrance, pure panic etched on his youthful face. Grimm, who had been close enough to watch the spectacle, also approached the wagon, his ears pricked with confusion.

"What just happened?" I asked. Fal just shook his head, unshed tears in his hazel eyes.

I took two seconds to rehouse Hail Mary back in my boot, and then I refocused my attention back on Fal. I grabbed his arms and gave a small shake. "Fal! What the hell? She just ... just ... disappeared! How?"

He met my eyes, and those depths still held fear, but also a little anger. "I don't know," he responded, his tone deliberately wooden.

Grimm let out a tiny growl, a small warning. I looked at him, expecting him to have his attention on our environment or Fal, but he was staring at me. I nodded, and let Fal go, knowing that I was being a little unreasonable. Even though I had just witnessed an unreasonable scene, I had to keep it together. After all—and I laughed inwardly at this thought—I was the grownup in the situation.

"Sorry," I breathed as I let his arms go. I took a step back and he clambered out of the interior. Fal looked around wildly, but no clues were to be found. "Fal, we won't go anywhere. Not until we figure out what happened. Okay?"

Fal nodded, pacing and running his fingers through his greasy black hair. I went over to him with a gentle touch on the shoulder this time. He stopped pacing and looked at me again.

"Has she ever disappeared before?' I asked him once I saw he was calming down.

He nodded after a couple of breaths. "Yes. I've woken up in the middle of the night and she was gone. I always assumed she was using the bathroom. Like last night. But sometimes I wasn't sure, since I couldn't seem to find her. I should have checked, but she was always back the next time I woke up."

"Okay, that's ... promising," I replied with forced cheer. I was desperately hoping he would latch onto this optimistic idea. Me? I still was not sure. I wasn't sure of anything, to be honest. "If she's gone away before and always returned, why would this time be any different?"

"Yeah, you're right," Fal agreed, although not wholeheartedly. He let out a shaky breath. "So, I guess we just sit here until she returns?" He looked over at me with a small smile, a silent gesture of genuine appreciation. The look suddenly transformed to one of concern when I raised my arm to shove a few stray wisps of hair out of my face. "Oh, you're bleeding!"

I had forgotten about the knife cut, what with all the vanishing people. Plus, adrenaline was a hell of a drug. I kept my arm raised and turned my forearm toward my face. Dried blood lined my arm, and the twisting motion had caused the cut to reopen. Bright red blood trickled down toward my elbow. Now that I had recalled my injury, pain came flooding back. "Oh yeah."

Fal jumped back like he was stung. "Do you have any water?" he asked as he headed toward the wagon.

"Uh, yeah, just inside the door. In a canteen," I directed, still staring at the bright red stuff that was now oozing down my arm to my elbow. I was glad to be wearing my summer shirt under my vest, which was short sleeved. Blood would have been a pain to wash out of the cream-colored linen. As it was, I noted with dismay that I had dripped blood onto my dark gray vest. That would take a bit of grooming to undo.

He found it quickly, unscrewed the cap, and handed it to my good hand. "I need a cloth."

"Use the … blanket?" I supplied, unsure.

He sprang back into the interior and grabbed the top blanket out, an old moss-green and rather holey affair. Fal sat down on the lip of the entrance, his feet dangling over. He patted the wagon floor next to him, motioning me to sit. Rather taken aback by his in-charge demeanor, I complied wordlessly. Fal saw the condition of the blanket and without compunction he tore a strip off the bottom.

"You going to pay for that?" I quipped.

Fal smirked but didn't retort. Instead, he tenderly took hold of my injured arm and held it flat, then dribbled water over the wound, washing away the new blood and the surrounding old. After hissing in pain, I regained my composure enough to see the wound sans blood. It was not too deep, and only a couple of inches long at the most, but the moment the water cleared it started welling up with blood again. I figured stitches were in my future. Too bad we were in the middle of nowhere.

"Here," Fal wrapped the blanket strip around my arm. "Put some pressure on it. I'll be right back."

Before I could ask him what he was doing, he took off to the right, into the surrounding woods. Grimm gave me a questioning look.

"I have no clue," I responded. I desperately wanted to transform and talk it over with Grimm, but I didn't dare, considering that Wren could magically appear again or Fal could come back instantly. I mulled it over before adding, "Want to make sure he's okay?"

Grimm chuffed an affirmative and followed in Fal's steps, bounding into the brush. I focused on my breathing, because now that I was alone with my thoughts, *damn my arm hurt*. I closed my eyes, willing my heart to slow a little. My adrenaline was still up from everything that had transpired in the last few minutes: the bad guys, the unexpected vanishing act, the knife slice. Today had just started and I already needed a nap.

I flicked my eyes open as Fal and Grimm jogged out of the bushes. I looked at my partner; he still showed confusion in his eyes. Fal looked pleased, however, which added to *my* confusion.

He held something in his hands with gentle reverence. As he approached me, I discerned it was a strip of moss. Fal sat next to me, carefully placing the moss on his lap while he pulled the knapsack off his back and rummaged through it. I expected him to pull out a needle and thread, but instead his objective was a small vial with clear liquid inside. My eyes narrowed as Fal unstopped the vial and ever so carefully shook out four drops onto the moss strip. Recorking the little bottle, he placed it back in his bag, gingerly lifted the moss, and gestured for my wounded arm.

"It needs stitches," I mumbled, hesitating to do his bidding.

Fal looked into my eyes, his own hazel ones showing annoyance with a heavy dose of concern. "Please trust me?"

What the heck, I was only out in the middle of nowhere with a teen I had met and arrested yesterday. But, despite everything, I did trust him. I just didn't trust my trust. I locked eyes with Grimm, who was watching the whole episode with his own brand of intensity. He knew what I was going through. He wagged his tail subtly, telling me to do as Fal wanted. Grimm was an excellent judge of character, and I trusted his gut over mine. I nodded my head once and then gave my attention and my arm to Fal.

Ever so gently, Fal grasped my wrist and removed the makeshift bandage, turning my arm until the red slit showed. He then carefully laid the moss green-side down over the wound. I expected this to hurt, but instead it soothed the pain. Fal mumbled something imperceptible under his breath, and a tingling warmth spread over the skin touching the moss. It felt amazing.

I sucked in a breath at the sensation. "You're an herbalist."

Fal wrapped the blanket strip around my arm tightly to keep the moss in place. He smiled at my words. "No, not really."

"But you have the gift."

He placed my arm back in my lap, finished with his ministration. "My mom was quite talented." He spoke as if it were a confession. "She had hoped to pass her knowledge to Wren, but then Wren turned out to have a different gift. Instead, I started to show signs when I was eleven. She started to mentor me shortly after, but I lost her too soon to learn much."

It made perfect sense now. The plants at the school that had no business being alive. And ...

"That was you!" I exclaimed suddenly. Realizing my statement was too vague to understand, I added, "The farmer's vegetable garden. It was dead except for the plants along the fence. You did that, didn't you?"

Fal almost looked embarrassed, ducking his head to hide his eyes from me. "I felt so guilty for what Wren had done. I thought that maybe I could repay the guy somehow, so I touched as many plants as I could while I ran."

"Incredible."

At that single word, Fal flushed a little, his pale cheeks turning a rosy hue. But the revelation that not only was his sister gifted, but Fal as well made me wonder: who exactly were these kids? And how did they find themselves in this predicament? I needed more answers.

"Fal, remember last night when I said I'd let my morals lead the way?" I asked hesitantly. He nodded. "I've come to the conclusion that incarceration is not in your cards. Yet." I tacked on this last word with a finger raised at the teen's growing grin. "I'm taking you to my friend. She's like you. Her place also happens to be on the way to Knobby Hill. I think she could possibly help you and this whole situation. I know I could certainly use the help."

Fal jumped up excitedly. "Thank you, Cressida! That's the best news we've gotten in a while. I'm sure Wren will think so too when she ..." His eager countenance fell into gloom at the recall of his missing sister.

I glanced at Grimm, who stood statue still watching everything. His eyes met mine and he cocked his head to the side slightly before turning his gaze back to the youth, whose face was back to full-blown worry. Wren had been gone for about fifteen minutes. Now that my wound was taken care of, Fal started pacing.

He did not have to suffer for long, however. No sooner had I risen from my seat on the wagon bed, I heard Fal gasp and practically yell, "Wren!"

I turned back around to see her sitting within the wagon in the same place she was last seen. No bandits were in sight. Fal lunged and wrapped his arms around her in a brotherly hug. She gazed at me with a queer expression on her face before slowly picking up her own arms to return his hug.

"I'm all right," she murmured into his shoulder.

"Where did you go?" her brother practically sobbed into her dirty hair. She became more lifelike as the seconds passed, her arms beginning to rub soothing circles on Fal's back.

"I took the bad men away," she whispered.

I suppressed a shiver. "Where did you take them, Wren?" I asked, trying to sound much calmer than I felt.

Wren made eye contact with me, and again, I felt a small amount of malice in her gaze.

"Away, to a place I can go. I was owed a favor."

Apparently, this answer wasn't giving just me the heebie-jee-bies. Grimm growled so softly I doubt anybody else heard it, and Fal sat up from his hug to look at his sister.

"What are you talking about, Wrenny? What place?"

Suddenly, the sullen girl melted away, replaced by a more normal Wren whose face pouted and burst into tears.

"I'm so tired, Fal!" she whined before burying her sobbing self into Fal's chest. He hugged her back, but also glanced at me with a very concerned expression.

"It's okay, Wren," he soothed. "We'll talk later."

I let the siblings be for just a minute before I began to feel awkward.

"So, who wants breakfast?" I asked.

Okay, I know I said I liked a little excitement in my life, but these last twenty-four hours had just about cured me of my adventuring ways. Scary little girls, escaping from a bounty hunter, whatever Wren's other trick happened to be ... couldn't a cat just get home? I started a very small fire and made eggs on toast with a skillet and some butter. Both siblings ate like it was the best meal they'd had in a long time, which, given their current circumstances, was probably the truth. We mostly ate in silence; Fal kept sneaking little shy glances either at me or at his sister, and Wren continued to creep me out by oscillating between sleepy and sad little girl to shooting me death glares every other bite. Grimm, as usual, was silent. He had found part of a deer carcass and was busy gnawing on the leg he had returned with.

With all the excitement and the much-needed breakfast for the siblings, we dallied for much longer than I had originally anticipated. It was a little after eight in the morning by the time we were packed up.

Luckily, once we were headed along the road, things seemed to be wonderfully dull for a few hours. Fal had decided to ride in the back with Wren, who was still sleepy from all of her tricks. I made sure they had some snacks and water for the road and left the lamp back there for them to have some light. That left me in the driver's seat with nothing to do but listen to the rhythmic clopping of Humbert's hooves and the constant rolling of the wagon's wheels underneath me. Grimm chose to walk.

Four hours into our journey called for a bathroom break. I bade Humbert to stop, and, once the wagon had ground to a safe halt, slid out of my seat. The sun was at its zenith in the sky, and for a moment I simply basked in the late-summer rays that kissed my skin through the overhead trees. This was the kind of day made for cats to lounge in sunspots for hours. If I were in my true form, I would have taken a moment to groom myself, but regrettably that would have to wait a bit.

I walked to the back of the wagon. Grimm sat patiently, panting slightly with perked ears. I hesitated at the closed doors. I hadn't bothered to lock them from the outside, and I contemplated opening them a bit to talk to the passengers within. On the off chance they wanted to keep their privacy, I settled for knocking, and lightly rapped my knuckles on the closed doors.

"Guys? Anybody need a bathroom break? Stretch some muscles?"

It's a good thing I have superb hearing, because the low murmurs coming back to me were barely audible. I heard a faint and masculine, "No thanks, we're good," from within. I shrugged and walked away from the wagon, over to Grimm.

"I'm going to go use the bathroom," I told him. He gave me a curt nod, but otherwise didn't move. Smart dog. He knew to stay and guard the wagon while I went to find a little privacy.

I absolutely hated relieving myself in human form.

Finding a small break in the roadside vegetation, I pushed my way off the road and down a slight embankment. I did a very thorough check of my surroundings. Satisfied that I was in complete privacy, I shimmered down. The relief at being my true self was rejuvenating.

First thing first, I did my business, making sure to cover it up well with earthy detritus to mask my scent. Having accomplished that minor task, I was planning on taking just a few stolen moments to groom myself before reverting and continuing our journey.

But suddenly I felt ... off. There was something in the air, like static, that was causing me to feel odd. Was a lightning storm about to hit? It would be a little strange for the weather to turn from a sunny day to a thunderstorm so quickly, but not unheard of for this time of year. The sky, however, showed no change to the weather. Utterly perplexed, I decided to go talk to Grimm.

The uncomfortable pressure in the air built as I trekked back to the road. Nearing it, I heard Grimm call my name. I burst out of the bushes at a run, truly freaked out.

Grimm met me by the side of the road from where I had emerged.

"What the hell is happening, Cress?" he growled with worry in his eyes.

"You feel it too?"

"Kind of. It's centered on you though. It's ten times worse now that I'm standing next to you." He sneezed.

I shook my body. "It's like an electrical storm. I feel terrible."

At these words, all of the fur on my body stood on end, like I was the world's largest dandelion puff. Grimm's eyes widened in alarm. "Cress! Shift right now!" he yelled as his ears flattened.

Who was I to argue? I did as he said.

The second I shimmered, a bolt of lightning hit with a re-sounding boom where I stood. In my semi-ethereal state, the electricity did no harm. But had I been one split-second slower or faster to change, I would have been one fried figure.

Grimm had dived away from me before the strike, so he was safe. I looked at my human body for signs of damage, but I was healthy and hale. My arm hairs were standing up, but they settled quickly as the feeling of static left the air. I let out a breath. "Whoa."

Grimm whined at me, like a question. I focused on him. "What in Freya's fur was that?" I shouted. Grimm just whined again in befuddlement. I took a deep breath, closed my eyes, and let it out slowly. "Okay, I need to talk to you. Hang on."

I morphed again. During the shimmer I felt, for the first time ever, a small amount of resistance at the change. Pushing through it, I opened my eyes as a cat. I blinked and swiveled my ears back in annoyance. "Strange."

Grimm surged forward and sniffed my body from head to tail protectively. "Are you okay? How do you feel?"

Poor guy, he was freaking out. "I'm fine, Grimm. Thank you for telling me to shift; I'm pretty sure you saved my life."

"Could you feel it as a human? Do you feel it now?"

"No and ... no. Wait," As soon as the words left me, I could once again feel a building in the air around me. "Furballs. Yes. It's happening again."

"Shift back now, Cress. Do it. And don't shift again until you can talk to Fleurette. Something's wrong."

"Thanks, oh obvious one. I hope to talk to you again soon." I didn't dare say more because the pressure was building, and I did not want to chance another possible smiting from the heavens. I shifted up, once again feeling a much more noticeable strain in the process.

The minute I was human, the static once again dissipated.

"It's gone again," I told Grimm. He whined with concern but also gave a half-hearted wag of his tail. I got down to my knees to rub his head. He licked my hand. "What would I do without you looking out for me?" I asked him softly. He just wagged his tail with a touch more enthusiasm.

Straightening, I sighed. Grimm's head suddenly swiveled to look at the wagon, his ears perking. During this whole episode I had forgotten about the fugitives in my wagon, as my focus was on not getting zapped by lighting. I spun just in time to see one of the doors move ever so slightly shut. Grimm let out a very low growl.

I turned back to him, a growing knot of panic in my gut. Grimm met my eyes. "Did they see?" I asked him in a hushed voice.

He drooped his ears a bit and let out a soft yip. That was a tentative yes.

Well, crap.

CHAPTER 16

This was the worst possible situation I could be in. My panic level was through the roof and my stomach felt like rebelling. Only two humans knew of my true nature, Fleurette and Lyle, and I had planned to keep it that way. At least until I found my true love, that is.

I took a deep breath and told myself to focus. Maybe I was overreacting, and nobody saw anything. I wouldn't know until I talked to them.

"Er, Fal? You in there?" I asked at the wagon door.

The immediate problem was that no one responded to my question, which ramped up my anxiety. *Breathe. Maybe they are asleep.*

"Fal?" I asked again, this time giving the door a little knock while willing my heart to stop beating out of my chest.

"Uh, yes?" Fal replied at a much higher pitch than was considered normal.

Oh, hairballs. Furry, furry flea dung hairballs. That was not a good sign.

"Everything all right in there?" I tried to sound concerned. Hell, I was concerned; I didn't need to act.

Another pause happened before he answered, "Yes, everything's fine. You bet."

Well, this was not going any better. The panic in his voice was crystal clear to me. I glanced at Grimm, who nodded his head once in a maneuver that plainly said I should go on with my questioning.

"Can I come in for a sec?" I asked.

No answer.

"Fal? Please?"

After a moment, I heard the unmistakable sound of a lock being turned slowly and carefully from the inside of the wagon. I checked my pocket, but the key was gone. That was when I recalled giving Fal the key last night. I had meant to get it back in the morning, but the surprise events had made me forget. I sighed at my own stupidity and slowly tried the handle just in case I was mistaken.

No go. I rattled the doors and sure enough they were latched tight. Now I was getting angry.

To add insult, Fal cheerfully replied, "No thanks, we're good."

Great. Just great. I had two fugitives who were locking me out of my own wagon.

"Fine," I retorted, trying to keep the agitation out of my voice. "Let me know when you want to talk."

I began to storm away, but stopped, turned back, and studied my wagon. Forming at least some sort of idea in my head, I found a fat stick that I jammed into the handles of both doors, effectively locking them from the outside. There. That way if they thought they could sneak out while I was driving, they were dead wrong.

Grimm snuffed his approval at my action. I nodded back at him and without another word I climbed back into my seat and urged Humbert forward.

I stewed in silence for a while, pondering just when my life had taken a turn for the worse. Here I was, transporting two humans that now didn't trust me as far as they could throw me. They both knew my ultimate secret, although how Wren had figured it out was still a huge mystery to me. To make matters worse, I apparently was stuck in my human form, which meant that I couldn't talk with Grimm about this. With Fal avoiding me and Grimm having a language barrier, I suddenly felt very alone. Loneliness was an abstract concept that, while palatable in my youth, now left a sour taste in my mouth. I had grown fond of companionship. Sweet Freya, when had that happened?

I needed someone to talk to, to rid myself of this newfound feeling of isolation. I eased Humbert to a stop.

"Hey, Grimm?" I called out. My partner appeared by the side of the wagon, ears alert and tail still. "I need a buddy," I told him with a small smile. I patted the bench next to me.

He didn't make a sound, but his eyes stared into mine with an "Are you kidding me?" kind of glare. He abhorred riding up front, claiming that he felt unstable and liable to fall off at every bump in the road.

I gave him my best doe eyed look. "Please?"

Grimm shook himself with resignation, huffed, and came around to the right side of the wagon. He leapt up with ease and inched his large canine body into a perfect sitting position next to me. He turned his head and snorted out of his nose.

"Yes, I *am* being ridiculous. I agree." I told him. I ordered Humbert to continue our journey. He obliged stoically, as usual. "But I'm going to go crazy if I don't talk to someone." I glanced at Grimm, who was facing forward, sniffing the air with a twitchy nose. "Even if it's a one-sided conversation."

I sighed. "Grimm, what am I going to do? My cover's blown. The kid is freaked out of his gourd. I mean, I would be too if I saw someone transform into a cat or vice versa. But it's not like he doesn't have magic. He has magic. I have magic too. It just means we're a bit more alike, right?"

Silence from my partner. "And it's not even like I can talk to you, really. I feel so cut off. I can't be myself without becoming cat flambé. I *need* your opinion on what might be causing it, but I need to be a cat to get that opinion! It's so aggravating knowing that I'm stuck this way. What happens if Fleurette can't figure it out?"

The longest I've ever gone without changing was a little over twelve hours. By the end of that stint my body felt like two tons of garbage in a grocery sack. It took a full twenty hours of being a cat to recuperate.

"And here I was making such progress with Fal," I continued, fully aware that now I was just moaning for the sake of moaning. "He locked me out! I locked him in! That doesn't exactly scream trust on either side, does it?"

Grimm still did not respond. He seemed to understand a great deal of what my human self said, despite not being able to understand other humans quite as well, but I never knew if that was due to him being so in tune with my body language. Regardless, I could not guarantee that he was getting even half of what I was saying, and there was no way of asking him, given my sudden handicap.

The vastness of my acquired solitude yawned before me with abrupt clarity. I allowed a trickle of self-pity to worm inside my heart, and the road before me unexpectedly swam with unshed tears. I was not usually one to let my emotions run away like this; instead, I corralled them like a sheepdog with his herd. But this time, I let them loose. I cried. Big fat teardrops ran down my face. I tried to ignore them. But damn me if my nose decided to also get in the act, and I had to sniffle lest I allow unmentionable substances free of my nostrils.

The sound, of course, alerted Grimm, and he swiveled his black head in my direction, his sunflower eyes wide with alarm. In one fell swoop he was nestled into my side, and his velvet tongue was washing the right side of my face of tears. I laughed through a sob and wrapped my arm around his shoulders.

"Thanks, partner," I told him, wiping the non-slobbered side of my face with my sleeve. "I needed that."

After the unexpected bursting of my emotional dam, I truly felt better. I couldn't pinpoint why, exactly, given that: A. My secret was still out with the Ramberts; B. I still didn't dare try to revert to my true self; and C. Um, every other miscellaneous problem my mind conjured up in my emotionally weakened state. But I was feeling more like my old self, the Cressida that kicked problems in the rear and took down names. I'd solve these problems, I was sure. Somehow.

And so, for another three hours, we rode in silence. I was still mulling things over in my head, but not at quite the frenetic pace my brain had set earlier. Grimm had stayed beside me, although at some point he had laid down on the bench seat and now looked like a precariously placed pile of fur. The potholes that had plagued the road were behind us, as was the forest, which signaled that our journey was almost to an end. I sighed a breath of relief that nothing bad could possibly happen so close to home base.

Famous last words. You'd think I'd learn.

CHAPTER 17

The window behind me, which was kept shut this entire time, slid open abruptly. The noise shocked me out of my wagon-rolling-induced lull and made Grimm jump from his sleep to the point where he had to scrabble on the bench to stay on the seat. I flipped the other half of my body quickly around and met two hazel eyes laced with panic from inside the wagon.

"Uh, Mi- Cressida?" Fal spoke hesitantly. It wasn't lost on me that he nearly reverted back to the polite name routine.

"Yes, Fal?"

"Um ... Wren's gone missing." His eyes shimmered with unshed tears.

I pulled on the reins abruptly. Humbert, unused to that sort of treatment, let out a nicker of disdain. I made a mental note to apologize later.

The idea of morphing into a cat in order to access the back quicker flashed through my mind for the briefest of moments, but I nixed the notion almost immediately. Instead, I hopped down and skedaddled to the back of the wagon, pulling the stick out with some difficulty—my improvised solution had worked so well that I had to let a couple of expletives loose while removing it—and trying to fling the doors wide. I say 'try' because they were still locked from the inside. If Wren had escaped, it was not through those doors.

"Hairy, hairy hairballs!" I cursed under my breath at what that meant. Louder, I called, "Fal? Please open the doors!"

Fal must have figured that the need for my help was greater than the fear of what I might be. Even while I was imploring him to let me in, he was undoing the latch. The doors flung open as Fal wriggled out of the back of the wagon, his body held rigid as he quickly wiped some tears from his face with his sleeve.

He wasn't making eye contact with me.

I sighed. "I know you saw something," I began slowly, "and I'm sorry it freaked you out. I never in a million years meant for you to see that. We do need to discuss it later, but right now all you need to know is I'm still the same person I was yesterday."

Fal took a moment to think this over. "You said we all have our secrets. I—I wasn't expecting something like that, but yesterday you protected Wren and me from the other bounty hunter, and you said you'd help us instead of turning us in. Your actions and words both speak to your true character." He looked up and met my eyes. He looked a bit sheepish. "I'm sorry I responded the way I did. I was ... scared, and I overreacted."

I stuck out my hand. "Mutual apologies accepted? Truce?"

He looked down at my proffered hand and hesitated just a fraction before giving a wan grin and accepting the handshake. His palm was warm and sweaty and the clean-freak cat in me couldn't help but wipe my hand on my trousers once it was free. Fal didn't seem to notice.

"Okay, what happened with Wren?" I asked.

Fal took a deep breath, as if to compose his turbulent thoughts. "After I, well, spied on you and locked the door, I stayed awake for a little while, but Wren was passed out the entire time. I eventually drifted off next to her. And then I awoke, just now, and she was gone!"

"Like before?" I asked, thinking of her folding herself and two men into nonexistence.

Fal nodded, his throat working in a nervous swallow.

I pinched the bridge of my human nose. "Look, I am having a very off day. That's putting it mildly. Let's just say that time is running out for me, and I can't hang around waiting for your sister to reappear." Ugh, that sounded harsh. "What I mean is, I need to get back to my friend. Something weird has happened to me. What are the chances that if Wren were to come back that she'd reappear inside the wagon, regardless of if it were moving? After all, she could have been gone for a while before you even noticed, meaning that the location of the wagon will have been different from this location."

The teen only nodded again, silently agreeing with me.

"We are very close to my friend's house," I continued once it was clear he wasn't going to debate my words. "Can we please just continue our journey in the hopes that Wren will show back up in the wagon and not on the ground somewhere behind us? Does that make any sense to you?"

"Okay, you're right," he finally agreed. I let out a silent thank you to the heavens. "But if she doesn't show, then what?"

"Then ... we retrace our steps and hope to find her."

"Fine. But I think you need to fill me in on some things while we are moving."

"Fine," I agreed, silently adding, *within reason*. "Grimm can ride in the back, and he'll let us know when Wren makes an appearance. Sound like a plan?"

"Yes."

"C'mon." I motioned with my head at the wagon. Together, we closed the doors after Grimm had jumped inside, and I locked the latch, placing the key in my vest pocket securely. Instead of climbing up into the seat as Fal did, however, I first walked up to Humbert's head. He looked a bit surprised to see me in front of his face. He snorted out a horsey blast into my hair.

"Humbert, I know this has been a long couple of days," I soothed, "but it is of utmost importance that we get back to Fleurette swiftly. I must insist that you go at a faster pace than usual. I promise I will up your pay for this bit of overtime."

Again, I doubt Humbert understood much if any of my human speech but talking to him made me feel better about the demands I was about to place on him. I joined Fal on the bench seat and picked up the reins.

"Forward, Humbert," I called out. He obliged at his normal pace. I flicked the reins, urging him to pick up just a little speed. He acquiesced, although I had a feeling he wasn't going to be happy with me once I could speak to him again. If I *could* speak to him again.

With the wagon moving at a satisfactory clip, I relaxed my hands a bit. Fal was staying awfully quiet beside me, so I glanced over at him. He was staring at me with an odd look on his countenance. Surprised, I furrowed my brow a bit.

"What? Is there something on my face?"

Fal immediately looked down, and I saw a small blush spread over his face. What in Gaia's good graces was that about? "Sorry, you look fine," he mumbled.

I snorted. My body was just starting to feel the strain from not reverting, I had dirt from the road all over my clothes and skin, I had sweat stains under my arms, I could smell *eau de highwayman* on me from our tussle this morning, my hair lay limp around my shoulders after having lost my hair tie at some point, and to top it all off I couldn't even give myself a quick groom to make it better. I might have to actually take a bath this evening. With water. I wanted to shudder at the thought.

"Thanks," I replied, my tone only slightly caustic.

Fal looked back at me. "What are you?"

I met his eye. "Getting straight to the point, aren't you?"

He shrugged his shoulders and gazed at one of the black streaks in my hair. Not with any sort of puzzlement or disgust, but rather with a sense of awe. Interesting.

He waited for my answer. I decided to deflect by asking a question of my own. "What exactly did you see?"

He pursed his lips and ran a hand through his pitch-black hair. "Let's see. I heard a weird explosion outside the wagon, opened the door, and saw you change into a white cat for just a moment. And then you transformed back."

Yep, that's pretty much what happened. There was no getting out of this one. I had officially broken Rule Number 1 *and* Number 2. Again.

"Yeah, that's about right," I agreed.

"So, you're a shifter?" Fal asked, intrigued. Shapeshifters, often shortened to just shifters, were people who could change into a specific animal shape at will. They used to be more numerous, but their population was decimated by the Shifter War over one hundred years ago. Now, they tended to stick to their own kind in small pockets of communities, and rarely interacted with other folks. It was unusual for the average person to meet one these days.

"Yes ..." I hedged. Technically, I was not, because a shifter was a person first, and animal second. I was the exact opposite. But I did not want to agree to any more. I was trying my hardest not to break the third rule.

Fal caught the hesitation in my voice. Clearly, he realized I was holding something back. "Are you mortal?" he asked.

"Yes, for sure," I answered quickly. That was an easy question to answer.

"A witch?"

I laughed, just a little. "No, definitely not. I'm ... unique."

Emboldened, Fal began to stare again. I kept my face forward but could see him from my peripheral vision.

He finally said, "I'll say. I should have known you were a supernatural. No regular human could look like you. Your eyes are too blue. Your face is too pretty."

Well. If I wasn't feeling self-conscious before, I sure was now. I glanced at the youth in time to see the pink tinge wash over his face at his own emboldened words.

I smiled awkwardly. "Thanks? I'll agree with the blue eyes, but otherwise I look like a normal human."

I think he murmured out an embarrassed "welcome." It was hard to hear, even with my enhanced hearing.

Okay, time to turn this awkwardness around and deflect. I patted him on the shoulder in a friendly gesture. "I promise to give you more answers at Fleurette's house."

Fal nodded, still not looking at me, evidently embarrassed. I had never truly been a teenager, but there was a part of me that could relate to what he was going through. I'm pretty sure I made a fool of myself the very first time I met Gavin St. Cloud, before I knew he was a jerk. I think I may have stared at him a little too long, which ultimately led to his assumption that I was a vacuous female. I am fairly sure I had more than changed his mind on the matter, but still ... I cringed every time I thought about it.

We lapsed into silence again, which was just fine by me.

Fal broke the silence. Apparently, my circumstances were just too interesting *not* to talk about. "I assume you didn't tell me sooner because you want to keep it a secret?"

I chuckled darkly. "You assume correctly. Until today, only two other people knew my secret."

"Is this Fleurette one of them?"

I nodded. The motion sent a tiny pang of pain into my skull. Huh. That was new.

"So, if she knows about you, you must trust her."

"I do. As a matter of fact, we met because I got caught in a trap and she saved me. She and her dad, Lyle. They're good people."

Fal looked intrigued. "Can you tell me about it? How you met?"

I looked at him, and then my watch. We were still a good distance away from home base. Why not? An interesting story would hopefully help pass the time.

"Sure. I was walking in the woods one day, as a cat, and I accidentally stepped in a snare set by a poacher."

That was a huge generalization of what actually happened. I had recently left the old barn that had been my only home, because I was almost a year old and wanted to see the world, instead of hiding from it like my mother. She wasn't thrilled with my choice, of course, but she allowed me to leave.

I wandered the forest and countryside as a cat for two months before I stumbled into that snare. It was meant for a small animal like a weasel or rabbit, but it worked just as well on a cat too. The noose tightened on my paw and whipped me up into the air. I screeched in pain and writhed like a fish on a hook before eventually coming to my senses.

"I changed out of my cat form and into a human to at least set my feet on the ground. The noose was extremely tight on my wrist, and I couldn't pull it off. That's when Fleurette stumbled upon me."

I smiled at the memory. As I tried to loosen the knot around my wrist, Fleurette had appeared and said, "That's not something you see every day."

She had been walking the woods in search of snares to destroy. She had already rescued a young rabbit from a different trap, which she carried. It had snuggled up to her as she approached me.

"I guess she had seen me change from a cat to a human, because she told me to transform into a cat so that she could help me get the noose off my wrist. I tried to deny it, but she can be very no nonsense. So, I did. And she got the damn snare off me," I told Fal.

I had loosened the noose just enough in my human form that when I shimmered down, I slipped right out. I landed on all four legs and felt a sharp pain in the foreleg that had been trapped.

"My wrist had been injured by the snare, so Fleurette helped me back to her house and her father Lyle patched me up. He's a veterinarian."

"So, she and her dad are good people?" Fal asked with a small amount of hesitation.

"I wouldn't have stuck around if they weren't. It wasn't just that they helped me, but there's something about them that made me want to stay. They care about me. I hadn't really had anyone care about me before I met them. Besides my mom, of course."

"It's nice to have that feeling," Fal agreed. "My parents were that way. Warm and welcoming. It made it all the harder when they died. I hope Wren and I can find a home with good people again."

I very badly wanted to ask Fal what happened to his parents and how he and Wren had found themselves homeless in the middle of nowhere. But, seeing the despondency on Fal's face, I bit my tongue. He would tell me when he was ready.

So, all I said instead was, "You will."

I couldn't believe how desperately I wanted to be done with this mishap-filled trek. It was going on five hours since the last time I had morphed, and because I had only been a cat for all of ten minutes, it was not enough time to have fully refreshed myself. More than anything, I wanted to see Fleurette, my only human friend, and tell her of my sudden issue. I wasn't sure if a simple herbalist would be able to help me, but perhaps she knew of a potion or had a friend she could direct me to. Simply getting these bottled emotions off my chest was something I was looking forward to.

I still did not have the foggiest idea about what I was going to tell Fal. Even the Williamses didn't know the whole story about what I was, and what my mother was. I could not trust Fal, and especially Wren, with the knowledge of how important I was to this world; how could I, if I could not even trust Fleurette with the truth?

And speaking of, where was Wren? I didn't even know how long she had been missing for, but surely it was longer than the first time she had disappeared. I certainly hoped I was right in my assumption that she would show up in the wagon, not miles away on the road where she originally departed.

All of these swirling thoughts did nothing to ease the hot ball of anxiety that had taken up residence in my chest. I wished I could shut my brain off during the last little bit of the journey.

Luckily for me, and thanks to Humbert's faster gait, we reached our destination much sooner than I had anticipated. Humbert rolled to a stop in his usual spot on the lawn, and I wearily clambered down. It was still plenty light out, but afternoon was swiftly giving away to the promised nip of evening. As Fal climbed down with an equally fatigued mien about him, the purple front door opened to display Fleurette, wearing her usual flowy skirt, loose blouse, and wild hair.

I smiled despite how drained I was. "You are a sight for sore eyes."

Fleurette glanced from me to Fal with a small smile gracing her beautifully plain face. "You brought company," she declared, nodding at Fal. "Won't you please come in?"

Fal hesitated, worry in his countenance. Fleurette gave him a knowing look. "Where is Grimm?" she asked me, still watching the youth.

"He's in back. We are waiting for one more to join us."

"I thought as much. Let's get her inside as well."

Fleurette's words knocked me for a loop. I glanced at Fal to see a similar look of stupefaction on his face. I turned to her. "How did you —"

Before I could get the whole question out, an ear-splitting bark burst out from inside the wagon, followed by a girlish shriek. Fal and I both turned and raced to the back doors, practically squabbling with our hands to open them. Without ceremony we both managed to fling them wide. Grimm bounded out, his hackles raised in alarm.

"Wren!" Fal yelled into the interior.

His sister was sobbing at the back, but at his voice she sat up and crawled toward the entrance. Tears created clean rivulets upon her dirty cheeks. She let out a gasping cry at the sight of Fal, who swept her up into a loving and soothing hug the moment she was close enough.

"Oh, Fal," she choked out between sobs.

"Hush, Wrenny, you're safe now," he cooed.

She squirmed at those words. "No," she disputed, and with more vehemence, "no, I'm not! And you're not either!" She turned her body slightly in his arms until she made eye contact with me. I was prepared for another glare but was shocked when instead I received only the face of a terrified girl.

"Please." She hiccupped. "Please, help me!"

I was dumbfounded.

"Me?" I squeaked.

She nodded, letting out hitching breaths. "I need help. She wants him! She wants to take Fal!"

Dread settled deep into my core. A hand rested on my shoulder. Fleurette had joined my side.

"What, Wren?" Fal asked, looking as flabbergasted as I felt.

Wren turned to meet her brother's worried eyes. "That wasn't part of the plan! But she wouldn't listen, and now she wants to take you too!" She turned back to me. "Don't let her, Miss Curtain! Please don't let her take my brother!"

Oh, Freya's feet. I had to ask the question. "Who, Wren? Who wants to take Fal?" I had a feeling I wasn't going to like the answer.

She let out another loud sob and hitched her breath once more. "Madam Coddle! Annie Coddle wants my brother!"

CHAPTER 18

A s bombshells tend to go, that one was pretty epic. There was a momentous pause in our group as we each processed Wren's words, and then, before any panicking could commence, Fleurette took charge.

"*Everybody, into the house*!" She roared authoritatively. She ran to scoop up the crying child from Fal's arms and led the way into the cottage, pausing at the interior doorway to make sure each and every one of us—except Humbert, of course—made it in before shutting it with a bang and latching it. She then strode to the spare bedroom with Wren still in her arms. The remaining three of us followed her, at a loss of what to do otherwise. My friend gently placed Wren on the bed, placing the palm of her hand on the girl's forehead.

"Shh," she murmured. Amazingly, Wren did calm. Her hitched breathing faded to more of a stutter, and her face smoothed. Fleurette, not leaving her side, softly said, "In the kitchen, on the wall shelf to the left of the entrance, there is a small green bottle with a purple ribbon tied around it. Will someone please fetch it for me?"

Fal glanced at me, and I nodded. Silently I crept from the room, down the hallway and to the kitchen. I knew which shelf she spoke of. It held an amazing assortment of bottles ranging in size from three inches to six inches high; some red, some blue, some green, and a few clear ones. I pinpointed each green bottle and noted that they all had a different hue of ribbon attached to the neck. I swiftly found one with a ribbon the color of lavender tied to it, plucked it from its shelf, and hurried back to the bedroom.

I hadn't missed anything, it seemed. I crossed over to Fleurette and handed her the bottle. She glanced at it, nodding her approval. She took her hand from Wren to uncork it, and then produced a napkin out of a pocket in her skirt. She tipped a very small amount of the contents onto the napkin and began gently rubbing Wren's forehead with it.

"Sleep," she murmured. Wren closed her eyes instantly, and her breathing deepened. Fleurette recorked the potion bottle and stood, placing it on the dresser behind her in order to pull a spare blanket from the foot of the bed over Wren's prone form.

"What's in that?" Fal asked in a half-whisper, veins of curiosity and fear mingling in his voice.

Fleurette smiled kindly at the teen. Having been on the receiving end of her smile, I knew the power of its easing effects. Fal visibly relaxed.

"It's a sleeping aid of my own design. She'll sleep without dreams for a number of hours and wake once she has been fully refreshed. She looks like she hasn't gotten proper rest in a number of days." Fleurette turned her gaze to me, frowning. "You look to be faring just as poorly as the girl."

I shrugged. "Long story."

"Come, let's let her sleep in peace." My friend made a shooing gesture with her hands to herd us out of the bedroom. "I'll make tea and you can fill me in."

Fal seemed reluctant to leave Wren's side. After everything those two had gone through, I couldn't blame him. As Fleurette and Grimm filed out of the bedroom, I crossed over to him. He had his hand over Wren's, stroking it with brotherly affection. I placed a hand on his shoulder. He looked up with a tinge of grief etched in his face.

"Fal, it's going to be okay. She's not going to go anywhere. C'mon."

He took one last look at his sister before standing and following me into the living room, where Grimm was taking up half the faded floral sofa, his posture relaxed but his ears and eyes alert. Grimm watched us with amber eyes as Fal plopped himself down in the gray wing back chair. I stayed standing.

"I think I'll go help Fleurette in the kitchen. You boys stay here."

I walked into the kitchen to find the kettle on the stove, and Fleurette busy cutting a large plate of meats and cheeses to pair with a healthy helping of crackers. At the smell of this simple fare, my stomach growled. Fleurette laughed at the sound.

"You look like hell," she said without preamble, not even looking up from her work.

"Thanks, I feel like it, too."

"What happened?"

"Oh, let's see," I began in low tones, "I tracked these two to an abandoned school, had a close encounter with a monster, nearly got caught by St. Cloud, got in a knife fight with two morons who were then whisked off to Freya knows where by that little girl, I narrowly escaped being fried by lightning, I can't change into a cat, and now apparently Annie Coddle is in the mix. So, yeah, I think it's safe to say I look and feel like hell."

Fleurette put the knife down and focused her attention on me. "Well, that's certainly a lot to take in all at once." She half-grinned despite the seriousness of it all, and a heavy dose of concern filled her eyes. She crossed over to the back door of the kitchen, a lovely stable-style with glass panes on the top. She opened the top half and threw it wide. Leaning out slightly, she called out, "Ruuuupert!"

The crow came fluttering over, landing awkwardly on the top of the lower door half. He oozed affection at Fleurette until he saw me. Rupert fluffed up his feathers and stared at me nervously.

"Rupert, be a love and tell Dad he needs to come over as quickly as he can. If he could bring over dinner that'd be even better." She gave the black bird a loving pet on the head, which Rupert leaned into before flapping off. Fleurette closed and latched the door half as soon as he was gone.

"What happened to your arm?" Fleurette asked, eyeing the bandage.

I rubbed at the non-injured topside of it. "Knife fight before breakfast," I said, keeping my tone casual. "Only the most normal part of my whole damned day."

Fleurette frowned and gently took my arm in hand. She picked at the knot. "Did you bandage it? Let's take a look."

"The boy, Fal, did the bandage. I think it needs stitches." But now that I thought about it, my arm didn't even hurt anymore.

Fleurette unwound the blanket strip. As it loosened, the moss clump fell to the floor, a large splotch of brownish red marring the green. My friend stared at it with interest before turning my freshly unbandaged arm over to look at the wound.

Where the wound used to be, anyway.

"Interesting," she commented as she ran a soft finger down the length of the pink scar. "You said this happened this morning? That's some pretty impressive healing magic."

Behind us, the kettle began to whistle. Fleurette moved gracefully from my side to lift it and fill the teapot on the tray, which was also filled with cups, a sugar basin, and cream. She picked up the tray and began walking toward the living room. Over her shoulder, she called, "Do you mind grabbing the food, dear? Thank you!"

With slightly less grace than Fleurette, I picked up the platter of snacks and followed her. Fleurette placed the tea tray down on the low table in the middle of the room, wasting no time in pouring out three cups of tea. I placed the charcuterie platter down next to the tray before taking up the spot next to Grimm on the sofa. Fleurette poured a large helping of cream into one of the cups, no sugar, and handed it to me. She knew me so well.

"How do you like your tea, dear?" she asked Fal.

He seemed thoroughly ill at ease. "One sugar, light on the cream please."

Fleurette followed these directions and handed the finished product to Fal, who took it and proceeded to look at it with distrust. As keen as ever, Fleurette noticed his hesitation.

"It's just black tea, nothing more," she said.

To prove her point, I took a loud sip from my own cup. "Mm, thank you Fleurette," I said.

Fal seemed to trust my judgment and took a small sip of his own. He visibly relaxed the moment he tasted the tea.

"Thank you," he murmured.

Fleurette smiled. "Oh, I nearly forgot!" She hurried back into the kitchen. She reemerged after a moment with a plate containing a large cooked ham bone with plenty of juicy pink meat still attached, and a large bowl that smelled of bone broth. "For you, Grimm," she said cheerfully, "but you can't eat this on my sofa."

Grimm, who had perked up once she had come back into the room, wasted no time sliding down from the cushions and gladly settling down in front of the door to scarf down his refreshments. Grimm's eagerness seemed to light a fire under Fal, who began digging into the food platter with equal aplomb. I too was famished, but my stomach was in knots, which diminished my willingness to eat. I simply picked up a slice of ham to nibble at while I sipped my tea.

Fleurette let us refuel in silence for the first few minutes.

"We have much to discuss and very little time. I think introductions are in order," she said, breaking the quiet atmosphere.

Silence.

"Er, Fal, this is my good friend Fleurette. Fleurette, this is Fal," I said.

"Fal? Short for Falcon? Last name Rambert? A pleasure to meet you," Fleurette declared, shocking both me and Fal into open-mouthed dumbness.

"That would make the girl in there your sister, Wren," Fleurette continued, "and your parents were Mathilda and Jason Rambert, correct? My deepest condolences."

Fal finally found his tongue again. "How ... Who ... What?" He paused, closing his eyes and taking deep breaths. He looked at Fleurette again. "Did you know my parents?" His tone was incredulous.

"Only by reputation. I never got the pleasure of meeting them in person," my herbalist friend responded.

I pinched the bridge of my nose. "Hang on," I interjected. "Fleurette, how do you know who he is?"

Fleurette looked slightly guilty as she stared into my eyes. But instead of answering, she turned back to Fal, whose confusion still shone clear upon his youthful face.

"Fal, there can be no hidden truths in this conversation. From any of us." She looked over at me briefly, pointedly. What was going on? "Can you please tell me what happened after your parents died? And I will answer all questions once you do."

In a daze, Fal's eyes moved back and forth, as if trying to rattle the memories out of his head. Finally, he spoke. "Very well." He sighed. "My parents passed away within twenty-four hours of each other, my father first and then my mother. Before she died, Mom told me to take care of Wren at all costs, and that she had already arranged for her sister to care for us in the event of their passing."

His eyes were already shiny.

"How did they die?" I asked, my tone soft.

He looked at me, anguish over the topic etched into his countenance. "Wasting sickness," he whispered with a hitch. "It happened very quickly.

"As soon as the funeral was over, we were placed on a train to travel to our aunt's house. Sixteen hours later, we arrived at Calipula in the Oracune Region, where our aunt was said to live. I should mention that we had never met her, although Mom had talked about her on occasion." Taking another breath, this one also hitching ever so slightly, he continued, "There was no one there to meet us at the train station. We asked around, but Calipula is a big city. It took us a whole day to track down her address. When we finally got there, someone was selling her furniture. You see, our aunt had also died."

I sucked in a breath. These poor children.

"There was a letter addressed to me from our deceased aunt, written just two days prior. In it, she told us that she was not long for the world and that we should seek out our great-uncle Gregory Elkins in the city of Dogwood, in Northern Oracune."

I nodded, getting a mental map in my brain. Calipula was over 150 miles south of Dogwood, no small traveling matter.

"We had never heard of this man, our great-uncle. But by this time, I was desperate to find any relative to live with. So, we hired a carriage to take us to Dogwood, but along the way they stole our remaining money and dumped us on the side of the road. We were able to hitch rides here and there, but as time went on Wren's disposition got more fragile, and I couldn't risk her exposing her powers to random strangers. So, we traveled on our own, and I had to steal things to help us out.

"By the time we got to Chargrove we were both exhausted. I decided we needed to rest once we found the abandoned school. We were there for about two weeks. And then Cressida found us. I'm sure she can fill you in on the rest."

"Oh, Fal," I whispered. "How long have you two been on your own?"

He seemed to be doing math in his head. "My parents died mid-July."

A month and a half. Those two had been orphaned and let loose in the world for a month and a half.

"Your parents didn't die from a wasting sickness," Fleurette spoke softly, hesitantly. "They were poisoned. Murdered."

"*What?*" Fal and I uttered at the same time.

"I'm sorry to be the one to tell you, and I hate to be blunt about these matters. But you need to know just how much in jeopardy you and your sister are. Your great-uncle, the honorable Mr. Elkins, is not a good man. He made sure your parents were given a fast-acting poison that mimicked the wasting disease. Your aunt too, I'm sure. Otherwise, her death is just too coincidental."

"How do you know this?" Fal breathed, frowning.

Instead of answering him, Fleurette looked at me. There was fear in her eyes. She smiled sadly, slid off her seat, and, on her knees, took hold of my hand.

"My dear friend, it is time for me to admit something. I have not been completely honest with you."

Oh, sweet Freya, where was this heading? My heart pounded a quick beat within my chest, but my mouth stayed silent.

"I have known exactly what you are since before I even met you."

I frowned, darting my eyes to Fal and back. "What exactly do you think I am?"

She pursed her lips, the glance I had given the teen not escaping her notice. "What I am about to reveal cannot be discussed with anyone else." She met my eyes, silently pleading forgiveness. "I would never openly share this knowledge, Cressida, but it is Fal's birthright to know, and he would have been told eventually, had his parents survived. Our secrets, you see, are intertwined."

She still had a grasp on my hand, her callused fingers warm but dry. Her thumb rubbed a soothing pattern over the top of mine. I met her eyes again and noted the regret and the pain of potential loss. The loss of my friendship. Whatever she was about to say, she didn't take it lightly. I truly did not have a clue what exactly she knew, but deep down I trusted her, and I trusted Fal too. I nodded. The relief on her face shone like a beacon. She smiled wanly and rose, resuming her seat in the rose-colored armchair.

"Fal," she began, "what do you know of Annie Coddle?"

He frowned. "Only that she's a myth, a boogeyman. A tale told to children to get them to behave. Our parents never used her as such, but I had heard of her from peers. 'Eat all your supper or Annie Coddle will come in the night and take you away.' That sort of thing."

Fleurette stroked her chin. "And Wren? Has she heard of her?"

"She must have. She was obviously having a nightmare about her when she came back from wherever she was. I don't recall ever telling her, though, and she was more cut off from peers due to her talent."

Fleurette bowed her head for a moment. Straightening her spine, she announced, "Annie Coddle is very real."

Fal half-guffawed. "You're joking."

"I wish I were." Fleurette turned to me but spoke to the room in general. "Annie Coddle is a witch who granted herself immortality about five hundred years ago as a means of ruling over this world with an iron fist. The only thing that stopped her was her cat familiar, Glivver, who managed to banish Annie to a different dimension. To keep Annie away, a cat from Glivver's direct line with a very special ability must always be present and continue the line."

My heart sped up to an extraordinary rapidity. She did know my secret. Not just a fraction of it either. Fleurette had just aired all of my laundry on one line.

"Cressida Curtain here is the last of this long line of cats. She is all that stands between Annie and our world. If she fails, our world is doomed."

When she put it that way, I sounded pretty damn important. I don't think I had ever thought of myself in that regard. It was humbling, exhilarating, and downright terrifying.

Fal stared at me. I grimaced. "Surprise," I mumbled.

He raised his eyebrows. "If I hadn't already seen you change into a cat, I think I'd have a harder time believing all of this. But how do I fit in? And my uncle?"

"And how do you know all this?" I added.

"Because," Fleurette spoke, "I am a GOG."

"I'm sorry?" I raised a finger in confusion. "Did you just say you are a god?"

Fleurette laughed slightly. "No, not a *god*, a *GOG*. It stands for Guardian of Glivver."

I blinked stupidly at her.

"Since Glivver's time, there has been a very secret organization in place to safeguard her legacy from general knowledge and to protect her lineage from any threats. It is known as the Guardians of Glivver Society, or GOGS for short. I am a member." She turned her head to Fal. "And so were your parents."

Fal didn't say a word but cradled his head in one hand at the revelation.

Fleurette turned to me. "Cressida, dear, you believe our first meeting to be happenstance. The truth is, I knew of your kind before we actually met. You see, I have been personally tasked with being your protector."

"So, you've known this whole time? I assumed you thought I was just a simple shapeshifter! When were you going to tell me the truth?" I was feeling a tad testy at this revelation.

She looked mildly uncomfortable. "Well, honestly, I never planned to tell you that I knew. So long as nothing threatened you, we would have continued on as the status quo. No cat of Glivver's has ever found out about GOGS until you."

"Wait. Wait, wait, wait." I pinched the bridge of my nose. "Are you telling me that there's been a ... a ... human protector for every single cat? Someone has been following me my entire life? My mother's?"

"Actually ..." Fleurette wavered, "we sort of lost track of your mother after she left your father. She was a wily one, and she hid you both well. You stayed off our radar until you wandered into my forest and my magic alerted me. I was supposed to keep my distance and not let you see me, only ..."

"For god's sake, what? What makes me so damn special?" I was at the end of my rope.

Fleurette never glanced away even as I spit those words at her. Rather, a solitary tear ran down her cheek. She smiled through the obvious emotional pain. "I saw you in the trap, and I rescued you. And having done so, I got to know you. And I came to cherish who you are, especially in human form. I was too selfish *not* to become your friend."

"Oh."

She wiped her tear away with a slightly shaky hand. "Refraining from telling you all this has been the single worst part of my life. I value you, Cressida, and I would never want to hurt you. My feelings for you are genuine, despite my omissions. But I know that a breach of trust is a serious crime in a friendship. If you want to walk away from all this, I understand."

In that moment I saw my friend's soul bared for the room to see. I knew how much the lie of omission had eaten away at her, and, while finally telling me the truth had set that part of her free, she was terrified that it would also cost her our friendship. And yet she would gladly pay that price if it meant I was happy.

I wouldn't let her pay that price. It wouldn't make me happy.

"Fleurette, nothing would make me more miserable than to lose your friendship. It may take me a moment to get used to the new truth, but I know your intentions are genuine. Besides, wouldn't it be a little hypocritical of me to condemn you from keeping a major part of your life a secret from me? I wasn't planning on ever telling you the whole truth about me either. I'm guilty too. So, guess what? I'm not going anywhere."

She actually let out a sob of relief at those words. I crossed over to her chair and hugged the stuffing out of my friend while she cried out some of her emotions onto my dirty vest. With the dirt, dust, and bloodstains, a few tears wouldn't be noticed upon it.

Once she had gained control over her emotions again, she left our hug. "Nobody is watching you at all times. You do have autonomy. I know you are a very independent being. And I should amend my initial statement. We only closely watch over a cat until she passes her duties down to her daughter. Usually, we have kept tabs on any living older cats, but as it stands, we only know the location of you and your mother. She hasn't mentioned to you where your grandmother might be, has she?"

I shook my head. "Mom's tight-lipped about the past. She only told me that it was safest for me to be born out in the wilderness." I chuckled, adding, "I guess that's why I'm so wild." Bad joke uttered, I continued, "I've never met my grandma, or any others down the line."

Fleurette nodded. "You *are* a wild one. Certainly, you have the most adventurous spirit from what I've seen of your mother and what I've heard of your lineage. It hasn't been easy to see you tackle such a high-risk occupation, to be honest. I can only do so much when you are here, and even less when you are out on a job. That's why I thanked the higher powers when you met Grimm almost immediately."

Grimm, who had been silently watching the entire exchange from the floor, wagged his tail and raised, then lowered, his ears at this sentence. Fleurette smiled at him. "Thank you for being there for Cressida when I cannot be, Grimm," she told him. He got up and padded over to lick her hand affectionately. It would seem that Grimm wasn't willing to end their friendship either. All was forgiven.

There was something that was nagging me, though. "Fleurette, you said that no cat before me has ever known about this GOG thing because they were never in danger. But you told me. Am I in danger?"

Fleurette sighed heavily. "Yes, dear, I'm afraid you are."

CHAPTER 19

Nobody likes hearing that they are in mortal danger. I may like a little excitement in my life, but this was just getting ridiculous.

"Okay, Fleurette, lay it on me," I demanded.

She gave a small shoulder shrug. "It's fairly obvious, isn't it? Annie Coddle is finally coming back."

I sighed the kind of sigh that starts at a full breath and empties to the diaphragm. "She's been gone for five hundred years. Why now? Why me?"

"I don't have much in terms of answers, sweetheart. But I'm slowly putting some things together."

"Such as?"

Fleurette pursed her lips in thought. "I think it's safe to assume that Annie Coddle has not been resting on her laurels this entire time. Based on everything I've learned about her, she has probably been working on the problem of how to make it back to this world for the last five hundred years." She turned to Fal, who had been watching our verbal volley with quiet thoughtfulness. He looked about as haggard as I felt. "Fal, I already know a little about Wren's talent, through my connection with GOGS. But there are obvious holes in my knowledge. What can you tell me about your sister's abilities?"

Fal took the time to explain everything that I had already come to know. As I listened to him, I fought a bite of jealousy that had taken root over how easily he was spilling his whole life story to someone he had just met an hour ago. At this stage of our acquaintance, it had been like pulling teeth for me to get information from him. But I concluded that Fal was probably just as beat down by all the weirdness of the last twenty-four hours and was probably more than willing to accept outside help by this point.

At the end of his reply, Fleurette nodded her head. "About when did her personality begin to change?"

"Let's see, it would have been about a month before our parents died—were murdered." Fal tested out the sound of those new words. I could see it left a very bitter taste in his mouth by the deep frown he wore.

"And she is able to fully project herself to a different dimension?" Fleurette continued.

Fal cocked his head to the side, reminiscent of a questioning dog. "I can't tell you where she goes. But she does disappear completely."

"And she's able to take things with her," I interjected, remembering the sudden fate of the two bandits she whisked away and didn't bring back. Fal nodded in agreement.

Fleurette nodded again at these words, as if whatever he said resounded with an unsaid theory. "Fal, has she ever mentioned strange or unusual dreams? Especially involving an older man with a silver beard?"

Fal furrowed his brow in thought. "No, she never mentioned it. She does have nightmares frequently, based on her tossing and turning and moaning while asleep. But she never told me about them. Why? Who is the man?"

Fleurette pursed her lips. "It would be your great-uncle. But without knowledge of fact, I prefer not to delve into that path just yet."

I suppressed an eye roll. She seemed to be skirting around the uncle issue, despite being the one to bring it up.

"You two have been through a lot these last couple of days. I'm going to say something that will not sit well with you, especially you, Fal." She winced. "It is my belief that Wren has become a puppet for the witch. You've had the enemy in your midst this whole time."

Fal gasped but didn't dispute her words.

"There is a good reason I put her to sleep right away. Yes, Wren is bone weary and in need of recharging, but also, as soon as I saw her in the wagon, I sensed a darkness within her. Her aura has been compromised." She turned to Fal with a mien of anguish. "I made her sleep so that she couldn't listen to our conversation."

"Heavy," I muttered. I pushed my unbrushed black strands out of my face to mingle with my pale blonde ones. "She knows I'm a cat. Wren does. I don't know how, but she does. Are you suggesting that because *she* knows, Annie knows too?"

This discussion was giving me a case of the heebie-jeebies. And here I hadn't liked the thought of the good guys spying on me. This was much worse.

Fleurette only nodded slowly as an answer.

I followed up. "So now what? What can we do for Wren? Keep her in a coma for the rest of her life?"

I was kidding, of course, but Fal shot me a dirty look at the suggestion. I frowned and shook my head subtly to give him the message that I was being sarcastic. His face smoothed out.

Fleurette gazed thoughtfully at Fal. "I am fairly certain that in order to use Wren as her puppet, Annie Coddle has performed a soulbond."

"A what now?" I interjected.

"A soulbond. There are two types of bonds. The first is created out of a pure love. The other is an unnatural procedure that defies the very basis of ethics."

No points for guessing which type Fleurette was thinking Annie Coddle did.

"She has fused her soul to Wren's by splicing out a small piece of Wren's soul and filling the void with a sliver of her own. In doing so, Annie Coddle has gained the ability to manipulate Wren's thoughts, feelings, and actions to some small extent, and can also see through Wren's eyes. The possession wouldn't be total, which is how Wren was able to warn us."

"So, my sister is still there? Mostly there?" Fal asked, his voice hopeful.

"Yes. If my guess is correct, there is a way to remove the piece of Annie's soul."

"Yes! Let's do it!" Fal jumped up enthusiastically.

Fleurette put a hand out to tamp down his eagerness. "Certainly, young man, but this will take some preparation. For both of us."

His face scrunched in confusion. "Me? What can I do?"

She gave him a level gaze. "A lot, actually. In fact, this procedure won't be doable without your help. To remove the tainted soul, I need special assistance and magical guidance from someone who carries a pure and absolute love for the afflicted person. In Wren's case, that's you."

"But I don't know how to do that!" he countered, a bit of a whine creeping into his voice and making it crack.

Fleurette smiled. "Hence, the preparation part. We will start the procedure first thing in the morning. Until then, I will show you everything you need to do and together we will prepare the magic."

Fal nodded. He was scared out of his wits over the thought of so much resting on him, but his desire to help his little sister overruled every doubt he was harboring. I was proud of him in this moment.

Fleurette continued, "I know we didn't discuss everything yet. I'm not trying to skirt around subjects, despite what you think, Cressida," she said pointedly to me, half accusing, half teasing. She turned back to Fal. "The matter of your great-uncle is important, but for now Wren's condition must take precedence. We must save her."

Fleurette glanced my way. "And you," she narrowed her eyes, "are in serious need of sleep. You should shift now. You and Grimm are welcome to use my bed tonight; I doubt I'll be needing it."

"But I can't!" I blurted, frazzled beyond belief.

She scrunched up her eyes in bafflement. "What do you mean, you can't?"

"Don't you remember my tirade in the kitchen? I'm pretty sure I mentioned this to you!"

"Yes, you might have," she admitted, squeezing her eyes shut and nodding, "but in my defense that was well over an hour ago and you threw a lot of things into that tirade. Some of the details may have been lost on me."

"An hour!" I ran my hands down my face with pressure, contorting my facial features in distress. "Freya's feet, I completely forgot about Humbert! I already forced him to trot today. Now he's been stuck on the lawn without proper care. He's going to be so angry with me!"

I turned for the door, but Fleurette put a hand on my shoulder. "Cress! It's okay. Dad's here and he's taking care of Humbert. Relax!"

The word 'relax' sometimes made me bristle. I wanted to tell my friend, in the friendliest way possible, to shove it, but instead I swallowed my words and made my way to the front window. Sure enough, Humbert was free of all restraints and getting curried by Lyle in the front yard. My metaphorical hackles lowered. "Oh. Thanks."

"Now, sit down, eat some more meat, and tell me what you mean by the words, 'you can't shift?'" She led me to the sofa, where Grimm had retaken his spot. He nuzzled his big furry body into me the moment I flopped down next to him. I stroked his ear absentmindedly while Fleurette plied me with more sliced ham.

Quickly I recounted the goings-on from earlier today; how the static built up around me in cat form until I was nearly zapped to death. "And it happened again the second time I was a cat. After that, I didn't want to try shifting again."

"Hmmm." Fleurette tapped her chin with her index finger, musing. "This reeks of dark magic. I suspect that Annie Coddle is trying to take you out—either directly with the lightning, or at the very least to weaken you so you won't be a threat." She shook her head. "Either way, it's best not to test anything tonight. Cress, go get in bed. I'm going to use my sleeping aid on you too."

Ugh, I had to fall asleep as a human? In all of my two-and-a-half years on this earth, I had never done that before. It sounded repugnant. But what choice did I have?

"Grimm, will you keep me company tonight?" I asked my partner next to me. He lowered his ears and snorted an affirmative. I patted his neck. "Thanks, pal."

Fleurette led the way to the back bedroom, her own personal sanctuary. I had never actually gone in here before, as the spare room was ours to use when sleeping over. The walls were a soft green color that radiated tranquility. The room, while larger than the spare bedroom, was just big enough for her full-sized bed (done up with a handmade quilt of blues, greens, and purples in a mandala pattern), armoire, dresser, and an old-fashioned full-length mirror tucked into the corner. A lace curtain covered the one window that looked out into the back property. And yes, there were more plants in here as well, their various shades of greenery competing with the wall color.

I sat on the edge of the bed, which gave a slight squeak at the pressure. Behind me, Grimm padded in and without preamble jumped up on the bed. The bed groaned again at his weight. Finally, Fal edged into the doorway, following us like a lost puppy with no clue of what to do.

Fleurette pulled a nightgown out of a dresser drawer and handed it to me. I took it but otherwise didn't move.

"It should fit you. Those clothes won't be very comfortable to wear to sleep," she said.

"Oh." I had forgotten that humans wore different clothes to bed. My handy interdimensional pocket simply stored the clothes for me while I was in my natural form, so I hardly ever had to think about changing clothes. I placed the gown on the bed, stood up, and began unbuttoning my vest. Once I had that shrugged off (good grief, it was a grimy mess!) I looked down to unbuckle my belt to slide my trousers off. Instantly Fleurette let out a little gasp. Alerted, I looked up to see Fal staring with a red face before looking quickly away and making tracks for the living room as if his rear end were on fire.

"Oops," I made an embarrassed face, realizing my faux paus. I had forgotten that humans typically had hang-ups over nudity; as a cat I was unclothed all the time, and it had entirely slipped my mind that undressing in front of other people, especially teenage boys, was usually frowned upon.

Fleurette was amused, her sun-kissed face grinning. "Don't worry, dear, but try not to cause our guest to spontaneously combust," she told me. She then slipped out of the room herself, shutting the door quietly behind her.

Grimm, who also didn't pay attention to human philosophies on decency, stayed on the bed and kept his yellow eyes on me, although he lowered his chin to the blanket. I continued to strip my disheveled garments off one by one, cringing at each new dirt or sweat stain that came to my attention. I was especially sad for my cream-colored linen shirt; there was a stark difference in color between where the vest covered it and where it was exposed. And even the protected places that were not grime-covered had unbelievable sweat stains to contend with. A good thirty minute grooming session would have righted this wrong in a jiffy. Instead, I was quite sure I'd have to throw these clothes away.

Well, maybe not my vest. That baby was a custom piece that I refused to give up on.

With the last sock off, I paused, allowing my naked human body to explore this unfamiliar state. The last time I had been this undressed was my first shift. It was somewhat ... freeing. I glanced to my left and discovered that I could see myself in the corner mirror. Curiosity got the better of me. I turned to the front to get a good look at myself. I studied my nude form, memorizing details of myself that I had honestly never seen before. As a cat, I had no appreciation of human physical attributions. All humans looked like ... well, hairless apes. As a human, however, my ability to discern a physically attractive individual from a less appealing one was at the forefront.

And, looking at myself naked for the first time ever, I learned something about myself.

I had a nice body.

I wasn't perfect, mind you. I was still petite, and my waist wasn't an hourglass so much as a carrot stick. And my breasts were practically nonexistent. But I had just enough curve to make me appear womanly, and I was toned thanks to the amount of exercise I received, both in cat and human form. I looked graceful as I turned this way and that.

But all good things must come to an end. Once I got over ogling myself in the mirror, I then focused on my face, which was a mistake. I looked like ten pounds of fertilizer in a five-pound bag. My normally vibrant eyes were sunken with giant dark smudges underneath. My complexion was pasty at best, not my usual healthy glow. And I could have started charging rats rent for my hair. Ugh.

This was not how a cat was supposed to look. Even as a human.

With that, the mirror's charm was broken. I swiftly donned the nightgown and crawled into the bed. Grimm, who had been watching me with disinterest, lifted his big head and turned it toward me. I frowned at him.

"Shut up," I admonished. "If you had a human body, you'd do the same thing." He simply stared for two seconds longer with eyes devoid of any emotion before resting his head again between his paws.

I nestled into the sheets as best as I could. I didn't feel comfortable, per se, with a general feeling of unease plaguing my human body, but I was starting to feel settled. And then Fleurette walked back into the bedroom. I gave her a cheekily fake smile.

She narrowed her eyes slightly. "Cress, it's nearly seven o'clock. When was the last time you used the bathroom?"

"Um, around noon?" I hazarded.

She pointed a single finger at me. "I'm basically going to be putting you into a magically-induced coma. You need an empty bladder. Go."

"But—" Fleurette moved to my side of the bed as if to physically yank me from my blankets. I hadn't paid attention to my bodily functions since the whole lightning fiasco, and I hadn't exactly been doing a bang-up job of drinking fluids, but now that she had mentioned it, the cup of tea I had consumed was suddenly making its presence known in my bladder. I moaned in a growly sort of way. "Fiiiiine."

As I got out of bed, feeling the draft of a cool breeze snake around my bare legs, I added, "But if Grimm is staying with me all night, he should go out one last time too."

"You're right. C'mon, Grimm," Fleurette ordered. Grimm shot me a look with his yellow eyes before jumping off the bed and padding out of the room. What can I say? Misery loves company.

Ablutions completed to Fleurette's standards, I toddled back onto the bed. From the window I could see that the sun hadn't entirely given up its clutches to the nighttime; a deepening gray permeated the small room. As early in the night as it was, however, I knew staying up was not an option for me. My eyes throbbed in my skull, and I could feel the birth of a nasty headache threatening. My entire body ached. This day had officially kicked my butt.

I did some quick mental calculations. I had changed into a human around six in the morning. I had taken a cat break at noon, but it had been cut tragically short. It hadn't been enough to recharge me, in any case. If it was seven in the evening now, that meant I had been more or less a human for a total of thirteen hours. That beat my previous record.

No wonder I felt horrible.

Grimm stalked in a moment later, smelling of late summertime. He resumed his spot on my right, turning his furry body in a full circle before settling down in the shape of a 'C,' his rump closest to me.

Fleurette followed my partner into the room, nodding her approval at me and Grimm. She sank down on the edge of the bed by my blanketed torso. Her nut-brown hair, loose and wavy, covered her face as she leaned her head down to extract something from her pocket. She straightened again, holding the small green bottle with the lavender ribbon and a piece of cloth.

"Sleepy time?" I asked her, my tone flippant.

She smiled, but it was a tired, sad smile. I did not like the look on her usually sunny face. "If you are ready, yes." She moved to extract the cork from the bottle.

I shot my left hand out and laid it on my friend's, to pause her action. She peered from our touching hands to my face, quickly hiding a look of surprise as she turned her eyes to mine.

"What is it, sweetheart?" She asked me, concern etching into her features.

I paused. "You won't do ... your thing ... with Wren ... without me present, will you?"

She smiled again, this time a bit warmer. "I wouldn't dream of it," she answered immediately, setting my mind at slightly more considerable ease than previously. "If I'm not mistaken, your fate and the fates of the Ramberts are intertwined. It would be ...unbeneficial to keep you from any step of the process. You have my word."

"Okay." I sighed, sinking back into the pillow and removing my hand.

"Um, Cress, dear, I just had a thought. Is there a chance that you will revert back into a cat in your sleep? Will you be fricasseed in the night?"

I chuckled. "Good question, but no. When I change shape, I need to be actively focusing on it, which means I am in full control. There's no way that can happen while I sleep. I'll stay this way until I can tell myself to shift."

"Good. Just thought I'd check." She took a deep breath. "Ready?"

I nodded, suddenly nervous. Sure, I trusted my friend, but this was not a typical day, and I suddenly wondered about what else could go wrong.

I needn't have worried. Fleurette removed the cork, dampened the cloth, and leaned over to rub it on my forehead. As she did so, the smell of green and earthy things hit my nose. I was about to puzzle out the identity of some of the plants used in this concoction as a cooling sensation sunk into the areas of contact. It felt nice, relaxing. I let my eyes drift shut. Was that mint? Lavender?

"Sleep," a detached voice said.

And suddenly I didn't care about what I was smelling.

I passed out.

CHAPTER 20

"Cressida, wake up!"

My body was shaking. The motion jump started my brain, and I tilted my head upward with panic, before realizing that there were two hands pressed against my side that were doing the rocking. I sank back down onto the pillow with a groan, my eyes still glued shut.

It had not been the best night's sleep, categorically, because I hadn't felt a thing all night long. As far as I could tell, Fleurette had just gotten me to sleep. Except now that I was actually thinking again, I *was* feeling more well-rested than before.

"C'mon, Cressida, rise and shine!" It was Fleurette, speak of the devil. I cracked an eye open. The room was mostly dark with a hint of morning light to make the darkness not as absolute. Fleurette sat by my bed, looking chipper. I growled.

"What time is it?"

"5:30 in the morning. Sorry, dear, but we need to get a jump on the day."

Normally waking up at 5:30 wasn't such a laborious chore. This morning was not one of those mornings. "I feel like I have a hangover."

She laughed at my misery. "You've never had a drink in your whole life. How would you know what a hangover feels like?"

"I can imagine that this is what one feels like," I retorted caustically. I sat up in bed and groaned. Now that reality was setting in again, I could feel all those aches creeping back. "Maybe I have a 'too-much-time-in-my-human-body' hangover."

"Could be." Fleurette picked up a cup from the dresser and handed it to me. "This might help."

I couldn't even fathom what the cup contained, other than a liquid, obviously. It hissed at me as tiny bubbles popped at the surface. It smelled like a mixture of citrus (gross) and bull piss (even worse). I scowled and tried to pass the cup back.

Fleurette guided my hand holding the cup back in front of my face. "Drink it; it will help."

"Let the record show that I hate you." I tilted the bubbly concoction down my throat, trying hard not to gag on the fruity yet salty abomination hitting my tongue. The carbonation tapped on the roof of my mouth as I forced myself to swallow repeatedly. My poor stomach flipped once at the abuse it was suffering, and then gave in, thankfully. I did not want to taste this poison in reverse. Once the beastly chore was finished, I thrust the empty cup at Fleurette, who graciously took it from me this time, and I wrinkled up my pert little nose with great distaste.

I could still feel the carbonation dancing in my belly, making me slightly nauseous. Soon enough, though, the bubbles stopped centering around my stomach and instead began to travel through my body, chasing away the human discomfort and sharpening my mind. My stomach stopped hurting as the sensation faded away. I pressed on my eyeballs through my lids and was delighted to find no lingering pain behind them. Suddenly alert, I threw back the covers and swung my legs over the side.

"Let the record show that I don't hate you," I amended cheerfully.

My friend smiled and patted my hand. "I thought you might come around. Please keep in mind the effects are temporary, but they should get you through a few hours, at least."

A few hours reprieve from feeling like a dung heap. I'd take it.

"Now," she continued briskly, "we have a lot to do. Go pee and get dressed and then meet us in the spare room. Your clothes are already in the bathroom." Fleurette swept out of the room but stopped in the doorway to add over her shoulder, "And make sure to fully dress *before* you meet Fal in the spare room. I don't think the poor boy could survive another strip tease."

"Oh, har, har, let's make fun of the cat!" I yelled after her.

At this point I realized Grimm was not present in the room. The big furball was probably the only one of us who actually had gotten a decent night's sleep.

I stretched and stood, feeling the freezing wood floor beneath my bare feet. Ugh, I missed my padded toes with fur to keep me warm. Being a human was just the worst.

I stumbled to the bathroom, yawning a bit despite Fleurette's potion having chased away the majority of my sleepiness. The bathroom was still too dark to see much, even with my enhanced vision. I grasped the pull chain to turn on the overhead light, which hummed softly as if the free energy was greeting me. Once my eyes adjusted to the soft glow, I turned my attention to the pile of clothes resting on the toilet seat. I let out a little gasp as I recognized my vest, free of all hideousness, resting on top of the pile. I grasped it in my hands, flinging out the folds to marvel at its cleanliness. I smooshed the fabric into my face, breathing in the clean scent. Smiling, I perused the rest of the pile. Sure enough, my trousers, socks, and even underwear were clean and neatly folded. The only piece of yesterday's outfit missing was my linen shirt, which had been replaced by a very similar linen shirt of a pale gray color.

Oh, that clever witch. I'm not sure what kind of magic Fleurette had used to accomplish this miracle.

I used the toilet and swiftly donned my outfit. I even brushed my hair with Fleurette's boar bristle brush and tied it back into a low ponytail to keep the strands out of my face. Lastly, I scrubbed my face—only slightly lamenting not being able to use my own tongue and paws in the process—and rinsed out my mouth with water.

"Time to get this show on the road," I commented to myself as I swung the door open.

Fal came around the hallway corner as I breezed out of the doorway. We came to a halt in front of each other. Even in the dimness of the hall I saw two small spots of color appear on his cheeks. He didn't look me in the face.

"Uh, good morning," I greeted him awkwardly. He mumbled a reply, still avoiding my gaze but for a split second of eye contact. He smelled clean, I realized, like the soap Fleurette used. He must have taken a shower last night after I had been put into my coma. His clothes had been cleaned as well. It was certainly an improvement over how he looked yesterday.

"Um, listen, about last night. I'm sorry if I made you uncomfortable. I ... am not used to being a human for such a long time. I sort of forgot the etiquette involved."

Fal did meet my gaze at those words, if only for a few seconds before looking away and running a hand through his messy dark hair. It spiked up adorably with his ruffling.

"Uh, yeah, that makes sense. I was just a bit shocked, is all. I thought maybe you were ..." he trailed off.

I turned my palms up in a gesture for him to finish his thought. Instead, he turned beet red before clearing his throat loudly. "Anyway, if it had been something else, I mean, you aren't that much older than me, right?"

Huh?

I narrowed my eyes at his nervous stammering. Seeing my look, he blurted, "You don't, obviously! But if you did ..."

"Fal, wait. Are you thinking that I might have started to get undressed in front of you because I wanted to seduce you?"

"Oh god!" The poor boy really did look like he'd spontaneously combust. "That sounds bad when you say it like that! No, I guess maybe the thought crossed my mind, but in my defense, you aren't that much older than me, right? Like three, four years older?"

I closed my eyes, feeling like my head was about to burst. "Try negative fourteen."

"Huh?"

I stared at him, willing his brain to catch up. He stared back in confusion until his eyes grew wide. "You ... you're only—"

"Two years old. Well, I'm actually about two and a half, but yes."

He looked utterly gobsmacked. "Oh."

I rolled my eyes. "Obviously, because I'm a cat, I age differently than you do. So, while I'm technically only two, I'm not a toddler. I'm an adult. So yes, in human years, in this body, I'm probably around the age of twenty-two."

"Oh." He looked a little weirded out by this information. I didn't necessarily blame him.

Fal looked up into my eyes. "You age differently from me. Do you think in a couple of years that we will be closer in age? I mean, to your current form?"

Dear Freya, did he just ask if we'd be peers in a couple of years?

"I'm not sure. I only age as a cat, so the more time I spend as a human the slower I age. So, I suppose it could be possible. Why?"

He gave a shy little smile and shrugged his shoulders. "Uh, no reason. Just curious."

"Mm-hm." I had a dawning suspicion that Fal was developing a bit of a crush on me. Bringing my suspicion to his attention might not be the kindest approach. I feigned ignorance. "Well, for now, I just wanted to say sorry. I was not trying any funny business. Chalk it up to brain fog and inexperience at being human. Okay?"

He nodded, still slightly embarrassed by how red his cheeks were. I gave him another look. "Can we forget about this whole conversation now?"

He let out a puff of air as a laugh. "Yes, please!"

"Done!" I smiled at the youth. "So, what are you up to then?"

"Oh! I nearly forgot!" he exclaimed, smacking his forehead. "Fleurette sent me to get you. It's time to help my sister."

"Well, lead the way," I answered.

"Alright, the gang's all here!" I announced with mock cheerfulness as I entered the spare bedroom. Fleurette was positioned at the head of the bed on the left, and Grimm sat like a guard dog at the foot. Fal, who had entered before me, took up position across from Fleurette on the right. It appeared Wren hadn't moved since last night.

Fleurette motioned her hand at a small plate of sliced ham resting at the foot of the bed. "Eat some breakfast."

I smiled winningly at her as I plucked a piece from the plate. "Meat. You sure know the way to a cat's heart."

She smirked at my comment but broke eye contact. Fal glanced at us both before shaking his head subtly.

Gazing at the teen, Fleurette grew serious. He met her gaze, and the carefree mood I had created in the room evaporated. I swallowed the sudden lump in my throat, the somber atmosphere infecting me as well. Fleurette cleared her own throat.

"Are you ready?" she asked Fal.

He nodded, fear lacing his features tightly together.

At his nonverbal response, Fleurette turned toward a small nightstand behind her, which had an assortment of objects upon it. I tried to peer around her to see what she was doing, but with my short stature and the witch's body in my way, I was still stymied.

Fleurette turned back toward the bed within a short time, however, which eased my curiosity. She had a bundle of herbs in her hand, wrapped end to end with string. The tip glowed with an ember as it emitted a lazy trail of smoke. The small room filled quickly with the scent of the burning aromatics. I assumed it would be repugnant, but rather, the smell was pleasant and evoked strong positive emotions within me. It was a scent of comfort, warmth, and love.

The smoke from the bundle curled upward in an eel-like fashion. Instead of dissipating over time, it instead unfurled slightly but kept its soft ribbon appearance. Fleurette smoothly waved the bundle in a pattern over her half of the bed, and the miasma formed a knitted blanket in the air. Once her side was complete, she handed the bundle to Fal, who took it with a slightly shaking hand. Copying the witch's movements, he too wove a velvety smoke pattern over his sister. The haze slowly condensed and settled over Wren, forming a misty cocoon around her sleeping figure.

As Fal finished the smoke tapestry, Fleurette produced a shallow bowl filled with a curious light green liquid. She held it ceremoniously over Wren. Her eyes met Fal's, and she spoke to him with those eyes, coaxing him to the next step.

She started a low chant, slowly at first, keeping eye contact with the youth. He joined in, haltingly at first but gaining confidence as it went on. Their chant grew louder. I felt a great anticipation in the air of the room, my heartbeat speeding up. I could not unglue my eyes from the scene.

Fleurette and Fal's harmonious chant reached an apex, their tone grown to a frantic volume. With one last shouted word, Fal plunged the smoking bundle burn-end first into the green liquid. The hiss of the quenched smoke was the last noise before complete silence blanketed the room.

I didn't dare sniffle or even move. To make a sound would have been sacrilege.

I did glance at Grimm. He clearly was feeling the same effects that I was.

When I brought my attention back to the bed, I did a double blink. Fleurette had moved the bowl to the side of it. The smoke still coalesced around Wren's sleeping form. Fleurette and Fal had linked hands over her. They both kept their eyes closed, heads bowed in concentration. All of this was to be expected. What I didn't expect was the soft glow that now emanated from the girl.

It was barely noticeable at first, a colorless glimmer within the heart of the smoke cocoon. While the radiance never brightened, it did increase in size until the body of the girl was obscured by a soft lavender luminosity. Once it had encompassed Wren, it rose upward and out of her body, keeping its girl-sized shape as it did. The radiance stopped once it was free of Wren, hovering in the air about a foot above the child and surrounding the held hands of the two people.

Both Fal and Fleurette opened their eyes in unison, as if by silent command. They gazed at the ghostly light before them. They unclasped their hands slowly and withdrew them to the perimeter of the glow, palms out as if to touch the light.

"Slowly," Fleurette whispered to the teen. Fal nodded, not taking his eyes off the ethereal form in front of him. With great gentleness the woman began running her hands along the edges of the light. Fal mirrored her on his side.

I didn't have a clue as to what was going on, but I did notice, after a minute of their massaging, a very small darkness appear within the radiance, located where the chest would be on a corporeal being.

It was slightly closer to Fal's side. He saw it too, after a few more seconds. "There!" he half-whispered with great enthusiasm.

Fleurette nodded encouragingly. "You know what you have to do." Slowly, as if not to spook the darkness, she reached to the side table and brought up a silver-handled blade. She carefully handed it to Fal without touching the lavender glow. "Call it up."

Fal grasped the blade in his sweaty hand and began another chant, this one more singsong than the first. Fleurette did not join in but kept her eyes on the lad with encouragement written on her face. Fal barely glanced at her but kept a close watch on the darkness as it began to surface out of the ethereal body.

As it became unburied, I saw that it was no bigger than my thumb, with clearly defined edges. While the body it had been housed within had an undefined softness, this tiny mass had clear definitions, like an ugly iridescent oil slick. Now that it was perched on top of the light, it writhed about. It was clearly parasitic, and it was angry to be bereft of its host.

With the purple-black mass nearly free of the glow, Fal's chanting broke. I glanced at his face, noting the disgust and fear that had stolen his voice. With the end of the chanting, the parasite once again started to burrow its way back into the ethereal body.

"No, Fal, don't give up!" Fleurette commanded. "If you lose it, you lose your sister. Fight!"

Fleurette's words broke the hesitancy in Fal's throat, and his chanting resumed with more fervor. The wormy mass struggled but rose again. As it cleared the body, there was one bit that still tightly grasped onto the light. It refused to let go.

"Now, Fal!" Fleurette ordered.

Fal's free hand darted forward and grabbed the oil slick as his chanting stopped. It writhed in his grasp, fighting to break free. With his other hand, he brought the blade under the mass and ever so carefully cut the darkness away from the light, making sure not to excise any of the lavender with the parasite. It was delicate surgery, to be sure.

The mass was completely free, and it writhed with unmasked fury. Fleurette produced an open glass jar, holding it out to Fal. He slammed the furious oily mass into the jar, and once his hand was out of the way, Fleurette screwed the lid on quickly.

I had been holding my breath during this procedure. Only now did I let it out in a whoosh of relief.

Fleurette apparently did the same. She smiled with exhaustion at Fal. "Now, you must coax her soul back. Only you can do this."

He nodded, his Adam's apple bobbing. Crawling carefully onto the bed beside his sister, he took hold of her still body, wrapping his arms about her in brotherly affection.

"Wren, don't leave me. Stay. Please," he crooned. He continued his pleading, hugging her tightly.

Slowly, the glowing form sunk back down. Fal did not stop his cajoling, but tears leaked out of his eyes as the lavender light came to rest inside of Wren's body again. Once it was firmly housed within her, Fleurette said a small chant and then waved her hands and fingers through the air above Wren in an intricate pattern.

The smoke cocoon that still enveloped Wren, and Fal partially too, lost its defined look and appeared more like a silvery fog as Fleurette made her movements. Finally, the herb woman stopped, bent over, and softly blew at the mist. Although her exhalation was mild, the mist rolled and tumbled away as if a great wind had disturbed it. It vanished into nothingness within seconds.

Wren moaned softly. Fal perked his head up, his glassy eyes widening. "Wren?"

She squinted an eye open slowly. "Fal?"

He choked back a sob with a watery smile on his face. She hesitantly smiled back, and Fal hugged his sister tight to his chest. She responded with an embrace of her own.

Damn the emotionally charged room; I suppressed the urge to shed my own tears at the scene. At the same time, I felt like an interloper. Deciding to give them a moment for their reunion, I exited the room. Grimm followed behind me, my ever-faithful black shadow.

We made our way to the living room sofa, myself flopping down upon it with great emotional heaviness, and Grimm nimbly jumping up next to me with immense care despite his size. He laid his furry head in my lap with a sigh. I absentmindedly stroked the fur between his ears.

Fleurette came out a few minutes later, her usually carefree face lined with worry and exhaustion. She smiled wanly at me as she fell into the chair across from me.

"I'm giving them a few minutes alone, but we have more to learn soon," she explained as she closed her eyes and leaned her head back into the chair.

"You look like hell," I observed, parroting what she had said to me the night before. She chuckled without opening her eyes. "Did you get any sleep last night?"

My friend sighed and stretched out her legs. "Not really. Preparations for this procedure took all night. I drank a lot of that energy potion to stay awake."

"Eww. I can't believe you could drink that much. That stuff tastes like a bull urinated orange juice. What is it made out of anyway?"

She chuckled again, shaking her head. "You really don't want to know."

"Fair enough." I switched topics. "So that scene I just witnessed. That was something. I didn't think you could do anything like that. It wouldn't seem like that would be in a lesser witch's power level."

She groaned at my observation. "It's not."

"What?"

She opened her eyes and looked at me. "I guess I have one more thing to confess to you."

"Oh man, more secrets?"

"It's the last one, I swear."

I exhaled heavily. "Okay, lay it on me."

Fleurette leaned forward in her seat, scrubbing a hand over her mouth to give herself a moment. "I ... have more power than I let on."

"So, you aren't a lesser witch?" I clarified. She shook her head to affirm my question. "So just how much power are we talking?"

"I'm still growing in power."

"Woah." Normally, a lesser witch or herbalist reached his or her full potential a few years after puberty. Many more powerful witches capped off in their mid-twenties. Fleurette was thirty-one and, according to her, still hadn't reached her full potential.

"It's not just you I've kept in the dark about this. Only my dad and GOGS know."

"GOGS?" I asked, raising an eyebrow. She had used the acronym last night, but it was just registering with me.

She laughed with embarrassment. "Guardians of Glivver Society."

I shook my head. "Five hundred years, and that was the best acronym you guys could come up with? Okay, not important. Why keep your power a secret?"

She pursed her lips as she looked away from me. "It's ... complicated. Part of it has to do with my mother. She was just as powerful as me when she left."

"You were eight, right?"

Fleurette nodded. "She was a part of GOGS at the time. But something happened, and she left. Or died. I'm not sure." She blew out a shaky breath. My heart lurched for the old pain that was dredged up. "The point is, she didn't stay long enough to see my powers develop. And Dad is definitely a mundy. It was his idea for me to downplay my abilities once they started to emerge."

This still wasn't making a ton of sense to me. "Is Lyle a GOG too?"

"He's an honorary member. Most members are magical in some way. But Dad's ties to my mom, and now me, allowed him to be in the loop."

"But why hide? I'm still missing something."

"Um, since we don't know what happened with Mom, Dad didn't want the same fate for me. A powerful witch tends to draw more attention than a lesser witch. In order for me to not go into hiding, I instead had to hide my abilities. And since magic is mostly hereditary, it made sense to everyone that I'd only be a lesser witch since my dad is non-magical."

"So, in other words, you are drawing the scent off of you in a magical sense?"

She laughed. "Yes, you animal, the metaphorical scent trail ends as long as I hide the bulk of my powers. Less scrutiny on me means I can be more useful as your guardian."

"Okay. I got it. Still, what happened in there isn't an everyday occurrence. How did you know to do that?"

"Keep in mind that I'm still learning. My studies have been much slower since I'm in hiding. But to answer your question, I knew this procedure was possible because I saw it done once before."

I dropped my brows. "When?"

She smirked without humor. "When I was a child."

"Huh?"

She nodded as if something more eloquent had come out of my mouth. "My mother performed this magic to heal someone's soul when I was young. Not the same problem," she amended hastily upon seeing my confusion. "The man was afflicted with a different soul curse. But everything else was the same."

"Did it work? When your mom did it?"

Her chest heaved with a grand sigh. "Yes and no. Mom was able to extract the curse. But the man didn't make it."

My eyes widened at the revelation. "What went wrong?"

She looked at me with reddened eyes. Clearly, it wasn't the happiest of memories. "His soul never settled back into his body. That's why I knew it was important for Fal to help me. Only pure love can save a soul from something like that." She shook her head as if to rattle the old memories back into hiding. "The bottom line is that ever since I was little, I have been cataloging spells and the like that my mother performed for future reference. I also inherited her books after she left. She was meticulous about writing down her methods. And even though my mother ultimately failed, I was confident our outcome would be different."

She stood. "Come on." She held out a hand to me. "Let's go check in on the siblings."

CHAPTER 21

W ren sat upright in the bed, propped up by pillows, with Fal by her side. The previous pallor of her face had dissipated, and a natural rosy glow had infused her cheeks during our absence. However, her face blanched for a split second when she locked eyes with me.

It was rather unnerving, frankly, to see her have such a visceral reaction to my presence. After all, we hadn't had the best track record. She had made it abundantly clear that she did not trust me. And she had acted like a creepy little girl with anger issues. In other words, I did not know what to expect from Wren.

And I really did not expect for her to simultaneously smile at me and burst into tears. She motioned me over as she wiped a stray tear from her cheek. I hesitantly approached.

Once I was close enough, she grabbed my right hand with affection.

"Miss Cressida," she began with a bit of a warble to her voice, "I feel so terrible at the way I've treated you. Can you forgive me?"

"Oh, well, I ..."

"I mean, you saved us, and I was awful the whole time. Not that I was fully me for all of it. I can't tell you how terrible it felt to not be in control of my own body. Still, though, I'm so sorry!" Another tear streaked down.

I patted our clasped hands with my left. "I understand, and there's no need to apologize. How are you feeling?"

Wren let out a hiccup. "Better. I can't tell you how horrible it's been."

Fleurette had come up behind me. She placed a hand on my shoulder as I sat on the bed. "Wren, what can you tell us?"

Wren took a moment to compose herself. "It started before Mom and Dad passed away. I was having a recurring dream. A man would come to me and show me how to open doors to other worlds."

"A man? Can you describe him?" Fleurette enquired, her tone gentle.

Wren's brow furrowed. "He was older, always smiling kindly, and he had a radiant glow about him. He had silver hair and a beard and perfectly straight teeth."

I exchanged looks with Fal. Concern etched his face as he thought back to what Fleurette had asked last night.

"You said he opened doors to other worlds," Fleurette probed again. "What do you mean by that?"

"They were just dreams, weren't they?" Wren questioned in a tiny voice.

"Sometimes dreams have deeper meanings," the witch murmured. "It is best to examine all angles so that we are armed with as much knowledge as we can glean."

Wren sighed. "In the dreams, he would take my hand and lead me to an actual closed door. We weren't in a room or anything, but there was always a door. He would tell me to unlatch my mind, and the door would open."

"What was on the other side of the door?" Fal asked.

"The universe," Wren replied. She thought a bit more. "I mean, it looked like the night sky, but with more colors and swirling stars. But I remember thinking it was the universe."

"What would happen after the door was opened?"

"At first, the dream would end there. But after a while, I would start to dream that we went through the door together. And each time we did, it would be a different place. Sometimes it was a meadow with the greenest grass I ever saw. Sometimes it would be a beach with an endless ocean." The girl's eyes had a faraway look as she remembered her dreams. "I came to love those dreams," she added wistfully. "They made me want to travel in real life. And so, I did."

"How do you mean?" Fleurette asked, still keeping her voice soft and comforting.

"It's like the dreams unlocked something in me," Wren described with a frown. "It's hard to explain. But I was really good at projecting by then. I could create scenes or transform myself. I just didn't know I could project myself to other worlds until the dreams showed me."

"And that's what you did?" Fleurette asked.

Wren nodded. "After each dream, I took myself to the particular world the man showed me. I actually got to see the green meadow and the beach. They were real places. But it took a lot of energy to do that, and I never wanted to worry my parents with my absence. So, I only left for a few minutes each time."

"Wren, do you understand just how unique your gift is?" Fleurette probed gently.

Wren shook her head but looked intrigued.

"To be a projectionist is a rare thing, and of all the known projectionists, only a small handful have been able to project themselves to other dimensions. They call those with your abilities 'world walkers.' It would not surprise me if you were the only world walker alive in our world right now."

Fal whistled softly. "But there have been others?"

Fleurette nodded. "Natural-born world walkers are extremely rare. Many times, when you hear of someone traveling to another dimension, there are more mechanics at play than simple talent. Tesla, for one, comes to mind. He managed to temporarily create a link between this world and his, even though he employed no magic. But he would not be defined as a world walker."

"What about the Grimm brothers?" I ventured. Grimm had once told me his master had named him after the famous Grimm brothers, a pair of writers who boasted that they could travel between dimensions, before they disappeared for good back in the 1700s. It was said that they claimed not to be of this world in the first place, but merely visiting. But there was no way to prove these claims at all.

Fleurette shook her head with a tiny frown. "I don't think they had true talent either. Rather, it is believed that they had help from the Fae."

"The Fae." I repeated in a deadpan. "As in faeries? They don't exist."

"I can assure you they are quite real. And never call a Fae person a 'faerie' to their face if you want to live. It's a rather derogatory term to most of them."

"Fine, the Fae," I amended with a wave of my hand. "What's their story, then?"

"They are only the most powerful magic users in all of the dimensions," Fleurette explained. "They have a home world, but they have a very high population of what they call 'dimension hoppers,' beings that are able to freely travel the dimensions. With this common ability, some Fae have colonized other worlds, sometimes temporarily, sometimes permanently. It's why there are tales of Fae in almost every world, even those that don't contain a lick of magic. The Fae have left their mark everywhere, whether you believe in them or not."

"Hm. I guess that makes sense," I conceded.

"So, to get back to your query, it was theorized that the Grimm brothers had the help of a Fae individual to somehow travel as extensively as they claimed. In this case, the Fae would have been the world walker, not the brothers."

Fal cut into the conversation. "So, Wren can dimension travel." He shook his head and directed his attention back to Wren. "And you never questioned whether or not it was safe?"

Wren looked abashed. "No. I suppose I should have, but I trusted the dream man. He only took me to beautiful and safe places. Until the last dream."

"Where did he take you?" Fleurette asked.

"When he opened the door and we stepped through, we were in a dark land of purples, blacks, and blues. I remember thinking that this dream felt different. I was a little scared and I told the man that. He just smiled and told me not all places were what they seemed, and this world was the most special of all."

"Did you go there in real life?" Fleurette asked with an edge of intensity.

Wren nodded with a gulp. "The very next day."

"What happened?"

"I appeared in a big throne room made of crystals. There was a woman in front of me, sitting on the throne. She smiled, and I was suddenly terrified." A tear raced down Wren's face at the recollection. "There's a gap in my memory after that. But then the woman said to visit her often, and I left."

I turned my head toward Fleurette, who exchanged an anxious look with me.

"After that, I didn't feel right, "Wren continued, frowning. "At first it was just a weird feeling here or there. But after a while I just didn't feel like me. I was angry a lot of the time for no good reason. I didn't want to project pretty or friendly things anymore. And I kept getting urges to go back to that place."

"How do you feel now?" Fleurette questioned softly.

Wren took a deep breath, hitching just a bit while she did. But a watery smile broke out on her face. "Like me again. Fal told me what you did. I can't thank you enough for saving me."

Fleurette looked troubled at the girl's words. "Wren, it's true your brother and I removed the bit of Annie's soul that was controlling you. But I'm afraid you are still in danger."

"What?!" Fal interjected. "How?"

Fleurette placed her hand over Wren's, which was still clasping mine. "Wren, Annie removed a small piece of your soul in order to bond the piece of hers to you. You are still missing that piece, and without it, you will die."

Fal hugged his sister to his body with that bit of news. "No!"

Fleurette moved her hand from ours and placed it on Fal's arm. "All hope is not lost, Fal," she soothed. She made sure to make eye contact with both siblings. "There is a solution."

She turned her attention back to the girl, who was once again white-faced. "I know it's difficult to talk about," she began, "but what exactly was your deal with Annie Coddle?"

Wren breathed a couple of times before answering. "Once I was not myself, it was so easy to do as Annie bid me. She told me that sometimes she would be 'borrowing' my eyes. I could always tell when she did this because it felt like there was a second person inside of me. But I was still in control.

"After a while, I would have blackouts. They seemed very short, but there would be gaps in my memory. I think those were the times Annie would have complete control of my body."

I shuddered. I couldn't help it. The hand on my shoulder gave a comforting squeeze.

"Annie couldn't ever control my gift. She asked me to start bringing her various ingredients from Mom's stash. That's how I learned I could permanently project objects to a different dimension."

Wren looked at me, fresh tears making her eyes glassy. "I think I killed my parents," she whispered.

Fal looked grief-stricken. "What do you mean, Wren?"

She could not look at her brother, but squeezed her eyes shut. The tears spilled out. "Annie gave me a potion and instructed me to put it in their drink. I did it, I think. I blacked out a little that evening. And they ... died ... three days later."

She broke down fully, curling into a ball away from her brother. Fal stayed motionless for a second before wrapping his body around hers.

"No, Wrenny, no," he murmured into her back. "*You* didn't do it. Annie did."

Wren sobbed, but turned to her brother at those words, embracing him in a tight hug as the two expressed their grief all over again.

It was enough to make me teary-eyed. I wiped my eyes on my sleeve.

After a few minutes, the siblings calmed. Fal sat back, rubbing his thumbs over Wren's cheeks to wipe away the tears. "I will never blame you, Wren," he told her. "I love you."

"I love you too, Fal," she returned.

They hugged once more before repositioning themselves against the headboard. A moment of awkward silence reigned in the room.

"So ..." I began, breaking the tension. "Where were we?"

Carefully avoiding the mention of deceased parents, Wren took up the conversation. "Once we were on our own, Annie told me to keep an eye out for a cat that could change into a human. I kind of thought she was crazy to bring that up."

"Oh sure, a mind-controlling witch living in another dimension isn't too far-fetched, but a simple shape-shifting cat is," I grumbled under my breath. Wren gave me an apologetic smile.

"It's how I recognized what you were so quickly. By that time, Annie could practically whisper thoughts in my ear. She saw you and she saw a cat always in close proximity, but never together in the same room. She helped me put two and two together. She knows what you are."

"Do you know what I am?" I asked her.

She nodded. "Sometimes I know things that Annie knows. Or at least I did when we were attached. I know that you are the only person that can stand up to her."

Her face fell. "I also did a bad thing."

I frowned at that simple statement. "Care to elaborate?"

She met my eyes sheepishly. "Do you remember the bathroom? At the school?"

I shuddered theatrically. "I try to forget it on a regular basis."

"I sort of ... plucked a few hairs from your tail."

I nodded. "I thought as much. What of it?"

Lowering her eyes, she mumbled, "IgavethemtoAnnieCoddle."

"Say what now?"

Taking a deep breath, she clarified, "I gave the hairs to Annie Coddle."

Well, that didn't sound good. I glanced at Fleurette. We both knew that personal possessions, such as things with your DNA in them, were worth more than gold to some magic users.

"That might explain a few things," my friend stated simply.

"Wren, when did you give them to her?" I asked, keeping my voice neutral even as I freaked out on the inside.

"When I took those two bad men away, I brought them to her. I thought she could keep them on her world for me if I traded her the hairs. She was so delighted though, not just with the hairs, but the fact that I could project people with me. It didn't feel like a trade at all, in the end."

"What did she do after that?" Fleurette asked.

Wren squirmed a bit. "She took the men away, saying she had a good use for them later. I didn't feel bad for them," she explained matter-of-factly. "I gave her exactly four hairs. She took three of them and made a potion then and there. I think ... she put a spell on you."

"I think you are right," I replied, fatigue washing over me. "I can't change to a cat right now without getting fried by lightning."

Fleurette steepled her fingers in front of her face in thought. "A simple solution to getting rid of the one being that could prevent her from returning. How on earth has she gotten that much magical oomph back though? Glivver stripped her of her power and sent her to a non-magical dimension. Or so I thought."

"That's what I've been told, too," I responded. "But that was five hundred years ago. Who knows what's happened since?"

"Indeed." Fleurette once again focused on Wren. "I know this is a lot to take in all at once, sweetheart. But one last question. You said something about Annie wanting Fal. Can you explain?"

Wren looked to her brother, who squeezed her hand in encouragement. "I guess by transporting the two men with me, I ... gave Annie ideas," she began hesitantly. "When I projected back later that day, she said she wanted me to bring my brother with me next time. It was the first time I felt fear with her since meeting her. She became very angry with me when I refused. She hurt me in here," she motioned to her chest, where the fragment of Annie's soul was once lodged, "and threatened me with all sorts

234

of nasty suggestions. I think she was trying to prevent me from leaving, because it took a lot of effort for me to return here."

"More than likely," Fleurette mused, lost in thought. "My guess is that she would have used your brother to make her return. The power of love," she glanced at the siblings, "is incredibly strong. Perhaps the most powerful of all. She would have capitalized on that. What she didn't expect is for you to rebel, Wren. She figured you were too deep under her spell by that time."

"But the power of love allowed me to escape?" Wren hedged.

Fleurette nodded. "A deep love for your brother, yes. Now then, as far as I see it, there's just one course of action. Wren, your soul needs to be healed before it's too late. You are the only one who can project yourself to the dimension in which it is housed. You need to go and collect it. And you are going to take Cressida with you."

CHAPTER 22

F leurette's words blanketed the room in utter silence. They also blanketed my heart in utter dread.

"Um, Fleurette, can I talk to you in the hallway?" I asked with forced cheerfulness.

She nodded and walked out. I patted Wren's hand with a fake smile on my face and then stood and walked out as well, with Grimm on my heels like my ever-present furry shadow.

Once we were in the hallway, I grabbed the witch's arm. "Are you crazy?" I hissed furiously.

Fleurette placed a hand on my back and guided me out to the living room. Once we were there, she turned to face me.

"What is your objection?" she asked in her completely calm manner.

"I can't face Annie Coddle! She'll kill me!"

Fleurette sighed. "Cressida, dear, you are the only one who can face Annie Coddle."

"No, I'm the only one that can prevent her from coming back," I countered. "I'm pretty sure she'll kill me the first chance she gets. Or have you already forgotten the lightning spell she placed on me?"

"Which is precisely why you need to be the one to go. Wren needs her soul piece back. You can't expect a young girl to do this alone, can you?"

"Then send Fal with her."

Fleurette shook her head. "That would be handing Annie exactly what she wants. You need to go and lift that spell and hopefully get back your remaining hair. Besides, the prophecy doesn't say *how* you prevent her from returning. Perhaps doing nothing won't stop her but standing up to her is what's expected of you."

I scrubbed my hands down my face. "I hate your logic," I grumbled. "Fiiiine. I'll go. But I don't have the foggiest clue what I'm supposed to do to stop her."

Fleurette gave me a friendly hug. "My advice? Help Wren get her soul back. Break the spell placed on you. And have faith that the rest will work out."

"Because if it doesn't, we are all screwed," I muttered.

"No pressure, right?" Fleurette gave a dark chuckle. "Seriously, though, Cress. This moment is what not only your short life but all of your ancestor's lives combined has been leading up to. You were born to do this. Don't doubt yourself now."

"Ugh, no pressure!" I moaned back.

The plan was set. We would wait another couple of hours to allow Wren to rest and regain her strength. Fleurette and Fal needed a nap as well, considering they were up all night. I would spend that time as a lump on the couch, fretting about my perceived impending doom.

They say that young people believe themselves to be immortal, and apparently that goes for young cats too. Up until this moment, I was happy to adventure out in the world with never a care. Even with my highly dangerous job, I had never felt like my life was in jeopardy.

Now, however, there was a large knot of dread in my stomach, and all I could think about was the fact that I could be dead in just a couple of hours.

Grimm could clearly sense my dark mood. He lay his heavy head on my lap, allowing me to pet his soft black ears as I contemplated my fate. His presence gave me a small sliver of comfort, but even that would be stripped away as he wasn't allowed to go with us.

"I miss our chats, buddy," I told him softly. "I hate being stuck in this form."

Grimm nuzzled my hand but could not give any other answer. I sighed.

A knock at the front door gave me a start. Fleurette was still sleeping, and it did not seem appropriate for either of the fugitives to answer the door. "I guess I'll get that," I said aloud.

I tenderly shoved the canine head out of my lap so that I could stand. The last thing I wanted now was for someone to bother me. Besides, who could it possibly be? We never got visitors out here.

I swung the door inward. And stared.

"Mom?" I asked incredulously.

I hadn't seen my mother in her human form for at least a year. While she still looked approximately how I remembered, her human form had aged considerably in that year. Her hair, longer than mine and a mix of brown and red that paralleled her calico colorations, was now streaked generously with white strands. Her green eyes were surrounded by a few wrinkles, and her face had lost some of the roundness I remembered. She looked to be solidly in her forties, now, instead of her early thirties as she had previously appeared.

She pursed her lips. "Don't stare. I know," she told me disapprovingly. But in the next instant she swept me up into a loving embrace.

I hugged her back tightly, tears running freely down my face. "I'm so happy to see you."

After a few seconds, she pulled away, looking me over with those all-seeing mom eyes. "Rupert filled me in," she told me as she led me back to the sofa. We both sat simultaneously, side by side. "You look like hell."

A laugh sputtered out of me. "So I've been told." Leave it to my mom to tell it like it is.

"So, this is what it takes to get you into your human form?" I asked her with sarcasm.

She smiled as she brushed my unruly black streaks out of my face. "I know that the last time we spoke I was rough on you," she said, sadness leaking into her words. "Cressida, I never want you to think that I'm not proud of you. In fact, far from it. I'm so very proud of your free spirit."

These words unleashed a fresh batch of tears from me.

"I'm hard on you sometimes because I'm not like you. I never wanted to look for danger. I just wanted a husband and a daughter and peace for the rest of my days. I sort of got that. And I guess I figured you would want that too for yourself."

She leaned toward me. "And I never wanted the prophecy to land on you. But even if it wasn't you and you had already passed on the responsibility, I wouldn't want that for my granddaughter either. I guess what I'm trying to say is that if it had to be anyone, you are the best choice available."

"What do you mean?"

"I mean, you have spunk, you have the drive, you have the necessary spirit to do this. I wouldn't have. We would have been screwed if this had happened just a few years earlier." She gave me a wry smile. "But you, you are the best possible choice. I know with all of my heart that fate picked the right cat for this job. You won't fail."

I sobbed and hugged her again. Somehow, my mother had lifted the feeling of dread within me and replaced it with hope.

"Thank you," I murmured into her shoulder.

She pulled back again, her own eyes shiny. She wiped her thumb over my cheek with affection. "One last thing," she said.

"What?"

"I'm sure Grimm has a few words for you, too. Hang tight." She shimmered into a cat, then gave her full attention to my partner.

After a few moments of a conversation I couldn't understand as a human, Mom retransformed.

"He says, and I quote, 'Stop being mopey and do your damn job. I chose you as my business partner because I know you are going to kick ass no matter what the job is. If you fail me now, I will be forced into early retirement because I refuse to work with anyone else. Come back to me, Cressida.'"

I stared at Grimm while Mom quoted those words. At the end, I grabbed the furry lunk's head in a fierce hug. His tail wagged at my touch. "You know just what to say," I told him. "I won't let you down, partner."

Okay, so I was still nervous. But instead of feeling like I was walking to my death, my natural confidence was back. I didn't know what to expect, but I was going to do the best I could no matter what. And dying was not on my to-do list.

I could tell Wren was also nervous, as she was once again entering the lion's den. But that girl also had a spunky spirit. Perhaps we were more alike than I originally thought.

Fleurette had lent Wren some of her clothes, with a few modifications due to the girl's smaller stature. She was more closely sized to me, but I simply did not have spare clothes since mine got magically washed every time I groomed myself as a cat. So, Wren now was sporting a loose shirt that hung like a tunic on her body, tied at the waist with a ribbon, and a pair of capri pants that came down to her ankles. Fleurette even braided Wren's hair to keep the long dark tresses out of her face.

My hair wasn't quite long enough and was too slippery to hold a decent braid. Instead, mine got the ponytail treatment.

I had Hail Mary still strapped inside my right boot, but otherwise we were not bringing anything else with us. There was no point when going up against a powerful witch. Besides, Wren could not wield a weapon, and her talents combined with my natural capabilities were hopefully enough.

We were surrounded by the people who meant the most to us: Grimm, Fal, Fleurette, my mom, and Lyle. Rupert perched on my friend's shoulder, looking as somber as the rest of us felt. I had already said my goodbyes to Humbert outside, not that he understood.

"Remember, the plan is to pretend that Wren is still controlled. Perhaps that way you can get close enough to find the soul piece and your tail hair," Fleurette said.

We both nodded in unison with grim determination.

Fleurette stepped forward and swept me into a hug. "Be safe," she whispered to me.

Out of the corner of my eye I saw Fal embrace his sister with gusto. Fleurette stepped back and Mom took her place.

"Come back to me," she said with a slight hitch in her voice. I tried not to shed any more tears as I gripped her tightly.

Lyle also offered a fatherly hug and words of encouragement as the others made their rounds with Wren. To my surprise, Fal stepped up to me after Lyle was finished. He stood before me awkwardly, as if debating to hug me. Finally, he opened his arms. I accepted the embrace after a second's hesitation.

"Please keep my sister safe," he murmured.

"With my life," I returned.

There was just one last goodbye to give. I stooped down to be eye level with my partner. "Grimm, it doesn't feel right to not have you by my side. I'm going to miss you."

He made a little whine and licked his lips before rushing me for a furry embrace. I buried my face in his fur, sending a little prayer to Freya and the universe that I would be reunited with this ragtag assortment of friends.

They were ... my family, strange as it was for a cat to admit. But the word felt right.

I released my grip on Grimm and straightened. I stepped back to Wren, smiling wanly at her as she returned the expression. She held out a hand. I stared at it for a second, took a deep breath, and grasped it with my own.

"Ready?" she asked me.

I nodded.

My world turned upside down.

CHAPTER 23

I t was over before I could even comprehend what had happened. But the disorientation passed, and the reality of it hit me hard. I fell to my knees, my head swimming. Wren put a comforting hand on my back.

"Sorry about that. The two men reacted the same way. I should have warned you," she apologized as I strained to regain my equilibrium.

"Yeah, that was the worst," I replied huskily, blinking my eyes rapidly. My head finally stopped spinning after a few minutes and I slowly stood up, making sure my stomach wasn't about to rebel. The contents stayed down, but the headache was back. Apparently Fleurette's energy potion was wearing off. Just fantastic.

Now that my body was feeling a bit back to normal, I looked around. We were outside, but absolutely nothing made sense to me. At first glance I thought it was nighttime. But upon further inspection, I changed my theory. The sky was a deep, dark purple, but there was also a sun in the sky that created a strange bluish glow over everything. This unearthly shine filtered down to highlight the alien landscape before us. I saw zero plant life: no trees, no grass, no shrubs dotting the terrain. There were gigantic mushrooms here and there, however, acting as a stand-in for trees in an otherwise barren land. The earth was black with jagged rock formations, and veins of blue crystals peeked out in places, glowing with the subtle light of the sun.

The overall look of the landscape was one of sharp angles and shadows. It was beautiful, but in a bleak, dreary sort of way. I shivered at the sight.

Wren seemed unaffected. "C'mon," she said quietly as she grabbed my sleeve. "I transported us a little ways away to give us extra time. Her castle is this way."

She led me down an obsidian path. I still gawked at my surroundings, taking in the unearthly light from the sun as it lit up the surrounding crystals.

"What is this place?" I asked her.

Wren shrugged. "Just another dimension. This one is definitely nothing like our own dimension, so it's pretty creepy. I don't think anything else lives here, though. But I don't know for sure. I've only been outside once before. Usually, I just pop right into the throne room."

I stared at her. "You seem to be taking this in stride."

She glanced my way before focusing back on the path before her. "I'm nervous, but I'm in my element, in a way. I've been here before. And what other choice is there?"

"True." I agreed. "Still, I'm impressed. You've got a good head on your shoulders."

"Thanks." She laughed a little uncertainly. "Let's hope my head stays on my shoulders by the end of this."

I frowned. I didn't want to dwell on the possibility that we would fail. "It will. It has too."

"Yep."

"Where is this castle, anyway?" I asked, looking around. The terrain hadn't changed in the slightest. I saw nothing in the landscape but more of those weird mushrooms and jagged rocks. One in particular was huge, rising out of the ground like a jagged blade ripping through flesh. It was directly in front of us, but still in the distance. I stared at the behemoth with apprehension.

"You're looking at it," Wren replied, nodding her head in the direction of my gaze.

"That's her castle?" I asked, incredulous.

Wren nodded. "Mm-hmm. Castle is a strong word, but inside looks more like one. It's basically a hollowed-out stone structure."

"Homey." I glanced around as we approached. A slight movement to the right caught my eye. I turned my head quickly, but only spotted a small pile of rocks. Frowning, I turned back. "Are you sure there's nothing else out here?"

"No, I'm not. I just never saw anything else." Wren amended.

"Great," I caustically replied, adding, "Can we pick up the pace?"

"What did you see?" Wren asked with a hint of apprehension.

I felt like eyes were on us. I turned back around, and I swear the pile of rocks had moved position. I grabbed Wren's arm.

"We aren't alone," I whispered. She stiffened at my words, but we did not stop walking.

"What do we do?" Wren asked, sounding more like a scared little girl instead of the in-charge persona she had adopted earlier.

"Keep walking and stay calm."

As we neared the castle, two piles of rocks suddenly appeared on either side of the path in front of us, their sharp crystal lances held glinting in the alien light. Staying calm was impossible. We both shrieked.

"Halt!" a masculine voice emitted from the pile of rocks on the left. We did, petrified.

As both entities approached us, I noticed that they were not made of rocks, but were in fact two men dressed in rock armor.

When lying on the ground, they had blended into the scenery seamlessly.

"You are trespassers. We are taking you to Mother. She is expecting you," the left-hand man informed us as he bound our wrists behind our backs with rope. Properly restrained, the two rock guards marched us into the depths of the castle.

"Castle" probably wasn't the best way of describing the dwelling. More like, "hollowed out rock formation sitting on top of a warren of tunnels." I felt like I was visiting mole people. The walls of the tunnel hallways were smooth, with many crystals peeking out. Surprisingly, the crystals gave off a soft blue-white light, even without the presence of the sun.

But once we got to what Wren had referred to as the throne room, I saw why she had mistaken it for a castle initially. It was a large room with a cathedral-like ceiling. Crystal skylights lined the top and more crystals lit the interior walls. Directly facing the doors from which we entered was a massive purple stone throne, with a rack of antlers mounted above it.

And a woman sat upon the throne.

"Bring them forward." Her voice was cracked and husky.

The lances held at our backs nudged us. Wren and I slowly marched down the center aisle.

Once we got close enough, I broke the silence. "Annie, babe, is that you? Immortality does not agree with you."

Being a cat, rodents have always fascinated me. When I was little, my mother would tell me about all sorts of different types of unusual rodents that existed in the world. And once I met up with Fleurette, she gifted me with a book about rodents, complete with pictures, as a birthday present. One chapter in that book was devoted to the naked mole rat, a curiously hairless little critter that lives in colonies under the ground. The one fact that really stuck with me was that the entire colony is ruled by a queen naked mole rat, the only female that is able to breed. This queen is always the largest mole rat in the colony.

Annie Coddle reminded me of a queen naked mole rat.

I could not discern her age, but she seemed to hover around early forties if I had to guess. She wasn't exactly obese, but her whole body looked soft and corpulent, including her rather long, doughy face with two piggy eyes that peered out angrily. She had curly auburn hair that was heavily streaked with white. Her mouth seemed too small for her face, and she kept her lips slightly open, exposing front teeth that were rather long and yellow, once more reminding me of a rodent's.

It was hard to tell what she was wearing, but I could swear it was a robe made of human hair woven together.

She narrowed her eyes at me in response to my comment, but then turned to Wren. She stared at her, eerily quiet, for a long moment.

"Let them free," she told the guard behind Wren without breaking eye contact with the girl.

As the guards fumbled to remove our restraints, Annie gave a small, chilling smile, highlighting those ill-fitting front teeth even more. "Wren, dear, you're back. And you brought the cat."

Well, so much for the element of surprise.

"Yes, ma'am," Wren replied meekly.

"How very ... brave ... of you, dear, for coming back so soon after you misbehaved." The threat in the statement was thinly veiled.

Wren gulped. "My apologies, Madam Coddle," she said with a small curtsy. "It was a shock to the system. I thought if I brought the cat instead of my brother, that might make you happy."

"Clever girl," the witch murmured. She turned her eyes to me. "You must be very strong to withstand the change. I had hoped to burn you to a crisp by now."

"Sorry to disappoint." I shrugged with feigned nonchalance. I peered at the disgusting dress as something caught my eye. A silver ball pendant hung around her neck. Something within flashed with a pure lavender light.

I'd bet anything it was the piece of Wren's soul.

Unfortunately, I was in no position to do anything about it.

Annie pursed her lips as she inspected me, oblivious to my own inspection of her.

"So," she finally uttered, "why are you really here?"

The question was directed at me, but Wren, bless her brave heart, answered, "I told you. I couldn't bring my brother, so I brought her instead."

"It isn't polite to lie to your elders, young lady," Annie replied icily, returning her gaze to Wren. She then focused her repugnant face back on me. "And you," she practically hissed, "I'm not sure what your angle is, but mark my words, you will see your death here."

Well, crap. I was very much hoping that Annie Coddle would turn out to be one of those incompetent villains that took no skill at all to bring down. Clearly, Annie was a sharper tack than that, unfortunately for us.

On Annie's right, I spied a small table which housed open vials, loose herbs, and a single colorless crystal a foot tall and four inches in diameter. Annie reached over and brushed her fingers down the crystal, almost in an absentminded manner.

"Wren, Wren, Wren," she cooed in her cracking ageless voice. "I don't want you going anywhere this time. Your eyes are blocked to me now. What did you do?"

Wren didn't answer but stared at her feet as if ashamed.

Annie grasped the silver pendant around her neck in the hand that didn't stroke the crystal. She cracked a smug smile, allowing a mien of evil to bloom on her face. "Let's keep you close for now," she decided, and then swiftly she raised her hand above the crystal and sliced her finger upon its sharp point. Flinging the wounded appendage at Wren, she shouted, "Sleep!"

The air around me crackled with unseen energy. Wren crumpled beside me. It took all of my effort not to scream her name.

With Wren out for the count, I was out of options. Truthfully, I didn't really have a plan anyway. I suppose I was hoping that once I saw Annie Coddle, my lineage's magic would kick in automatically. But, quite unfortunately, I still had no clue what that magic was.

But I still wasn't completely helpless.

I thanked Freya in my head as I realized that neither Wren nor myself had been searched when we had been taken into custody. I had just one more trick, and it was hidden in my boot.

With more grace than I thought my human body could muster, I bent down, retrieved Hail Mary, and straightened.

"It's not nice to pick on little girls!" I yelled as I flung my knife straight for Annie's heart.

It flew through the air, blade over handle, with perfect aim. And stopped just a foot shy of Annie's body.

My eyes couldn't quite believe what I had witnessed. Hail Mary hovered. My heart lurched when my brain finally caught up. Annie's magic had somehow stopped the blade from hitting its mark.

The witch looked at the weapon thoughtfully as it stayed poised before her. After a few seconds, she casually plucked it from the air with her unbloodied hand and observed it closely.

"Interesting. This is a refined charm indeed. You have some powerful friends."

"That's right," I blustered.

Annie Coddle shot me a sly look, a slight grin beginning to form upon her lips. She stood up and casually strolled over to

Wren's form. "Too bad they aren't here, then. You might have stood a chance."

She leaned over Wren and picked up a limp hand. And then she pierced Wren's forefinger with Hail Mary.

"No!" I shouted before I could stop myself. Annie dropped Wren's hand, which landed with a boneless thud. The punctured fingertip welled with crimson blood. Blood that was now coating Hail Mary and activating its enchantment.

Annie straightened. Still smiling, she licked her own bloody finger, the one she had sliced on the strange crystal. As she removed her finger from her tongue, her face turned sour. "You," she yelled at the guard behind me, "which one are you?"

"It's Groban, Mother," he replied with reverence.

She waved her hand in a dismissing gesture. "Take this one to the dungeons." She sneered. "We'll see if things get more fun when she's more worn out."

"Yes, Mother."

Groban grabbed my arms and led me out of the throne room. He placed the sharp crystal blade against my back, a threat not to try anything heroic. I turned to take one last look at Wren's recumbent form on the floor, and then I swiveled to meet Annie's eyes. I narrowed mine menacingly. She just smiled evilly and wiggled her fingers at me in a "toodle-oo" gesture as Groban manhandled me out of the room.

CHAPTER 24

B ack in the maze of tunnels, I tried my luck with Groban. I figured that Annie seemed to have a shabby relationship with him, so maybe I could persuade him to help me out.

"So, you said your name is Groban?" I asked conversationally. No answer.

"Well, uh, Groban, where in Gaia's greenness did you come from? I didn't think anyone else was supposed to be here."

Just when I didn't think he'd answer, he responded, "From Mother."

"Mother? Do you mean Annie Coddle?"

"Yes, they are one and the same."

Well, that was an odd leadership title. "She kind of treated you like dirt out there. Why listen to her?"

We did not pause our walk through the tunnel—which was decidedly slanting downhill—but he seemed to consider my question.

"Because she is life. Without her, I would not exist. I owe her everything."

"Okay, then. So, I take it I can't convince you to help us out? Not even a little bit?"

I could sense the head shake behind me. "No. Mother must be obeyed. We dare not face the consequences."

"Worth a shot." I muttered.

Groban did not offer any more words of wisdom, not that I quite understood what little he had said. We continued to trek down for quite a while, weaving deftly through the maze of tunnels, until finally our path ended at a door. He pushed me into a wall with one strong arm while the other took a keychain and unlocked the door before us.

Once the door was opened, I was manhandled inside. It was indeed a dungeon in here. Rows of prison cells lined the wall, at least ten in all. Wasting no time, my guard took me to the nearest cell and pushed me in through the opening, before shutting the cage with a loud clank and turning the key. His job done, he swiftly exited like an automaton.

"Wait!" I called to his retreating back, "you forgot the mint on my pillow!"

My quip didn't even slow him down.

Once the door to the dungeon had clanked shut and locked, I let out a loud sigh. Now that the adrenaline of the events had subsided, I could once more take note of every ache and pain in my body. My head hurt, my eyes were strained, and my muscles groaned. The bad news was it was only getting worse. I slid down the cell wall to rest on my butt, keeping my eyes closed.

"You're not the usual," a high-pitched voice in front of me said.

I opened my eyes to see a small woman watching me through the bars. She was being housed in the cell adjacent to mine. High cheekbones and big violet eyes graced her face, which had a slight greenish hue to it. Her hair was a dark forest green, and it lay limply in long disheveled tresses. Her gossamer dress was torn and dirty.

"What do you mean? I'm not the usual?" I asked her, not moving a muscle from my spot in exhaustion.

"I mean, you are clearly not Fae. You aren't one of her daughters, either." The petite woman studied me.

"Whose daughter?"

She laughed. "Who else? Madam Annie, of course."

"Wait a moment." I sat up, intrigued. "Annie Coddle has children? She's actually a mother?"

The woman before me squinted her large eyes. "Where did you come from?"

"Elsewhere. Please, answer my question," I practically begged her.

She cocked her head. "Well, yes, all of the people living here are either Madam's children or grandchildren."

"Ewww," I uttered, jumping to my feet. "She really is a naked mole rat queen!"

The woman cocked her head in confusion. I waved it off. "Not important," I told her. I thought about the ramifications of Annie having children. Despite not knowing the details personally, I did know the basics on procreation. "How is it possible, though?"

She frowned at me. I shook my head. "I don't mean it quite that literally. Nor do I want that mental image. Ever. I mean, this world was supposed to be abandoned. Who the heck is the father?"

"Oh." The woman nodded. "That's easy. I'm from a dimension of Fae. This world is used as a prison for the worst kind of Fae criminals. Madame Annie takes advantage of this fact."

Well, I'll be darned, Fleurette was right. Fae did exist.

I'm not sure which part of her sentence surprised me more, though, the fact that there was a whole dimension of Fae, or the fact that they were using this place for their own nefarious plans.

I'm pretty sure my eyes bugged out at her. "Since when has it been used as a prison?"

She screwed up her greenish face in thought. "Since, oh, about four-hundred and seventy years ago."

"Well, that's just fantastic," I groaned sarcastically. "This dimension was supposed to be magic-free to keep Annie here forever. Clearly, she has *some* magic. How did this happen?"

The Fae woman scrunched up her face. "You seem to be a fountain of knowledge when it comes to Madam Annie," she said, her tone accusatory. "Care to explain? I think I've been more than forthcoming."

I closed my aching eyes and pinched the bridge of my nose. "My ancestor was the one that sent her here," I told her, reopening my eyes to look at her, "Annie was banished here without any magic powers, and the place was supposed to be magic-free. And people-free, for that matter."

"Oh, I see," the friendly demeanor was back again. "Well, the Fae council chose this dimension as a terminal prison because it *was* non-magical. It basically sucks Fae dry of any residual magic, which kills us faster. I don't think they knew Annie Coddle was here when they chose it. And since none of the blowhards has ever stepped foot here since making it their prison, still no one knows she's here."

"Bureaucracy at its finest," I muttered. The woman nodded in agreement. Something occurred to me. "If this is a prison, what are you doing here?"

She shrugged. "Oh, I'm a prisoner too. I was sent here about three weeks ago."

I almost didn't want to ask, but curiosity got to me. "What did you do?"

She winked at me, and then replied, "I ate all of my siblings."

"Ohhhhh ... kay," I responded, trying my hardest to keep from sounding horrified.

She laughed. Her incisors were sharp, like shark teeth. "It sounds worse than it is. I can see intentions deep inside of people. My siblings had dark intentions, so I ate them. It was the best possible outcome. But the council didn't see things my way. So here I am."

Here she was. I looked around my cage for a moment, taking stock of my surroundings. It was barren of everything but a big stone bowl in one corner, and a pile of rags that I assumed to be a bed in another. The right-hand wall was solid stone, and the other three sides were comprised of bars. On closer inspection, they were fashioned from stone, not metal, and it appeared that the bars and cells had also been carved from a solid piece of stone.

The Fae female in front of me stuck a dirty greenish hand through said bars, offering it to me. "I'm Dunisha."

I hesitated for a split second before taking the proffered hand, not wanting to offend the apparent serial killer in front of me. Shaking her hand, I said, "Cressida."

Handshake done, we both stepped back from the bars again. "Don't worry, Cressida, I can see your intentions. They shine bright with goodness. I don't want to eat you." Dunisha winked at me, her cheeky smile unnervingly pointy.

"Thanks for that," I told her. "I can't read intentions. You've been here for three weeks. How did you end up in the dungeon?"

"Oh, that," she waved a hand in the air. "Madam always snags the fresh meat as soon as they arrive. From what I've gleaned, the men she usually takes for herself, unless she's currently pregnant. The women are reserved for her sons. They're just wearing me down first before I'm put to breed."

"Ugh, barf," I retorted. "That's disgusting. And I don't get it. Why does she want to keep popping out babies? Based on her interaction with her son the guard, she's not a very fit mother."

"She's creating magic, of course."

"Come again?" I was intrigued.

Dunisha nodded. "Creating a life also creates a very small amount of magic. Normally it's so slight that it's like a drop in the ocean, but here in this barren land a drop adds up. She's storing this magic somehow. But it's such a tiny amount that she has to keep breeding for it to pile up."

"Interesting." As much as I didn't want to picture Annie doing anything remotely romantic with someone, it *was* fascinating. And clearly, based on the sleep spell she placed on Wren, it was working. Annie had built up a good amount of magic over the last five hundred years. "But how is she able to store it?"

Dunisha shook her head. "I don't know. This world naturally sucks up magic like a sponge, ridding it from the environment and rendering it null. Madam Annie has clearly found a way around that. She's also collected everything from every unfortunate person that comes her way. Any herbs, potions, metals; you name it, she saves it. And when people die, she makes potions out of their body parts."

"Waste not, want not," I muttered.

"She knows what she's doing, that's for sure," Dunisha agreed with a little too much cheerfulness for my comfort.

A bolt of pain shot through my skull, making me wince and screw my eyes shut. It faded as quickly as it had come, but a throbbing ache stayed put. I sighed in frustration. Clearly, without being able to revert to my cat form, I was failing in the health department. And fast.

"Well, Dunisha, this has been the most disturbing conversation I've ever had, and I've had some doozies lately," I told my fellow detainee with forced cheer. "But I can't stick around. I need to get out of here. Any ideas?"

She frowned at me. "Seriously?"

"Yeah, seriously." A lance of pain pierced my left eye from the back. I winked it closed with a grimace. "It's my destiny to save my world, and by proxy all the other worlds, by keeping Annie here, and I can't really do my job from inside a cell."

She furrowed her brow at me in thought. She may have been the one to eat her family members, but I could tell that she was considering me to be the crazy one in this situation. "What's in it for me?" she asked.

"Um, I'd love your help. I also need to get my hands on Annie's pendant. You know, the one around her neck? It's really important."

"Why?" Dunisha countered with narrowed eyes.

In for a pound, at this point. "I traveled here with a little girl. A part of her soul is inside of it, and if I don't get it back, she'll die. And she's my ride back to my dimension, so I need her to not die."

The Fae woman considered my words and then she visibly brightened. "She can dimension hop? Okay, I'll help you, but only if you take me with you back to your dimension."

I should have seen that one coming.

"Oh, um..." I hesitated. Should I accept the bargain and let a Fae murderer loose on my dimension, or should I decline and try to get out on my own? And even if I accept, what were the odds that she could even do anything to help me? And what if she really was acting for the good of her world by eating her siblings, and was wrongly incarcerated?

So many questions. So little time. My left eye throbbed again.

So, I went with my gut's deep-down feeling. "Deal."

"That was a struggle, wasn't it?" Dunisha said with a wry smile. "Good thing I can see that you intend to keep your promise, otherwise I might not have trusted you enough to actually help."

Gulp. "Good thing," I agreed wanly. Dunisha smiled more broadly, displaying those sharp little teeth.

"Do you have a plan?" she asked.

"Other than kicking Annie's butt to kingdom come? No."

"I see." The Fae screwed up her face. "So, I'm to be the brains of this operation?"

I shrugged. "I think I just need help with getting out of these cages. Once that's done, I'll have more say."

"And how exactly do you propose we break out?"

If I could become a cat, I could breeze through these bars and be done with it. I contemplated doing just that, but ultimately decided that the risk of being barbequed before I could turn back to human was too great. Especially since my shimmer was being weirdly sticky.

I didn't want to give away my secret to my nice new criminal friend, anyway. So instead, I suggested, "I was sort of hoping you had a trick up your sleeve that could get us out."

She frowned at me. I smiled winningly at her in response. Finally, Dunisha rolled her eyes. "I told myself I'd never do it again. But Groban, based on his intentions, is to be my intended."

"Pun intended?" I interjected.

She sent me a half-hearted glare, but then changed it to a smile. "Groban is nothing more than an automaton of Annie's. Not literally, but the man has no character. Except when it comes to me. He has a sweet spot for me. I think I can work with that."

"Excellent!" I exclaimed, clapping my hands together once. The pop of the clap sent a throb of pain through my skull. Oops. "How soon will he be coming back?"

"I couldn't say," Dunisha said with a little head shake. I sighed loudly. Time was running out for me, I could tell.

For once, however, luck seemed to be on my side. We stewed in our cells for only twenty more minutes before the telltale sound of a key in the lock met our ears. The two of us sprung apart, me to the rag bundle in the corner and Dunisha to the door of her cell. Groban entered on cue, holding a plate of what I guessed was food. He made a beeline for us.

Dunisha scowled widely at me from over her shoulder. I frowned in response at the malicious look she had given me for no apparent reason. Turning back to the guard, she made her voice saccharine sweet. "Groban? Could I talk to you?"

Groban had witnessed her scowl. He hesitantly approached her cell. "What is it, prisoner?"

Oh yeah, he was sweet on her, alright. I could totally tell by the monotone voice he used on everyone else, and that sweet nickname he called her. I wanted to snort aloud but kept it in.

"I was wondering if you'd be willing to move me to a different cell. This new creature is bothering me greatly." She piled on the cute damsel in distress vibe as she said this.

"No." Groban responded.

"Please?" she wheedled. "She keeps trying to touch me and talk to me, and I just want to be left alone. There are so many empty cells, surely it wouldn't hurt to put me a few down from her."

Groban paused, considering.

Dunisha added, "I would be ever so grateful. I'd consider this a favor to repay once we are betrothed. Or even now."

Groban's mask didn't slip, but his eyes took on a twinkle of interest at her words. He paused a second longer before giving a curt nod and reaching for the keys attached to his belt. Finding the right one, he unlatched her door with efficiency.

As it swung out, Dunisha stepped forward. She was now turned toward Groban, so that I could see both of their side profiles. She had a charming "come hither" mien on her face. She reached her arms out enchantingly.

"Thank you, my sweet," she cooed. Groban stepped forward to claim his prize.

Dunisha's lower jaw unhooked, and she lunged forward faster than I could blink. Her mouth grew impossibly wide as she sunk it over Groban's head and closed her jaw. With a sickening crunch, she straightened her body as Groban's decapitated neck spurted blood like a fountain before collapsing into a heap on the floor.

Dunisha swallowed with a significant head tilt up. She turned to smile at me, her mouth once again looking normally proportioned, although her teeth were now bloody.

I was going to have nightmares for weeks.

"Holy furballs," I muttered. "That was ... something."

Dunisha let out a girlish laugh, completely at odds with the horrifying scene I had just witnessed. She bent over and unlatched the key ring from Groban's dead body.

I stood, but I didn't take a step forward even as my cell door swung wide with freedom. "On second thought, maybe I'm safer staying in here."

Dunisha rolled her eyes but smiled playfully at me as she beckoned me out of the cell. I stepped forward and out, keeping my eyes on the Fae woman as I skirted around both her and the headless corpse. "Remind me to never get on your bad side."

She winked at me. "Don't worry, you're safe with me. Besides, that takes a lot out of me. I couldn't do that again any time soon."

"Good to know." I rubbed my hand down my mouth tiredly. I pointed to the key ring in her hand. "Keys to the kingdom?"

She nodded. "Shall we?"

CHAPTER 25

Now that Dunisha had kept her end of our bargain and freed us, she expected me to uphold mine and come up with an awesome plan on the spot. I was still a tad shell-shocked from witnessing the Fae lady's unsettling talent, and my pain and exhaustion were growing worse by the moment, so unfortunately my mind was staying a blank slate. But I was not about to tell my companion that, for fear that she might go back on her word of not harming me. After all, my new friend was still too new to trust one hundred percent.

So instead, I bluffed, and did a recap instead. "Okay, here are our tasks. One, find Wren."

"Who?"

"My friend. The girl who dimension hops." I shook my head to get rid of the fuzzies invading my thoughts. It didn't really work, but it did serve to unbalance me for a moment. I placed a hand on a wall to steady myself before continuing. "The last time I saw her, she was in the throne room, hit by a sleeping spell. But she may have been moved by now."

I snapped my fingers as if I knew what I was doing. "Let's make our way toward the throne room and check out other rooms as we go. Maybe we'll run into Wren in the process."

"Okay, then," Dunisha agreed dubiously.

Admittedly, it was a weak plan, but in my exhaustion-addled state, it was the best I could do.

Cautiously, we exited the dungeon, making sure there were no other guards milling about in the underground tunnel before locking the door behind us and venturing slowly upward.

I realized that during my descent to the dungeon, I had been so busy talking to Groban that I hadn't actually paid much attention to my surroundings. Now I was kicking myself, as there were offshoot tunnels galore. A couple looked too small to lead to anything significant, but at times we had to make the difficult choice to either go down a different tunnel or stay on the given path. With my foggy mind, I let Dunisha do most of the deciding.

Many of the tunnels did not lead to much. Once, we came to what appeared to be a nursery, with a handful of infants and toddlers being cared for by a small group of women. I assumed these were all Annie's children, young and old, with perhaps a grandchild or two as well. The whole idea of this eusocial society that Annie had created gave me the shudders. It was fine for ants and bees, and even naked mole rats, but from an immortal human witch? Creepsville.

Luckily for us, no one saw us peeking our heads into the door, and so we were able to backtrack out of the tunnel without raising any alarms.

After wandering for half an hour, we came upon a locked door within the main tunnel. Dunisha held the key ring and studied the keys upon it to determine the right one.

Footsteps sounded down the hallway, coming from a higher elevation.

"Quick!" I hissed at her.

She fumbled for a key, tried it, and then tried to grasp another as the first didn't work.

The footsteps grew louder.

Third time was the charm. The door flew open, and we piled in haphazardly. Dunisha pushed the door shut with a loud thunk. I cringed at the sound.

"Do you think they heard us?" she whispered to me.

From outside, a male voice, muffled by the closed door, spoke. "Did you hear that?"

"Yes," said another masculine voice.

I glared at Dunisha. "Yes, I think they heard us," I whispered back. Her eyes grew wide with fear.

I turned, giving the room a once-over for hiding spots. It seemed to be a storage room, with shelves lining the wall. Each shelf housed bottles of all shapes and colors. Tiny labels were stuck to the bottles.

Dunisha ran over to the nearest shelf. "It's her potion room!" she whispered excitedly. She started stuffing bottles up her sleeves with vigor.

I picked up the nearest bottle. The label read, "Essence of Elf Tongue." I nearly gagged.

Dunisha side-eyed me. "Don't just stand there!" she admonished. "Start collecting them!"

I didn't give her request a second thought but began shoving various vials into the pockets of my vest. My vision swam as I did so, with little tiny black motes dancing like flies before me. I shook my head to be rid of them.

The door behind us flew open, revealing two male guards with lances.

"You there, halt!" the one on the left shouted.

His voice sounded familiar. I peered at him before uttering in surprise, "Groban?"

He frowned in confusion, but it was Dunisha that spoke. "No, that's Gorban. His twin."

Leaning toward me and barely moving her mouth, she muttered, "And ix-nay on the ecapitation-day."

I rolled my eyes despite myself. I hoped Annie had never taken the time to explain Pig Latin to her offspring.

But the guards only got a split second to even comprehend what the Fae woman had said, because my companion grabbed a handful of potions off the shelf and hurled them at the guards with a loud, "Take that!"

Most of the vials broke on contact, and a strange thick fog sprung up from the combination of mixed potions. It looked promising, so I followed suit, grabbing five bottles off the shelf and hurling them at Groban's twin.

Admittedly, I did not put enough oomph into my throw. Only two of the bottles broke upon hitting Gorban. Clearly, my body was failing me in all sorts of ways.

But, once combined with the continued lobs that Dunisha kept contributing, a large enough multicolored plume of fog enveloped both men. They paused their attack, looking at the swirling miasma, before starting to yell and bat it away ineffectively with their hands. We paused our attack as well, watching as the misty substance crawled up the hapless guards, until they were hidden from our view completely.

And then, in synchronicity, they both fell to the floor. Whether or not they were dead, I couldn't tell.

I stared at their unmoving bodies in shock, unsure of what I had just witnessed. Luckily for me, Dunisha's brain still worked.

"C'mon!" she urged, grabbing my arm. "We have to get out of here!"

Snapping to, I realized that here we were, on the far side of a small room that was now inhabited by a possibly killer fog. If we stayed put, surely the room would get swamped by the stuff. The Fae woman had an excellent point.

We scampered toward the door, holding our breath once we got close to the fog, and leaping over the prostate guards to freedom. Once we cleared the doorway, Dunisha turned with grace and slammed the door shut, trapping the potion-created mess within the room. Only then, did she breathe a sigh of relief.

I, on the other hand, felt quite light-headed and generally miserable. I tried to take a step forward but ended up crashing my right side into the wall of the tunnel.

Dunisha stepped forward with concern and plucked at my sleeve. "Are you alright?"

As another lance of molten pain shot through my head, I squeezed my eyes shut. "No." I answered simply. It was all I could manage.

My companion might have said more to me, but at that moment my ears filled with buzzing, like angry bees. I swiftly opened my eyes, but dark motes covered their surface. I reached a hand out in panic.

My body was suddenly horizontal, thumping heavily to the ground. My ears still buzzed, muffling the crack of my head against the hard-packed earth.

I had run out of time.

Everything went black.

I woke up slowly, feeling strangely at peace. No aches, no pains. In fact, I couldn't even feel my body.

But I could move, so I must have had a body still. I sat up, dazed but unafraid.

I assumed that I was back as a cat, since I was once again pain free. But upon further inspection, I saw that I still had hands and clothing upon my body. The mystery deepened.

I looked around, but it was like my brain couldn't process what I was seeing. I was in a vast whiteness. Everything around me was undefined, and if I focused on a certain point, it seemed to become even more vague. Scowling, I tried to find a viewpoint that wouldn't twist and squiggle away.

My eyes landed on a cat.

I squinted at it, and, in opposition to the surroundings, its form became more corporeal the longer I stared.

The cat was sitting before me, watching me with a bemused expression, its fluffy tail wrapped daintily around its front paws. It was long haired, but sleek, with what I could only describe as silver fur. As the image of the cat resolved further, I could make out a marbled tabby pattern of a slightly darker shade etched on its body.

It was the most beautiful cat I'd ever seen, and we cats don't take such statements lightly.

The cat waited a few seconds before standing, stretching nimbly and showily, and then letting out a petite mew in my direction. When I did not respond, the cat disappeared into a shimmery mass and then transformed to a woman.

"Hello, Granddaughter," she said with a smile.

CHAPTER 26

I frowned at the woman in confusion. I had never met my grandmother, and as far as I knew she was still alive. Plus, this woman looked to be only a handful of years older than me. She had a kind face with large blue eyes and long silver-blonde hair that ran down her back in a silky wave. If I did the math, my grandmother should have appeared to be in her early fifties.

She saw my confusion and let out a harmless chuckle. "Well, 'granddaughter' isn't exactly accurate," she admitted with a tilt of her head, "more like, 'great-granddaughter seventy times removed,' or so. To be honest, I lost count after twenty-five."

My eyes opened wide in understanding. "Glivver?"

She smiled again, warm and welcoming. "Well, Gilva at the moment. You are unfortunately in the wrong body to converse more naturally, so I compensated."

She was so carefree with her comments, while I was still trying to process.

"But how?" I asked, practically stumbling on my words. A lump of dread filled my stomach. "Oh no. I'm dead, aren't I? That's why I'm here. That's why I can see you. I mean, dying wasn't as terrible as I thought it would be, but that means I've failed. I've failed and Annie's going to come back after all and—"

"Shhh." During my anxious word vomit, Gilva had sidled up next to me. She placed a dainty pale hand over mine. I quieted immediately. She patted my hand in assurance. "You aren't dead."

Relief flooded me. I let out a whoosh of breath.

"But"—Gilva held up a finger—"you *are* in danger."

"And there's the other shoe," I muttered.

My ancestor smiled at my comment.

Shrugging my shoulders, I added, "So, if I'm not dead, where am I? How are you here? Not that I'm complaining, because I haven't felt this refreshed in quite a long time, but I am very confused."

"To be expected." She took a breath, schooling her features. "Honestly, this was a part of the legacy that I had never expected. Do you know anything about familiars?"

I thought for a moment. "Not really."

Gilva nodded. "Not surprising. They are exceedingly rare. And there is a lot of misinformation out there. To put it simply, a familiar is an energy spirit from a different plane of existence. Sometimes our individual frequencies resonate with the frequencies of magic users on other planes. If the magic user is powerful enough, he or she can call us out of our realm and into that magic user's. When this happens, we form an immediate bond, and we take on a true shape."

"So, you bonded with Annie Coddle?" I clarified.

She grimaced. "Yes, unfortunately. It is not a love bond or a personality bond, or anything like that, otherwise we never would have been paired. Each living being has a fairly unique energy, or frequency. Think of a massive piano that stretches for an eternity, with thousands upon millions playing the piano all at the same time. Each plays their own tune with their own chords and tempo. Now, imagine a second piano in a different world, with other beings doing the same. If somebody from one plane plays the same exact song as someone in another, the notes come together and harmonize, and that causes the two beings to be pulled together."

"I suppose that makes sense."

"Sometimes, when the two personalities come together and they are in disagreement, one of the two parties can bend the other to their way of thinking. Over time, of course."

"Of course." I had heard stories of familiars who had corrupted their witch over time. It was the main reason that familiars tended to be thought of as demons by the mundy crowd. Similarly, I could see a strong witch being able to change their familiar to better align with their morals. "Clearly, that wasn't the case with you and Annie."

"Oh no." Gilva chortled a bit. "We two had only one thing in common: our extreme stubbornness. I refused to give in to her evil ways, and in turn she denied every attempt I made at making her into a better person. In the end, her superior magic enslaved me."

"As fascinating as this is," I interjected, trying to keep my tone sincerely respectful, "what does this have to do with all this?" I motioned my hands at my opaque surroundings.

"You are an impatient one, aren't you?" Gilva laughed. I squirmed with slight embarrassment. "Well, dear one, I'll get on with it. You see, if you understand where familiars come from, it will make more sense.

"A familiar is tied to its magic user for the duration of the magic user's life. Once he or she dies, the familiar loses its attachment to that plane of existence and goes back to being a spirit of energy again with the other familiars."

"Oh." I could now see where this was going. "But Annie never died."

She nodded wisely. "And so, I should have still been tied to her. But instead, I sacrificed my immortality to stop her evil plans. When I eventually died, I assumed I would just ... stop being. Instead, I was resurrected, in a way, as a guardian of my descendants."

"So, you've been here all along, watching my every move?" That thought was somehow even more unsettling than GOGS watching over me.

She shook her head mirthfully. "No, dear me! Most of the time I reside as I once was, an energy being. Like that, I consume all information, but I don't necessarily have an active consciousness."

"Then how are you here?"

"Because this is the exception to that rule."

I pinched the bridge of my nose. "Please explain."

She winked at me. "If, for any reason, one of my descendants is close to death, I can stage an intervention."

"An intervention?"

"A second chance, if you will."

"Meaning what, exactly?" I asked her.

"Meaning, I can give you two things. The first is a pep talk, I believe is the saying these days."

I stared at her. "Have you done this before?" I had never once heard of one of my ancestors talking of encountering Glivver. Perhaps it was because I was the first descendant to meet Annie Coddle in the last five centuries.

Gilva let out a chuckle at my question. "Truthfully? Only once. Your relative from about a hundred and twenty years ago. Her name was Mildred."

"Glad I didn't get saddled with that moniker," I muttered. "What happened to her?"

"Nothing bad, compared to what you're dealing with. She fell out of a tree."

"As a cat?" Tree-related clumsiness while in cat form was a true crime.

She smiled. "Yes. She was not the most graceful thing ever. Or the brightest, for that matter."

I laughed in surprise. Gilva returned my reaction with a shoulder shrug and a cheeky smile. "What? I'm allowed to choose favorites."

I sobered slightly. "Do I make the cut?"

She grinned and patted my hand. "My dear, let me fill you in on a little secret." She leaned in toward me in mock confidence. "Even though we look nothing alike, you remind me of, well, me. And I like me a lot. You have got spunk, drive, and a strong will. All of these are excellent qualities to have when you are facing off against you-know-who."

"Well, that's a relief," I responded with a sigh.

Gilva straightened back up beside me. "Now for the second thing I can do during this intervention. I am going to give you a little boost. It will be enough to refresh you temporarily, but time is of the essence once you awaken."

"But what am I supposed to do?" Now that Gilva was talking about sending me back, the old panic was starting to creep back in.

"Do?" Gilva creased her brow at me.

I huffed a breath. "All my life, I've known that it may one day be my destiny to defeat Annie Coddle, but never once have I ever heard how. How can I possibly stop her plan? What do I do?"

"Oh." Gilva shrugged dismissively. "Child, most of what you do must come from you. I, unfortunately, can't give you all of the answers."

I let out a little grumble.

"But," my ancestor continued, "I can give you a little leg up. Do you know the transition phase between cat and human?"

I scrunched up my face. "You mean the shimmer?"

"The shimmer?" Gilva looked thoughtfully at me. "I suppose that is an excellent name for it. Yes. Do you know what it is?"

"Not really. I always figured it was just the in-between stage of transforming." I had never even given it much thought, truthfully.

"It is, but also, the shimmer is a phase that most closely resembles my familiar state. You no longer have a corporeal body when you shimmer. But I imagine it only lasts a split second for you."

"Well, yes, although the last time I tried to change, it was ... harder. It felt, well, sticky."

Gilva nodded as if this made sense. But she didn't elaborate. Instead, she forged on. "My advice? If your life is threatened again, do not just change forms. Surrender to the shimmer. *Be* the shimmer."

"Be the shimmer?" I parroted back with confusion. "What kind of advice is that?"

She smiled and leaned forward to plant a tender kiss on my hair. "The best I can do," she replied softly. "Stay safe, Cressida. And remember, the universe never gives us more than we can handle. You were born to do this. I have faith in you."

Before I could get another word out, my vision washed out with whiteness before everything went dark.

"Cressida? Cressida!"

I slowly registered that my name was being called rather urgently. My body twitched in response, but this sent a pang of pain throughout, from head to legs. I groaned.

Oh good. I was still alive.

Cautiously, I peeled my eyelids apart. Dunisha's frenzied face appeared before me. When she saw me stir, she breathed a sigh of relief.

"Thank goodness! I thought you had died!"

I grimaced as my head let out a twinge. "I think I might have, just a little," I replied, as I strained to sit upright. "How long was I out?"

"Not long, just a few minutes." She reached a hand around my back to help me into a sitting position.

I thought about her words. While Gilva's domain seemed a bit timeless, it still felt like I was gone for much longer. Interesting.

Also interesting: I still felt like death, even though Gilva had given me a boost. Apparently, she wasn't joking when she told me it was temporary. Which meant that time was a-wasting.

I struggled to stand. Dunisha lent me her arm for support as I hobbled to my unsteady feet. Once I was more or less vertical, I tugged on the arm that was helping me remain upright. "C'mon, let's get going."

"Where?" Confusion laced her reply.

"Time to kick some ass. We have to get to the throne room."

"Now?" Her face was incredulous. "No offense, but I don't see you doing much ass kicking. You can barely stand."

"Yeah, it's a problem." I rubbed my forehead, trying to massage away the headache. It did not work. "But if I don't do it now, chances are good I'm going to die again really soon. And this time it might be more permanent. So, it's now or never."

Dunisha gave me a once-over as she continued to hold onto me. "If you say so."

"Excellent." I waved a hand at the tunnel we were in. "Lead the way."

And so, with Dunisha helping to support my still unsteady body, we made our way slowly up the tunnel incline. It would appear that we had finally found the correct path out of the underground maze. As we progressed, I felt a little better. I surmised that my boost was perhaps simply slow acting, and had taken a while to fully kick in. By the time the tunnel ended in front of a pair of familiar wide double doors, I was well enough to fully stand on my own without any shooting pains.

We both paused on the outside of the doors. I shot a glance at Dunisha, who returned the look.

"Are you ready?" I asked her.

She nodded. "As I'll ever be."

I began to count softly, nodding my head at each number. "One ... two..."

"Three!" That last number we proclaimed quietly in unison. We each grasped a door handle and pushed our respective doors wide open before we marched in with determination.

I'm sure it felt cooler than it looked.

Our forced entry was only seen by one person. And she had been standing on her throne, fondling the mounted antlers lovingly. I grimaced at the odd scene, but Annie had turned swiftly at the intrusion, even as she kept one hand rubbing a tine. She did not look guilty, just extremely annoyed at the interruption.

"You!" she shouted at us as we approached.

"Us!" I yelled back.

We stopped a few feet from her throne. Annie smirked menacingly, swiveling her fleshy body around and carefully maneuvering down from the stone seat. Once back on the ground, she sat with confidence.

"Any cleverness I'd grant you on your escape is forfeit by your complete stupidity for coming here." She grinned mockingly. "As a matter of fact, I was just about to call you in here anyway."

"Oh really? I just bet," I bluffed with exaggerated swagger. I narrowed my eyes at the witch. "How convenient for you."

"Truly, it is." Annie sighed as she lounged on her throne. She smacked her lips together, making a wet popping sound that made me cringe. "I even planned to have a bit of a reunion. Guards!"

This last word was yelled shrilly by her rusty voice. It made me wince. Through a smaller side door that I hadn't noticed until now, two more of her offspring walked in, carrying a limp figure between them. The form weakly raised her head. Though her hair hung down in her face, I knew who she was.

"Wren, are you okay?" I called.

"Of course she is, you silly cat!" Annie admonished me. "She is the key to my freedom. Once I get rid of you, that is."

At my side, Dunisha nudged me and whispered, "Is that the dimension hopper?" I nodded as imperceptibly as possible. The Fae woman whispered to me again, "Then this is our chance to get out of here!"

Before I could react, Dunisha yelled and charged at Annie. Flabbergasted, I watched as she reached a hand out, already unhooking her lower jaw.

Ah, the good old bite-your-enemy's-head-off routine.

Except it didn't go as my Fae companion had planned. Despite Annie's slothful demeanor, the moment Dunisha was within reach, the witch whipped out a hand like a cobra and grabbed the woman around her neck before her jaw grew too wide. Dunisha let out a choked gasp.

With a bored expression, Annie swirled her free fingers over the Fae. Instantly, a golden haze lifted through Dunisha's skull and siphoned over to the clear crystal I had noticed earlier. The crystal sucked the shimmering mist up like a sponge. Within seconds, Dunisha had stopped emitting the haze, and every particle had been vacuumed up by the crystal, which had taken on a warm tint, like a lightbulb, but now looked clear again.

Speaking of lightbulbs, one clicked on in my brain. The crystal was the source of Annie's power. Somehow, she had taken one of the natural crystals, the ones that already sucked up magic, but had perverted it to her own use.

Dunisha's magic fully drained, Annie cast her off to the floor. The Fae woman hit the ground and bounced once, like a rag doll. She stayed prone on the ground, just a couple of feet from me.

I glanced at Annie, who had gone back to lounging as if nothing had happened. Risking her wrath, I rushed to my companion. Her eyes were closed, but they cracked open when I put a hand on her cheek.

"Dunisha?" I asked tentatively.

She smiled wanly. "I tried," she whispered. She had no energy. "Sorry I botched it."

"No, it's okay," I soothed, wracking my brain for a way to save her.

She could not even shake her head, but I could sense that she was telling me not to bother.

"I was living on borrowed time anyway." Her voice was strained. "At least now you know where the magic is stored. In the end, I did help you out."

I let out a tiny sob. Dunisha was rapidly fading before me.

"Thank you," I told her with a watery smile.

She gave me a hint of a smile back. "Thank you for having the best of intentions."

It was the last thing she said before closing her eyes. She did not open them again.

I straightened my body back up, wiping the tears away with an angry fist. My mind was in turmoil. I hadn't known the green-skinned woman for very long, but damn me if she hadn't already wriggled into my heart. Plus, I had never lost someone on my watch, friend or otherwise. I was furious at Annie for breaking my streak. My ass-kicking urge was back with a vengeance.

Annie glanced at the murderous look on my face. "Tut, kitty-cat," she rasped out mockingly. "Keep your claws in. You are in no position to threaten me."

I glared at her. "I think I'm in a fine position, thank you very much."

"Oh?" Annie turned her head toward Wren, who was still being held up by the two guards. "I think you are forgetting about our little friend over there."

My heart lurched. But my face did not show my fear. "I think you're bluffing. You need Wren to live for your own needs. You said so yourself."

Annie threw her head back and laughed raucously. My right eye twitched. The witch stopped laughing just as quickly as she started, her changing mood giving me mental whiplash.

"Are you really that stupid?" she taunted me. She waved a fleshy hand at Dunisha's corpse. "You were in a better position before this thing gave me her magic essence. But now, I'm free no matter what."

I said nothing, only stared.

Annie did not need prompting, however. "You see, I can either leave with Wren now, but only after you die, or I can kill you both and make my own portal, since you two will have given me just enough magical oomph to get the job done."

"So, I'm to die either way?" I clarified.

"Yes." Annie smacked her lips again as she smirked at me. "Your death is necessary. After all, you are the only one that can stop me. I have to get you out of the way first."

"Makes sense, I suppose," I agreed grudgingly. "But what makes you think I'm going to go so easily?"

She waved a hand in Wren's direction but didn't bother looking at her. "Because you are too soft-hearted to doom an innocent little girl." Annie then took said hand and pierced her fingertip on the sharp point of her magic crystal. A tiny drop of blood oozed down the crystalline side. She withdrew something from the folds of her dress, muttered something I didn't understand over it, and dropped the object.

It was Hail Mary.

Hail Mary floated in the air again. It turned a lazy half-circle, pointing its blade directly at Wren. Annie wiggled her bloody finger, and the knife took a small leap forward, like a rabid dog on a leash.

My heart dropped. Annie undoubtedly knew that because the blade had already tasted Wren's blood, the knife's next move would most likely be fatal. I had been outmaneuvered by my own weapon.

Annie wriggled her hand questioningly in the air, like a dead fish, and raised a barely-there eyebrow at me.

I panicked. "Okay, you're right!"

Annie lowered her bloody hand with a satisfied smile on her lips. "Well, then, get on with it."

She wasn't going to kill me herself? "What am I supposed to do?"

Annie huffed in frustration. "Are you so dense that you forgot your little problem? All you have to do is turn into a cat. I do believe electrocution is a pretty quick way to go. I could have made this so much harder for you."

"Oh, well, thank you for that favor," I muttered.

Wren's voice rose weakly from her spot. "No, Cressida! Don't!"

I turned to her in sadness. "I promised your brother."

She let out a small sob and lowered her head.

Annie harrumphed. "Tick-tock, time's a-wasting."

I glowered at her. Taking a deep breath, I closed my eyes. I recalled what Gilva said. "Surrender," I breathed quietly to myself.

"I will not." Annie must have heard, and thought I was talking to her.

I ignored her. Taking one last cleansing breath, I started the shimmer. As before, it was difficult to transition through it, but I pushed at the stickiness, willing it to let me in.

Be the shimmer.

After two seconds, much longer than it usually took, I opened my eyes with an odd mixture of relief at being a cat again, and dread at the knowledge that I was about to be killed.

Unless ...

I could already feel the mounting energy around me. The static in the air made my fur stand up. Annie cackled with glee, anticipating the moment she got to watch me be snuffed out of existence.

I had to time this perfectly.

"Be the shimmer, be the shimmer," I chanted to myself, aware that no one would understand me.

The roiling static coalesced around my feline form. The impending doom came to a resounding head.

I had no clue what I was doing. But in that moment, I gave myself up, either for success or failure. I surrendered.

Just as I felt the power of the spell coalesce and materialize into the lightning bolt, I shimmered.

CHAPTER 27

I shimmered, giving in to the sensation.
I used the stickiness and held on to it.

I had no eyes, but I saw all.

I had no body, but I simultaneously felt nothing and everything at once.

I was nothing.

I was everything.

I *became* the shimmer.

The lightning bolt struck the shimmer and continued to hammer pure energy into it.

But, as a being of pure energy myself, it did not consume me. I consumed it.

In my new state of consciousness, I saw and heard Annie shriek in fury as she rose from her throne. Instinctively, I knew it was a bad idea to let her do much else. So, I threw some of my extra energy her way in the form of a mini lightning bolt.

Simultaneously, I made sure to throw bolts at the guards holding Wren. I had tremendous precision with my throws.

Lastly, I hurled a big bolt of energy at Annie's beloved crystal.

Annie screamed in pain and crumpled in front of her throne, clutching at her chest where I had zapped her. Both guards also fell, releasing Wren, who fell to her knees but looked in wonder at my new state of being. And the clear crystal, the reason for Annie's success in this damned dimension, exploded into a million pieces, blowing debris all the way across the room.

And through it all, I continued to suck in the magically made lightning, consuming every last bit.

Until the spell Annie had put on me ran out, that is.

Once the last of the loose energy had been devoured by me, I let go of the stickiness and finished my transformation into my human body. It was that simple.

Feeling amazingly refreshed, I rushed to Wren's side. She grasped my hand and got to her feet shakily.

"How?" she asked me with wonder.

I shrugged. "New trick," I hazarded. I glanced at the two downed guards. "Are you okay?"

She nodded, also giving her guards a glance with distaste. "Let's get out of here."

"Wait," I dislodged myself from her grasp. There was one more thing to do.

I meandered over toward Annie, tiny pieces of exploded crystal crunching beneath my boots. She had gone completely still, lying prostrate on her back with her legs at odd angles beneath her. Her arm and face on one side had been nicked by countless crystal shards, and many of the cuts bled freely. The pallor under her skin, however, was quite pale. I couldn't tell if she was dead, although I assumed she wasn't. After all, an immortal being might be impossible to kill.

Cautiously, I approached her body. There, around her neck, lay the locket, which glinted lavender through the cracks. Wren's soul was still inside, waiting to be freed from its prison.

When the witch stayed unmoving at my approach, I grew braver. Reaching a hand down, I grasped the locket and readied myself to tug it off her neck.

Annie's hand shot out and grabbed me by the wrist in an iron hold. I gasped and tried to wrench my arm back, but I couldn't budge from her grip. Annie opened her eyes and stared deep into mine, her blood-pocked face a furious mask.

"You stupid cat," she hissed. I watched in pure terror as she lifted her other hand, which held something tiny between bloody thumb and forefinger.

A single cat hair.

Annie's voice grew mystically deep, loud, and clear in the cavernous room. "I curse you," she boomed.

"*I curse you, Descendant of Glivver, that from this day forward, and for the rest of your life, you will never fall in love with a man. Without true love, the line of Glivver will die with you!*"

The single hair in her fingers burst into flames. At the same time, a deep pain lanced my chest as the words she spoke etched into my mind with certainty. I gasped again, clutching my chest with my free hand. I expected to find a grievous wound, a gaping maw of flesh and bone, but upon tactile inspection I found that my skin remained whole.

I looked at Annie's face again with panic. She smiled wickedly at my expression and forcefully released my wrist, nearly flinging me back in the process. But I at least had the wherewithal to hold on to the locket, and with the last of my strength, I wrenched it loose from her neck.

I scooted backward on my butt to get some distance from the witch. Annie found my terror utterly entertaining, and lay her head back on the floor, laughing into the air. I looked at my wrist. It was red and sore from her grasp, and she had smeared her own blood all over it with her grip.

The sight of this red stain panicked me anew. Witch's blood was a powerful thing.

Annie stopped laughing long enough to yell at me, "You're doomed! I did it! Once you are gone, I'm free!" Her voice was no longer booming but sounded strained instead.

She continued to cackle and spew insults my way, but seemed to lack the energy to move off of the ground. I slowly stood, noting a lingering ache within my chest, a metaphysical wound upon my soul, I realized. A curse.

I was cursed.

But I also noted that now was not the time to dwell upon that fact. Now was the time to escape.

I hobbled back over to Wren. She had watched the whole episode, and now turned to me with fear-laden eyes. But she reached out for me. Grasping her in a hug, I gritted out, "Get us out of here."

She complied instantly.

CHAPTER 28

M y vision refocused into the sight of the familiar and comforting living room in Fleurette's house. Releasing Wren from my grasp, I fell to my knees as the room spun a bit. I felt hands on my back but couldn't tell who was there.

"Cressida?" Someone, possibly Fleurette, called my name. I shook my head, closing my eyes. I didn't want to talk.

Instead, I released my death grip on the locket, placidly placing it away from my body with an outstretched hand. And then I shimmered into a cat.

I could hear the voices around me, but paid the human speak no mind. I would deal with them later. For now, I needed to rest.

A large wet nose brushed against my head. On my other side, I heard a familiar purr. My mother.

"Come on, Cressida, let's get you to bed," she said.

I let my partner and my mother guide me away from the human activity and into the spare room. Jumping up on the bed, I curled myself into a tiny ball of fluff, tucking my tail over my face to block out the world.

The bed dipped as Grimm jumped up next to me. He positioned himself silently at my back. This small act instantly put me at ease. To make it even better, Mom stretched out before me, resting her nose on my neck and purring loudly. Sandwiched between the two animals I cared for the most, I drifted off into a deep and dreamless sleep.

It was dark in the room when I awoke. I had barely moved from my curled-up position, and I now felt cramped. I stretched both sets of legs out as far as I could, arching my back as I flopped to one side. I yawned widely.

"Feeling better?" my partner chuckled by way of greeting. He was still positioned at my back, I noted with contentment.

I washed my face, focusing on the area around my eyes. "Grimm. You are a sight for sore eyes."

He chuckled again. "I'm a black dog in a dark room. And you are rubbing your eyes right now. How much of me can you really see?"

My ears flattened, mostly in a mocking way. "Enough."

Grimm gave me a big lick upside the head. I shook my head to fluff the fur back out. Amusement rolled off Grimm.

"I'm glad you are back. I was worried."

"Me too." I glanced around. "Where's Mom?"

Grimm yawned. "Your mother said if she stayed here any longer, she'd smell like a dog. She left you in my care a little while ago."

I flicked the tip of my tail. That sounded just like something she would say.

I glanced around the room, noting that it was indeed dark outside. "What time is it?"

Grimm gave out a small snort. "Time is a human thing. You know that."

"I also know that you have become very adept at telling it when there's food involved," I retorted caustically. "So, when was the last time you ate?"

Grimm groaned as he flopped his large body over onto his side. I sat up and stretched my spine upward at the shoulders.

"It's night," he finally answered as I began to give myself a thorough grooming. "The humans are still awake, though."

At the mention of the humans, my heart gave a little lurch. "Is everything ... did Wren ...?" Apparently, words were hard in my state.

Grimm nosed my face to shush me. "Wren is fine," he assured me. "They already healed her soul."

I sighed heavily with relief. Head bumping Grimm's nose tip with affection, I asked, "Did they talk about anything yet?"

"A little," he admitted, "but I stayed here with you. Besides, you know it's hard for me to follow conversations, especially when you aren't there. I figured I'd get a better picture with you present."

I went back to grooming. "I need to talk to them, but first thing's first."

I cleaned every inch of my furry body with the utmost care and attention to detail, from the tips of my eyebrow whiskers to the cracks of my toes. At last, when I felt sufficiently clean for the first time in what felt like ages, I jumped off the bed.

Before I transformed, though, I turned back to Grimm, who was still on the bed, watching me. "Are you coming?"

He snorted and stood. "I was fairly comfortable. But if I must." He jumped off the bed behind me.

I chuckled at his obvious sarcasm. I knew that my partner would rather be neutered than miss out on this story.

I shimmered, noting with pleasure that the stickiness of the transformation was once again absent. In the back of my mind, I wondered if the sensation had been caused by Annie's lightning spell, or if it was my body's way of preparing me for the magic that had ultimately saved my life and thwarted Annie.

Once I was human, I took a moment to appreciate the vast improvement of my countenance since the last time. My body was pain-free, my mind unfoggy. I patted my vest and trousers, noting with relish the fresh, clean feel of my clothing.

I also noted some unfamiliar bulges in the pockets of my vest. As I ventured into the dimly lit hallway, I fumbled my hands into said pockets. My fingers brushed against a hard surface, warmed by my body heat. I pulled the object out.

A stab of memory jolted me at the sight of the small blue bottle in my hands. Only now did I remember that I had stuffed various vials into my pockets while Dunisha and I were holed up in the potions room.

At the thought of my deceased cohort, another stab jolted me, but this one of pain and regret. She had given her life to me, a risky endeavor, but surely one that had paid off. I would never forget her sacrifice.

I fished out five little bottles from my pocket, all variations of blue and green. I stared at the colorful objects indecisively, before deciding that the best thing to do would be to gift them to Fleurette. I briskly walked into the kitchen and set them on the shelf with Fleurette's many vials. My stolen goods seemed to blend right into Fleurette's collection. Satisfied, I ventured out into the living room, Grimm on my heels.

Fal and Wren were snuggled together on the sofa facing me. Their eyes simultaneously lit up upon my entrance. Fleurette, who took up her favorite armchair opposite them, must have seen their reaction. She swiveled around in her chair, peering over the edge.

"Cressida," she greeted me with a glad smile, "you're up!"

I returned her smile, my heart feeling lighter for the presence of my human allies. Fleurette stood as I approached and engulfed me in a hug. Wren, while weariness marred her young face, still jumped up to hug me with enthusiasm. Only Fal refrained, but he grinned sheepishly and gave me a friendly head nod.

Once my mobbing was through, I made my way to the other chair next to my witch friend. Despite being asleep for—I checked my pocket watch—nine hours or so, the act of sinking into the plush chair still felt so good.

Wren had settled back into her brother, leaning her head sleepily against his side, but still looking the happiest I had ever seen her. Fleurette hadn't sat back down after hugging me but had slinked off into the kitchen. She now returned with a giant turkey sandwich, which she presented grandly into my lap.

"Thanks," I uttered with appreciation before swiftly consuming the sandwich. I hadn't realized just how hungry I was until the smell of oven roasted meat struck my nostrils.

Once my plate was empty, Fleurette turned her whole attention on me. "It's getting late, Cress dear, but we were waiting up for you. Do you have the energy to tell your tale?"

I gulped, the sandwich bits inside of me giving a minor lurch. But I mentally shook my head at my fear. "Yes, can do."

And so, I relived my ordeal by talking about it. Wren had already filled Fal and Fleurette in on some of it, but since she had been asleep for much of the time, her tale was not as action packed. She had also apparently not understood much of what happened once she had been brought back to the throne room. When I got to that part of my story, she interjected a lot, with, "Oh, that's why you were afraid of the knife?" and "I couldn't tell what you were anymore; I explained you as a ball of shimmering dust motes." It was evident that she was riveted by the new perspective on events.

I kept my cool throughout, detaching my emotions from the telling. Once I got to the part of Annie grabbing me, however, my voice choked.

"Cressida?" Fleurette reached a hand out to touch my arm. My name on her lips held concern.

"Sorry." I took a deep breath and purposefully didn't look at anybody. Grimm, who had heard the change in my demeanor, instantly got up from his position beside my chair and placed his great shaggy head in my lap. I stroked his ear, feeling his support strengthen my resolve.

I continued with less warble in my tone, "Annie ... did something. A curse."

Fleurette sucked in a breath.

I could see Wren nodding out of the corner of my eye. "I heard it. It was hard *not* to hear it. Madam was really loud."

Fleurette patted my arm again. Her lovely brown eyes held great concern. "Do you want to talk about it?"

I contemplated her question but shook my head. "I think I need a little time. To process it."

My friend nodded her agreement. "It's late. Wren, you look like you're about to drop. Why don't you take the guest bed tonight? And Fal, you can sleep in my bed."

Fal sat up a little straighter. "Oh no, Ma'am, I couldn't—"

"You can and you will. I'll crash on the sofa for tonight with the nonhumans." She pursed her lips at the young man. "And it's Fleurette, not 'Ma'am,' to you."

Fal at least knew when to stop arguing. "Alright."

The siblings slowly got up to make their separate ways to bed. Fleurette turned to me. "To be continued," she said with a concerned air before shuffling off to gather bedding supplies for herself.

I sighed, knowing my friend wouldn't drop it. And, as much as I wanted to pretend that the curse hadn't happened, I knew it was important to discuss the ramifications.

Shimmering down to my cat body, I settled in one of the armchairs. Despite having slept much of the day away, exhaustion still plagued me. I fell asleep before Fleurette made it back to the sofa.

Sleep, however, didn't stay with me. I awoke suddenly, sure that only a couple of hours had passed. The house was dark and silent.

Wait, almost silent. Someone was crying, muffled but distinct.

I stretched my body upward, arching my spine to its highest peak, before jumping off the chair. I barely missed landing on Grimm's head, as he had chosen to curl his big body around my chair.

"Cress?" He opened his eyes sleepily but didn't raise his head up.

"Sorry, partner," I mumbled. "Go back to sleep. I think I hear Wren."

Grimm let out a sigh, the air from his nostrils skittering across the wooden floor. He closed his eyes again, content to allow me to investigate alone.

I padded down the hallway to the spare bedroom. The door was shut. The sound of sobbing was much more distinct now that I was just outside of the room.

I transformed, grabbed the knob, and slowly turned it. The door's hinges squeaked ever so slightly as I pushed the door a fraction open.

"Wren?" I whispered into the dark interior.

The girl grew silent suddenly. I almost felt bad for intruding on her privacy, as touched with melancholy as it was. She let out a sniffle. "Cressida?"

"It's me." I opened the door a little wider. "Can I come in?"

Wren sniffled again. I imagined I could hear her wiping at her face and nose hurriedly. But she replied, "Sure."

At her invite, I quietly pushed myself into the room, mindful of squeaking hinges and protesting floorboards. I made my way carefully to the bedside, sitting on the edge. Once seated, I asked, "Are you okay?"

Wren gave another sniff, this one sounding a bit drier than the last two. "I keep having nightmares," she admitted. "Even though I was asleep for most of it, my mind keeps coming up with awful stuff that could have happened while I was out. Her face keeps popping up. Like she's looking for me."

"Oh, sweetie," I cooed, for the first time feeling an almost maternal protectiveness for the child. I reached my hand out and grasped hers, silently issuing some of my strength into her. "I know in the past your dreams have been more than dreams, but we severed her connection to you. She can't find you again."

More tears fell. Their salty tang dampened my senses.

"I know. But I'm still scared."

"Me too, kid. Me too." I gave her hand a squeeze.

"Cressida?" Wren's voice sounded so small and lost, and haltingly hesitant. "Would you ... stay with me? Just for tonight?"

My heart gave a little squeeze at the request. I liked this Wren. She was so much better than the manipulative puppet.

"Of course," I answered without hesitation. In fact, I might have a trick up my sleeve to help you get back to sleep."

Wren's relief was palpable. "Thanks," she replied with a yawn. "You're a good friend."

Aww.

I scooched my body onto the bed more, and then transformed into my true self. Wren had wriggled back down into the covers, making herself comfortable. I waited until she had situated herself, and then carefully I crept over to the hollow made by the curve of her stomach and legs. I situated myself into a ball, nestled against her. And then I began to purr a soft, peaceful rhythm.

Wren sighed with contentment.

"Thanks, Cressida," she murmured. She lifted her hand to stroke my fur. Truth be told, I had never allowed a human to pet me before. My old self would have felt it as a violation of my personal space. But Wren's gentle touch felt very nice. Perhaps in the future I'd let her pet me again.

Wren gave one last stroke before curling up her arm. Her breaths evened out shortly.

With a full heart, I, too, drifted off to the sound of my purrs.

CHAPTER 29

I was back in the whiteness, except instead of it feeling so vast, it seemed somehow confined. Not in a suffocating way, but cozy.

The last thing I remembered was purring Wren to sleep. How did I get here?

And there was Glivver again, her silver fur sleek and shining in this comfortable void. She cocked her head to the side in a perplexed manner upon seeing me.

"Wait," I said, mirroring her confusion. "Did I die again?" Despite this harrowing thought, I was still at peace, as if the whiteness kept me calm and levelheaded no matter what.

Glivver laughed. "No, silly, but I *am* surprised to see you again."

"This has never happened before?"

"Never." She stretched her front legs out and gracefully padded toward me on dainty feet. "I do believe you are dreaming. I have never been visited during dreams. This is a new experience for me as well."

I contemplated her words. "Maybe my near-death experience somehow ... connected us together. Like opening a door that had previously been unlocked?"

"It's as good an explanation as any," Glivver agreed. She rubbed her head against mine affectionately. "By the way, I'm very proud of you. You did so well!"

Even through the uplifting and calming effects of this place, my heart gave a tiny lurch. "Except for that last bit."

Glivver's expression turned serious. "Granddaughter, there was no way of knowing. Destiny is a funny thing. Yours is still being written. And, you should know, it is not the end for you. You are a bright and intelligent cat. And you have powerful allies, as it turns out. Keep faith. You will get through this."

Her words soothed my troubles. "Thank you. I suppose you were right before, so I will listen to you about this too."

"Like I said, intelligent. Freya forbid what would have happened if Mildred had been the one to go up against Annie!"

"If I am allowed to visit you in my dreams, what would you like me to address you as?" I asked her, curious about this new and highly unusual relationship.

She gave her unnaturally blue eyes a slow blink. "Oh, no need to get fancy. I know I call you "granddaughter," which I hope you do not mind, but seeing as how I don't look like an ancient crone, I am not a fan of being called 'grandmother.' For now, I think Glivver will do just fine. Or Gilva, if I happen to be in my human form."

"I don't mind you calling me granddaughter, but feel free to call me Cressida, too."

"It's a deal, Cressida." She began grooming the top of my head, purring softly. "And, just so you know, I will always be happy to have you visit me, but please keep in mind that I am a relic of the past. I do not want you to lose sight of yourself by coming here. Do not ignore your life over someone who has already lived hers."

"I think I understand." Her purring was making me sleepy, which seemed ludicrous given that I was already asleep and dreaming. However, the warm fuzzies of the moment were pleasant, so I went with it. I closed my eyes and settled into a comfy position.

"Sleep well, child," I heard my ancestor tell me, before I drifted off.

Sleep well I did. As a matter of fact, once I left Glivver, I didn't have any more dreams, and I awoke in the early dawn light, refreshed and light of heart. I was still on the spare bed, nestled against Wren's sleeping form, although she had turned the other way at some point.

I stood and stretched, and then quietly leapt off the bed and padded out into the main room.

Fleurette was awake on the couch, although she must have just awoken, as she was still nestled down in the blankets. She smiled when she saw me enter.

Grimm was flat on the floor, long legs sprawled. I crept up to his head and batted his nose, careful to keep my claws sheathed. He gave a tiny start and let out a rumbling groan as he stretched his legs even further out.

"Morning, Cress."

"It is, isn't it?" I replied cheekily. "C'mon, lazybones, let's go outside."

Grimm took a deep breath, his shaggy chest rising impressively. Then he got his legs under him and pushed himself up to his feet. He gave his body a little shake once he did.

Fleurette finally began to extract herself from her blanket cocoon. She sighed and stretched too, before getting up to open the door for us. She was obliging that way.

Grimm and I pranced out into the front area, each going our separate ways to do our individual business. It was a glorious morning, with a faint pattern of dew on the ground but a promise in the warming air of another late summer sunny day. From nearby trees and shrubs, birds added a symphony of trills and tweets.

Perhaps, though, it was only glorious because I was alive to see it. I waved the thought away, preferring to bask in happier thoughts.

Once I had come back from my secret potty spot (it wasn't in any of Fleurette's flower beds—she would have killed me), I turned back to the front porch for morning ablutions. The sun was just starting to rise, and a small sliver of light bloomed on the wooden beams. I chose that spot to start my grooming.

Within fifteen minutes I was wrapping up my cleansing ritual. The front door opened with perfect timing, and Fleurette, wrapped in her old ratty robe, shuffled out of her house, balancing a cup of coffee and a plate of toast in one hand.

I shimmered, feeling fresh as a daisy, and wrangled the plate of toast from her carefully, to make it easier for her to sit. She smiled at me as she settled down on the top of the steps. I sat next to her, placing the toast in my lap for a moment before offering it back to her.

She nodded her head towards the proffered plate. "Thanks, but that's for you."

I glanced at the toast, which glistened with melted butter. My stomach let out a gurgle of approval. I took a giant bite. "Thanks," I mouthed around the delicious toast.

Fleurette smiled at my uncouth manners and sipped her coffee. "The Ramberts are still sleeping. I figured they need all the rest they can get."

I vocalized my agreement as I inhaled my toast. Fleurette let me eat in silence. Her eyes scanned her property, noting my dog companion as he patrolled the area with gusto and occasionally marked something with his own unique odor. And by that, I meant lifting his leg and peeing on everything.

I let out a grunt. "Dogs."

Fleurette took another dainty sip. "Cats do it too."

I scoffed. "I certainly don't!"

"Tomcats certainly do. Remember that ginger fellow that used to frequent the garden? My back shed smelled like piss for months."

"That's because tomcats are disgusting," I pointed out matter-of-factly.

Fleurette raised her eyebrows at me. "That's your own species you are bad-mouthing, you know."

I nodded as I chewed on the last bite of toast. I swallowed. "And that's why I'm allowed to say it. Tomcats are gross. All leather skin, jowls, and let's not forget the barbs on the penis. I thank my lucky stars that I will only be reproducing in my human form."

As the last sentence left my mouth, my heart lurched. Would I be able to reproduce at all? Time to come clean. "Speaking of that last bit ..." I sighed.

Fleurette focused her attention on me. "The curse?"

I gulped and nodded, a flare of panic racing through my chest.

She cocked her head to the side, examining me. "Are you certain it is a curse? Could she have just been trying to scare you?"

The words Annie spoke thundered in my brain as I thought about them. I opened my mouth to let them out. "*I curse you,*

Descendant of Glivver, that from this day forward, and for the rest of your life, you will never fall in love with a man. Without true love, the line of Glivver will die with you!"

"Hmm," Fleurette said. "It's etched into your soul, isn't it? I'm afraid you are right, dear. That's a curse if I ever heard one."

I groaned. "So, I'm doomed." I stated flatly, letting my head fall into my hands with a huff.

"Not necessarily." My friend's voice had a wry edge to it. I lifted my head to peek at her. She was watching me closely. "Curses, of course, are not good things, but they also aren't set in stone. There can be ... loopholes."

"Loopholes?" I felt a tiny glimmer of hope.

Fleurette nodded. "The most obvious answer is that you are already in love with someone. I know it's a bit personal, but Cressida, is there anyone out there that you may have feelings for?"

I scrunched my mouth to the side in thought. Unbidden, a mental image of Gavin St. Cloud floated into my brain. But the thought that I could possibly be in love with him, of all people, repelled my sensibilities. I waved his image away and shook my head.

"Sorry, no."

Fleurette shrugged her shoulders. "It was worth a shot. Okay, the next most obvious thing, then. Usually, the loophole is in the wording of the curse. Can you repeat the curse again?"

I did, slowly. Fleurette's eyes glazed over in thought as she listened. When I finished, she nodded.

"Off the top of my head, the line about never falling in love with a man sounds promising. What if ... the man you should fall in love with is not a man yet?"

"Are you insinuating that I'm a ... cougar?" I half-joked.

Fleurette chuckled. At least she found me humorous. "Think about it. You are still quite young, and if you spend the majority of your time as a human, you'll hardly age. So, if you meet someone less mature than you, fall in love, and then he becomes a man, that breaks the curse, right?"

"Fleurette, I don't care how you spin it. It makes me, a grown woman, sound like a dirty lech trying to seduce a youngster. That's just ickville."

My friend huffed a little. "Cressida, we are dealing with magic variables that don't usually factor in. I'm not telling you to "go seduce a youngster." Many times, true love is built upon friendship. I'm asking you to have an open mind about these things. Take Fal, for instance. If he were a few years older, would you say he might be a candidate?"

"Okay, I will seriously think about it." I closed my eyes and thought of Fal, who I had only known for a couple of days. Who clearly harbored a bit of a crush on me. Who was sweet and nice, and ... "Nope." I said aloud with a small headshake. "I like Fal, but I feel more of a sisterly affection for him if I feel anything. No matchmaking there for me."

"It was worth a shot." Fleurette became quiet, resuming the consumption of her cooling coffee. She had an odd look on her face but didn't say anything else.

I lowered my eyebrows at her. "What?"

"Hmm?" She played dumb. "I didn't say anything."

I rolled my eyes. "But you want to. C'mon, spill it."

She sighed and stopped hiding her face with her coffee mug. "Okay, but remember, we are just brainstorming here."

"You're reluctant after coming up with the teenager matchmaking idea?" I scoffed. "Now I *have* to hear it."

"Okay, what if ..." She paused as if to gather strength. "It's not a man because it's a different gender?"

I let out a little laugh. "Huh? But that would mean ..." I trailed off when I met Fleurette's eyes. They looked searching, wistful. Lonely.

In the almost two years that I had known Fleurette, she had never had a boyfriend. Never had a date, even. My mind traveled back to a conversation we had not even a week ago.

"I mean, look at you! Here you are older than me, at thirty-one, and still single. It's not like you are rushing all over Gaia's green world trying to find a man!"

"Well, that's a little different."

"What makes it different?"

"Because this is a small town and nobody is right for me here, and I don't have the chance to get out and see the world like you do. So, it looks like the single life is for me."

"That doesn't mean you'll be single forever. If it's fated to be, Mr. Right will find you."

"I wish I had your optimism."

I was such an idiot. She had practically spelled it out to me, but I had been oblivious.

"Oh, I see." I said carefully. She still stared into my eyes, almost beseechingly. I shook my head. "No, that's not the answer."

She dropped her gaze then, nodding at my words but with an air of sadness about her.

I hastily added, "Not because I'm against it. I don't care, love is love. But it's not an option for me personally."

"Fair enough."

She was being standoffish now.

"Fleurette? I'm sorry I never put two and two together before. Call me dense if you like. I really don't care what your leanings are. But I have to ask. Are you ... attracted ... to me?"

She let out a little laugh and buried her head in her hands. "Great Gaia," she groaned before straightening and meeting my eye with a twinkle. "I'm not saying I wouldn't be curious if you gave me the green light, but no. I value you as a friend only. You aren't exactly my type."

"Ouch." I teased with a smile. "Just as well, though. I don't think a different gender is the solution to our problem. I have to be able to reproduce with my true love, after all."

"True." She became serious again. "But Cress, dear, you truly don't mind? About me?"

"Pshaw." I waved my hand to dismiss her insecurity. "It makes no difference to me. You are still my gorgeous, talented, and loving friend, even if I know now that you think I'm hideous."

She slapped my shoulder lightly in response. "I never said that. You are a stunning creature, you vain animal. I just prefer darker hair."

"I see. I'll be sure to be on the lookout for someone more suitable, then. Don't blame me if the raven-haired beauties start flocking to your door."

She sighed theatrically but gave me a sunny smile as she nudged my shoulder with hers affectionately. "Thanks."

"Any time, friend. Never be afraid to be yourself with me. I know I won't be."

Our conversation was interrupted by two young voices in the living room.

Fleurette sighed. "Sounds like the siblings are up. I should go make them some breakfast too." She gathered my empty plate and her mug. "We need to come up with a plan for them as well. And Cress?" She looked at me with a sad smile. "Don't lose hope. We will find a way around the curse. That's a promise."

She got up from her spot then, and a cold emptiness engulfed my right side at her absence. Despite that, there was a new warmth in my chest that lifted my spirits.

Hope.

CHAPTER 30

Despite the seemingly tidy conclusion that my defeat of Annie had wrought, there was still one very big loose end to tie up. And they were sitting with us at dinner.

"It's been three days since we broke Annie's spell. We have to turn you in, Fal."

This came from Fleurette, who uttered those uncharacteristic words with a heavy sigh. Although just moments before the kitchen table had been alive with small talk and the scrape of forks against plates, now the room was silent.

I let the silence envelop us for an awkward moment before yelling, "What the hell, Flo?"

Fal and Wren also began protesting. While my outburst was in anger, the siblings had resorted to whines and pleas.

"Did we outstay our welcome?" Wren asked tearfully.

I didn't blame them. These last three days were probably the happiest, and most stable times for the duo since losing their parents.

Fleurette raised a hand to shoulder height to silence us. "You misunderstand me. What I mean is, we must untangle the legal web Fal has been placed in."

"Why can't we just keep hiding here?" Fal asked.

My friend smiled at the teen. "I was hoping for a more permanent solution. I would be too fearful of somebody eventually sniffing you out. Besides"—she turned to glance at me—"if it was found out that Cressida, a reputable bounty hunter, had a manager who was harboring the very criminal she had set out to find, her livelihood would be ruined."

Fal nodded, twisting his lips to the side in thought. "Makes sense. Should we leave, then?"

I began to protest, but Fleurette cut me off. "Of course not. In fact, the whole reason I want to take you to the courthouse, is a rather selfish desire to ..." She paused.

"What?" Fal asked, intrigued.

Fleurette gazed at him. "I've been alone in this house ever since I moved in. Yes, my father lives down the road, and yes, I sometimes have the company of Cressida and Grimm. But I also feel like there's a hole in my life. Having you and Wren here these last few days? The hole felt filled. Not only that, but I am a witch without an apprentice. Fal, you show great potential, not just in herbal magic, but in the more powerful arts as well."

Fal's eyes widened. "I do? You would want to teach me?"

Fleurette nodded. She turned her eyes on Wren. "Both of you, actually. But Wren, your particular flavor of magic is rare. I may not personally have the tools to help you succeed, but I believe I can at least give you the guidance you need, and at the very least I have connections to other powerful witches through GOGS." Fleurette took a breath. "In other words, Fal and Wren, I would love to become your official guardian. I know I can never take the place of your parents, but I would love to be given the chance to have you as my wards and give you a home with love, magical benefits, and stability. I can only hope that you two would also desire this."

She nearly flinched when her small speech was met with silence. My heart went out to my friend, who had bared her soul to these kids and faced potential rejection.

Thankfully, the silence was extremely short lived, as both Fal and Wren spewed forth words simultaneously.

"Of course, we want to stay with you!"

"This is the best thing ever!"

"Oh, thank you, Fleurette!"

"You're the best!"

Wren leapt to her feet and practically flew onto Fleurette's lap. Fal, being older and more reserved, stayed seated, but the smile on his face shone with gratitude.

Fleurette laughed as she hugged Wren back. "All right, all right," she chuckled, "but there's still that little wrinkle to address."

I had stayed silent during all of this, observing the growing happiness with a light heart. The mood turned somber again at Fleurette's words. I glanced at Grimm, who was sitting beside me. He stared back with serious yellow eyes. I knew he would be doing his best to follow the conversation, even though he could only pick out a few words. Body language and moods spoke volumes, however, and I knew he had no trouble following the gist of this conversation.

Refocusing my attention back to the humans, I cleared my throat. "I guess I have to be the bad guy in this situation?"

Fleurette shook her head, her fluffy brown hair bouncy with the movement. "Bad guy, no. But I will need your assistance. And a little outside help as well. I already contacted one of my fellow members who specializes in legal aid. We are meeting tomorrow to go over our strategy. After that, I think it's best we get this over with as soon as possible."

True to her word, Fleurette left early the next day and was out until late afternoon. When she returned, she seemed in good spirits.

"Lawrence will be meeting us at the courthouse at 4:45," she declared. I had no clue who this Lawrence was, but I decided to stow my questions for now. Fleurette continued, "Let's eat a quick dinner and be off. Fal, Wren, you two will be riding in the wagon with Grimm. Cress, dear, you and I will be in the driver's seat."

After that statement, it was a flurry of preparing a hasty meal, consuming it, hitching up Humbert, and trotting down Rabbit Hole Road at a less than relaxing pace.

Once we were underway, I could not hold back my curiosity anymore. "What's the plan, Flo?"

She chuckled. "You know I hate that nickname."

"It's a good thing I only use it on you when I am vaguely annoyed with you. So, spill. What's the plan?"

Fleurette laughed. "Fine! Thanks to the preparation that my fellow GOGS member went through, we have a fairly solid case on our hands. But there's a side quest we are on. I need to know who exactly put the bounty out. You said that you had asked for the information, and they were being secretive about it?"

I nodded when she turned her head in my direction.

She pursed her lips as she studied me. "Feel like letting your true self out and doing a bit of sleuthing while I plead my case?"

"Sounds like fun."

Lawrence turned out to be a sandy haired man in his mid-forties with a bit of a paunch and a friendly smile. He was a GOG who also had a law degree. Lucky us.

After letting the siblings and Grimm out of the back of the wagon, we six marched into the courthouse just a few minutes shy of its public closing time. I assumed Fleurette and Lawrence had timed our arrival on purpose, for the hallways were mostly empty. The evening guard tried to keep his expression set to neutral, but I could still sense the aggravation of having to check a large group in at closing time.

As he waved his orb over Fleurette in front of me, I began to reach into my boot by habit, only to remember that Hail Mary no longer resided in its usual spot. I sighed and straightened.

Having been checked in, we made our way to the bounty office, pushing the door open and filing into the small room. I hadn't bothered to ask the guard who was working the office today, because he clearly wasn't in the mood for banter. I had a brief amount of time to wonder who it was before a hard, feminine voice filled the tiny room.

"*Get that dog out of here!*"

Ah. It was Miss Clark.

I opened the door again to usher my partner out to the hallway like a good model citizen. Hopefully, that would win us brownie points for what my friend was about to pull.

Fal and Wren, both looking nervous, sat on the waiting bench by the wall, which opened up a little more walking room for the three remaining bodies. I surged forward and took my place at the gilded window.

"Miss Clark, how good to see you again!" I gushed rather uncharacteristically.

"Miss Curtain, we close in two minutes. This had better be good." The clerk's acerbic tone made me internally flinch. I pressed on.

"Oh, it is. You see, I have completed this bounty." I slid the folded-up paper under the cage.

She sniffed with disapproval, unfolded the paper, read it, and glanced first at me, and then at the siblings, over the paper's top.

"Miss Curtain," she began with that stuffy tone as she slid the rumpled paper back under the slot for me to take back, "since this office is about to close, you need to follow after-hours protocol and take this boy to the jailhouse."

"Oh, but I'm afraid this case is not typical in the slightest," Fleurette butted in, stepping forward as I pocketed the paper.

Miss Clark gave my friend a once-over, keeping a slight look of disgust on her pallid features. "And you are?"

Fleurette stepped fully up to the counter. "Fleurette Williams, Miss Curtain's manager. And this"—she gestured to Lawrence, who also stepped up to the just behind Fleurette—"is Mr. Lawrence Farthing, Esquire."

The clerk paled ever so slightly but I had to give her credit for not breaking her hard demeanor. "And?" she demanded.

Lawrence pushed to the front. "Madam, there is a grave matter of dispute over the authenticity and claim of the bounty placed on this young man's head. I must insist that a consultation happen immediately out in the hallway."

Apparently, the term 'Esquire' had a lot of pull with Miss Clark. She froze with indecision for a couple of seconds before blowing out an annoyed breath. "Very well. But I insist this young man be watched by the guard while we talk."

"Agreed," said Lawrence amiably. "And the guard can watch his sister while we talk. This involves her as well."

Muttering under her breath, Miss Clark fumbled for a key ring that was attached at her waist. She unlocked her door to the hallway, opened it, and called out, "This way, please." She did not leave her small room but watched us instead.

Lawrence walked back to the waiting room door and held it open as Fal, Wren, and Fleurette filed out. He glanced at me, and I could feel the unfriendly gaze of Miss Clark on my back. I shrugged my shoulders and sat on the bench that had previously held the siblings.

"My part is done. I'd like to wait in here if I may," I said.

Lawrence smiled and tipped his head in acknowledgment before exiting the room and shutting the door behind him. I spared a glance toward the clerk, who simply walked out of her own door. I heard the tell-tale sound of a key locking that door.

I stayed put, using my superior ears to determine what was happening outside this room. There was the muffled voice of stuffy-britches Clark telling Fleurette and Lawrence to stay put while she marched the Ramberts over to the guard. There were her prim footsteps just a minute later as she returned. Another muffled yet snooty command to follow her into an adjacent room. A doorknob jiggled nearby as she unlocked and opened it, followed by a curt closing.

That was my cue. I transformed swiftly and ran to the counter. Bunching my muscles neatly underneath me, I sprang upward and landed on the small surface area in front of the barred window.

This was the tricky part. Using my whiskers, I measured the space between the golden bars. Even turning my head sideways, the fit was simply too tight for my body to squeeze through. That left only one option.

Through the back wall, I could hear snippets of the conversation. As I very carefully squeezed under the cage through the slot left open for exchange of papers and money, I overheard Lawrence claiming that the Ramberts had left a will with his company that stated Fleurette was the rightful guardian of the children. Miss Clark's response was more muffled. I sucked in my belly, my small primordial pouch dragging on the counter as I finally wiggled through the narrow space.

Dropping down, I wasted no time regaining my human form. I turned to the filing cabinet to my right.

"Miss Williams is willing to give these children a home," the lawyer continued through the wall, "and she is also willing to pay whatever fine is necessary for these ridiculous charges to be dropped."

I pulled the rumpled dossier, the one for a nameless teen boy who had stolen items and battered an old man over the head, from my vest pocket. I ignored everything written upon it except for the long number typed in a very small typeface at the bottom. 974332. Fal's bounty case number. Scanning the files before me, I searched for the matching number.

"As much as you have everything in order, I still cannot divulge any information. That is classified!" Miss Clark practically screeched through the wall.

I chuckled under my breath. *No need to divulge it, Miss Clark.* I had found the folder.

I pulled it out of the cabinet. Inside the folder were extra copies of the dossier. I flipped those aside and finally found what I was looking for: the bounty application.

It sounded like the next-door meeting was wrapping up. I quickly started reading. "Application date, August 1 ... location, Chargrove, O.R ... name of applicant, Gregory Elkins—*Gregory Elkins?*"

The supposed uncle was the independent contractor? Things just got interesting.

I kept reading, but the rest was regurgitated information about how the source wished to remain anonymous, and so on and so forth. All this I had already gleaned from Angie. Just as well. I heard the door of the meeting room start to open.

Quickly, I closed the folder and shoved it back into its spot in the filing cabinet. As a key slid into the knob by my left, I shut the filing cabinet as softly as I could.

"I just need a few signatures for now. Please meet me in the waiting room," Miss Clark declared as she fumbled with the lock. I shimmered down.

Just in the nick of time. The door opened as Miss Clark began walking in. While her body was still blocking the doorway, I lowered myself until my belly practically dragged on the ground and slinked out the open door, keeping myself as close to the righthand wall as possible.

"What in the world?" Miss Clark demanded, clearly having seen a glimpse of me as I exited around her feet.

Before she could swivel her head back out into the hallway, Fleurette swiftly opened the bounty office waiting room door, allowing me to make a speedy entrance. As soon as I was back in the room I shimmered to a human, as my clever friend kept Miss Clark's attention out in the hallway with an innocent-sounding, "Is everything alright, Miss Clark?"

"Did you just see a cat?" A mystified Miss Clark asked her. I settled back on the bench as Fleurette replied in the negative.

The stuffy woman reentered her little room, looking around and then glancing at me. I pretended to be half asleep for a second before meeting her eye with a confused look. Miss Clark glared around her as Fleurette and Lawrence entered the room, also feigning confusion over the clerk's demeanor.

After a couple of seconds, she let out, "I could have sworn I saw …" but she did not finish her sentence. Miss Clark let the matter drop with a sharp shake of her head.

I had to bite the inside of my cheek to keep from smiling.

It was officially case closed.

That night, the Rambert siblings came home with us, but only after Fleurette, Fal, and Wren signed all sorts of papers. I let my mind space out on that part due to boredom. The only thing I signed was the paper stating that I officially captured the "criminal" and "collected the bounty." I say these things in quotes because in actuality the bounty was forfeit due to extenuating circumstances. I was more than okay with this.

When I told Fleurette about what I had discovered in regard to who put the bounty out in the first place, she actually laughed.

"It doesn't surprise me," she said with a touch of ruefulness. "I looked into the Ramberts' family tree. As I suspected, they don't have a great-uncle. Since Elkin's plan to pose as their uncle didn't get those two into his clutches, he resorted to playing dirty. And I suspect he's not finished trying. I'm not sure what his motive is in all of this, but we'll have to be careful."

A week later, Fleurette had a court date with Fal and Wren. I was not invited. I did lend them the use of Humbert and the wagon, however, since I had decided to take a small hiatus from my profession. Just to make sure everything was sorted out.

When they returned from court, all three were smiles. "It's official!" trilled Fleurette. "Fal and Wren are now my wards." She beamed as she wrapped an arm around the shoulders of both kids. They smiled widely and leaned into her. My heart sang at the sight.

There were many details to work out still, such as permanent sleeping arrangements. The house only had two bedrooms and the siblings couldn't feasibly share a room, but Fleurette had plans to transform one of the outbuildings into a little sleeping cabin for Fal. He was delighted at the prospect. It seemed that everything would work out quite well for everyone involved.

That evening, Fleurette threw a family party to celebrate. Lyle came with my mother in tow, who actually changed into a human for part of the shindig. Lawrence came too but left early before dinner was served because he was traveling back to wherever he had come from. He did not divulge where that might be to me. Those GOGs were a secretive lot.

After a most delicious dinner, we retired to the cramped living room for after dinner tea. As we chatted about anything and everything, my vest pocket vibrated. I pulled out my message mirror, flipping the leather cover open.

"NEIGHBORING TOWN HAS WW PROBLEM. REQUEST ASSISTANCE FROM C CURTAIN." It was signed by Sheriff Jones of Veradale.

"Werewolf problem ..." I muttered to myself. I glanced at Grimm, who was stationed next to me. He had heard the vibration too and perked his ears in expectancy. "Ready to get back to work?" I asked him. He wriggled his sitting bottom with anticipation and let out a tiny whine. "Yeah, me too, buddy," I answered. The time off had been nice, but we both had been growing antsy from the lack of work. It was time to get back out there.

Picking up my teacup and a stirring spoon, I rapped them gently together, the spoon making a tiny tinkling sound on the porcelain. All eyes swiveled to me, and conversation dwindled to silence. I cleared my throat.

"Grimm and I are leaving first thing in the morning for a job," I stated to the crowd. A couple mumbles of sadness reached me. I ignored them. "I have something important to say to all of you. Being a cat, I always thought of myself as a loner. I assumed I would make it in this world by only relying on myself. That I didn't need friends, or a family for that matter."

Silence met this statement. I swallowed a suspicious lump in my throat. "But I was wrong. It started with Fleurette and Lyle, who showed me that some humans could be trusted. And then Grimm, my faithful partner. Mom, of course, has always been there for me, even if she doesn't approve of my actions."

Mom scoffed at those words, but also smiled.

"I thought early on that being alone was how I was supposed to live my life." I stared at the people in the room, meeting the eyes of first Lyle, then Mom, then Fleurette, and lastly Wren and Fal. I placed a loving hand on top of Grimm's head to include him too. "I am so glad that this wasn't the case. If anything, these last few weeks have only proven how much that wasn't how I wanted to spend my life. I am honored to call you all my family, no matter how unusual it may be. And, as my family, I'd like to bestow a token upon you."

I transformed back into a cat and leapt up onto a side table in front of everybody. I sat down in a statuesque pose, head held high, tail curled around my feet. I met the gaze of each member of the room. And then, with my ears perked forward, I slowly closed my eyes. And kept them closed.

Silence reigned.

Still keeping my eyes closed contentedly, I heard Fal whisper, "What's happening?"

It was my mom that answered, and she spoke just loudly enough for everyone in the room to hear. "Cats are very suspicious by nature, and only in the most trusted company will a cat deliberately close her eyes. It is considered the highest honor a cat can bestow to close her eyes at you."

Another small stretch of silence. I imagined they were digesting my mother's words. Finally, Wren let out a little, "Aww!"

"To Cressida!" Lyle suddenly shouted. The outburst nearly made me open my eyes, but I refrained, only tucking my ears back for a second. "To Cressida!" "Hear, hear!" followed in Lyle's wake.

I basked in the praise that my ears brought me. As I continued to bestow my respect upon this motley group of people and animals, I reflected upon the happenings of these last couple of weeks. I had bested my enemy, a witch that hadn't shown her face in five hundred years. I had gained the love and trust of two more humans and discovered a whole secret society that would forever have my back. Sure, I had been cursed in the process, and I was still processing this fact, but more importantly, I had also been blessed with a sense of camaraderie and family.

Overall, just another successful job.

ACKNOWLEDGMENTS

Dreams don't often come true overnight. Timing is often a huge factor—at least it was for me. Even though I have wanted to publish a novel for many years, I had to jump over a lot of hurdles just to get to a point where I could take the time to write. For me, my time hurdles were college, jobs, marriage, and raising my daughters from babies to school-aged children. But throughout it all, the dream held fast.

My main character Cressida has been hanging out in my head for at least ten years. I'm so glad I was finally able to liberate her, and I'm excited to continue her story in the rest of the series. But it takes more than one person to show her to the world at large. Publishing a book seemingly takes an army!

First, my thanks go to my parents, who raised me to believe in my vivid imagination and never to stifle it. And that goes for my husband Matt as well, who has supported my flights of fancy wholeheartedly. He was also my first beta reader and gave me the confidence to show my manuscript to more people. Appreciation goes to my wonderful friend Jennica, for also cheering me on the whole way and for being my sounding board whenever I needed a sympathetic ear. And for Rachel, my beta reader, who gave me a major boost of confidence when she loved my story.

For the professionals I hired during my publishing journey, I am so appreciative of your much-needed assistance! My editor Tina Beier is amazing and really polished my book beautifully. I couldn't have done it without you, Tina! Angelee van Allman, thank you for the gorgeous cover art. I can't wait to see what you do for the next book! And many thanks to Cynthia Ley for proofreading the whole thing. You all were so helpful during this journey.

A special shout-out goes to the Northwest Independent Writer's Association. Its fellow members were incredibly helpful and supportive any time I needed questions answered. Thank you, NIWA!

And lastly, thank you to my readers. You took a chance on a new author, and for that I am very grateful. I hope this literary journey found you happy at the end.

About the Author

R. Lindsay Carter wanted to be a zookeeper when she was a girl. Now, she is content to stick with her small menagerie at home, which includes her supportive husband and her two daughters. When she isn't in the throes of writing, you can find R. Lindsay creating art, reading, gardening, ignoring household chores, and otherwise lounging about, usually with her lap taken up by her dog and/or one of her three cats. Born and raised in the Pacific Northwest, R. Lindsay happily lives in Oregon.

BOOKS BY R. LINDSAY CARTER

The Familiar's Legacy:
Unfamiliar Territory
Relative Truths (coming November 2022)

CONNECT

Follow R. Lindsay Carter for all the latest news!

Social Media:

https://www.rlindsaycarter.com

https://www.facebook.com/rlindsaycarter

https://www.instagram.com/author_rlindsaycarter

Newsletter:

https://tinyletter.com/rlindsaycarter

Printed in the USA
CPSIA information can be obtained
at www.ICGtesting.com
LVHW051312190923
758575LV00003B/7

9 798985 907223